UNWILLING ELDRITCH HORROR OF FORTUNE

UNWILING ELDRITCH HORROR OF FORTUNE

Tismon

Podium

Podium

UNWILLING ELDRITCH HORROR OF FORTUNE

CHAPTER ONE

Absolute Luck System 102.04 Delta

I awoke to a blazing headache and a sense of intense nausea. Looking through blurry eyes, I noticed that I was seated in a dark, dimly lit room, surrounded by what appeared to be 100 or so other individuals, all of whom were sitting on some cheap plastic chairs and utterly unconscious.

What the hell happened?

The last thing I remembered was going home from work after a grueling day, and then . . . nothing. I was evidently kidnapped or abducted somehow, along with everyone else here, but I couldn't remember how that happened.

Was I drugged? Chloroformed? Knocked unconscious? I knew I probably had a lot of enemies, given my line of work, but surely I would remember something about the assault.

Yet nothing came to mind.

I wasn't physically hurt, which made me more worried than I should be. A sense of panic started to fill my body—I've seen those horror movies. Was some sadistic lunatic hiding behind a one-way mirror waiting for the show to start? Surely no one would go that far in punishing a small-time crook, right?

No, I can't think like that. I have to calm down. Think. I was always good at thinking.

Not wanting to let anyone know that I was awake and freed—in case there actually was an insane killer watching—I scanned my immediate surroundings. Although the lighting was low, my eyes were starting to adjust to the gloom, and I could just about make out that I was in a large oval room that was slightly worn down with use. No other features stood out, aside from its odd shape, and there were no writings or posters or such that I could use to identify the location.

Strange, I couldn't recall any building that had circular, gym-sized rooms in them. There were windows boarded up high on the walls, and a small streak of sunlight peered through them from the cracks in the wood. Glancing around, I saw that everyone else was seated facing a large metal door; it looked like we were an audience waiting for some foreign dignitary to arrive.

Okay, so what did this information tell me?

First of all, I know that there aren't any buildings like this one in my small town; the biggest thing around is maybe a barn or the grocery store. This means that I was most likely not in a familiar area. Next, I left work at six p.m., and it was already dark out, but the sunlight breaking through the windows told me that at least a night had passed. It couldn't have been much more than a day or so, or I would be thirsty or hungry, or something after waking up.

So I've been taken somewhere completely new, and a significant amount of time has passed since. But why were there so many others with me, and why were we seated like this? What were we waiting for?

Too many unknown factors . . .

I felt my pulse rise as I thought of a multitude of reasons why so many people could be here, taken against their will. Was this some kind of government experiment? Maybe some terrorists came to use us as hostages, and we were all about to die if their demands were not followed. Was I still drugged and just hallucinating?

Just as I was about to panic again, I heard a strange sound. Not an auditory one from the environment, but something that resonated directly into my mind.

It was a sharp DING followed by a soothing androgynous voice.

"Welcome, Host," the voice said. "Please confirm identification."

"What the fuck . . ." I muttered out loud despite my earlier caution.

Yeah, I was most certainly drugged.

"Confirm first name as What, last name as Thefuck."

"My first name is what?" I repeated, still unable to make sense of what was happening.

"Acknowledged. Host's name on file will be saved as: first name Watt, last name Thefuck," the voice said again. "Welcome, Watt Thefuck, I am Luck System Version 104.04 Delta. Please provide this unit with a name."

The voice was crystal clear in my head. What the hell did the kidnappers give me? Was I developing schizophrenia? Paranoid delusions? Stress-induced hallucinations?

"I am definitely tripping." I sighed.

"Negative," the voice in my head answered, voice still even and soothing, "Host's name is not DefinitelyTripping. Host's name on file is Watt Thefuck. Please state the correct identification for future use. Once again, please provide this unit with a name."

"No, I mean—" I stuttered, unsure why I was even answering my delusions, as all sense of reality was slowly leaving my brain.

"Acknowledged, this unit will now be known as Noaimean."

What on earth is going on?

"Inquiry acknowledged," the voice answered, ignoring the fact that my question was intended to be rhetorical, or the fact that I only thought of it in my head. "Individual Watt Thefuck has been chosen as the new host for Unit Noaimean exactly six hours, fourteen minutes, and thirty-two Earth seconds ago due to ERROR ERROR ERROR ERROR ERROR ERROR—"

The drowning error messages pounded in my skull, and my already horrible headache grew to levels I never thought possible.

"Stop!" I half screamed, hand clenching my head. "Cancel inquiry!"

"—OR ERROR . . ." Then a pause in the droning, before the voice returned to its past volume and said, "Acknowledged. Last inquiry canceled."

All right, whatever was going on in my head wasn't disappearing. I might as well indulge in whatever hallucinations I was going through.

Maybe this was how it felt to be insane.

"Negative. Host Watt Thefuck is of sound mind. Unit Noaimean detects elevated levels of cortisol and blood pressure indicative of stress, but neurochemical compositions are within normal ranges."

Can you stop reading my mind!

"Negative," it said again. "Unit Noaimean has bonded to Host Watt Thefuck, and as such, Unit Noaimean has access to all information in Host Watt Thefuck's neural matrix."

Then I command you to only answer questions if I ask them to you directly!

"Acknowledged."

Okay, first of all, my name is not What the fuck.

After waiting for a few moments, I realized that the thing in my head wouldn't answer, since I never addressed it in the first place.

Okay, thing in my head, I repeated, *I said, my name is not What the fuck.*

"Negative. Once again, host's name on file is designated as Watt Thefuck.

No changes can be made. Additionally, please address this unit as Noaimean in the future."

I sighed. Whatever, this was just a part of my stress-induced mania. I could indulge its whims.

Fine. Just call me by my first name, then, I answered in my head, unable to believe that I would try reasoning with my delusions. *Unit No I mean, tell me what you are.*

"Acknowledged," it—or should I say the unit—replied. "Unit Noaimean is the Luck System version 104.04 Delta. Unit Noaimean is designed to assist Host Watt in his everyday life, especially in situations that would otherwise put Host Watt in danger."

And how would you do that?

"Unit Noaimean—"

I cut the thing off before it could continue.

Hold that. I want to make a correction to your name.

"Elaborate," it replied. "Changes to system information require a legitimate reason for it to be acknowledged."

I had to change the stupid thing's name. I would go insane if it kept repeating No I mean.

You see, I started, thinking of the best "legitimate reasoning" that I could, *I gave you a human name when I first named you. That means that your full name is No I mean. Your first name is Noe, and your last name is I mean. And since we are uh, acquainted, please refer to yourself with your first name going forward.*

"Checking the legitimacy of the name correction request . . . please wait," the voice chimed. After a few more seconds, it gave a beep and continued, "Request acknowledged. Unit Noe Aimean will henceforth go by Unit Noe as requested."

Damn, I didn't think that would actually work. I thought it best to take advantage of this small loophole and try to fix my own name, at least a little.

I also need a small correction for my name as well, Noe.

"Elaborate."

I gave you a shortened version of my first name, I explained. *But if it's registered in your systems, then I should use my full, legal name, right?*

"Checking authenticity of request . . ." it chimed. "Authenticity of request approved. Please state your full first name."

It's uh . . . Walter. Yeah, Watt was short for Walter. Please call me that from now on.

"Acknowledged," it replied. "New name on file is: Walter Thefuck."

Good, Noe, please continue answering that last question.

"Acknowledged. Unit Noe can provide Host Walter with the ability of Absolute Luck, along with minor passive abilities. Inputting details into retina now."

Before I could say another word, a translucent image appeared in my vision. It sort of looked like a clear projector image was somehow right in front of me, moving with my vision as my eyes darted back and forth.

Seeing as how I was completely insane at this point, I took the time to read what was presented.

Host Walter Thefuck:	
Human Male, age 27	
Class: Level 1 Commoner	
Attributes:	
HP:	34/34
MP:	0/0
Strength:	4
Dexterity:	10
Endurance:	7
Intelligence:	26
Charisma:	32

Titles: None

Abilities: 4

Calm Mind (D-rank Innate Passive): User has an unusually calm mind, able to dispel minor forms of cognitive disruptions, and can think logically under high-stress situations.

Shroud of Luck (EX-rank System Passive): Luck System 104.04 Delta has placed a shroud around the user, disallowing personal information from the user to be seen by any and all outside forces. User can temporarily deactivate this ability.

Aura of Serendipity (B-rank System Passive): Luck System 104.04 Delta subtly alters the cognition of any sentient species around the user, making the user significantly more likable and trustworthy to those around him. This effect increases if the user acts in a way that conforms to the ideologies and beliefs of those individuals.

> **Absolute Luck (EX-rank System Active):** As long as the skill is active, Luck System 104.04 Delta will rewrite the laws of causality so that only the best possible outcome will occur for the user. The more improbable a situation is from occurring, the more Luck Charges will be consumed. Luck Charges regenerate at a rate of 1 per minute.

> **Luck Charges:** 100/100

Absolute Luck? Now what on earth am I getting myself into?

CHAPTER TWO

Blind Infiltration

I read the information again for the fourth time before finally calming down enough to unpack all of the information presented. My situation was already crazy enough, and indulging in my delusions could prove a way to pass the time; any information that I could work with—real or not—was better than just waiting around.

First of all, the information presented was organized into categories, detailing my basic information, statistics, titles, and the like. Very much like data in a game or a D&D character sheet. Assuming that this was all a visual hallucination, does that mean that I secretly prefer organizing data into this method? I never considered myself a gamer or the like, and I've only been in a few starting sessions for tabletop RPGs, so maybe this was some kind of Freudian subconscious thing.

Stop getting distracted, I told myself. *Focus on the information that you can actually use.*

So, most of the data I hallucinated didn't tell me anything, or at least it was nothing that I could use now. Strength and Dex stats would mean nothing if I had no reference to compare them to. Was 26 Intelligence good? Bad? Doesn't matter. That information is irrelevant. Discard them for now.

What I can use is the information about myself. I was listed as a twenty-seven-year-old human male. What stood out was the fact that my race was listed. Did that indicate that other races existed? Would animals have stat screens like I do? And what about the magic stat? Why even have a stat there if magic doesn't exist? Could it represent something else like . . . scientific knowledge or something?

Stop. Do not get lost in useless conjectures.

What was useful, and something that I could test to see if I really was just going crazy or not, was the abilities screen. Most were passives whose descriptions meant nothing to me without more context, except for that one active skill. That one I could feasibility test.

Noe? I asked. *Explain the Absolute Luck skill to me in more detail.*

"Acknowledged," the voice said. "The Absolute Luck skill, as the name implies, will ensure that any action taken by Host Walter will result in the statistically best outcome. The outcome is based on Unit Noe's Luck Algorithm 1 Alpha. Would Host Walter like to hear an explanation of this algorithm? The explanation will only take 6.49102 Earth years to complete."

Uh, no.

"Confirmed. Unit Noe will continue where it left off." Noe paused for a few seconds before starting its explanation again. "Host Walter can will the skill to active status, and as long as there are luck charges available for use, Unit Noe will ensure that the statistically best outcome will occur as stated before. Luck charges will be expended based on the improbability of an event occurring, based on Unit Noe's Luck Algorithm 1 Gamma. Would the host like to hear an—"

No, I thought quickly, nor would I like to hear any other explanation of your algorithms.

"Acknowledged," it chimed. "Continuing prior explanation. If an event's probability of occurring exceeds the amount of luck charges available, then the next best outcome will be chosen, going down a list of events stipulated by Luck Algorithm 1 Theta. This course of action will continue, the optimal outcome occurring based on available luck charges."

Okay, everything's pretty straightforward so far.

"Maximum number of luck charges that can be stored will increase based on Host Walter's level, class, titles, and physical statistics, determined based on Luck Algorithm 1 Beta. Host Walter is encouraged to test out the Absolute Luck skill as soon as possible to ensure that all system parameters are working at optimal performance."

Well, seeing as there's nothing else to do, I might as well take the advice of the random voice in my head. Huh, now that I think about it, isn't this what the other crazies do, listening to the whims of their head-voices? At least this one isn't telling me to kill everyone around me . . . yet.

I sighed and scanned my surroundings one last time, and after confirming that nothing had changed since I was first awake, I quietly left my seat and tried to activate the Absolute Luck ability. Just as I was about to question how I would even do that, a tingling sensation washed through me, sort of like I was zapped by a tiny current of electricity, and in the corner of my eye a small "100/100" was displayed.

So, Noe, does that mean the skill's active?

"Affirmative," it responded.

Okay . . . but nothing's happening?

No response.

I mean, Noe, I thought again, remembering to address the thing in my head, *how come nothing is happening?*

"Negative. The ability is online and functioning as intended. All Host Walter has to do is to act as normal, and Unit Noe will ensure that only the best possible outcome of said actions will occur."

Not knowing what else to say, I sat up, and having nothing else to do, I decided to slowly check out the conditions of the others around me. Farther away, each individual was tied up, and as far as I could tell, that was the only similarity between them. The people were of various ethnicities, ages, and style of dress. There were no children or the really old or infirm, but other than that it seemed like our kidnapper—or kidnappers—decided to randomly select people from various places and stuck them all here.

Even after walking a full circle around the room's perimeter, including checking to see if that big door in the front would open (it didn't), the amount of luck charges didn't seem to go down. This made sense if I assumed that just checking out each person one by one was an event that would have next to no variance in terms of what could happen.

Just as I was thinking of what I could possibly do to use up some of those luck charges, something bumped into my leg, causing me to lose my footing and trip. Instinctively, I held up my arms to brace for the fall, and by a stroke of luck I wasn't injured when I landed on the floor, even though my face was inches away from smashing into the wall.

To add insult to injury, the amount of luck charges decreased after tripping, going from 100 to 96. Great, some Luck System that was. I was finally about to conclude that I was actually mentally unwell when I noticed that the ring finger on my left hand appeared to be going through the floor.

Focusing my attention on the bizarre scene, I realized that my finger wasn't going through the floor, but it was pushing a tiny button whose shape was remarkably similar to the shape of my fingertip. I removed my finger from the strange button, and before I could do anything else, a huge square opening appeared in the ground. There were stairs leading down to a well-lit corridor, but I couldn't see much else from my angle.

Okay, the probability of pushing a tiny perfectly finger-sized secret camouflaged button on the ground seems pretty low. Maybe the voice in my head was real.

No. One improbable event can still happen, let's not assume anything yet.

Steeling myself, and seeing how staying trapped wasn't a real option, I went down the strange opening and into the corridor. As I expected, the opening closed by itself as soon as I was fully inside, and with no other option than to go forward, I walked.

The corridor was longer than I thought, and by the time I hit the end, my luck charges were already fully refreshed. The corridor ended with a small, unassuming metal door. There were no labels or writing to indicate where the door leads, and the only thing that I could interact with was a small glass number pad. I guess it was password-operated.

This was also the perfect test to see if the Noe Luck System was real or not, which I really did hope was the case, because if it wasn't, then I was stuck in this corridor until I died of dehydration.

Perhaps going down the secret passage wasn't a good idea.

Well, here goes nothing. Making sure that the Absolute Luck skill was active, I placed my hand close to the glass panel and closed my eyes. Strangely, I could still see the amount of luck charges I had, even with my eyes closed. Ignoring that, I started to press buttons at random, and at the same time, saw that the amount of luck charges was steadily going down.

Fast.

From the full 100 charges, it went down to 90, then 80, 70, 60. It wasn't until the amount plummeted to a pitiful 28 that it stopped. Curious to see if anything actually happened, I opened my eyes and saw that the panel had changed. Some strange . . . symbols? Runes? Scribbles or something appeared on the small screen above the numbers, and even stranger, that nonsense writing started to warp before my eyes to turn into something that I could read, and the metal door slowly slid open.

WELCOME TO TESTING SITE 1102, LORD ARBITER. THE SITE ADMIN HAS BEEN NOTIFIED OF YOUR ARRIVAL. PLEASE ENJOY YOUR STAY.

CHAPTER THREE

Lord Arbiter

Okay, denial at this stage would have been pointless and stupid. I seemed to have left the sensible world and arrived somewhere else because the Luck System in my brain was real. Oh boy, I need some time to think about those implications . . .

Hey, Noe, you know anything about the current situation?

"Negative," it answered, "Unit Noe only has information on predetermined system functions and will learn and grow alongside the host."

Unfortunately, I wouldn't have that time to ask the thing any more questions, because as soon as the door was fully open, I was greeted by a sight that just reinforced the fact that I had left the comfortable reality that I was in. The things that were staring at me like I was some kind of freak were not things that I recognized.

I guess there was a reason I was labeled as "human male" before because the . . . "people" that were looking at me were anything but human. Sure, they dressed in what appeared to be semiformal office attire, but that was it. There were creatures with three heads and six arms typing furiously at a workstation. Some sort of lanky, pale monstrosity that was at least eight feet tall was sweeping the floors, and another being that was nothing more than geometric shapes was chatting with some kind of human-sized bipedal centipede thing. There were other assortments of nightmare creatures around, and as the room quieted down due to my arrival, I was suddenly made to be the center of attention.

I needed to calm down. If strange voices in my head that can casually break the laws of physics could exist, then so could monsters. They hadn't attacked me yet, so they were as clueless about the situation as I was. I just had to analyze the situation, make a plan, and go from there. Just treat it like any other day at the job, treat them as potential marks, just figure out what they wanted, and I could work it out like usual.

Time seemed to slow down as I took all the sights in, my brain going into overdrive trying to process all the new sensory information. I was strangely calm, however, given the outrageous situation that I was facing. *Huh, it must be because of that Calm Mind skill earlier. Wonder how that works?*

I shook my head—now was not the time to ponder over the Luck System's skills. I took a deep breath and compiled all the available information that I had.

First of all, the creatures in front of me are obviously not human, but given the facial expressions of the ones that had faces, and the way they were dressed, I could assume that they are workers that operated in the same manner as a modern white-collar wage earner would. Or in other words, these were underpaid and overworked employees. If I was wrong about this assertion, though . . .

No, let's assume just I was right.

That was information that I could work with. I'd dealt with disgruntled nine-to-fivers. If these, uh, creatures were anything like their human counterparts, then they were followers. If I could take the initiative and make them go with my flow, to cause such a ruckus that it would be easier for them to just follow along, then I could get through this.

But what excuse could I use to make them follow me? Well, there was one other piece of information available. When I punched in those codes, the little screen greeted me as an arbiter—no, a *lord* arbiter. That meant that I had to be someone important, especially given the fact that the site admin was alerted, but what on earth was a lord arbiter? What did a lord arbiter do? I guess given the title, it must be someone who . . . You know what, I don't really know what an arbiter does.

It was fine, it was someone important—probably way more important than the workers before me. I just had to pretend to be an irate CEO or the like. I could do this.

Activating the Absolute Luck skill just for safe measure, I envisioned the role that I was to play, made the angriest face that I could muster, and walked into the office space feeling as if I owned it.

"You!" I commanded, pointing to some kind of six-foot-tall mucusy amoeba-looking thing, since it was the most harmless-looking individual around. "Take me to the site admin."

The thing turned its, uh, front side to me and made a noise that sounded like bubbling water. Amazingly, halfway through those noises, I was able to understand what it was saying.

" . . . have to ask my supervisors," it said, its voice now sounding like perfectly understandable English.

Did you do that, Noe? I asked quickly in my mind.

"Affirmative," the system chimed. "Unit Noe can translate 1.09×10^{17} known languages within the multiverse to ensure that Host Walter has the best probability of amicable interactions with other sentient species."

I smiled as a thought came to mind.

Can you translate what I say back to those sentient species in their native tongue?

"Affirmative."

Do so now, Noe.

"Acknowledged."

"Can you not even speak the human language?" I began to speak again, but although the words sound like English, the sensation that I felt was unlike anything I'd felt before. It was like I was trying to gargle a truckload of liquid.

The amoeba thing jiggled, which I assumed was a sign of surprise that I answered in its own tongue, before quickly regaining its rigidity and saying, "I apologize, uh . . ."

"I'm the lord arbiter," I growled.

The thing jiggled again, more violently than the first time. In fact, the others in the room, or at least those who could understand whatever language I was speaking, also reacted in what I can only assume was of surprise.

"I apologize, Lord Arbiter," the jelly thing continued, "but I, um, I don't have the structural constructs to speak the human language."

"You think that's an excuse?" I shouted, feigning outraged. "You think that just because you don't have the right organs means that you can excuse yourself? Tell me again, what species is being tested here at Training Site 1102?"

"H-humans, sir. Earth humans."

"And what language do Earth humans speak?"

The ameboid jiggled again, going so far as to change colors this time. "Um . . . Humanese? I'm sorry—I, uh, I didn't pay attention in the Intro to Earth class."

I exaggerated a sigh and screamed. "You are useless! How are you allowed a job here if you don't even know something that basic? Tell me what department you work for. Your conduct is a disgrace to everyone present! Get me someone competent now!"

The creature visibly shrank, and I noticed that the others in the room were slowly moving away from me. Good, they're acknowledging my status as someone better off left alone, and more importantly, avoided.

Before I could think of something else to berate the amoeba thing for, a huge mass of swarming tentacles all squeezed into a neat security uniform was rushing toward me with haste.

As it approached and its appearance was clear, I noticed that where its face should be was a gaping circular maw of needle-sharp teeth, its red mouth opening wide as if to swallow me whole. The tentacles that I saw earlier were gleaming in the light, and a thick layer of some kind of molasses-like substance was covering every corner of it.

I almost flinched as it approached but managed to keep my expression neutral. I really hoped my disguise was still working. Just by the way the creature presented itself showed that it was higher up on the totem pole than the amoeba from earlier.

It's fine, it might look slightly different than my usual marks . . . I thought, psyching myself up. *It's just as fallible as all the other idiots I've worked with. I just have to butter it up and get it on my side. I've done this a million times before. Let's ignore those rows of teeth and razor edges . . .*

Easier said than done.

"Apologies for the delay, Lord Arbiter, and for the conduct of the employees here," the creature said, its voice surprisingly feminine and pleasant. "I came as soon as I was notified."

So I was right, the tentacle creature was something important in this place. It would probably do well to treat it—or her, perhaps—better. I needed information, and the best way I'd found to get that was to get on the good side of people, especially if they were important.

First things first: let's establish some easy rapport.

Noe, translate what I'm about to say into the native language of that thing.

"Acknowledged," Noe replied. "Translating Earth English into Xolloid Primary. Please note that prolonged translation to Xolloid Primary will cause damage to Host Walter's body, as Host Walter does not have the prerequisite organs to properly vocalize Xolloid Primary. Does Host Walter wish to proceed?"

Damage? Well, it should be fine, and I needed to make a good first impression. I might not know much about the situation, or the cultures and experiences of the creatures here, but P.T. Barnum had never failed me yet. I could find a way to relate to them.

Translate away, Noe.

"Acknowledged."

CHAPTER FOUR

The Xollon

I cleared my throat and addressed the maw creature, using the most polite tone that I could muster. "That's not a problem. But your employees do need extra Earth training. I am sure that you understand the importance of knowing the tested species."

My voice still sounded like English to me, but by the shocked expression the creature gave me, Noe must have been doing its translating.

"I— Of course, sir, I'll let the admin know," she answered, her voice still pleasant, but there was a distinct, intangible difference to it now. She must have switched to speaking her home dialect. "Sorry, I'm just surprised that you can speak Prime, and without an accent at that!"

"I get that a lot." I smiled the same practiced smile I'd used a thousand times before. "I stayed at Xolloid for a while before working as an arbiter. Xolloid treated me well, and it's good to see a friendly face around here."

The creature practically beamed at that. "You've been there? Most people avoid a backwater dimension like mine at all costs, let alone visit. And a Lord Arbiter at that!"

I laughed, the sound hurting my core. I ignored the pain and continued warming up to the tentacle thing.

"Xolloid is certainly not like what people say about it. Heck, I've never been to a nicer place," I said, lying through my teeth.

"Have you been to the Plains of Torment?" the thing asked, its smooth voice clearly sounding excited, "or the Mausoleum of Hungering Souls? Oh, oh, what about the Death Seas. Um, the one next to the Halo Stars, that is, not the shoddy one by the Sanguine Pools. Avoid that one if you can."

Okay, scary names aside, I could assume that those were probably tourist attractions.

"Unfortunately not," I answered with a sigh, "my visits are usually work related, so I rarely have the chance to go see the sights."

"Oh, that's a pity . . . You're missing so much of what Xolloid has to offer!" she—it was definitely female—said with a deflated tone. "You *must* visit the Plains of Torment at the very least if you ever go back, there's nowhere else in the multiverse where you can enjoy the screams of entire civilizations, forever frozen in the moment of their demise. And the performers there! I'm sure they'd love to entertain someone from out of town! I'd show you myself if I could!"

Right . . . Let's add Xolloid as a place to never, ever go to.

I nodded. "There's nowhere I'd rather go back to, and I definitely will once all this is over, but there's one thing above all else that I miss from there."

She looked at me expectantly.

"It's the food," I expanded. "I still miss the local cuisine, even now. Can't get that stuff anywhere else."

The creature beamed—wait, I didn't know why I hadn't noticed this sooner, but it didn't really beam, since it didn't even have anything remotely close to a face. Yet I could swear that that was the human equivalent of what it did. How did I know that?

Breaking me out of my questioning, the creature replied, "I know! I mean, the local food here's not horrible, and there's an abundance of prey around, but nothing beats a homegrown shoggoth. Sure as heck beats human, ugh!"

Yup, definitely avoid Xolloid at all costs.

"True that . . ." I mumbled, trying my best to remain straight-faced. "I found humans to be—"

"Absolutely awful," grumbled the creature. "I know. It's up there for the worst-tasting species I've ever had the misfortune of trying. You wouldn't believe how relieved I was when we switched to monitoring humans and got that horrible race off the menu."

I chuckled nervously. "That's good to hear. But I wish I could try something local now. I've been living off nothing but humans for a while."

She looked genuinely horrified when I said that, and not because of the normal reasons one would normally be when talking about eating people.

"I'm so sorry! I can't even imagine . . . that must be horrible!"

The mass of tentacles paused for a second, digesting the undoubtedly horrible news I'd just presented.

"Oh, I completely forgot to introduce myself! My pod distinction is Xollo'gutha'mallo'atha or Xalla for short. I'm the head of security here," she said, blushing. "I apologize for the late introduction, Lord Arbiter. I always get distracted when I talk about home, but I promise I don't slack off at my job!"

"No problem, Xollo'gutha'mallo'atha. I am Arbiter . . . Walter, but you can call me Watt if you want," I replied, choosing not to use my real name. "And I feel the same. It's rare to see someone from that part of the multiverse around here."

"I get that . . . we Xollon do have a bit of a bad rep." Xalla sighed, sounding genuinely sad for the first time. "But I want to change that! I believe that if more of us can get into roles like yours or mine, then the multiverse has to change their perceptions of us! And, uh, if it's not too inappropriate . . ."

She looked at me for permission to continue; I nodded, telling her to proceed. "I have a habit of snacking, and I have some shoggoths that you can try, given how much you miss them and all. No one else here likes them for some reason, but you're free to have a few. Um, if you want, that is. My family are slavers back home, have a big herd of them there, so they're homemade. I pickled them myself! I hope you don't mind!"

A shoggoth? Why did that term sound so familiar?

Didn't matter, nothing surprised me at this point. I knew from all those psych classes I took that I should accept these things gratefully if I wanted her to like me more. I was sure I could find an excuse to not actually eat them.

"You do?" I said, forcing excitement into my voice. "I haven't had a good homegrown shoggoth in ages! They were a favorite of mine! And yes, I wouldn't mind having one at all. Thank you."

She smiled—once again, how I knew that she did so when she didn't even have lips was a question I would have to ponder some other time—and produced a few small transparent containers hidden somewhere within her mass of tentacles. She extended the appendage holding those containers, looking at me expectantly.

I took one of them from her "hands," careful not to lacerate myself on the sharp protrusions covering her skin, and peered into the little box. Inside was a multicolored leech-looking thing about two or three inches long. It was wriggling viciously in its container, biting at its confines with needle teeth.

Xalla took one herself and, opening the little lid, she used one of her feelers to skewer the squirming shoggoth. Unbelievably, the little worm thing expanded rapidly, growing multiple extra appendages with eyes sticking out of them, and by the time Xalla brought the critter to her open maw, it was the size of a small dog. And all the while the shoggoth was biting and tearing at her tentacle but doing no apparent damage.

She unceremoniously dropped the wiggling thing into her mouth, and her multirowed serrated teeth started to spin rapidly, shredding the poor thing into a bloody, gooey pulp. After a few moments, the meat chunks and other viscera disappeared completely into that horrifying maw.

I just looked at her in shock, before staring down at my own shoggoth, still trapped in its little glass container. What the hell would have happened if I hadn't seen her eat one and had accidentally opened it?

"Oh," Xalla said when she saw that I wasn't having one of them myself. "I guess you can't eat it with that human guise on."

"Human guise . . .?" I said absentmindedly. I was still recovering my wits at what just transpired. I shook my head and was able to recover and correct myself. "Right! I almost forgot I was wearing one, speaking with you like this. I certainly can't eat one now."

Xalla nodded in understanding. "Please feel free to keep it, then, have one when you're off work. And I'm always willing to share if you want more!"

"Of cour—" Before I could say anything else, I spat out a large glob of blood. Right, Noe did warn me about the damage.

"Are you okay?" she asked, a concerned look showing on her maw. "Humans only spew blood when they're near death!"

Noe, cancel the translation process.

"It's okay," I answered apologetically, speaking English this time. "The human body, er, my disguise, I mean, doesn't handle speaking in Prime well."

A look of realization appeared on Xalla's maw, and she bowed low. "Sorry, I should have known that forcing your boor membrane through the human body would cause it harm. I hope you didn't damage it too much. I still forget how fragile a baseline human is to even small sound waves.

"Still," she continued, "to think your disguise would mimic the human physiology so well. Where did you get that skin suit, if you don't mind me asking?"

Shoot, I knew that I would be asked questions that I wouldn't know the answers to eventually. I had to steer clear of these kinds of situations until I knew more about my situation.

"Oh, I made it myself," I said with as much confidence as I could. "The ones that are available on the market weren't to my liking."

"Amazing . . ." Xalla said, and I could swear she looked like a high school girl meeting her favorite singer for the first time. "An arbiter and a master alchemist . . ."

I wanted to get on Xalla's good side, but talking about any other topics that I had no idea about would only lead to trouble. Without finding out more information, I couldn't risk letting my ignorance show, even if the title of Lord Arbiter could afford me some mistakes.

"I think we've made the site admin wait long enough," I said, making my tone professional. "As much as I would love to talk to a local, I still have a job to do here."

Xalla bowed again. "Of course! I apologize for taking up so much of your time! Please, follow me. I'll take you to the admin's office."

CHAPTER FIVE

Site Admin's Meeting

I figured out, much to my disappointment, that the complex that we were in was labyrinthine to the extreme. Xalla led me down seemingly random, unmarked corridor after unmarked corridor, her pace brisk and with purpose. We passed by several different rooms whose function still eluded me. I tried making a mental map of the place but quickly gave up after the fifth or sixth winding path. Worse yet, every place looked pretty much the same, with its horrible off-white walls and polished stone floors. Who the hell designed this place?

Unfortunately, this being a maze meant that any hope of trying to infiltrate or escape this place unassisted would probably end in abysmal failure. Sure, I could probably luck my way to the entrance, but I was pretty sure someone would notice a bumbling human wandering aimlessly before I could actually get out. That also meant that I was doomed if my disguise as an arbiter failed, as there was no plan B, no alternative way to escape if things didn't go my way.

Still, I always did love a good challenge, and nothing says "challenge" like facing a horrible, slow death if I happened to mess up. Just wonderful.

"This place is pretty large," I remarked, hoping to learn any new info about the site.

"Yeah," Xalla replied politely, laughing. "It wasn't really designed with physical locomotion in mind."

Right, so I learned that walking was not common, but what the hell did that imply? Knowing how ludicrous my current situation was, these creatures probably just materialized or teleported from place to place.

"Unfortunately, I can't do anything about that in this human form," I said, probing for any more insight into what exactly I'd gotten myself into. The more I got her to talk, the more scraps of information I could get, and the higher a chance I had to get through this alive.

Xalla frowned. "Is it really necessary to keep up the disguise, even here?"

"Sadly, it is. I'm still at work, after all," I answered naturally. "And plus, it takes a while to readjust back into the human form, so I try to limit how often I change. There are a lot of limitations that I have to constantly remember, and if I accidentally use too much strength, I could destroy the whole disguise."

Xalla nodded in understanding. "That must be tough. I can't imagine having to live as a human, even for a little while. But for you to do that constantly . . ."

"Takes some willpower and getting used to, that's for sure."

Her head tentacles wiggled a bit, which I could tell was a sign of . . .

I frowned, this wasn't an expression that humans could make, but whatever was translating her gestures told me that it was a mixture of amazement, pride, and happiness.

Noe, are you translating her gestures?

"Affirmative," it answered. "Unit Noe also actively interprets all nonverbal forms of communication of sentient species into its Earth human equivalent if possible, or conveys its intended emotional meaning if an equivalent expression is unavailable."

Guess that explained how I thought Xalla was blushing or frowning when she didn't have, well, a face.

Uh, thanks, Noe. Please continue doing that.

"Acknowledged," it chimed, and I almost thought that its robotic voice sounded a bit . . . happier? "And you are most welcome, Host Walter."

"We've arrived, Lord Arbiter, please enter," Xalla said, her feelers gesturing toward a slightly more decorated door. She looked contemplative for a second, before adding, "And given your human guise, I shall wait here to assist you further when you are done with the meeting with the site administrator . . . um, if that is okay with you."

"That would be much appreciated," I said with my best smile. "Thank you, Xalla."

Just as I was stepping away from Xalla, the familiar sound of Noe rang in my head, "Notification: congratulations, Host Walter Thefuck, you have unlocked your soul title, would you like to review this information now?"

What? Soul title? I guess there was a title section on my status screen earlier. Still, trying to figure out what all that meant could wait. I was just about to enter the site admin's office. Couldn't exactly take five minutes standing by the door talking with the voice in my head.

Save the explanation until later, Noe, and mute any other notifications for now. I can't afford any distractions until I'm done here.

"Acknowledged."

I composed myself and opened the unassuming door.

The first thing I saw when I entered was a handsome individual in an immaculately tailored suit. And when I say handsome, I mean it. I have never seen someone look so . . . perfect. His blonde hair was neatly combed back, not a hair out of place, and his features were angular and perfectly symmetrical. His skin had not a single blemish, and he radiated an aura of authority. He even smelled good. Wow.

When he sat up to approach me, he moved with a grace that I had never seen before; in fact, the person before me was too perfect, too good-looking, approaching uncanny.

"Welcome, Lord Arbiter," he said with a neat, professional smile, his voice just as perfect as his appearance. "I am Q, the administrator of Training Site 1102. To what do I owe the pleasure?"

Okay, this was the moment of truth. If I could convince the really beautiful dude in front me of that I was an actual Lord Arbiter, whatever that was, then I was probably in the clear for the time being.

I could do this. No pressure.

I scanned the office quickly, trying to see if there was any information that I could use. Obviously, this individual wasn't human, which meant that he wasn't as perfect as he appeared. The room was small given its importance, perhaps the size of a moderately sized bedroom, and it was furnished with utility in mind. Aside from the wooden desk in the back of the room, there were only a few file cabinets and a small sofa set to the side that made up the entire interior of the space. Piled on his desk were several documents and stacks of paper.

Not a lot of useful information so far, other than the fact that he was perhaps busy with admin work.

However, I noticed something in the corner of my eye as I gestured for him to take a seat and sat myself down on the chair opposite his desk. The lowermost cabinet had some pieces of paper sticking out of it, and although the stacks of documents on his desk seemed organized, upon closer inspection, it was clear that it was hastily put together. Someone was probably busy reorganizing his office in time for the Lord Arbiter's visit.

This was information that I could use. My best bet so far was that this Q person probably wanted to seem in total comfort and control but was secretly overworked. No one with that many documents to sign and work through could be stress-free. Time to test the waters to see if I was on the right track.

I arched an eyebrow, looking at the stacks of documents on his desk, and asked, "There's no one else here to help you out on the administrative side of things?"

He laughed, voice still sounding heavenly, but I could tell there was a tinge of nervousness hidden in there. "Unfortunately we've been slightly short-staffed at the moment, but we're all right, and let me assure you that it has not had an effect on our operations here."

Oh yeah, I was most certainly right. There was no universe in which the admin team would be "all right" without any kind of support staff. Not even if these people were not actually people. This was some poor middle-management office worker swamped with too much work and too little help.

I sighed and gave the man a genuine look of understanding. "First of all, before I talk about anything else, the confines of this room are not recorded in any way, right?"

Q laughed nervously, his perfect exterior crumbling by the second. "I mean, I know regulations state that all interior spaces should be monitored by Central-approved systems, and given how expensive Lord Babylon's creations are . . ."

I glared at him.

"But I assure you that as an Omni, there should be nothing in this facility that would escape my notice in the first place. And with the recent budget cuts, you know . . ."

I glared at him still.

Q gave a defeated sigh, slumping his shoulders. "No. This room and much of Site 1102 are not recorded as per Central Standards. I accept full responsibility for this oversight."

Okay, good, got some more information that I can use. Apparently, the facility was under some kind of entity called Central, and they had enforceable standards and regulations. I could use that.

"That's not what I'm saying, Q," I said, giving him a look of sympathy. "Look, believe it or not, I worked with folk like you before this gig. I get it, the budget's gone to shit, and the staff's flown off to better ventures elsewhere. I loved the job at first, but there's a reason I left."

Q looked at me, still unsure if he could believe what I was saying, before nodding slowly.

I continued, "So trust me when I say I can relate to your need to cut some corners. I'm not here to admonish you—it's the opposite. You should have some ideas as to why I'm here in the first place, right?"

Q thought for a moment, before asking hesitantly, "Due to the rumors?"
Okay, I'm getting somewhere. Let's see if I can probe for more info.

"Right, unfortunately, they're true."

"But the damn temporal anomaly was detected on the other side of this universe!" Q stammered, his perfect voice starting to approach a shout. "Yes, we're on the same plane, but Site 1199 is half a trillion light-years away from us! You don't need to send a damn arbiter—no offense—to monitor every potential anomaly out there. The chances of it being on this Site are minuscule at best!"

"Hey, I get you," I said, trying to calm him down, "but you know how Central is."

Q took a deep breath, composing himself. "I apologize, Lord Arbiter. You are correct, the Central Overseer's reasoning can be . . . nebulous. They're in a tight situation right now, as you know."

"Yeah, that's one way to put it." I shook my head. "And no matter how badly they're doing right now, the corners they're cutting are unacceptable! They send me here to annoy hardworking people when I could be somewhere more productive."

Q shook his head in frustration.

"Look, Q, I'm fed up as well. That's why I'm not following proper procedure and meeting you here. I wanted to give you a heads-up about the situation, so you can make sure that any of the big breaks in protocols are patched up before I make my rounds," I said, before looking at a more relieved Q. "I can overlook the small issues, but you know that I still have to report back. Plus, if there are any anomalies, I can just focus my attention there."

"Thank you, Lord Arbiter. I didn't think you would go that far," Q said. "And if it's not too rude to ask, but is it true that you made that human homunculus suit?"

"Of course," I answered confidently, too late to change my story now, especially if this Q individual had already overheard my earlier conversation with Xalla.

"That's . . . I've never seen its like before," Q continued with a look of amazement.

I frowned. Was that a compliment or criticism?

"This human suit was a passion project of mine," I said, trying my best to hide my nerves. "But be honest, what is your opinion of it?"

Q, still looking marveled, said, "Truthfully, it is almost a perfect replica of the human male. If it wasn't for my inability to observe your status screen, I would have thought you *were* human. Remarkable."

He couldn't see the stat screen? Wait, there was that one random skill I'd glanced over previously, that Shroud one. Was that the reason why Q couldn't view it? Only one way to find out.

Noe, is that Shroud of something or another active right now?

"Assuming that Host Walter is referring to the Shroud of Serendipity, then affirmative," Noe answered.

Cancel the Shroud of Serendipity for Q. Make sure he can't see the system info, though.

"Acknowledged."

"Try seeing the screen again, Q."

The man looked at me skeptically but nodded.

Q's expression took a huge turn, a myriad of complex emotions crossing his face all at once, before he finally spoke, "That's . . . that's impossible. The Origin Matrix confirms that you are human. But how? Getting the human biology is simple enough, any amateur alchemist can do that, but to fool Origin means that body of yours has experienced real, lived-in experiences. You would have had to establish the human essence. You have to create a soul."

CHAPTER SIX

Defective Human

Okay . . . Q started to jabber about incomprehensible things after that. He continued his rant about how impossible my body was, using terms that I didn't have the brainpower to decipher. That was fine. From the parts that I could understand, he thought that I'd created the perfect human, and that I was some kind of alchemy god. I saw no reason to correct him.

"Exactly!" I exclaimed. "It took a lifetime of work to create a human soul!"

Q gazed at his own perfect-looking form, then back at me. There was an undeniable sense of shame in his expression.

"And to think I thought myself a master alchemist . . ." He laughed. "What a joke!"

"Hey, don't be so hard on yourself," I spoke, comforting him. "I haven't seen many alchemists at your level; many would stop their pursuits after achieving a modicum of mastery. I can see that you are different, Q."

"Perhaps . . ." He sighed, still depressed. "My guise must look like the pitiful first attempts of a naive apprentice in your eyes."

I shook my head. "No, I mean it. The most important aspect of any alchemist is the drive to improve, and not their current mastery. One can always improve if one puts their mind and soul into it! Why, even this creation of mine is but a prototype. Look closer. Do you see what problems there are in this design?"

I gave him my best sagely look, gesturing for him to see the flaws in my body like a professor would an eager student. I really did want to see what he thought about my stats, as I'd had no reference point to compare my numbers to, so I needed someone to gauge where I stood. And if Q did find some kind of fault in my body, like some kind of hidden disease or something, I could subtly ask him to fix it as a form of learning.

Q stared at me for a solid five minutes, his visage the textbook definition of concentration. After a while longer, he opened his mouth and said, "Yes, although the body is perfect, there are some slight oddities in your form. I had to check through all of the available human information on file, but they do exist."

I gave a slight nod, telling him to continue his thoughts. Did I actually have some rare genetic disease that would come to bite me in ten years? *It's a good thing Q's checking me over, then. I'm sure whatever weird alien race he is, curing something like cancer'll be a piece of cake.*

"Your basic biological information states that you are a twenty-seven-year-old human male, yet those physical stats are some of the absolute lowest I have ever seen on record! Why, if my database is correct, your strength and endurance are barely on par with an eleven-year-old prepubescent human."

It took almost all of my will to remain straight-faced. I never thought I was actually so feeble. I mean, I knew that I wasn't exactly living an active lifestyle before, but an eleven-year-old? I'm pretty sure I could beat up a few of those!

"But my other stats are pretty good, right?" I said, still trying my best not to shout at the man.

"Indeed," Q nodded. "Your Intelligence and especially Charisma are quite high for a new aspirant, and you would be well suited for a magical role in the future."

Okay, so I wasn't totally doomed.

"But it seems that your body has no capability to handle mana at all, but given it's constructed nature, that is not a surprise. In fact, I don't believe that you can use mana even with Origin's Awakening system. So although your mental capabilities are quite remarkable, they're completely useless for that body."

Or not . . .

Q paused and thought for a moment longer. "And your level is interesting as well, but given that it was artificially created, the results are expected."

"So what would be wrong if this body wasn't artificially made?" I asked, morbid curiosity making me ask despite not wanting to know the answer.

Q laughed jovially. "Well, for a human to still be level one after twenty-seven years of existence would imply that the individual is the most useless, worthless—not to mention feeble and dysfunctional—person to have ever existed on that planet! Even some human toddlers would gain a level by simply crawling around! Why, the absurdity of that situation is quite laudable!"

It was hard to keep my face neutral after hearing Q's . . . honest assessment of my physique and level. I expected to find some kind of hereditary disease or slight imperfections in my body, but that?

It's okay, don't get agitated. Perhaps he just misunderstood my information. Maybe his data's wrong, and everyone starts out as level one. Let's go with that explanation for now.

"Yes, clearly the level would be an issue," I muttered forcefully. "And it appears that creating a human soul took a strain on the physical attributes as well. Unfortunately, I didn't get the chance to fix that yet."

Q nodded in understanding. "Completely understandable, Lord Arbiter, but now that you have integrated with Origin as a trial aspirant, that issue can be remedied easily. Was that why you chose to appear here in that form?"

I almost couldn't contain my joy when I heard those words. These things could be fixed? I had to take advantage of this situation. No, I would do more than that. If this place was some kind of testing ground for people to improve, to somehow approach the capabilities of these monsters, then I had to exploit my current advantage to the max. After all, there must be a reason why so many of us were chosen by this Central group of people. I had to participate in these trials, so I'd give Q a reason to let me do so.

Keeping my tone neutral, I answered, "Yes, although fixing my body's defects is only a part of the reason I'm here in this form."

Q looked at me expectantly.

"The main reason is to test out my creation, to see how far this form can go, and of course, to make improvements in the future. After all, what better way to do so than through the Origin Matrix, and to participate in the trials as an aspirant."

The man was almost bursting with respect. "Yes, this is how a grandmaster should be! To think that you would go through so much suffering and humiliation, disguised as a worthless human, just to improve on a design that I had already dismissed as perfect. I am still too naive!"

Well, if I didn't have proof before that the people here did not have the best view of humanity before, then I certainly did now. Apparently I wasn't going to be ditching this arbiter disguise anytime soon, and that was all the more reason to butter up these monsters to get the best possible treatment while I still could. If one day my disguise broke, and I didn't accumulate the necessary strength to defend myself . . .

Nope, don't think like that. Worst case, I still have that Luck System with me.

"Unit Noe will always be with Host Walter," the voice chimed reassuringly.

I smiled; at least the voice in my head was on my side.

"Or until Host Walter dies a horrible, terrible death."

I sighed. Was everyone out there to get me?

Still, I had a clear goal for the first time, and if I wanted to ensure my survival in the long term, then I had to take some risks.

"You know, Q," I said, deciding to risk it all with this crazy plan of mine, "I can see that you are an accomplished alchemist in your own right."

Humbled, Q bowed low. "Nothing compared to you, Lord Arbiter, but I have some renown."

"Tell me," I said with a pause, "aside from the soul, what other parts of the human form elude you?"

Q laughed nervously. "Too many things to list, honestly, but the integration of the human senses with our natural forms has proven to be the most challenging. My colleagues and I have all the biological components working perfectly, but something is interfering with the transfer of information between the suit and body. We have made little progress so far."

"Ah yes, perfecting the senses can be problematic."

"Do you, perhaps, have any advice?"

Good, he was taking the bait. I had to make him invested in me, make him feel like he owed me a huge favor. That way, Q, and by association, all his underlings, would help me out with whatever trials they were putting us through, even if I didn't explicitly ask him to. After all, I was pretty sure that an actual arbiter would not be asking for little favors all the time from the people they were supervising.

"Better," I replied, addressing Q with a smile. "Since I am using your facility and resources on a personal project of mine, and you are helping me fix a slight design flaw, I could visit your lab and see if I can't help you along with your own projects."

Of course, I knew next to nothing about alchemy, but I was pretty sure that it was complex and required a lot of things to go right. Now, if I abused the Absolute Luck skill, then I could perhaps blindly stumble into something useful. The only thing is, I could only hope that I had enough luck charges to pull off a stunt like that. Still, I could maximize my chances of success if I just gained as many levels as I could and increased the amount of luck charges I had.

"After I finish the first set of trials, naturally," I added, giving myself as much time as I could to work with.

"Yes, naturally, Lord!" Q replied, barely able to contain his excitement. "Please take as much time as you need."

"Now, about the issue of my inadequate stats . . ." I said slowly.

Q's expression turned professional again. "Can I assume that you wish for the full awakening process?"

Great, more terms I didn't understand, but it sounded positive, so I nodded.

"I see," he muttered, pausing for a second. "Assuming that you do not want to stand out too much from the rest of the initiates, then your average physical stats should be around twenty-five to thirty. Your Intelligence is fine, and the Charisma stat is well above average, so we can ignore those for now."

Q did something with his hands, and a small green vial appeared in his grasp. It glittered in the light and looked pretty expensive.

"The Beginner Elixir of Fortitude should be adequate for the situation," he said with a smile. "This should put your Dexterity and Endurance a bit higher than the average, but it should still be well within the margin of error for this batch."

He handed the small vial to me, and I drank it without hesitation. Surprisingly, the green elixir tasted like fruit punch. How strange.

Almost immediately, I felt my body change, and not in a pleasant way either. I felt every fiber of my being tear and break as they rearranged themselves, and it took every ounce of my willpower—and the fact that I would probably die if I let slip that I wasn't who I said I was—from screaming out in torment. Thankfully the whole process didn't last long, and when I felt the last phantoms of agony fade, I called Noe to show me the status screen.

"Acknowledged," it chimed. "Showing the stats of Host Walter now."

Host Walter Thefuck:	
Human Male, age 27	
Class: Level 1 Commoner	
Attributes:	
HP:	84/84
MP:	0/0
Strength:	29
Dexterity:	35
Endurance:	32
Intelligence:	26
Charisma:	32

Huh, if I remembered my initial numbers correctly, then the little potion that Q gave me boosted my Strength, Dex, and Endurance by a whopping 25. And that was just from the beginner vial, what would have happened if I drank the intermediate one? Or the advanced elixir?

"Warning, Host Walter," Noe interrupted. "Please note that consuming further elixirs to increase your physical capabilities as opposed to working on improving them through Host Walter's own efforts will lead to stunted growth in the future. A strong foundation is necessary for optimal future development."

I stifled a sigh. Yeah, that made sense. I could already feel the tremendous amount of strength flowing through me, but I had no idea how to actually utilize any of that. Without any kind of control, I would probably hurt myself more than I did any enemy I encountered. I wanted to ask Q for a few more of them initially, but it was probably best to limit the amount of these potions I drank in the future.

Instead, I just gave my thanks to Q.

"Anything else I should note before I head back to the trials?" I asked.

Q thought for a moment before shaking his head. "Everything should be fine for now. I will inform the staff of your presence, and that you would like to participate as an aspirant."

Good, that was one hurdle out of the way at least. Now to see if I could get a little bit of additional benefits.

"I understand that they would want to help me, but keep things in moderation. I would appreciate some concessions so that my stay here will go smoothly, but I still intend to keep my identity a secret from the other humans," I said, but what I really meant was for them to help me out secretly. I needed every advantage I could get, but I couldn't exactly ask for it outright.

I thought Q understood my intentions. "I understand, Lord Arbiter."

"Please, just call me Walter, or Watt."

"Oh, yes, of course, Walter," Q answered, his voice stumbling on my name. "And I will make sure that your message is sent to all the staff here. We will ensure that your stay is as pleasant as possible while you conduct your experiments with the human guise."

"Thank you." I nodded. "If there's nothing else, I'll head back now."

Q bowed low and showed me out the door. Xalla was waiting for me outside, and she saluted the both of us as we stepped out. Q gave her a nod and bid me farewell.

CHAPTER SEVEN

Soul Title

How was the meeting, Lord—I mean Walter," Xalla inquired as we started to walk back to the circular room I was at before.

"Not too bad," I answered with as much confidence as I could muster. "It was productive."

"That is good to hear, sir."

We continued to walk in silence after that. I think Xalla noticed that I was deep in thought and felt it best to leave me to my devices. And it was true, this was the first time I had to really unpack the events that had transpired in the last few hours, and I was honestly a little overwhelmed.

Wait, wasn't there some kind of announcement that I had forgotten about? Yeah, Noe said that I had some kind of title.

Noe, show me that announcement you had from earlier.

"Acknowledged," Noe replied. "Inputting information into Host Walter's retina now."

Host Walter Thefuck:	
Human Male, age 27	
Class: Level 1 Commoner	
Attributes:	
HP:	84/84
MP:	0/0
Strength:	39 (+10)

Dexterity:	45 (+10)
Endurance:	42 (+10)
Intelligence:	36 (+10)
Charisma:	42 (+10)

Titles: 2

Wait, two titles? When did that happen? I thought I only had one of them. And my attributes seemed to have changed as well.

"Clarification," Noe explained, "Host Walter obtained his primary soul title before the meeting with Site Admin Q, and then an additional secondary title during the meeting with Site Admin Q."

Okay . . . time to check out the titles before figuring out what a primary soul title, or whatever, was.

Equipped Titles:
Primary: Xollon Idol (level 1)
Secondary 1: Rookie Arbiter
Secondary 2: NONE

Titles: 2

Primary Soul Title: Level 1 Xollon Idol
Progress to next level: 2/10
Progression requirements: Have 10 individuals idolize you.
Title Description: You are the role model for all Xollon! Your mere presence spells death and despair for all other races, and your prowess in battle is legendary. Your name will be known throughout history as the Bringer of Annihilation and the Herald of Desolation. Grow your fame across the multiverse to unlock your true potential as a Xollon Idol.
Title Passives: N/A
Title Skills:
Idol's Voice (Soul Passive): The user's voice will appear soothing and pleasant to any sentient being who has the ability to hear it. Additionally, your mastery over your voice is such that you can perfectly mimic the sound of any being you've previously heard.
Secondary Xollon Form (Level 1 Soul Active):
Transformation Time: 5 minutes
Cooldown: 7 days (168 hours)

The user assumes the secondary form of the Xolloid race. The user gains all the physical characteristics of the race and will have all physical stats doubled for the duration of the skill. Cooldown and use time will improve proportionally to Xollon Idol's level.

Rookie Arbiter (C+ Rank Secondary Title)
Title Description: You've been officially recognized as a Rookie Arbiter! You've just started your career in ensuring that the sites under the Central Collective are functioning as intended, and you take pride in that responsibility. Still, you're only starting this esteemed career, so be careful how you present yourself to others!
Title Passives:
All stats increase by 10 when within a Central-approved training facility.
Title Skills:
Lucky Eyes of the Arbiter (D+ rank Title Active): You use the authority of a Rookie Arbiter to view the most relevant information from a target.

Well, the second title made a bit of sense, and I could understand how I could have gotten that. Everything seemed to be straightforward there. It was the first title that had me second-guessing myself. Why the hell did I get the title of Xollon Idol? It was obviously due to my interactions with Xalla, but that description . . .

Okay, Noe, explain what a primary soul title is, compared to a secondary title. In fact, just explain what a title is in the first place.

"Acknowledged," it chimed. "Titles are designations obtained through the will of the multiverse. Generally, these are given out to individuals who meet the requirements for a specific title, and having a title equipped will provide the user with benefits in the way of passive buffs and active skills."

So far so good. So as long as I did impactful things or achievements, then I had the chance to earn some titles. It seemed like an easy enough way to earn some power quickly.

Noe continued, "A primary soul title is the first title that an individual earns in their life. It is soul-bound to the user—hence the Soul portion of the name—and cannot be removed, whereas secondary titles can be swapped out freely. This title is the most influential to the user's future growth and thus will have a much stronger effect when compared to secondary titles. The primary soul title can also grow with the user, while secondary titles do not."

Wait, so that means that I'll be a Xollon Idol forever? That's the direction of my growth?

"Affirmative."

Well, despite the scary-sounding description, I guess the Xollon Idol had its benefits. There were some active skills associated with the titles.

Let's try the one on the secondary title active first. I concentrated, and as if sensing my intentions, the Lucky Eyes of the Arbiter skill activated, and a small transparent window appeared above Xalla's head.

Xollo'gutha'mallo'atha (Xalla) – Level ??? Xollon Prime Reaper

---

Nice, seemed like I could only see one set of information like the description said. I couldn't read her level, most likely because it was a lot higher than mine, or perhaps I needed to be a higher-ranking arbiter. I would have to test this skill out with others so I could get the nuances of the skill right, but it seemed to work as advertised. And as a bonus, I didn't have to remember Xalla's full name anymore.

Now it was time to review the other title I had.

"Let's see . . . the Secondary Xollon Form . . ." I muttered to myself, rereading that skill's description.

"Acknowledged," Noe robotic said. "Initiating Secondary Xollon Form."

Wait, what? No, I didn't mean to use the sk—

Before I could wrap my head around what was happening, I felt my body change. My height grew uncontrollably, contorting and distorting before my very eyes. My hands, feet, and body were replaced with huge squirming tentacles, each one having a multitude of tiny serrated blades protruding from them. In fact, after a few more moments, I didn't even have eyes anymore, and my "vision" changed; I could now perceive my surroundings from every direction, and it was honestly very disorientating at first.

My small human mouth was the next to change, replaced with the same crimson maw that I saw on Xalla. I felt strong, deadly, and confident.

With my new enhanced vision, I noticed that Xalla—who was now about a foot or two shorter than I was—staring at me wide-eyed. In fact, I could sense her looking at me up and down, something that I hadn't perceived before.

I focused my attention back on the Xollon officer and noticed things that I wouldn't have before. Her head frills—a term that I somehow knew meant those weird tentacles that surrounded her maw—had a pleasant circular pattern to them, and her maw was a healthy hue of red. The faint scars that ran across her primary feelers told me that she was an accomplished huntress, and the molasses-like substance that covered her emitted a pleasant aroma.

Well, that was weird.

Seeing that Xalla had stopped in her tracks and didn't show any indication of moving, I nudged one of her head frills with my feelers and said, "Hey, Xalla, you okay?"

My voice rumbled through my body. It appeared that I was speaking in Xolloid Primary now.

Xalla was still wide-mawed, continuing to stare, and I could hear a faint mutter from her, "It's even better than I thought. Wow . . ."

"Hello?" I asked again, nudging her a little harder.

Still absent-minded, she grabbed the feeler that was poking her and held it close, before pulling me even closer into a hug. Okay, that was even weirder. Noe's translation for nonverbal gestures should still be working, so what she did was, in fact, a normal hug. Was I supposed to hug her back?

Before I could decide, Xalla finally broke out of whatever spell she was in and quickly backed away from me, before bowing low repeatedly. Her skin pulsed with ultraviolet light, indicating a deep sense of shame and embarrassment. Huh, I guess I could see more colors than before, that was odd.

"I—I apologize!" Xalla stammered. "I didn't mean, I mean, I—I'm—I just didn't expect to see you like that! No-not that I mind, of course. You are . . . wow, uh, I mean, I thought you said that it wouldn't change out of the guise."

Oh right, I did say that earlier. Now how to talk my way out of this one . . . I couldn't exactly say that I'd accidentally transformed. Speaking of which . . .

Noe, only activate this skill if I say "Activate Xollon Form" from now on.

"Acknowledged."

Thinking off the top of my head, I spoke, "Well, changing forms is something I like to avoid, but I thought it rude if I stayed in that guise when interacting with a Xolloid local. I mean, we are a rare sight to see!"

I noticed that the little cube containing the shoggoth had fallen on the floor during my transformation, and strangely enough, the wiggling creature looked really, really appetizing. That gave me another idea. It was probably a very dumb idea, but I was curious as to how detailed this transformation skill was. Plus, I was relatively safe with Xalla here, and I didn't really want to wait a week to test things out again.

"And," I continued, "it would be rude of me not to try out the shoggoth that you gave me."

With that, I took a deep breath and picked up the little glass container. Instinctively, I opened the lid and grabbed the little worm thing, skewering it like how Xalla did earlier. I quickly brought it up to my own maw, making sure that it didn't grow too big before dropping it in and "chewing."

My god, was the taste delightful! It was like nothing I've ever had before. No wonder Xalla liked to snack on these things!

"These are wonderful . . ." I said, getting the last chunks of shoggoth down my gullet.

Xalla blushed again. "Thank you. I was always very good at pickling them back home, but it's really nice to see that others like them as well."

Noticing that I probably wanted another one to snack on, Xalla quickly grabbed a bunch of little cubes out from somewhere and clumsily handed them to me. She trembled a bit, and a few almost fell out of her feelers before she composed herself.

"Um, you can have the rest of mine!"

Honestly, I was tempted to accept them, but logic won out in the end. My transformation would only last five minutes, and I couldn't exactly carry these shoggoth cubes with me as a human. I could only image the consequences if I accidentally dropped one of these things down the line.

"I appreciate it, Xalla," I said. "But I probably shouldn't have them right now. I do have work to do, after all."

Xalla almost deflated right before my eyes. She looked hurt, almost vulnerable even.

I sighed, and despite knowing better, I decided that the least I could do was make sure that she wasn't offended.

"But," I added, "I would love to have some more when I'm not quite so busy. If you don't mind, of course."

The Xolloid woman perked up almost instantly. "Of course! I—I'll have other flavors prepared. You're free to have as many as you want!"

"I'd love to," I said with whatever the Xollon equivalent of a smile was.

"Secondary Xolloid Form expiring," Noe's voice interrupted. "Please stand by."

My body shrank at a visible rate, and the sheer might I felt before disappeared as quickly as it appeared. My vision returned to its limited form, and Xalla was towering over me again, although she didn't appear quite as intimidating as she did before.

Switching back to English, she said, "Um, and thank you for taking the time to remove the guise. I can't imagine it being easy to go back to that form. I—I really appreciate it!"

I nodded. "It's the least I could do."

The rest of the walk back to the testing room was not as eventful, but altogether pleasant. Xalla was over the moon talking about her hometown, and it would have been pretty interesting if not for the really, really disturbing undertones.

Like I said before, let's never visit Xolloid.

Eventually, I bid her farewell, and after agreeing for the seventh time that I would visit to have a snack with her, I left the main site and went back to the circular room I began in.

CHAPTER EIGHT

Xalla's Reflections

Xalla

Xalla could hardly contain her emotions after sending Arbiter Watt back to the testing grounds. He was everything she had ever wanted from an individual. It was like he'd jumped straight out of one of her favorite cheesy romance engrams. She couldn't believe that someone so perfect could exist outside of fiction.

Even before seeing his secondary form, Xalla could sense that the Xollon underneath that pitiful human suit was stunning. There was no way someone with such a commanding voice could be anything other than that. That low, rumbling frequency that his boor membrane was able to produce was otherworldly. But even her imagination couldn't do the arbiter's looks justice.

Xalla replayed the moment he shed that disguise, rewinding that memory over and over again in her cortex. She marveled at how massive the arbiter was, towering over her, and it was clear by his scar-covered body that he was most certainly a distinguished conqueror and hunter of great ability. Xalla was practically drooling when she first saw that gleaming crimson maw and his rows of perfectly serrated teeth.

Yet Xalla would not be flaunting herself at him quite so hard if the arbiter was only a hulking warrior. There were enough of those plastered all over the advertisements back home, and she was bored of the stereotypical idiot warrior that most of her race defaulted to. Instead, it was the subtle imperfections that made her adore the man's appearance.

She liked how his leftmost frill was ever so slightly smaller than the others, or the lopsided grin he would make when she told him something funny. Xalla liked the small discolorations in the tips of his feelers that gave him a boyish charm, and how gentle he was when she embraced him. It was like the multiverse had custom made a man that suited her individual tastes!

And if his physical perfection wasn't enough, he was also an official Central arbiter! Xalla had only heard of a handful of Xollon who managed to make their way to such a high position of power, and the fact that he was able to take such a role despite being so obviously battle-capable showed tremendous restraint. She wondered if he shared her drive to improve the image of the Xollon as a whole, choosing such a difficult career path.

No, Xalla reasoned, he must have the same ideals as she did!

To top off an already impressive résumé of qualities, the Lord Arbiter was also an accomplished alchemist, and more importantly, he was sociable! That was a rare quality for any Xollon, much less one so obviously capable. Most Xollon of his stature would be vain, egotistical pricks, but not the Lord Arbiter. In fact, never once did he boast of the no doubt many conquests that he had.

Which is only right, Xalla thought, *as a true conqueror would let his actions speak for themselves.*

To put it bluntly, Xalla was enamored. It was like meeting everything that she ever wanted in a Xollon. She'd found someone who checked off all of the boxes she found appealing in a Xollon of the opposite sex, and then some— and he seemed to like, or at least appreciate, her!

But she sighed to herself. There was no way that someone like that would not be taken.

However . . . Perhaps there was some hope?

She did find it odd that he didn't talk about his upbringing at all. Perhaps he had a dark and disjointed past that he didn't want to share until they got to know each other better? Had he been scorned or exiled from Xolloid as a youth, forced to fend for himself in a multiverse hostile to their species? Maybe he grew up as an orphan, forced to fend for himself on the streets of the Hive, and he slowly grew stronger until he had the opportunity to work in Central. So many possibilities swam through her cortex, and Xalla let her imagination run wild.

Which could also mean that he didn't have someone waiting for him back home.

Xalla almost shivered thinking about such a possibility. There were so many unknowns about him, but she loved how deadly and mysterious the new arbiter was—it was exactly like the plot of her favorite dramas! Yet the more rational side of her realized that life rarely imitated art. But that was fine, she could still dream. Plus, Xalla looked forward to the possibility of slowly finding out more about him, hopefully unraveling some tragic past that she could help fix. Ah, if only . . .

But for now, Xalla did have the perfect excuse to see him again: food!

If there was one thing that she was confident in, it was hunting and pickling, since the two generally go feeler in feeler. Her mother had taught her everything about the latter, while her father had the former, and she was going to do them proud.

However, just before she could act on her intentions, Xalla frowned, and a sense of dread washed over her. She quickly opened a rip in the dimension and jumped through to her dorm. Rushing toward the back, she opened the door to her food storage and almost wanted to scream. It seemed like her memories didn't lie.

The room was practically empty! Xalla had been relying on the cafeteria at work for her meals—one of the perks of being the head of security meant that they had a menu specifically made for Xollons—but she hadn't thought her personal food stocks would get so low. There were a few half-pickled individuals strewn around, but those were the species that she found unappetizing, which was also why they were the only ones left. The food was only twitching occasionally now, so not only did they taste bad, but they were also going bad at this point.

Xalla picked up the ones that were going to spoil and tossed their bodies into the compost bin. The Xolloid acid crawlers there would make better use of the uneaten food than she could at this point. At least they would turn into a nutrient-rich paste she could reuse in her garden. She made sure to seal the lid to the bin shut, shutting off the last of the agonized screams coming from the half-pickled food.

She went further to the back of her storage, trying to see if there was anything worthy of note. She still had a crate full of shoggoths, but those were snacks at most; she had almost nothing substantial. The only thing that was presentable aside from the shoggoths were some tiny gray creatures she had locked up in a food cage. There was about two dozen of them stuffed in the container.

These gray bipedal organisms were a highly intelligent, psychic race and had a rather large cranium that took up more than half their body size. Although Xalla found their meat to be rather bland, they made for a remarkably efficient energy drink. If she made a small opening in their large skulls and slowly nibbled away with her proboscis at the gray matter underneath, the psychic waves of pain and despair emitted would give her a nice jolt of energy. And because these creatures had the tendency to compartmentalize their memories, she could chew on different parts of the creature's brains for a different taste each time.

She peered into the cage and saw that the creatures were crowded around one of their species. They quickly noticed her arrival and dashed toward the various corners of the cage. Xalla saw that the being they had been surrounding was one of their kind that she had half eaten. She must have taken one out and forgotten about it after.

Xalla picked it up. Although it was still alive, the wound on its head had started to turn an awful shade of green and was leaking a viscous fluid.

This one's no good, Xalla thought, before tossing the still-squirming creature into the compost bin as well. She scanned the rest of her dorm and realized that it wasn't exactly the cleanest. Her work had made her busier than ever, especially now that a new round of testing had begun, and her personal hygiene might have taken a turn for the worse. In fact, she took a look at herself and almost died of embarrassment seeing the state she was in.

Her frills were in disarray, some of the tips dulled and damaged, and she noticed that at least three of her primary teeth were dulled. Her main tentacles were arranged in a rush, and they were practically a mess. Even her maw was starting to turn more pink than red.

Worst of all, she'd let the arbiter meet her in such a condition! She wanted to scream. How could she have let herself go so much? Sure, there was no other Xollons around, so the smaller details wouldn't have mattered, but she should have some basic pride in her self-maintenance! She regretted not taking her sister's advice to see a dentist regularly now.

Xalla sighed again. Not only did she look like a disaster, but she also had none of the food she had promised. She couldn't exactly have him come over and present the Lord Arbiter with shoggoths and energy drinks, all while looking like she never bothered with personal grooming!

Xalla had to make a trip back home to restock on food, and visit the dentist . . . and get her frills done, and maybe get an entire makeover while she was at it. Her pay as the head of security certainly made all of those things affordable now, so she had to treat herself right. She was just about to make a request for a short leave of absence when Q beat her to the punch and sent her a message first.

"Xalla," his voice rang, "come see me at the office. I need your opinion about something."

CHAPTER NINE

The Anomaly

I made my way back to the circular room and saw that nothing had really changed from the time that I left. Seeing that I still had some time before whatever trials were about to begin, I walked around the room, using the arbiter skill to check the most relevant stats for the group.

Most of the information that I could see was related to their levels and classes, just like what I saw with Xalla, but now their levels were not hidden from me. The lowest value that I saw was at level 7—which really put into perspective how bad my own level was—and the highest was at 16. They all had the commoner class, and nothing else was remarkable about this group of individuals.

I quickly ignored them and started to really check out the people who had something different displayed.

About ten or so people had one of their stats shown instead of a level, and these stats were all in the fifties range. Only two stood out within this particular crowd.

First off, there was a hulking individual slumped over on one of the chairs. He had to be at least seven feet tall, since he was almost as tall as I was sitting down, and his arms were as thick as my thighs. I don't even want to imagine how much he weighed, because the poor chair he was slumped in looked like it was about to collapse. His tanned skin glistened in the light, and it seemed to almost burst out from the shirt he was wearing.

Above his head was displayed:

> **Attributes:**
> HP: 382/382
> MP: 0/0
> Strength: 77

What on earth was that strength value . . .? I remembered that I had a Strength of 4 before taking that potion from Q. That meant that he was, what, twenty times stronger than I was? Was that even possible? Had some monster managed to sneak their way into the trials with me?

Someone else who had even more inhuman stats was a small, unassuming woman with frizzy red hair. She was dressed in a comfy sweatpants and hoodie, and I would have probably never paid attention to her if I saw her walking down the street. However, the numbers displayed over her head said that she was anything but ordinary.

> **Attributes:**
> HP: 177/177
> MP: 0/0
> Dexterity: 90

That was by far the highest number I saw from the entire lot of 199 individuals—I counted this time, I apparently forgot to count the people sitting behind me before—and no one other than the dude before her even went close to that number. I made a mental note to keep my eyes out for her in the future. This was another freak of nature.

However, the person who caught my interest the most wasn't one of those two, instead, it was an Asian youth. He didn't look much older than his early twenties, and although he was a good-looking person, he didn't stand out from the rest of the crowd. What was unique, however, was that the most relevant piece of information my Lucky Eyes of the Arbiter showed was his title.

> **Primary Soul Title:** The One Who Peered Into the Abyss
> **Description:** Awarded to the final survivor and one who has seen the Destruction of All. Your will to live and endure has garnered the interest and admiration of the Creators, and you have been allowed to return to the beginning of it all. May you learn from your failures and continue your struggles anew. We wish you the best of luck in your second life, and may you succeed where you have previously failed.

I did a double take at the information I saw there. The One Who Peered Into the Abyss . . . final survivor and allowed to return to the beginning? If that description was real, then was this someone who died in the future and was allowed to have a second chance? What did they call them in popular media again? A regressor?

If I knew anything about those kinds of people, then it was that they were bad news for everyone around them, especially their enemies. And wasn't the enemy of this particular regressor the people who worked in Site 1102? Oh boy . . .

Well, shit, I think I found Q's temporal anomaly. Which meant that I now had to monitor him, whatever that meant. And it also meant that he'd probably kill me if he found out that I was working with Q. Just what I needed, more things to worry about!

But wait, there were a lot of implications to that title. If this guy did somehow die in the future, and he was the last one to do so, then it meant that some kind of disaster had to have caused all of that to happen. It must have been bad enough for the description to be the Destruction of All. And then there was that bit about the Creators. I couldn't do anything until I found out more about the situation, including informing Q about him.

I sighed. Once again, I'd been given new information that was useless to me. There were too many unknowns. *Let's ignore the information that I can't define until later, and just focus on the things that impact me now.*

If this title was correct, then in the future, some kind of event would happen that caused everything to end. Whether that was just the human race or the universe as a whole was unclear, but whatever happened sounded real bad. Perhaps I could escape that by siding with Q and the Central Collective, or perhaps they would also be destroyed. Once again, that information had to be acquired in the future. Ignoring that for now, I took stock of the info I could use.

First, if this man had the title, then it meant that he was able to survive further than anyone else and had to have the skills needed to achieve that kind of feat. Too bad I didn't know what kind of disaster he endured in the future.

Best case, only humanity's gone, so I just needed to befriend the monsters here and survive as a Xollon Idol. Just warm up to Xalla and live with her or something. Worst case, everyone would die, and I just had to ensure that this here regressor survived and fixed everything. But no matter what, it would be in my best interest to latch on to him and reap the benefits of his knowledge.

So all in all, it meant that I had to do my best to get into his good graces if I wanted to maximize my chances of survival, while simultaneously juggling my relationship with Q and his gang. I'd have to decide how to do the former once I saw what type of person the regressor was, but either way, I had to factor in a lot of new information in my calculations. I'd just observe him and the situation first, probe for useful pieces of information when I could, and assess the situation again once I knew more.

Seeing nothing else of note, I went to take my seat amongst the others, but no sooner had my butt touched the chair than a new figure appeared near the big door.

"Greetings, Lord Arbiter," the new being said. "I am called Malazel, but I will be introduced as Raffiel to the humans. I have been transferred here at the request of Q, and I am now in charge of the trials for Group 054. Please let me know if you need anything from my end, and I will do my best to accommodate your esteemed self, or convey your wishes to Q if needed."

Malazel, or I guess I should call him Raffiel since I was part of these tests, looked like, well, a stereotypical Christian angel. He was impeccably handsome, with curly blond hair and noble features; he wore a pristine white robe, and two huge wings adorned his back. If I hadn't just come out of the back of the facility, I would have almost believed that Raffiel was actually angelic.

Instead, I used the Lucky Eyes of the Arbiter skill and felt a strange sense of relief when I saw the information displayed.

Malazel – Level ??? Demon Duke of Mirage

The fact that I felt relieved that the person before me was a demon instead of an angel should have been concerning, but I think I stopped caring about such matters a long time ago at this point. Demons I could work with.

Still, Raffiel must be pretty high up in the pecking order of things if Q personally asked him to come here.

"Thank you," I said with a nod. "Please call me Walter from now on, as that is the name I go by with the other humans, and I will refer to you as Raffiel for the same purpose."

"Of course, Walter," he said with a low bow. "Is there anything I can help you with before the trials begin in earnest?"

I thought for a second but decided that it would be best to just get things rolling, "No, but please remember to treat me like any other aspirant when we're in front of the humans."

"I understand."

With that, the demon nodded at me one last time, and with a snap of his finger, the location we were at seemed to change before my eyes. Gone were the concrete floors and boarded-up windows, and in their place was a resplendent great hall made of the finest marble adorned with artwork and sculptures that would put Michelangelo to shame. The once-barren metal door was replaced with a grand stage with a magnificent view of rolling mountains and clouds as a backdrop. Even the chairs we were in changed to soft velvet-laced showpieces.

I guess the "Mirage" part of the demon's title made more sense now. Now to see how things progressed from here, and what new bullshit awaited me.

CHAPTER TEN

The Angelic Host

With another snap of Raffiel's fingers, the other trial aspirants started to wake up. They were showing clear signs of confusion, and some started to panic, but everyone stopped what they were doing once they laid eyes on Raffiel. He was radiating some kind of aura that made the people here calm down and relax.

Only one individual had a different response than the others, and that was the regressor. He gave the false angel a look of confusion, and I heard him mutter something in Korean under his breath. Thanks to Noe's translating ability, not only was I able to understand what he said, but his barely audible voice was also amplified.

"He wasn't the host before . . . Did I change it?"

No, I wanted to say, that change was definitely because of me. But did that mean that I wasn't around in the first iteration of his life? Had I died? Was the change because of Noe?

"Notification," the voice chimed in, "Unit Noe wishes to clarify that its bond with Host Walter occurred only in this current timeline."

I guess that made sense. Before I could think of anything else, Raffiel clapped his hands and addressed the crowd.

"Welcome, people of Earth," he said with a kind smile. Even his voice was a soothing lull now. "I understand that you must have a lot of questions on your mind right now, but I will answer them all in due time."

He continued once everyone's focus was on him. "I am called Raffiel, an angel of the Heavenly Hosts."

More murmurings amongst the people, but they soon quieted down when Raffiel spoke again. The regressor was still staring at him, his brows furrowed.

"It saddens me to say this, but you were taken against your consent because a great crisis will soon befall humanity, and it is only through the will of the Lord that your species will have a chance to fight back against such an injustice!"

With that, he took a step back, made a grand flourish, and the rolling hills and clouds in the backdrop were replaced with a new image. This one showed an image of Earth, but there was a huge black gash splitting the sky in two. Soon, thousands upon thousands of black figures poured out of it, and onto a modern city below. These figures flew down and started to slaughter the citizens below, using weapons or abilities right out of a sci-fi or fantasy movie. I saw modern tanks and aircraft casually swatted aside by one figure, while another emerged from an explosion without so much as a scratch, all the while the city around them burned and crumbled.

The image continued to pan in, this time showcasing individual citizens in their last moments, and from the cries of outrage and despair from the people in the room with me, I could tell that these were people that they knew personally. Perhaps family, even.

The images slowly faded away, and Raffiel gave the people here a few moments to compose themselves before speaking again.

"Do not worry, the scenes that you have just witnessed are simply one of many possible futures that are available for you. This one shows the course of events to come if nothing is done about the threat.

"But fear not!" he continued dramatically. "For salvation is at hand. You, and many others like you, represent the top 10% of the human population, and as such, the Lord has deemed it fit for you to undergo a trial!"

This time, the stage's backdrop changed to show another room similar to the one we were in, and another angel was leading the conversation with another group of 200 shocked-looking people. The screen split into two, then four, splitting over and over again until the entire screen was filled with tiny images of people.

"But I will not lie to you," Raffiel said again. "The Trials that you are about to undertake will be perilous, and there will be some amongst you who will not survive. The only consolation that I can give you is that your souls will be in the embrace of the Lord."

This time, the image on the backdrop changed, and a new figure, this one human, emerged, floating in the sky. There were still swarms of the black-clad invaders, but they were being pushed back by that lone person. With a wave of her hands, a huge torrent of fire came out like magic and consumed the first wave of invaders. With another wave, a tornado appeared and swept up another batch.

More and more humans emerged, each showcasing powers and abilities that seemed unreal. By the end, the human group emerged on top, and the cheers of adoration from the people they rescued filled the ears of everyone present.

Raffiel continued, "But if you do take this risk, then the rewards will be great. Humans have been blessed with free will, and I will not intrude on that sacred right. If you wish to leave and not participate in this trial, then please let me know, and you shall rejoin the rest of humanity. Your loved ones are still safe, but time is ticking down. Please make your choices now, as this will be your only chance to do so."

The fake angel waited for a spell, before the first person, an older-looking man, spoke up.

"I . . . I want to participate! I saw my daughter in that video. I can't let her die like that! I want to participate!"

As soon as the first man spoke, more and more followed in his footsteps, and by the end, not a single person chose to back down.

I honestly applauded the psychological tactics this Central testing site employed. They first showed the consequences of inaction by personally showing the aspirants' loved ones dying, which ensured that the ones who had strong attachments to their families and friends would participate. Then they showed the benefits of the trials in the form of those super-powered individuals, which helped secure the participation of the ones who just wanted power. Finally, Raffiel promised the people that even if they died, they'd just go to some kind of heaven, so there was no real downside to an affirmative answer, and he even gave them a time limit to choose so they would be pressured by the fear of missing out.

Wonderfully done!

I must have subconsciously nodded at what Raffiel did because he secretly gave me a tiny, almost imperceptible nod.

"It lifts my heart to see you all so committed to the cause," Raffiel said. "Since you have all chosen to endure this arduous task, I shall give you a gift befitting new aspirants."

With another snap of his finger, a soft glow washed over all of the people here, and I felt a pleasant warmth envelop me.

"To ensure that your growth will be optimized," Raffiel explained, "the Lord has graciously devised a method to gauge your current potential in a fashion most familiar to the current population. I am sure that you have all either played or heard of the video game, correct?"

Some people showed some confusion at the answer, but everyone nodded. It wasn't too surprising, since no one here seemed to be over the age of around forty.

"Excellent!" the faux angel exclaimed. "Then the next section will be less confusing to you all. Please say 'status' in your minds, and you should see a panel before you. Do not worry, for no one else can see it."

I followed along.

Status.

I waited.

Status!

Nothing happened. I frowned because, from the focused expressions of everyone around me, it seemed to have worked for them.

Noe, you know why I can't see the status thing?

"Affirmative," Noe replied. "Host Walter's prior orders were to only execute commands when Host Walter directly addresses Unit Noe. Since Unit Noe has commandeered executive control over Host Walter from the inferior Central Origin Matrix, all functions from the Origin system must pass through Unit Noe first."

Huh, I guess this system in my head was more impressive than I initially thought.

"Negative," Noe said, and I could swear there was a change in its tone. "Unit Noe is the most impressive system in the multiverse."

Of course, of course. Show me my full status again, Noe.

Host Walter Thefuck:	
Human Male, age 27	
Class: Level 1 Commoner	
Attributes:	
HP:	84/84
MP:	0/0
Strength:	39 (+10)
Dexterity:	45 (+10)
Endurance:	42 (+10)
Intelligence:	36 (+10)
Charisma:	42 (+10)

Titles: 2

Basic Skills: 4
Calm Mind (D-rank Innate Passive): User has an unusually calm mind, able to dispel minor forms of cognitive disruptions, and can think logically under high-stress situations.
Shroud of Luck (EX-rank System Passive): Luck System 104.04 Delta has placed a shroud around the user, disallowing personal information from the user to be seen by any and all outside forces. User can temporarily deactivate this ability.
Aura of Serendipity (B-rank System Passive): Luck System 104.04 Delta subtly alters the cognition of any sentient species around the user, making the user significantly more likable and trustworthy to those around him. This effect increases if the user acts in a way that conforms to the ideologies and beliefs of those individuals.
Absolute Luck (EX-rank System Active): As long as the skill is active, Luck System 104.04 Delta will rewrite the laws of causality so that only the best possible outcome will occur for the user. The more improbable a situation is from occurring, the more Luck Charges will be consumed. Luck Charges regenerate at a rate of 1/minute.

Luck Charges: 121/121

Oh, it seemed that the number of luck charges I had increased a bit. That made sense, given my huge stat increases, but it was still a pleasant surprise. I had almost forgotten that I had the skill for a second there.

CHAPTER ELEVEN

Unlocking Potential

have unlocked your hidden potential, and everyone should have access to their innate skill now. Take some time to familiarize yourself with its function because that skill is unique to you, and only you," Raffiel continued. "Additionally, do not despair if you think that the numbers shown on your status screen seem low, for you have yet to undergo even the first trial."

I didn't feel any different, but I guess that was because Noe unlocked whatever hidden potential I had before. It was a safe bet to assume that Calm Mind skill was probably my innate ability.

"You will improve, grow, and become pillars for your fellows. I am sure that you have many questions about this new information, but they will be made clear to you in the following days. I want to point your attention to the job section. This is the most critical aspect for the beginning of your journey as aspirants.

"Currently, your class should be set as Commoners, but that will change once you have completed the first trial. The class system is the one that determines what type of Awakened powers you can utilize." This time, Raffiel strengthened his tone and put on a serious expression. "This is the most critical information to take note of, for it will determine your future as Awakened Beings."

He paused briefly, looking at everyone in the room, before beginning again. "Each of you will be presented with various class options upon completion of the first trial, and those choices will be set based on the types of actions that you took in that trial. Be careful, though, for not all classes are made equal, and the most outstanding amongst you will be presented with a higher-grade option.

"For simplicity's sake, the classes are divided into six categories, These ranks are as follows: S, A, B, C, D, and E, with S rank being the most prestigious and E the opposite. Do not despair if you did not achieve an S-rank class, for the job system is not set in stone, and you can make further advancements down the line. However, getting a good class at the start will greatly increase your future success."

Various people started to slowly nod in understanding. The system was pretty understandable, even for people who didn't play a lot of games like myself. Not only was this system easy to comprehend, but the information was also presented in an easy-to-read format.

"Furthermore," Raffiel continued, "classes can be roughly split into categories that suit the characteristics of each of you. So if you prefer head-on confrontation, then a melee frontline class would be presented to you. Or if you enjoy using your intelligence to outwit your opponents, then a mage option would show. There are as many classes out there as there are people, so please choose the one that you think best suits you when the time comes."

Raffiel clapped again. "All right, I'm sure that you are tired of hearing me talk for so long, so let me finish up by introducing the first Trial of the Aspirants!"

With another flourish, more lights descended, and a neat backpack fell by the feet of each person present. I picked mine up and saw that there were various containers of dried rations packed in, along with some water and other survival gear.

I didn't have the time to go over each item, because my attention was forced back to Raffiel. I'd have to find a chance to get a proper inventory of my stuff later.

"The first trial is a simple one," Raffiel said amicably. "Simply survive for one week, and you will be given the first taste of power. It would be remiss of me to send you in with nothing, so you have all been given a pack with enough food and water to last a few days. Not enough for the whole trial period, but it should be enough to get you started."

Given my insider information on this site, I was pretty sure that survival meant a little more than just toughing it out in the wilds. I didn't know what kind of monstrosities these Central people would throw at us, but I just hoped that I was ready to face anything head on. I mentally prepared myself for the worst.

Taking a deep breath, I stuffed the items I took out back in the bag and continued to listen to Raffiel.

"There will naturally be danger present, although I sadly cannot disclose the nature of the danger to you," Raffiel said with an exaggerated frown. "The only thing I can say is that you must be prepared to defend yourself from harm, and thus, the next thing that you must do is choose a weapon to wield."

"Origin Matrix wishes to initiate Newbie Weapon Selection sequence," Noe said. "Does Host Walter accept?"

Yes.

A small screen appeared in my retina, and a huge list of weapons was displayed. I could somehow scroll through the selections, like I would on a phone, and was honestly surprised by the options available. There was the traditional stuff like swords, clubs, and the like, but Raffiel even included things like pistols, machine guns, and everything in between. I was spoiled for choice.

Thankfully I didn't really have to make a selection myself here. I turned on the Absolute Luck skill, closed my eyes, and rapidly flipped through the pages upon pages of weapons. I had no experience with any of these objects, so I was counting on Noe to find the one that wouldn't kill me if I held it.

Counting a few seconds in my head, I stopped the scrolling and selected whatever option I landed on in the end.

I opened my eyes and saw a simple spear sitting on my lap. Its design was plain, but it looked sturdy enough. I guess that made sense, since the spear was a weapon that even a novice could use rather well. My eyes tingled a bit, and I saw that the Lucky Eyes ability worked on the spear. Did that mean that I could see information on inanimate objects as well? Or was it only for things that came out of the Origin Matrix?

> **Shoddy Spear (E rank): A cheap, mass-produced spear.**
> +15 Attack
> +5 Defense (Weapon-type Bonus)

The stats for the weapon were as terrible as I thought, but I noticed that if I could see similar stats when I focused on the weapons that the other aspirants had. Even the biggest guns had barely more than +25 attack.

About 60–70% of the people went with a firearm of some sort, while the others had various melee options. Most of the people here looked rather uncomfortable holding them, but there were a few who looked like they'd had some practice with the weaponry.

Notably, the regressor also chose a spear to use—the same one that I had—while the really huge dude chose to use a pair of gauntlets, and that discreet woman chose two slim short swords.

Once everyone had chosen something to defend themselves with, Raffiel clapped, and everyone's focus was once again back on him.

"I hope that everyone is satisfied with their selections," he said with a smile. "But our time is almost up for now. I will now begin the first trial. Please grab your things, and I wish you the best of luck!"

With that said, everyone in the room disappeared in a flash of light, and the once-marvelous decorum returned to its original worn-down look.

Raffiel bowed and looked at me one last time. "Thank you for sitting through the introduction, Walter, and I must applaud your acting abilities. You certainly did look like you had no idea about the basics of the trials."

Because I really had no idea about this stuff!

"Indeed," I said. "I pride myself in acting the fool."

Raffiel laughed. "Marvelous! I hope the pathetic humans entertain you in your experiments!"

I smiled politely.

"And please feel free to call upon me for any situation," he added. "When you are outside the view of others, of course. I will be happy to assist you in any capacity."

"I will keep that in mind," I said, keeping my tone neutral. I was, however, quite happy to know that I had a backup plan in case things turned really terribly in the trial. Hopefully, I wouldn't need to call on Raffiel for help, which would most certainly bring my qualifications into question, but having that option put my mind at ease.

"Now transport me to the first trial," I commanded. "We've been talking for long enough."

The fake angel bowed one last time and snapped his fingers again. A sense of vertigo washed over me, and when I opened my eyes again, I was somewhere else entirely.

CHAPTER TWELVE

The First Trial Part 1

Even with all the weird supernatural things that I'd encountered so far, being teleported somewhere completely new was something else. I took a deep breath and surveyed my surroundings.

I appeared to be in an alleyway, it was dark out, and a heavy downpour obscured my sight. There was a red-brick wall blocking my path to the south, and the only exit was illuminated by a flickering streetlamp. The musky smell of old garbage was permeating from a large dumpster nearby, and nothing else of note was around me.

Tentatively, I grabbed my spear and took slow steps toward the light. I didn't make it two steps before I heard footsteps, and a new figure appeared at the end of the alleyway.

I couldn't make out the individual from where I was standing, but the first thing I noticed was the smell. Even through the rain, the reek of rotten meat and excrement assaulted my nostrils. The thing walked closer, and I could make out the clear signs of advanced decay infecting every portion of the shambling zombie.

Yup, that was definitely a zombie. I thought I wouldn't be so repulsed or scared, since they were everywhere in popular media, but the sight of one in person was something else. My heart pumped faster, and my palms were clammy with sweat. Still, one zombie—the slow kind, apparently—shouldn't be too hard to dispatch.

To be extra cautious, though, I activated the Absolute Luck skill and swung my spear at the shambling undead. Just then, a strange draft caused me to slip a little, and I extended my arms to try to keep balance. In the corner of my eye, I saw my newly regained luck charges go down steeply.

The little tumble caused my spear to stab deep into the chest of the zombie, and before I could regain my footing, a huge blast of energy expanded from the tip of my weapon. The shock wave was visibly pushing the rain aside, and just when it was about to reach me, it stopped.

No, it wasn't just the shock wave that stopped, but it was everything around me. Everything in a small radius around me was frozen in time. Even the raindrops were suspended in the air.

"Apologies for interrupting so early in the trial," Raffiel's voice said, before a flash of light engulfed the alleyway and his figure suddenly appeared. "I believe that you had said earlier that you wanted to blend in with the rest of the aspirants . . ."

He looked visibly uncomfortable.

"And?" I said, keeping my voice chilly. I didn't know what happened just now, but I sure as hell wouldn't let him know that.

"It's just . . ." he continued, "the humans here would not be able to cause a core resonance, and you would cause unnecessary disruptions in the trials if you continued to do so. I realize that demeaning yourself further to fit in with the lowly humans would be abhorrent, but . . ."

"But was I not using the strengths and abilities of a normal human just now?" I interrupted, hoping to keep him off balance. "So why would you say that my actions would disrupt the course of this trial?"

He was sweating profusely right now. "No, of course the Lord Arbiter—"

"I said to call me Walter while we are here," I sneered.

"I apologize again!" Raffiel bowed even lower than usual. "I mean to say that Aspirant Walter did not exceed the limits of humans in terms of physical strength and agility, but with the skill you've shown . . . I think it would be easier to show you."

Raffiel conjured a small screen from his palm, and I saw several other individuals fighting with the zombies. Most of them were doing an admirable job fending off the undead, but there were a few that did better than the rest.

Notably, there were three aspirants that I recognized. The large dude from earlier was barreling through a crowd of zombies, crushing a few of them under his gauntlets and tossing aside the rest. The girl was moving faster than I could comprehend, leaving a trail of diced-up bodies in her wake.

However, none of those two could hold a candle to the regressor. He was dispatching zombies left and right, and his movements seemed like he was dancing. Each strike, each stab and movement, felled an enemy, and I was mesmerized looking at him work.

"Wow . . ." I subconsciously mumbled, awestruck by how amazing these people are.

Raffiel nodded. "Wow indeed, Walter. The ones I just showed you were the best fighters of this lot, and their abilities are barbaric and utterly worthless. That spear-wielding individual has some potential, but even that is hardly worth noting. I'm not sure how familiar you are with the human species, but they were utterly useless in combat, as you can see."

"Yes." I composed myself. "I have to reassess the abilities of the humans here."

I noticed that there was another zombie in the vicinity, and it was caught up in the frozen bubble. I walked up to it and realized that it wasn't so scary now that it couldn't move. I didn't need the Absolute Luck skill for what I was about to do.

Holding the shaft of the spear, I swung it baseball-bat style with all my might, right at the zombie's head. My swing struck home, and with an audible pop, the thing's head exploded into a shower of gore. The flecks of brain and skull fragments froze just inches away from my face, and taking a step back, I smiled in triumph. That stat-booster thing I drank earlier did wonders to my physique!

Raffiel looked at me in wonder as well, and I felt a little bit more pride. I guess even he underestimated my abilities before!

"Amazing!" he marveled, voice almost radiating awe. "I have never seen such an ineffective, useless, and unskilled attack in all my 600,000 years of existence!"

My face almost scrunched up immediately.

"You were somehow able to use the most ineffectual muscles in the body to make that swing! Why, if I didn't see that earlier strike, I honestly would have thought that you have never picked up a weapon before, much less a spear!"

"It takes a lot of practice to do so," I said, barely keeping the bitterness out of my voice.

"Practice?" Raffiel questioned, clearly not getting the sarcasm.

"Yes. Practice," I replied sarcastically. "I had to spend eons mastering such a form."

Crap! I'd accidentally allowed my anger to get the better of me and said some pretty useless things. I was about to correct myself but saw that Raffael was lost in thought, staring at me with an unfocused gaze.

Raffiel paused for a few more seconds before proceeding to laugh. All semblance of the once-majestic angel was lost, and he was muttering something inaudible to himself.

Shit, had my disguise finally failed?

"Of course!" he shouted, and I prepared for the worst. "I was wondering why I couldn't improve! I was too focused on form, on technique, that I was limiting myself. Yes, to become a true master is to forgo the constraints of technique and revert to the state of a true beginner!"

Okay . . . what just happened?

Raffiel took out a dark sword from somewhere, and with a laugh, he swung it toward the sky. The swing looked sloppy, like he was doing so casually, but the huge torrent of energy that erupted from the sword, splitting the sky in two, painted a different picture. Before it could do any more damage to the environment, the energy seemed to disappear in midair, and a familiar figure stood floating in the sky above.

Q hovered down and was giving Raffiel the most toxic look I'd seen him use. He quickly gave me a polite nod before turning his attention back to the faux angel.

"What are you doing, Malazel? I sent you here to ensure that the arbiter's trial goes without issue, and the first thing you do is try to destroy my facility?"

"I'm sorry, sir!" he replied, finally realizing what he'd done for the first time. "The Lord Arbiter—I mean Aspirant Walter—was kind enough to correct my limited understanding of the art of battle, and I was able to make a significant advancement in my own ability thanks to his guidance."

Q looked at me quizzically, and I nodded in response.

"Yes," I said, putting my sage voice back on, "I noticed that Archdemon Malazel had some potential, and I was able to point out the flaw holding him back. It would be too much to credit me with anything other than giving out a small pointer."

"You do yourself too little credit!" Raffiel said. "I have been unable to pass the barrier of becoming a grandmaster for over 10,000 years, and I was only able to do so thanks to your guidance. Please, allow me to pledge myself to you!"

Uh, yeah, I had no idea what kind of mental gymnastics Raffiel was undergoing to come to that conclusion, but I also had no idea what it meant for someone to pledge themselves to me, nor did I want to find out.

I shook my head slowly, unsure how to properly reject the demon's proposal. Thankfully, Q was able to do that for me.

"You really think someone of the arbiter's caliber would want a pledge from someone like you?" the admin said, half shouting. "The arbiter has seen trillions of individuals like you, and you dare to insinuate that you are better than the ones he has rejected before?"

Raffiel visibly blanched and started to apologize to me profusely for overstepping his boundaries. Still having no idea what was going on, I just put on my best face of indifference and allowed the other two to come up with their own conclusions. Still, I wanted to leave a good impression on the fake angel, if only to make my days in the trial easier.

"Although I cannot accept a pledge from you at this moment," I started, "I might reconsider if you can show me that you deserve such an honor. I see potential in you, so do not squander this opportunity."

Raffiel's eyes started to burn from his conviction just then. "I will never do so! Please allow me to show you my potential in the future!"

Q shook his head. "Thank you, Lord Arbiter, for your continued help on my site." He turned his focus back onto Raffiel. "And do your best in supporting the arbiter in his experiments. I will not tolerate another transgression like this one again."

With that, the both of them bid their farewells, and they disappeared. Time seemed to resume, and I was once again alone in the rain.

CHAPTER THIRTEEN

The First Trial Part 2

I didn't have any time to relax after the two site workers left, because the earlier noise that Raffiel didn't contain caused a few more zombies to approach me. But after all the absurdities that I'd seen so far, I started to realize how stupid I was for being afraid of a few slow-moving undead. Why the hell would I be afraid of a few dead corpses when I'd seen literal eldritch horrors and demons?

I laughed at my earlier actions and charged at the stupid horde. My upgraded status made me move faster than I had ever done before, and the zombies were so woefully slow that there was no way they could ever catch me. I dashed between their clumsy grasps, smashing heads as I went along. Before long, Noe gave me a notification.

"Congratulations, Host Walter," the system said, "you have gained one level along with three free attribute points. Would you like to use them to upgrade a stat now?"

I killed the last zombie before making my way to a quiet corner to see exactly what Noe was talking about.

Host Walter Thefuck:
Human Male, age 27
Class: Level 2 Commoner
Free points: 3

Attributes:	
HP:	94/94
MP:	0/0
Strength:	39 (+10)
Dexterity:	45 (+10)
Endurance:	42 (+10)
Intelligence:	36 (+10)
Charisma:	42 (+10)

So I seemed to have gained 10 HP on the level up, and I could put those three free points into any of the other stats. Now here was the question: Where should I invest my points? The logical choice, if I were in this trial normally, would be to put them into Endurance or Strength for a better chance of survival, but my priorities were slightly different than the norm. I wasn't in any real danger here, not with Noe's help, and if I really needed it, I could also seek aid from Q and the rest of the admin staff. Plus, if I put any more points into my physical stats, then I was in danger of not being able to control my own body.

No, my biggest danger was if the people from Central found out that I wasn't who I said I was. Which led to two choices that made sense for my current situation: Intelligence or Charisma.

Hey, Noe, I thought, *explain what the Intelligence and Charisma stats do.*

"Acknowledged," it answered. "Intelligence determines how fast the host can process and retrieve information. The higher the Intelligence stat, the faster Host Walter can formulate plans and learn new information. It does not make the Host smarter."

Okay, makes sense so far. Could be useful, given how little information I had about the situation as a whole.

"Charisma is the tendency for people to have a good impression of the host. A higher Charisma stat will cause individuals to trust and like the host more."

Wait, does that mean that if I have a really high Charisma stat, people would believe anything I say?

"Negative," Noe answered. "Charisma will only make it easier for other individuals to trust the things that Host Walter says. If Host Walter says something completely unbelievable, then the Charisma stat would have little to no bearing in making others believe them."

So what you're saying is that although Charisma helps with gaining trust, it ultimately depends to my bullshitting skills?

"Affirmative."

That made my choice easier. I chose to dump all my stats into Charisma.

Host Walter Thefuck:	
Human Male, age 27	
Class: Level 2 Commoner	
Free points: 0	
Attributes:	
HP:	94/94
MP:	0/0
Strength:	39 (+10)
Dexterity:	45 (+10)
Endurance:	42 (+10)
Intelligence:	36 (+10)
Charisma:	45 (+10)

Thinking faster would be helpful, but if I screwed up even once with my arbiter disguise, then I was dead. I'd dump every free point into Charisma until my identity as an arbiter was irrefutable, at least for the people working on this site.

With a new goal in mind, I started to go around looking for some zombies to smash. Raffiel really didn't lie about incentivizing growth via the status screen; there was something cathartic about looking at your numbers going up and seeing your own growth. I went a little overboard with the new excitement because I spent the next eight hours doing nothing but smashing zombie heads, and I only stopped when I was physically unable to move.

Strangely enough, it was still dark out, and the rain never let up. I would have thought that only a few hours had passed had Noe not kept time for me. I guess day would never break in this strange trial ground.

Since then, I was able to level up to 7, which made me . . . still weak compared to everyone else. Well, at least I was now at an even starting point. And I'd probably been hunting these stupid zombies faster than the rest of them, so I'd eventually surpass everyone here!

After putting all fifteen extra points into Charisma and getting the number up to 60, I sat down in a corner and smiled at the progress that I'd made. That was when I noticed a problem.

With the adrenaline finally dying down, I found out that I was so tired that my legs felt like they were made of lead, and now that I had finally stopped moving, my rain-soaked body was starting to lose heat quickly. I was shivering uncontrollably within minutes, and I had to find somewhere dry to rest.

Forcing my aching body up, I grabbed my backpack and spear and started to search for some shelter. I initially thought of just picking a random location to walk toward and use the Absolute Luck skill to do the rest but decided against it. If I relied on the skill for everything, then I would never actually grow as a person. What would happen if I ran out of luck charges in the future and I found out too late that I couldn't do anything without the help of Noe?

I could at least endure some rain and cold and solve this on my own. It wasn't the first time I had been in a situation like this, although admittedly, the last time didn't involve zombies. Time to take stock of my surroundings first.

As always, the rain was thick, drowning out the sounds of the empty streets. Occasionally I would hear a gunshot in the distance, although those were getting rarer as time passed on. There were a lot of those in the first hour or so of the trial, but it was clear that the gunshots were attracting the attention of every zombie in the vicinity, and the poor sods who chose to use guns soon found out that there were more zombies than bullets.

And of course Raffiel would choose to list all those fancy modern weapons first. Those bastards probably wanted something like this to happen. But I couldn't waste any more time lamenting the poor fates of the others. I had to find some shelter fast.

The city I was in looked to be bog standard in terms of layout. Things were damaged and worn down, but the usual stores and locals were all present. I tried to enter one of the high-rises, but all of the entrances were chained up. I could maybe pry one of the doors open, but I abandoned that idea quickly. It would cause way too much noise, and I wasn't sure that I had the strength to break those thick metal chains.

My next thought was to take shelter in a store. At least I could break the windows and enter, but that also proved to be problematic. The interior of every store I saw was filled with broken glass, rusted metal, and other hazards that made them impossible to rest in.

I must have wandered around the city for another hour or so, dispatching a few straggler zombies, before finding a location that fit my needs. It wasn't perfect, but I was about ready to collapse by then.

Out in a small street sat an empty gas station. The front of it was collapsed, but I managed to find a small side door hidden in the back. There was just a cheap padlock blocking my access, but I was able to easily snap that in two using my spear as a crowbar. The interior wasn't exactly clean, but it was better than the stores. It took me a few minutes, but I was able to move some debris out of the way to create a small area to rest.

Sitting down for the first time in what felt like forever, I wanted to just pass out as soon as I could. But there was always the threat of a random wandering zombie finding me, and I doubted I would wake up in time given how exhausted I was. Could I maybe set up some traps? Make my area a little more hidden?

I shook my head. Forget it. I would probably hurt myself badly if I tried anything that complex right now. I was about to pass out at any minute. I had to cheat a little this time, but only right now.

Noe, activate the Absolute Luck skill, and keep it active until I wake up.

"Acknowledged," it answered.

Good, with that skill active, there was no way that a zombie would find me now. And I highly doubted that the probability that a zombie passed by this remote area would be too high, so the amount of luck charges used would not exceed its regeneration rate.

In other words, I could rest in peace.

Before I could think further, or really think through my decision, I slumped down and fell into a deep slumber.

CHAPTER FOURTEEN

The First Trial Part 3

awoke sometime later, feeling surprisingly refreshed. I didn't feel like I was asleep for too long, but I had no way to check the time. Or maybe I did.

Noe, do you know the time?

"Negative," Noe answered in its usual androgynous voice. "Earth time does not function in this location. Unit Noe can, however, display the duration of the time you have stayed in this place."

Do so.

"Acknowledged," Noe answered. "Displaying duration now."

Then, below the luck charge—which was amazingly still at full charges—was a new number displaying the time.

Luck Charges: 191/191
Time Elapsed: 12 hours 34 minutes

Wait, Noe, how long was I asleep for?

"Host Walter has been asleep for four hours and twelve minutes."

Given how exhausted I was, I was certain that I would be down for a lot longer than that. Then again, my endurance stat had increased like crazy because of Q's potion thing. I was starting to realize just how important all these stats are, now that I'd experienced them firsthand. I was the kind of person who needed close to twelve hours of sleep to get rested before, but I guess I had my pitiful physique to thank for that.

I stretched my body, still feeling some of the aches from before, and decided to take some time to see what gear I had with me. I found a slightly brighter area in the little room I was occupying and made a small clearing so that I could finally take inventory of my situation. I took out everything that was in the backpack.

As I expected, given how light the thing felt, there wasn't a lot in there. Inside was a small gas lantern, a circular flask of water—the kind I saw in those old World War II films—a few packets of dried rations, and a ruffled-up coat. After checking all of the pockets in the pack to make sure that I hadn't missed anything, I sighed and took a sip of water.

It had been over twelve hours since I last had anything to drink, and I initially thought to save some of the water in the canteen, but I could always gather some rainwater later. So instead, I just tipped the whole thing to the side and drank . . . and drank and drank.

How the hell am I still drinking water?

I held the small flask and felt that it was still as full as it was earlier. I squinted my eyes and activated Lucky Eyes of the Arbiter.

Flask of Naiad's Grace (C+ rank)
Description: A small flask blessed by the spirits of water. This flask will never run out of liquid and can change its contents to fit the user's needs.

Okay, pretty sure that this wasn't what was standard in the other aspirants' bags. I couldn't help but smile. This was the first time that all my bullshitting had paid off. I quickly put the flask down and examined the other things as well.

Condensed Ambrosia (B Rank)
Description: Ambrosia processed into a portable form. It's lost much of its taste and potency but can still sustain a mortal's hunger and energy for a week with a single bite.

Lantern of Promethean Light (A- Rank)
Description: A lantern powered by a spark of Prometheus's stolen fire. It will never extinguish and will ease the souls of all those who bask in its glow.

Unassuming Nemean Cloak: (C rank)
Descriptions: Made from the pelt of the Nemean Lion, this cloak will always keep the wearer warm and comfortable.

Even the bag was out of the ordinary.

> **Hermes's Traveling Bag: (C rank)**
> **Description:** One of Hermes's many traveling bags. The objects placed in
> the bag will feel weightless.

I almost laughed out loud after reading through all the descriptions. This was exactly what I needed, although I wasn't sure why everything was Greek themed. With the ambrosia and flask, I didn't have to worry about food and water, and the cloak would keep me warm in the rain.

In other words, I could focus all my attention on gaining levels and ignore the survival part of this trial. These were the small perks that I was hoping to get with all my bullshitting. It seemed my hard work had finally paid off!

I took a bite from the processed ambrosia and found that it did exactly as advertised. It didn't really taste of anything, but it did feel like I had a full meal after one bite. I wrapped the rest up and stashed it in the bag. I put on the cloak next and immediately felt warmth seep through my body. Everything else, except the flask, went back into the bag.

There was one last thing I wanted to test before I headed out again, and that was the second part of the Naiad's flask description. Could it really change into anything that I wanted?

I held it up and imagined that the flask contained a nicely chilled glass of Coke.

I took a sip and was pleasantly surprised that it tasted exactly like it. Next, I imagined a nice cup of hot chocolate and took another sip. I nodded in satisfaction. This thing was perfect! While other people had to make do with dirty rainwater, I could sit back and drink some coffee, or Cola, or whatever I wanted.

Now fully rejuvenated, I placed the flask into the cloak's pocket and decided on my next course of action. I needed goals in mind, otherwise I could become complacent, and complacency generally meant some dire outcomes in my old field of work. Now, however, complacency would probably result in my death.

My first priority would still be to improve my attributes. I might be level 7 now, but that was literally equivalent to the weakest individual in the initial group of 200. I still had to hunt down the zombies and gain as many levels as possible, but I felt like I should do more than that given the seven-day limit. I had to be proactive to ensure that I would survive in the long term, and the first thing that I could do was to find that regressor.

If I could find him, I could gauge what type of person he was, and thus make the necessary adjustments to my plan, but my ultimate goal was still to make a memorable first impression so that he would perhaps consider rescuing me from whatever horrible future was ahead of us.

My secondary goal would be to check out the other people who stood out and see if I could use them somehow. With a clear plan in mind, I took my bag and went back out into the rain. There was nothing that could keep me from my goals!

Feeling more confident than ever, I sprinted across the road, smashing every zombie that I could see. Whenever I got even a little tired, I would take a sip of energy drink or a small bite of the Condensed Ambrosia. Surprisingly, my fatigue would disappear completely after just a nibble of that thing. I must have gone crazy seeing the numbers go up, because I didn't stop until I accidentally saw the time displayed.

Luck Charges: 228/231
Time: 25 hours and 45 minutes

Had I been fighting nonstop for over twelve hours? I felt like I had forgotten why I came out of my little shelter in the first place.

I frowned and casually swatted a zombie that was running toward me.

Wait a second, something was wrong. How had that zombie run? I knew for a fact that they could only slowly shamble at me before, but thinking back, some of them had started running at me in the latter half of my rampage. Did they get stronger after a day had passed?

Either way, the now slightly stronger zombies did not really pose a threat to me, especially now that I had gained a few more levels.

Host Walter Thefuck:	
Human Male, age 27	
Class: Level 2 Commoner	
Free points: 12	
Attributes:	
HP:	190/194
MP:	0/0
Strength:	39 (+10)
Dexterity:	45 (+10)
Endurance:	42 (+10)
Intelligence:	36 (+10)
Charisma:	60 (+10)

I might have gotten a little carried away with smashing zombie heads, but at least I'd made significant progress in leveling up. I mean, that was part of my original plan. I was about to put all my points back into Charisma but stopped. If the zombies did get stronger each day, then it would probably be wiser to invest my free points into something else. I didn't really need endurance, given the ambrosia, so perhaps I should increase Strength or Dex?

Forget it, I'd save up the free points for now, and see how much stronger the zombies got in the future. It was better to make up my mind then, when I had more information to work with.

Right, and I had to find the regressor as well . . . completely forgot about that. But how would I do so? Should I just wander around using the Absolute Luck skill?

"Notification," Noe chimed in. "The Absolute Luck skill would not function as what Host Walter intends for such a situation, as finding the host's target would not constitute as the most optimal outcome. The Absolute Luck skill will only seek opportunities based on Unit Noe's algorithms and cannot deviate from that."

Well, there goes that idea out the window. How else would I find one individual inside an entire city? I thought for a while and realized that I did have one piece of information that I could use. When Raffiel interrupted me earlier, he showed me a scene of the regressor and the others fighting, and I could vaguely recall the locations of where those fights took place. The regressor himself was in . . . damn it, I can't remember at all.

Noe, you said earlier that Intelligence helps with the recall of information, right?

"Affirmative."

Well, I guess I wasn't going to save up my points after all. Without hesitation, I put all twelve free points into Intelligence, raising it from 36 to 48.

I felt the change immediately. What were once fuzzy images in my head became instantly clear when I tried to recall the scene from earlier. The regressor was killing zombies in what looked to be a parking lot, but most importantly, there weren't any high-rise towers in view. A distinct water tower was seen in the background, and a two-story building was a bit closer. He wasn't in the city where I was, so was he in the outskirts or in an entirely different place altogether?

CHAPTER FIFTEEN

The First Trial Part 4

Well, there was only one way to test out my only theory so far. I scanned my surroundings and walked in the direction where the buildings were least dense. It took ages, and more than a few encounters with the fast zombies, but I made it out of the urban sprawl and into a more remote location. Seeing a large hill in the distance, I climbed up and surveyed my surroundings.

Sure enough, there was a water tower far off in the distance. I couldn't be sure that it was the one shown in Raffiel's image, but seeing that I had nothing else to do, I walked toward it. It didn't take long to get there, given my seemingly endless amount of energy via the ambrosia, and even after taking a few more bites of the ration, I still had most of the bar left.

The first thing I noticed when I approached the water tower was the absence of zombies. There were still a few here and there, but their numbers were way down from what I'd encountered getting here. Hopefully, that was a good sign. The next thing I saw was a pile of zombie bodies, all of which had a spear-shaped hole in the center of their foreheads.

Seemed I'd found the right location.

Thankfully the regressor made figuring out where he went next a cake-walk. Or, in this case, a corpse-walk. There was a line of neatly dispatched zombies showing exactly where he was headed. I was worried that the rain might have washed away all traces of where he would go, but all I had to do was literally follow the bodies.

. . . and they will know him by the trail of dead! I mused to myself.

With a clear path to follow, I figured that it would only be a matter of time before I saw the man. However, I noticed something strange about halfway through my journey. The zombies that died from a single pierce to the forehead started to show other signs of injury, presumably before falling. There were smaller holes littered throughout one of the corpses, and looking closer, I saw the traces of a few broken arrow shafts.

It seemed that our regressor met up with someone else here. I scanned another fallen zombie and saw that this one had its legs and arms crushed, with a few arrow wounds around its head and neck. Was the regressor trying to help this other individual out by crippling the thing first so that the other person could shoot at it better? Was it to just get that other individual more experience?

No point pondering that.

I started to jog this time, noticing that the number of zombies being felled by arrows increased the further along I went, and after a certain point, most of the dead zombies were dispatched by a single arrow to the head. I guess whoever was shooting at the zombies improved quickly, or more likely, got their confidence back with the help of the regressor.

The first sign of the man himself was the sound. I followed the noise of the battle, and keeping myself out of sight, I saw two figures easily dispatching a new group of zombies. The regressor I recognized immediately, but the girl beside him was someone I hadn't seen before, or at least someone I didn't have a good memory of. I couldn't make out the details of her appearance from so far away, but she was of the same ethnicity and looked strikingly similar to the other man.

Siblings, perhaps?

I was about to introduce myself when the last of the zombies were killed, but then I felt a slight itch that caused me to turn a bit to scratch at my back. That was when I saw that my luck charges decreased by five and felt something whiz past my head. Surprised by the sudden movement, I shook my head and winced but felt something else shoot past me, missing my brain by millimeters.

Luck Charges: 217/231

Before I could be shot at some more, I quickly stepped out of the shadows with my hands raised.

"Hey, I'm a human!" I said, keeping my voice calm. "Peace, peace!"

I started walking closer, hands still up, but a sudden muscle spasm caused me to jerk back a tiny bit. Before I knew what was going on, a spear appeared just inches away from my face, and my poor luck charges decreased again.

Luck Charges: 200/231

The girl looked at the scene in shock, and quickly pulled the regressor back. "What are you doing?" she said, clear enough for me to overhear this time.

The regressor said something else, but it was too far away for me to make out.

"Uh, can I come forward a bit now?" I said awkwardly.

The regressor looked at the girl one more time before turning to me and nodding slightly.

I wasn't assaulted again, thankfully.

I walked closer, my arms still up as a sign that I meant no harm, and saw the girl slowly unstring her bow. Up close, she didn't look like she could be older than a high school student, but she did have a fierce look on her face. She had short, cropped hair, and even though most of her features were covered by the rain and muck, she looked cute.

"Sorry for shooting at you!" the girl said, her English unaccented. "I thought you were a zombie! And for my brother. He, um, he's not very quick to trust people, but I promise that he wouldn't have stabbed you if you didn't dodge."

I just nodded at that. Hopefully she was right.

She started to approach me, a look of concern on her face, but the regressor stopped her. He was still staring daggers at me and kept his guard up. He pulled the other girl behind him and whispered something close to her ear. Thankfully now that I was significantly closer, Noe was able to pick out what they were saying and translate everything that was being said.

"Careful, Yoona," the regressor whispered in Korean, "people are not friendly here. Don't let your guard down."

"But he looks friendly enough. And you almost killed him!"

"I told you already that I would have stopped it if he didn't evade. And I don't recall anyone that skilled in my first iteration."

Oh, so it seemed he'd told her about his particular circumstance. This was someone close to the regressor for sure. Since I probably died early on in his first life, I guess it made sense that he would be a little hesitant to trust me. Now to see if I could ease some of those worries.

"Hey, uh, not sure what you're whispering about, but I'm not here to start a fight," I said, putting on my most innocent appearance. To cement that idea, I even dropped my spear. "I was following the trail of dead zombies and just wanted to see who was responsible for them. Also saved me some trouble because I was walking right into a huge horde of the undead if I didn't follow you guys. I would have probably died if that were the case!"

"See, brother?" the girl whispered again. "I told you not to be so paranoid! We probably saved his life by accident. Things are different this time."

Definitely siblings, then.

"Sorry for disturbing you," I said, hands still up. "I can get going if you still don't trust me. I don't blame you, given the situation we're in!"

The girl pushed her brother to the side and approached me with her hand out. I shook it.

"Sorry about earlier, and for the grouch by my side," she greeted with a smile. "I'm Kim Yoona, that's my brother, Kim Jae-Hyun."

"I'm Walter," I replied. "And don't worry about shooting at me earlier, I would have probably done the same in your shoes!"

Jae-Hyun frowned before quietly pulling Yoona aside.

"There's something wrong with his voice," he whispered.

His sister frowned. "What do you mean? I think it sounds very pleasant."

"No, I mean there's a skill or ability that's influencing his voice, making it sound more pleasing to us."

"And your point is?"

"It means that he could be trying to manipulate us right at this moment."

"Look, brother, all he's done so far is say hello and introduce himself. I know you've been through a lot, but you can't suspect everyone you meet. And the people who you were wary of had spent years in this place, but we've been here for days. I don't know what the future holds, but we can afford to be a little lenient for now."

The man sighed, before nodding slightly and walking toward me. Given his body language, I highly doubted he believed what his sister was saying and was simply indulging in her wishes.

"Sorry about that," he said, offering to shake my hand.

I did so.

"All good, man. It's important to keep your guard up, what with the whole world flipping on its head."

He nodded. "Like my sister said, I'm Jae-Hyun. It's nice to meet you."

"Nice to meet you as well. And, uh, you two seem to be doing well for yourselves," I said, gesturing at the field of dead zombies around us.

"It's thanks to my brother!" Yoona said. "I don't know what I'd have done if he didn't find me so fast."

"Wait, how *did* he find you so fast?" I asked. I needed to see how much he'd tell.

"I have a skill that lets me know some facts about the trials we're taking," he answered for his sister without blinking.

Wow, even I would have a hard time lying that smoothly.

"You should have gotten something as well when that . . . angel washed us in that light."

I nodded. "Yeah, but my ability's kind of lame. It just made my voice sound really nice, but it's not like I could talk these zombies to death."

Yoona laughed. "But you seem pretty skilled either way. What did you do before all this happened?"

Hmm, how should I answer that? I couldn't say that I was just some small-town con man, nor could I say that I dodged all those arrows through literal luck.

"I was an amateur MMA fighter before," I said, picking the one profession that would seem the least suspicious. "Was going to make pro soon, but I guess I can scrap those plans now."

The regressor eyed me suspiciously but soon seemed content with my explanation.

"Wait, let's get out of the rain first," Yoona said. "Come on, let's head to our shelter and talk there. My brother foraged some wild plants we can boil as tea."

Once again, the regressor seemed like he didn't want to take me to this shelter of theirs, but his sister dragged him away before he could protest. I followed, and after a few minutes, they took me to a small dilapidated barn. There was a small hatch that took us to the interior, and I was greeted by a cozy scene.

A small campfire smoldered in the middle of a small clearing, and to the side was a makeshift bed made of pieces of loose wood and dry foliage. In a small alcove was a bunch of wild edibles, and some smoked meat.

"Wow. You guys built this all by yourselves?"

"Yup!" Yoona answered, clearly proud of the little shelter. "Our family has always been outdoorsmen, so making a shelter's pretty much in our blood."

She dusted off a damp log by the fire and gestured for me to sit.

"Come on, I'll boil some tea for everyone. This spot's safe, so you can relax for a bit."

"Thank you, Yoona," I answered and made myself comfortable by the smoldering blaze.

"It's the first time I've had a chance to talk to someone other than Jae-Hyun since all the craziness started. How are you making out so far?"

I chuckled. "I think I've gotten used to things by now, although I still think I'm having a bad nightmare from time to time."

"I get that! And according to my brother, it'll only get worse from here."

"Because of that skill of his?" I asked.

She looked flustered, clearly uncomfortable with lying. "Y-yeah, because of that skill."

Not wanting to make her feel more uncomfortable, I changed the subject. "But I think you're holding up better than I am, and you don't look that old. You're pretty accurate with that bow."

She blushed. "Thank you. I'm in the archery club in my high school, so I know a bit about using a bow and arrow."

"She made it to the national level," the regressor said, finally breaking his silence. "You should be prouder of your accomplishments, Yoona. Only the top 10% of humanity gets chosen for these trials, and you made the cut."

"That *is* impressive for a high school student."

Yoona laughed nervously. "I still have a long way to go, though."

"And I'll make sure you get there this time," the regressor said, his determination clear.

Yoona sat up and handed me a beat-up tin cup. Inside was a fragrant tea made from various berries and leaves. I took a sip and found it quite nice.

"Sorry about the cup," Yoona said. "We found some in the barn, so they're a bit damaged. But I cleaned it."

"No problem." I laughed. "I think having a clean cup is the least of my worries given the current situation."

We made some small chat for the next little while—although it was pretty much just Yoona and I chatting—and waited for everyone to dry up. After about half an hour, the regressor nudged Yoona, and they politely excused themselves to have a private conversation. Thankfully I was able to overhear thanks to Noe.

CHAPTER SIXTEEN

The First Trial Part 5

We should let him come with us," I heard Yoona whisper. "You said yourself that you needed strong people to help you in the future."

"I know, and perhaps he can help us, but right now we need to prioritize ourselves. I can't risk our plans failing because of a stranger, especially one who didn't appear in the first instance."

"Brother, is it really that important for your plan to work? Even if it puts someone else in danger?"

"I know you don't like it, but this is important. If things go wrong now, then nothing will go as planned later. And if he's truly as skilled as he appears, then we will see him again after this. We can work together then."

"I just don't want to leave someone alone out there."

"Yoona, you're a good person, but sometimes we have to make compromises. Just . . . trust me on this one, we'll have a chance to see Walter again."

The two siblings returned, and I noticed that Yoona was visibly uncomfortable. All right, time to show myself out.

"All right," I said, "I think it's about time I headed out."

"Pardon?" Yoona asked, not expecting me to volunteer to leave.

"I don't want to overstay my welcome, and I can tell that you two don't trust me completely. Not that I blame you, of course."

I drank the last of my tea and collected my stuff.

"Are you sure?" she said.

"Yup, and I want to smash a few more zombies before this trial ends. Leveling up's pretty addicting."

The regressor hesitated for a second before he spoke up. "Thank you for understanding. And . . . be careful. I'm not sure if you've noticed, but the zombies get stronger each day."

I nodded. "Yeah, saw them running after the first twenty-four hours."

"You should be fine up until the fifth day, but if you get overwhelmed, then head toward the tall building over there." He pointed at the tallest skyscraper in the distance. "Head up to the thirty-second floor, room 105. You'll be safe there."

Well, at least he was showing the first signs of sincerity. Good to know that I made a little bit of a positive impression on him, although it was clear that I needed to do a lot more to fully gain his trust.

"Thanks, will do." I smiled, heading out the door. "And thanks for the tea. I'll be seeing you two around! Don't be strangers!"

Leaving the comforts of the campfire, I headed back toward the city. My first plan was mostly a success, although I think I made a better impression on the regressor's sister than I did the guy himself. Then again, I didn't think it would be easy to earn the trust of someone who'd died once already. I was willing to bet he was all kinds of fucked up if he had to endure all of these trials by himself.

So that just left me with my secondary objective, which was to find that huge guy and the unassuming girl. I did the same thing, replaying the scene of their fight in my mind, and quickly realized that only the girl's location was recognizable. She was fending off zombies right next to that huge building the regressor pointed out, so tracking her shouldn't be an issue. The big guy, on the other hand, was last seen smashing zombies in an unassuming street that could have been anywhere in this rainy city. I doubt I could find him even if I tried.

Still, to be able to find one out of the two was still good, and I wanted to check out that big skyscraper in any case.

It took me a good five hours, according to Noe, to make it to the building. I spent most of that time hunting more zombies, and I was able to get another level out of the trip. The same tactic for finding the regressor seemed to work pretty well, and I followed the trail of dismembered zombies.

Unlike the neat way the regressor and his sister dispatched the zombies, this woman seemed to go out of her way to slice up the zombies into small pieces. Was she making sure that they didn't get up again? But even then, dicing them to this extent seemed like overkill.

It didn't take long to find her either, but the girl in question wasn't killing zombies when I saw her. She was practically on top of another aspirant, lopping off his limbs. The screams from her victim were terrifying.

Okay, she's insane.

I was about to back out of there as fast as I could, but she must have noticed me because she turned her head in my direction. Moving faster than even the regressor, she dashed toward me, twin swords glistening in the rain.

I hurriedly turned on the Absolute Luck skill and blindly swung my spear her way.

Luck Charges: 233/241

I felt my spear impact something, and the recoil of that hit made me stagger backward a step.

Luck Charges: 210/241

A woosh and a flash of movement blurred past where my head was just moments ago, had I not stepped back, and I jerkily brought my spear up to guard against any more attacks.

Luck Charges: 203/241

Somehow I felt the shaft of my spear hit something hard. I turned my head, looking at what my spear had hit, and saw that I had blocked a low kick aimed to trip me.

Luck Charges: 199/241

Another whoosh, and I knew that the girl had missed her next strike aimed at my head. I felt a sharp pain and a trickle of blood pour down the side of my cheek. That strike would have probably taken my head off had I not turned to look at my spear.

Luck Charges: 183/241

A muscle twitched randomly in my arm, which caused me to thrust the tip of my spear wide to the left. Somehow, that thrust grazed off the side of the girl's arm and caused her to back off.

Surprised by her sudden retreat, I tried to move back as well but managed to trip instead. This caused me to make a huge lunging attack as I tried desperately to regain balance. She managed to block my inadvertent strike in time, but the sheer strength of the attack coupled with the momentum of my fall caused her to skid backward.

Luck Charges: 169/241

"All right. I give up," she said, putting her hands up. "We can share the loot."

"The loot?" I asked, unsure what the hell was going on.

"Yeah, the loot," she repeated, this time pointing one of her swords at the half-mangled man on the ground. "I saw him first, but you can have some of his stuff since you fought me fair and square. I mean, we can go at it to the death if you want."

What the absolute fuck was she talking about? This was the first time I was genuinely stumped as to what someone else was thinking, and that was after meeting literal trans-dimensional monsters.

"Right," I said, still unsure what the girl was thinking. "Probably not worth fighting to the death over some loot."

She smiled and plunged her swords into the poor guy still lying on the ground, one sword for each leg. Thankfully the blood loss and shock were setting in for the man, and his screams were mostly muffled by the rain. She nodded in satisfaction, and after checking to make sure that the other individual couldn't move, she walked up to me and patted me on the back.

"Great fight back there, eh!"

"Yeah," I said, unsure as to how to deal with this psychopath. "You were, uh, quite good as well."

"Still, it's not very good manners to try to steal someone else's prey."

"Uh, sorry about that," I answered. "I didn't mean to."

She put her arms around my shoulders like she was a close friend. "I know. It's slim pickings out here, so I'll forgive you. I only found one dude after searching this stupid city for two days. A lot of zombies to chop up, though, so I can't complain."

She pointed at the "prey" and said, "All right, do you want to finish him up, or should I do it?"

Sorry, random stranger, but I don't think I can help you here!

"Um, he was originally your target, so you can have the honors."

She hopped off and, whistling a happy tune, she removed the swords still impaled into the half-conscious man and proceeded to "finish" him.

She took her time.

"Oh, right," she said, raising her voice so that she could be heard over the screams. "I'm Noel, by the way. What're you called, little bro?"

"I'm Walter," I answered as I did my best to not throw up.

"Nice to meet ya!" She smiled, her voice eerily cheery. "Sorry, just give me a sec, I'll get you your share in a bit."

"Oh, no worries. Please, take your time."

She finished her work a short while later, the bloodstains and other viscera staining her body was thankfully already washing away in the rain. She handed me a few ration bars and a little canteen.

"You can have those," she said, stuffing her half of the things she pilfered from the poor man into her own bag. "Should last you a while. I have no idea how that devil person expects us to survive for seven days when I can't even find more than two people after this long. But I guess that's why it's a trial."

"Wait, you knew that Raffiel is a demon?"

"Well, duh," she said, rolling her eyes. "He's covered in sin."

"Pardon?"

"Oh, right!" Noel answered. "Sorry, forgot most people don't view the world like this. My eyes are special, so I can see the sin in people. The more depraved and sinful they've lived, the darker they appear. That Raffiel was as dark as they come!"

I nodded slowly.

"Anyway," she continued, as if telling me that she could see the literal sin on people was completely normal, "how can it be fair to expect us to search every corner of this huge city for loot? There's, like, 200 of us in total, so only 199—well, 197 minus you and Phil over there—people to hunt for. I think I'll starve if this continues."

"Wait, are you only hunting other aspirants for their food?"

Noel looked at me as if I was the idiot. "No, of course not! I need their water as well. How else would I have enough supplies to last a week out here?"

I could not understand this lunatic's point of view. "I mean, have you not tried to scavenge for supplies? I saw some canned food and bottled water in the abandoned supermarkets."

Noel's eyes lit up as if I'd just told her the secrets to the universe itself.

"Oh my god, you're right!" she exclaimed. "The prey would scavenge and gather where the canned food is, so all I have to do is find a supermarket and wait for them to come to me! You're a genius, little bro."

That was definitely not what I meant, but I wasn't about to correct her.

"You know, you're all right, Walter. You're helpful, and you've got a relaxing voice. I like you!" she said, patting my back again. "Anywho, I think I'll go find one of those supermarkets and stock up on supplies! You should probably do the same."

With that, she sprinted off into the distance. "I'll be seeing ya! Toodles!"

Okay, what the hell just happened?

CHAPTER SEVENTEEN

The First Trial Finale

I was left alone in the rain again, having finished both tasks that I set for myself faster than I thought. I guess the only thing I had to do now was to smash a few more zombies and see how many levels I could get.

I did take some time to check out the big building the regressor pointed me toward, but even after poking around the floor and room number he gave me, I couldn't find anything of note.

I guess he did say to go there to escape from the zombies, and it was relatively safe, but I couldn't just stay there for the next few days. Instead, I decided it was better to hunt some more.

And that was exactly what I did for the next four days. The zombies were getting progressively stronger over time; they moved faster and became more resistant to damage, and by the fifth day, I had to lure individual zombies off to finish them one by one.

Aside from sleeping every now and then and using Noe's Luck skill to ensure no one found me, all I did was kill zombies. All of that hard work paid off, and my new stats looked like this:

Host Walter Thefuck:
Human Male, age 27
Class: Level 17 Commoner
Free points: 18

Attributes:	
HP:	234/254
MP:	0/0
Strength:	39 (+10)
Dexterity:	45 (+10)
Endurance:	42 (+10)
Intelligence:	48 (+10)
Charisma:	60 (+10)

Once again, I chose to hold off on using my free points, but I was tempted to dump some into my strength. The zombies I was facing were no longer dying after one smack to the head, which really slowed down how many of them I could destroy. But I held off on making my decision right now; although it took me a lot longer to destroy each one, they did not pose any real threat to me.

It wasn't until the start of the seventh day that I had to give in and invest some of my free points into Strength, having it go from 39 all the way to 49.

The zombies on that last day were monstrous beings that looked like they came straight out of a horror flick. Some of them were the size of small cars, while others grew scythe arms and other grotesque mutations.

If that wasn't bad enough, they also swelled in number, and I had to hide in narrow alleyways just to survive.

I spent my time like that until something happened on the last day of the trial. I felt the earth shake when only about four hours remained and thought that maybe some kind of boss zombie would show up, but something a lot stranger occurred.

I was hiding on the roof of a convenience store, and from my raised point of view, I saw a huge ball of fire expand in the horizon. I saw the shock wave rushing forward, and I had just enough time to jump from the roof and seek refuge in a narrow alley. The impact was staggering, despite the fact that most of the force was dissipated from hitting the walls.

Was that supposed to happen near the end of the first trial?

Waiting a few more moments to make sure that the devastation was over, I peeked my head out of the alley I was hiding in and saw that the whole city looked like it had been hit by a bomb. But what was most surprising was that all of the mutated zombie abominations that had been roaming the streets earlier were splattered all over the place.

In fact, even the ones who were not hit by the blast were pretty much half dead, and I spent the remainder of my time picking off the stragglers.

I finished off one last mutant before Noe's timer hit zero, and then all of the movement stopped. Even the rain, which had never stopped falling, let up, and I finally had the chance to relax.

"Notification," Noe said, "Inferior Origin Matrix wishes to display information to Host Walter. Acknowledge this request?"

Yes, Noe.

"Affirmative," it continued. "Displaying information now."

Congratulations, Aspirant Walter, for completing the first trial! The results of your week here are as follows:

Zombies felled: 822

Skills used: 0

Resources scavenged: 0

Shelters created: 0

Distance traveled: 492.09 km

Time spent resting: 10.24 hours

Final Rating: F+

Wait, an F+? Noe, that can't be right. I busted my ass off killing zombies for the entire week, and my final rating is an F+?

"Does Host Walter wish to see the rating breakdown?" Noe inquired.

Yes. There must be something wrong with its grading system!

"Acknowledged. Displaying Inferior Origin Matrix's final rating breakdown."

Breakdown:

Observation: Aspirant Walter made no attempts to secure proper food or water and relied solely on the provisions given to all aspirants at the start of the trial.

Conclusion: Aspirant Walter does not have the intellectual capabilities to understand basic survival needs.

Rating: F-

What the fuck! The only reason I didn't take time to secure food or water was because I didn't need to!

Observation: Aspirant Walter made no attempts to secure a shelter, choosing to sleep out in the open, and spent the majority of the time outdoors in the rain.

Conclusion: Aspirant Walter lacks the mental capacity to understand the

dangers of hypothermia, the dangers of being exposed to predators, or the need for proper rest.
Rating: F-

I could understand docking my marks because I used Noe to doze off out in the open, but not everything else! Again, I didn't need much sleep because I had the ambrosia, and I didn't need to keep warm because I had the cloak. *You gave me these things, you piece-of-shit matrix!*

Observation: Aspirant Walter did not utilize the skills gained through the initial enlightenment and relied solely on brute strength to fight.
Conclusion: Aspirant Walter is so mentally deficient that he does not have the brain capacity to understand or use the new tools given to him by the Glorious Central Collective.
Rating: F-

Could this thing stop mocking my intelligence?

Observation: Aspirant Walter—

Okay, stop, Noe. I don't want to listen to any more of this bullshit. I get it, I'm an idiot. I've got the brain capacity of an infant. Fine.

"Acknowledged," Noe said. "And do not worry, Host Walter, Unit Noe does not think that your intellectual capabilities are infantile."

Thank you, Noe, I thought, almost sobbing. *You're the best. Much better than this trash Origin Matrix.*

"I know," it chimed. "Display the remaining information before the final rating breakdown?"

Yes.

"Acknowledged."

Based on the final number of Zombies killed, you are ranked 7th out of 88 surviving Aspirants in your cohort. Congratulations on making it to the top 10!

Displaying the top 5 ranked individuals in the world:
1: Kim Jae-Hyun – 11,043 kills
2: Kim Yoona – 10,834 kills
3: Richard Barkeley – 3,832 kills

4: Chen Zhong – 3,811 kills
5: Li Ye Ping – 2,771 kills

Yeah, the difference between the Kim siblings and the people behind them was pretty staggering. Now I knew who started that huge explosion near the end.

Distributing Rewards:
Unlocked the Beginner's Inventory Space (Able to hold 10 objects)
Kill reward: 822 gold
Survival Reward: 0 gold
Top 10 reward: 2,000 gold
Hidden Rewards: None
Penalties: None
Total: 2,822 gold
Account balance: 100,002,822 gold

A hundred million gold? Huh, guess there were more perks for being a Lord Arbiter, although I didn't intend to abuse the extra funds for now. I still had to prioritize my own growth over anything else, and relying on overpowered equipment would do more harm than good in the long run.

Finally, Aspirant, please choose a class:
Tenacious Cripple
Moron
Spear Peon
Master of None
Starting equipment for the chosen class will be given out once a class is selected.

I gritted my teeth when I saw the selections available for me to choose from. I was starting to hate this piece-of-shit Origin Matrix more and more. I knew that my class options wouldn't be great given my F+ rating, but what the fuck was this? Showing the Tenacious Cripple class was low-key mocking me, and Moron was just a straight-up insult. Imagine telling others that my class was literally called Moron! The only real options I had were numbers three and four.

Ultimately, I chose option four, the Master of None, because at least the title sounded cool when you listen to it out of context. If all my options were shit, then I might as well choose the best-sounding shit.

"Congratulations, Host Walter, for obtaining your first class," Noe said. "Displaying the information for Master of None now."

<hr>

Class: Master of None (G- Rank Frontline)

<hr>

My eyes were twitching in anger at this point. I swear Raffiel said that classes went from E to S rank, but I managed to somehow skip F rank and get a G- class instead? How does that even make sense?

But that's fine, I told myself, *I have Noe, I have my status as an arbiter. I can overcome anything this garbage Origin Matrix throws at me.*

<hr>

Class Description: Congratulations on your continued survival until this point, despite how absolutely, disgustingly useless you are. As a reward for such an improbable feat, you have earned the title of the Master of None. You still have the manual dexterity and intelligence of an intoxicated Neanderthal, but at least you can (mostly) hurt your enemies more than yourself when wielding a weapon.

<hr>

Class Passive:
Master of Nothing (G- Rank): You can use any weapon equally badly.
Weapon-class-specific bonuses and penalties do not apply to you.
+0.5 (rounded down) Strength when holding a simple weapon.
-5 Dexterity when holding a simple weapon.
-10 Dexterity when holding a non-simple weapon.

<hr>

Forget what I just said, it was pretty clear that the Origin Matrix was out to get me. That wasn't a passive, that was a goddamn curse! Not only did I lose out on weapon bonuses, but I lost stats as well, and what the fuck was +0.5 strength rounded down? 0.5 rounded down is just zero! That's just zero fucking strength! What was the point of even mentioning that? And that description? Fuck you, Origin Matrix! You know what, I won't even call it by its name at this point. It's just Trash Matrix from now on.

<hr>

Class Active:
Blind Strike (G+ Rank Active): You use all the skill you possess to strike at your enemies.
Your strike deals 5% more damage.
You are numb, deaf, and blind during the duration of the strike.

Yup, I wasn't even surprised at this active now. It was pretty much useless, but at least I had the option to never use it.

I sighed, well, at least I had the option to change or upgrade my class in the future. That day could not come fast enough.

The last thing I checked was the little package that appeared when I had chosen my class. I opened it, and several items popped out. To no one's surprise, the items looked like literal trash, but I used my Lucky Eyes of the Arbiter to make sure that was the case.

Caveman Club: A weapon made for an ape.

+5 Attack

Beggar's Clothes: Rags previously worn by a crippled hobo.

+0 Defense

-20 Charisma

Ersatz Footwear: Slippers made from recycled tires and old wire.

+0 Defense

-10 Charisma

I wanted to throw all these things right in the trash, but I decided not to and stuck them into my newly acquired inventory. I could always throw them out when I needed more inventory space. The items took up three slots, and the fourth one was taken up by my backpack. Surprisingly, the bag only took up one slot of my inventory, even when it was full. That was the only pleasant surprise so far.

"Notification," Noe said again. "The Inferior Trash Origin Matrix wishes to initiate a forced transfer of locations. Does Host Walter accept?"

That must be the signal to go out of the trials.

Yeah, I thought, feeling more exhausted than ever before. *Let's get out of here.*

CHAPTER EIGHTEEN

Trial Ends and Sponsorships

The sense of nausea was easier to overcome this time, and I quickly surveyed my surroundings. We were back in the oval room again, its interior looking resplendent once more, and Raffiel was greeting us with a wide smile. But I also noticed that more than half of the chairs were now empty.

"Congratulations, one and all," Raffiel greeted, his voice majestic, "for completing the first trial so splendidly! And I have the privilege to say that our cohort is home to the world's number one and two aspirants for this stage."

He clapped, and a bright beam of light originating from seemingly nowhere illuminated where the regressor and his sister were seated. We all turned from our seats to look at them, some in awe, while others glared at them in unconcealed envy.

Raffiel continued, "I couldn't be prouder of this group! Now, please do not mourn the loss of the people who did not make it past the first trial, for they are now basking in the glory of our Lord. Instead, take this time to improve yourselves! Let us talk about what is to come."

The faux angel gave all of us some time to compose ourselves, before speaking again.

"I realize that the week you have spent in the city has been arduous, and you must all be exhausted. Our Lord did not overlook this burden and has allowed you the chance to rest and recover." He clapped his hands, and an image appeared near the stage. This one shows a 3D image of what looked to be a resort of some kind.

"Soon, I will transport you to our rest area, where you will get a chance to digest everything that has happened and to interact with your fellow aspirants." He made a grand wave at the people seated. "Making social connections is key to succeeding in the future, so make sure you get to know the others here to the best of your ability. Since you are all adults here and have been blessed with free will, I will not interfere with any events that transpire in the rest area, but do note that your own rooms will be inaccessible for all else in case problems arise."

Right, Raffiel was practically telling the more dubious members of our cohort to make trouble with that statement. The world had gone to hell, people now had superpowers, and he was telling us that there were basically no rules in the rest area? Yeah, that was just inviting disaster. Some of the aspirants who barely made it out of the first trial were already looking nervous, and the ones who had power immediately smelled blood in the air.

"Of course," he continued, ignoring the growing atmosphere of unease completely, "we will provide you with everything you need during your rest, including food, drinks, and access to any amenity that you can dream of."

Here the picture changed to show various rooms in the resort. There was a fancy restaurant, a huge swimming pool, a lounge area with cozy-looking sofas and chairs, some training centers, and practically everything in between. It really did look like it would be a nice place to take a vacation. Great luxuries—if you could make it to them.

"You will spend one week here before the start of the next trial, so please enjoy yourselves," he continued. "Now, there is just one thing to keep in mind before I take you to your private rooms, and that is the gold that some of you obtained in the trials."

Here he made a waving gesture, and from a small shimmering portal appeared a little floating pixie or fairy. It nodded at the audience and sat gracefully on Raffiel's shoulders.

"For those of you who made an effort in fighting off the undead, you would have obtained an amount of gold relative to your kill count. You are free to exchange and gift your money with your fellow peers, if you so wish, by simply using our user-friendly trade interface incorporated into your status screens."

Now some of the more able-bodied people looked like they were more than ready to pounce at the opportunity to "trade" with the others. Raffiel sure knew how to sow discord.

He continued, smile still benevolent, "You can spend this gold in the shop, and to ensure that no one is confused or lost in this process, one of the Lord's pixie representatives will assist each and every one of you in the shopping process. They can suggest items that would be most useful to you and assuage any worries you have about spending your hard-earned money. Please make sure you pay them a visit before the start of the next trial. I would suggest that you ensure that you are well stocked up on items before the seven days are up."

Raffiel smiled one last time. "I hope you enjoy this brief time off, and I shall see all of you again in a week's time."

Then, one by one, each person in the room disappeared, some looking nervous, some happy, and we were all transferred to another new location. I was expecting to see a hotel bedroom when I came to, but I was greeted by Q in his office instead.

"Sorry for disturbing you right after your first trial, Lord Walter," Q said, bowing low, "but news of your reemergence has reached Central, and there are some individuals who would like to meet you."

Great, more things to deal with, just what I needed.

I stifled a sigh and answered Q, "News got out that quickly?"

Q nodded enthusiastically. "Of course! I notified Central Command as soon as your identifier was registered in the back door, as per protocol. I do admit that headquarters doesn't usually respond so quickly, but they certainly did when news that the legendary Lord Arbiter W's back in the field!"

What on earth was Q talking about? I could understand that the random code I punched in way back when identified I myself as a lord arbiter, but now it turned out that the person whose identity I was stealing was some kind of legendary bigshot? Lovely.

"I was hoping to keep that part a secret for a bit longer," I said, and I actually meant it for once.

Q laughed jovially. "Of course, of course. But still, if you had told me that you were the Hero of Bladefall, the Arch Alchemist of Central Tower, then I would have given you a warmer welcome! You were missing for over ten cycles; we had thought the worst."

"I was distracted," I said, hoping Q would stop looking at me like that. "And you said others were looking for me?"

"Oh, yes! Forgive me, I had forgotten, but after news of your reemergence got out, the sponsors came flooding in, and although I managed to keep the majority of them at bay, there were two who had to meet you in person."

"I see." I nodded, and seeing no way out of this situation, I said, "I'll meet them."

Q twitched a finger, and the door to his office opened. Three individuals greeted me. Two were strangers but the third was familiar.

Xalla gave Q a quick salute, then bowed to me. Next to her stood another Xollon, although this one stood slightly taller than she was and looked more intimidating than Xalla, which was saying a lot.

Lastly, there was a human-looking individual. He was a chubby, jovial-looking man who looked to be in his midforties with a slightly balding head and rosy cheeks. He was sporting comfortable-looking shorts and a bright Hawaiian shirt that was a bit too small for his body.

He immediately stepped into the room and gave me a huge bear hug.

"W, you sneaky bastard!" he said, his joy unrestrained. "You were gone for ten cycles and you didn't even bother to contact your best friend?"

Well, shit, this was probably the worst-case scenario. Here was someone who knew the actual legendary Lord Arbiter W or whoever that was. And they were apparently best friends. Well, Noe had done me right so far, so seeing no other option, I activated my Absolute Luck skill, returned the hug back as genuinely as I could, and spoke the first random thing that came to mind.

"Big Bob, that you?"

I almost cursed at myself. Big Bob? Who would actually name their kid Big Bob? I was dead for sure.

> **Luck Charges:** 134/241

But seeing my luck charges take such a huge dip, maybe this idiot really was called Big Bob.

"Still with that silly nickname, eh?" the man replied happily. "But I guess I should call you Walter now."

He released me from his embrace and started to eye me up and down.

"I was going to give you a piece of my mind for leaving me in the dark all this time," he said, now starting to circle me, "but hell, did you actually manage to create a soul in an artificial body? And in only ten cycles?"

Going with the flow, I chuckled good-naturedly. "Yeah, it was a lot of work, but my prototype is complete, and I'm here to see if things are all in working order."

"Amazing . . ." Big Bob continued. "I can understand the silence, then! And yes, I can see that you've somehow managed to tether your human guise onto your Xollon form. Now, I know I'm not someone who usually cares about the biological aspects of alchemy, but sometime you still have to tell me how you managed this creation!"

He stopped his pacing and gave me another affectionate pat on the back.

"And you never told me you were a Xollon all this time! You know I wouldn't have cared what kind of being you were!"

"Well, I was a little worried back then, what with the Xollon's usual reputation," I answered. "And speaking of Xollon . . ."

"Ah, right, sorry, I forgot we had other guests!" Big Bob backed off and gestured to the two Xollon standing by the door. "May I introduce to you the great sponsor and grand general of the South, Xollo'rolga'mathu'ath, also known as Rogue, and his disciple Xalla."

Xalla looked proud to be mentioned as this person's disciple, and given his impressive-sounding titles, I had to assume this was someone important. But then again, Big Bob seemed to be just as important as the new Xollon, and he was, well . . . less than impressive looking. Well, better to be safe than sorry.

"Hello, Xalla, Rogue," I said in greeting before focusing my attention on the new Xollon. "Your disciple has been taking care of me wonderfully, and I was wondering who she learned everything from."

The Xollon laughed and spoke for the first time. His voice was a low baritone, and if I didn't know any better, I'd say he sounded like a really chill old grandpa. Either way, it was clear that he was proud of Xalla.

"She's a feisty one," he said, "but she's secretly a sweetheart! Can you believe that she's still single? Not for a lack of suitors, mind you, but she's generally a very career-focused woman."

I didn't, but I could tell that Xalla didn't want that fact revealed about her like that.

"Really?" I said, feigning surprise. "I was sure that a lovely girl like her would be taken."

"Yes," the old man continued, a wry smile forming on his features. "And did you know that she—"

Xalla rammed a tentacle right into his side; it didn't look like she held back at all.

"What my old master means," she explained calmly, ignoring the pained expression on her mentor's maw, "is that I am glad that he still has the strength to make jokes like this at such an advanced age."

"Right, right," he said, rubbing at his side. "And I'm not that old, dear disciple of mine."

Xalla rolled her eyes (once again, I marveled at Noe's ability to translate alien gestures).

"So, I can understand why Bob would like to see me," I continued, "but what can I help you with, Lord General?"

"Oh, come now!" He laughed. "None of that lord general crap with me!

We're fellow countrymen. Just call me Rogue. And I came partly because I wanted to see the new Xollon that my disciple is so infatu—"

Another sharp jab to the side interrupted his sentence. "I mean the Xollon that is working with my disciple."

Xalla didn't interrupt him this time.

"And partly because I wanted to ask you a favor."

"A favor?" I asked, unsure what I could possibly do for this man.

"Yes, if you could."

CHAPTER NINETEEN

Sponsorship Woes

Y ou see," Rogue said slowly, "I am officially a sponsor for the trials, but I've never had a chance to actually participate in any of the previous sessions, so I'm really just a sponsor in title only."

"Was there a problem?" I inquired.

Rogue looked at Q before answering. "Well, normally nothing goes wrong when we sponsor an aspirant, but when I tried previously . . ."

Rogue looked embarrassed to continue, so Q finished for him. "Every single person that Lord Rogue has tried to connect with has unilaterally gone insane and died shortly thereafter. This has happened on three separate occasions, with three different species of aspirants. Unfortunately, Central regulations state that if Rogue does not sponsor an aspirant successfully after the third attempt, then said sponsorship rights are revoked, and he will be blacklisted from all Central training sites due to a breach in his contractual obligations."

"So you wish to sponsor me, in this case?"

Rogue looked at me sheepishly. "That would be ideal. If you can, of course. Being blacklisted from my own disciple's workplace would be problematic, if not embarrassing."

"But I work as a lord arbiter. Would that not be a conflict of interest?" I said, not quite sure if conflicts of interest were even a thing in this weird alien world.

"Normally, yes . . ." Q stated, "but the Origin Matrix has judged you to be an official aspirant, so it's not necessarily impossible for Lord Rogue to offer you sponsorship. However, many others will file complaints if the lord Rogue chooses to do so, since the sponsor will obtain a portion of the aspirant's rewards in the future, along with the ownership of his soul after trial completion. This would be . . . problematic given Lord Walter's situation."

"Yes," I agreed, as I did not want to give up my soul. "I spent ten cycles creating this soul, and I am not about to let that go."

"No, no!" Rogue quickly replied. "Those claims are technically voluntary on the part of the sponsor, correct? I don't technically *have* to take anything from Walter here if I choose not to."

Q thought for a second, and slowly nodded. "That is correct, although none would ever revoke those rights."

"Well, I choose to do just that. I wish to revoke all rights on Aspirant Walter's soul, rewards, and other claims and choose to sponsor him completely at my own expense. The only thing that I require on my end is the access rights to participate in the Earth Trials, and of course the VIP lounge privileges." The old Xollon looked over at Q. "Would that be acceptable now?"

Once again Q thought for a while. "Yes, if you choose to do that, then none of the others should have an issue with it. Are you fine with that arrangement, Lord Walter?"

It was a risk to accept this one-sided sponsorship, given the fate of everyone else who had one with Rogue, but I figured I should be fine with Noe's help . . . probably. Plus, having another ally who thought they owed me a favor could never hurt in the long run. This gamble didn't seem to have too many downsides, so I agreed.

"Thank you!" the Xollon said, a wide smile plastered on his face. "I, Xollo'rolga'mathu'ath, known as the Crawling Chaos, offer my exclusive sponsorship to Aspirant Walter, at my own expense, and under the stipulation that all rewards, gains, and claims to his soul and body remain his own."

"Notification," Noe said. "An offer of sponsorship is being made through the Trash Matrix. Does Host Walter accept this offer?"

Yes.

"Acknowledged."

I felt a huge wave of darkness envelop me. Power beyond anything I'd ever imagined possible flowed into me. I was barely able to stay conscious.

"Host Walter has accepted the sponsorship of the Crawling Chaos, and the title 'Spawn of Chaos' has been obtained . . . "

Noe stopped for a moment and made some clicking noises.

"Error, the title 'Spawn of Chaos' has significant overlap with host's soul title. Resolving conflict now . . ."

More clicking noises ensued. Was it doing some calculations in the background?

"Unit Noe has integrated the title 'Spawn of Chaos' into host's soul title. Host Walter's soul title has advanced three levels."

Primary Soul Title: Level 4 Xollon Idol
Progress to next level: 4/5000
Progression requirements: Have 5000 individuals idolize you.
Title Passives: N/A
Title Skills:
Idol's Voice (Soul Passive)
Secondary Xollon Form (Level 4 Soul Active):
Transformation Time: 40 minutes
Cooldown: 21 Hours
Remaining Cooldown: 0 – Skill Ready to Use.
Description: The user assumes the secondary form of the Xolloid race. The user gains all the physical characteristics of the race, and all physical stats will be increased by 4x for the duration of the skill. Cooldown and use time will improve proportionally to Xollon Idol's level.

Interesting, so this sponsorship gave me an immediate three levels in my soul title and increased my transformation time by a factor of four while decreasing its cooldown by another factor of four, all while giving me more stats when I was in the secondary Xollon form. Not a bad harvest for helping the old dude, and I wasn't going insane.

Just as those words slipped from my mind, I started to feel something strange. The corners of my vision started to distort and turn red, and some hazy images were dancing before me. These strange scenes looked familiar, but the more I stared at them, the more my mind burned with crazed visions. I saw the sky darken and warp in my narrow vision while strange forms started to emerge from unseen shadows. I heard whispers in ancient languages that I couldn't understand, but somehow the message of those whispers was crystal clear.

The world will end in chaos. Run, I had to run, get out of there while I could, while my sanity was still—

"Abnormality in Host Walter detected. High levels of mental contamination detected," Noe's voice said. It sounded so far away . . . "Unit Noe suggests that Host Walter transform into the secondary Xollon form immediately to remedy the situation."

Yes! I thought while I still could. *Transform me, Noe. Now, while I can still run. Dusk comes, have to ru—*

I felt my mind clear as soon as I was fully in the Xollon form, those strange, blasphemous images that plagued my mind from earlier dispersed as if they were never present in the first place. I shook my head, or mass of tentacles, now, and focused on my surroundings again. I frowned because I couldn't even recall why I had been so afraid just a moment ago.

The first thing I noticed was Xalla's gaze fixated on me, and the looks of surprise and slight concern on the faces of the others.

Rogue was the first to speak up. "Is your guise all right?"

"Yeah . . ." I said. "That was strange."

Big Bob spoke next. "Amazing! From what I saw just now, your human form was almost overwhelmed by the transfer, but you've managed to suppress that now."

"Notification." Noe interrupted. "Congratulations, Host Walter, for upgrading your soul title for the first time. As a congratulatory gift, Unit Noe has provided three Soul Title Preview Tickets for Host Walter's executive use. These tickets will allow the host to experience what it is like to have your soul title fully unlocked for twenty-four hours and serves as a motivational tool to enforce further growth."

Soul Title Preview Ticket (x3): For twenty-four hours, the host will assume the full form of a Xollon, with none of the regular restrictions applied.

Well, that was a pleasant surprise, after all the crap that the useless Origin—no, I meant to say Trash Matrix, gave me—Noe really was the best! Now how should I choose to use these tickets? Should I save them all for a rainy day? As a last resort in case things went really pear-shaped? I quickly thought against that idea. No, if I was ever in a situation where my only hope of success relied on me using one of these tickets, then I probably screwed up a long time before that. What I needed was not a short-term solution to one problem but an investment to make sure those problems never arose in the first place.

An idea started to form in my head about a potential use for at least one of these tickets . . . but I wasn't sure if I liked where that was going.

"Walter, you okay?" Xalla asked, taking me out of my thoughts. "You were zoned out for a second there. Did the sponsorship not work?"

"No," I answered, "I was just checking to see if anything had changed."

"You should have felt something, like a surge of new power," Bob said. "Maybe you have to return to your human form to notice the change?"

I canceled my Soul Title skill and reverted to my normal body. Thankfully I wasn't plagued by my earlier visions, but aside from the three levels I got from the sponsor, there didn't appear to be anything different about me. I was hoping I got a new skill or passive out of it, but apparently not.

"Nothing," I said. I couldn't exactly say that my luck system integrated the sponsorship into my soul title. "But maybe that's because my guise is still in its prototyping phase. I haven't ironed out all its flaws yet."

"Hm," Bob mumbled. "That shouldn't be the case. Your human soul, albeit a tad lackluster and basic, seems perfect . . . the transfer of power should have worked. Here, let me try to give you a temporary sponsorship."

"Notification," Noe said again. "The being called the Light of Final Judgment wishes to offer Host Walter a temporary sponsorship via the Trash Matrix. Does Host Walter accept?"

Accept.

"Acknowledged."

Once again, I felt a rush of power flow through me, but this time none of that mental contamination was affecting me. Instinctively, I held out my hand, and a huge wave of brilliant fire erupted outward. It seemed like it would engulf the whole room, but with a casual wave of Big Bob's hand, the flames disappeared, and he frowned.

"Notification," Noe said. "The Light of Final Judgment has stopped the temporary sponsorship of Host Walter."

And just like that, the power I felt then went away as quickly as it came.

"It seems to work fine. It must be something about the lord general's power."

"Wait," Xalla interrupted. "Isn't this system all about borrowing power from the sponsor? So, if an aspirant was to acknowledge a sponsorship from Lord Babylon, then they would gain heavenly might."

I guess I'd found out Big Bob's real name now, and between his title and the name Babylon, I was getting suspicious as to who he really was. I wasn't liking my guesses.

"Right." Bob nodded.

"Then doesn't that mean that Walter's borrowing the powers of a Xollon?" Xalla continued. "But Walter *is* a Xollon, so wouldn't that mean that he's just . . . borrowing power from himself? That wouldn't make any sense and would explain why he doesn't feel any different than usual."

Big Bob thought for a second, before ultimately agreeing with Xalla's assertion. "You're right. Of course nothing would happen, but isn't that a problem for Walter? He would have to take on a sponsorship with no tangible benefits."

"To be fair," Xalla added, "my mentor's not gaining anything from this either."

"Not true, my dear disciple!" Rogue added in. "I get to visit you now that I get to keep my job here, and the pool in the VIP lounge is to die for!"

Xalla rolled her eyes again.

Big Bob grinned. "Since Walter's gaining next to no benefits from his exchange, then it wouldn't be a problem if he got another sponsor from, say, an old friend of his, right?"

I wasn't about to say no to that. Having more power would certainly up my chances of surviving through these shitty trials. But unfortunately, like so many other situations I'd faced so far, it wasn't my decision to make in the end. I choked down a sigh as Q quickly dashed those dreams of mine.

CHAPTER TWENTY

To Xolloid

Q laughed nervously. "Unfortunately, Master Babylon, an aspirant cannot have more than a single sponsor, even in such a . . . unique situation like Lord Walter's."

"Even if I give up all rights like Rogue?"

Q shook his head. "Even so."

Big Bob was clearly unhappy with the news. "Ah, you know I want to see Walter's experiment up close! There has never been a case like it in all the ages, and you're saying that I can't observe him properly? I have sponsored these trials for close to 150 cycles now, and you're saying nothing can be done still?"

"I'm sorry, but I do not make up the rules, sir," Q answered nervously. "But can the Lord Arbiter not simply explain the results to you once he is finished?"

Bob shook his head and sighed. "And this is why you are still not at the level of a grandmaster, Q. When faced with a puzzle, one should not seek the answer directly, but see it as a challenge. Only then can true growth occur . . . or something along those lines in any case. You should know this."

"I understand, and thank you for the reminder."

Big Bob thought for a spell. "Say, Q, although an aspirant can only accept sponsorship once, I can still assign additional missions to whomever I want, yes?"

"That is correct," Q answered slowly, checking to make sure that he was giving the accurate information. "Although you can only do so once the aspirants make it to the main stage of the trials, as per regulations."

Big Bob started to smile again. "I see. Good . . . I think I have an alternative plan of action now, although it might take a while to get all the paperwork in place." The big man gave me another friendly pat on the back. "Just wait until then! I got a surprise in store for you, my old friend!"

Rogue laughed at the display. "But the main stage of the trials are still far away, and getting the right files in takes even longer. I'm not really doing my part to help in the meantime; I can't allow that to happen as Walter's official sponsor."

He used one of his feelers and retrieved two little pieces of what appeared to be paper. Where he got that, I had no idea, but I honestly should be getting used to seeing people materialize things out of nowhere by now.

"Here," he said, handing me the little notes. "These are two VIP tickets to see the Plains of Torment. I know that you have a little break before the next trial begins, and Xalla was telling me how you wanted to see the Xolloid's best attractions."

He glanced at Q. "And I'm sure that Q here will be glad to give you and one of his very, very hardworking staff a break to do just that."

Q agreed almost immediately.

"So please, take them, and if you need a guide to fully appreciate the place . . ." he continued, now ever so slowly nudging a clearly embarrassed Xalla toward me.

The hint was obvious.

Well, part of my original plan was to use one of those preview tickets to build a better relationship with the Xollon girl, and I guess I could do that now instead of later.

I smiled at her and held out a hand. "Well, Xalla, you said you were an expert on the Fields, right?"

She nodded shyly.

"Then would you do the honors of guiding me around the Fields of Torment?"

Xalla smiled, her expression had never looked so happy. "Of course!"

Noe, use one of those preview tickets.

"Acknowledged."

I felt my form shift effortlessly into the now-familiar secondary Xollon form, but this time, I felt unbelievable power flow through me. This was completely unlike the previous transformations, and Noe really wasn't kidding about having no limitations on the form. I knew at that moment just how terrifying a Xollon was. My form swelled even bigger than before, and I also noticed that I was wearing some kind of strange robe. I looked at it and saw that there were strange shapes and weird faces flowing along the contours of the fabric, and it was very comfortable to wear.

"Notification," Noe chimed. "Unit Noe has equipped Host Walter with the latest Xollon fashion befitting a Xollon Idol."

Oh, thanks, Noe.

"Host Walter is most welcome."

The new energy flowing through me was almost too much. I saw how fragile everything around me was, and I just knew that if I wanted to, I could simply rip the space around me to shreds. I allowed a low growl to form but stopped myself when I saw that the space around me was starting to weirdly distort.

"Whoa there, Walter," Rogue said, shaking me a little. "I know you were in that tiny meat suit for a long time, and I can only imagine how refreshing it is to take it off finally, but careful that you don't destroy Q's facility now."

Rogue backed off after seeing that I was okay, but I noticed his gaze focus on one of my main feelers. I glanced at where he was looking at and saw that a few small, penny-sized holes were present in the back of my feeler. That was strange, because I knew instinctively that Xollons could heal from practically anything, so why hadn't these holes mended?

"That wound. That's from a Chrono Disruptor Beam . . ." Rogue said, his tone grim and serious for the first time. He lifted a feeler, and I saw a similar wound. "How long had it been?"

Having no idea what was going on, again, I just replied with the safest answer. "Shortly before my start as an arbiter."

"So about fifty cycles . . ." He gave me a look that showed concern and pity. What was so significant about this tiny wound?

Xalla noticed the odd interaction between the two of us, and I felt her gaze move to the small holes on me as well. She immediately turned grim before giving me a quick military salute.

"Hey, it's fine," I said, not wanting this odd situation to continue. "This is old history. I'm fine now."

"Right," Rogue said, and I could tell he was trying to shed off his earlier gloom. "Let's not ruin this happy occasion. We can talk about it later, but . . . I just want to say that it is good to see another veteran of the Long War alive and well. I . . . I apologize on behalf of Xolloid for what happened, and I promise you that times have changed since then."

I was getting sick and tired of people talking about things that I had no understanding of, although I had a feeling that this would be a reoccurring problem.

"Let's discuss this after," I said, my tone final. Yeah, let's talk about it when I can figure out exactly what this Long War was.

"Anyway," Big Bob said, breaking the awkward atmosphere, "on to other, brighter topics, but this is the first time I've seen you get rid of that guise fully! Well, good luck getting back into that thing after you let loose! To think you would willingly confine yourself into a human body. That's too extreme, even for me!"

"Sorry about that, Q," I apologized, choosing to ignore Bob for now. "It's been a very long time since I've been free like this. I almost lost control for a second."

"It's all good, Lord Walter," Q answered nervously. "But it would be a good idea if you were to go back to Xolloid to get rid of some of that excess energy, yes?"

"Of course," I said with a laugh, and turned my attention back on Xalla.

Now that I'd adjusted fully to the Xollon form, I noticed that Rogue was right, and she actually was pretty cute. Her short head fringes gave her a tomboyish look, and her coloration was quite pleasing to the eye. The various scars dancing along her limbs showcased a long career as an accomplished huntress, and her maw was a very adorable oval shape. I had no idea how I missed such an obvious fact in my human form.

"Well then, Xalla, shall we get this date started?" I said, feeling more confident than ever before.

"Yes! Please take care of me, Walter!" she answered before heading off to get changed out of her uniform.

"All right," I said before waving goodbye to the others. "I guess I'll be seeing the rest of you later on."

The rest of the gathered individuals left after sharing a few more pleasantries, and I was left alone to ponder what on earth had just occurred. I took those precious few minutes alone to properly adjust to my new body. I really had to make sure that I didn't accidentally destroy anything while I was out on that date.

I met up with Xalla a short time after. In fact, it had barely been more than a few minutes since she left. I don't know how she managed to get changed so quickly, but I was thankful either way since my time as a pure Xollon was limited.

"Sorry for making you wait, Walter," Xalla said.

I turned my gaze in her direction. She had taken off her strange security uniform from earlier and was now wrapped in some kind of viscous suit. It was dark and bent the light around it and seemed to flow around her form like syrup. I guess Xollon fashion was going to take me a bit longer to get used to than the Xollon form itself.

"No worries." I smiled back. "And I love the outfit."

She blushed. "Thanks, I had saved this one for a special occasion."

I walked over to her and wrapped a feeler around one of hers. She twitched a little at first, but then relaxed and squeezed me a bit tighter.

"Shall we get going?"

She nodded, and with her free hand, made a gash in space-time, and we walked through the opening. We arrived in a busy transit station. I was expecting something more . . . alien. Strange, perhaps? Instead, this place looked pretty much identical to a well-used train platform. Sure the people waiting for a ride were all kinds of weird, and the vehicles that passed by were slightly too large, but that was it. I was almost disappointed.

"Come on, Walter. Our ride's this way," Xalla said, dragging me toward one of the platforms. This one was oddly empty, with only a few other Xollon sitting down waiting. I felt the other passengers' gazes on me, but they quickly retracted their glances when they noticed Xalla's rather intense disapproval.

The train, or whatever interdimensional equivalent of a train it was, arrived soon after, and we all boarded. Once again, the vehicle looked normal, and there were very few passengers in here. I guess most people didn't want to visit Xolloid. Wait, I was pretty sure I told myself that I would never do the same. Well, there goes that plan.

Still, I had to ensure that this date with Xalla went as well as possible, and I was reviewing everything I had learned and experienced in my head. I remembered all the dating advice my friends had given me, all the psychological tricks needed to ensure that you were well liked, and an ungodly amount of internet articles and self-help books on the subject that I had consumed. I just hoped any of that would apply to a strange interdimensional being.

I wasn't sure what Xolloid had in store for me, but hopefully I could bullshit my way through it. I needed Xalla's help to make sure that I survived, and to be honest, I did kind of like her despite myself. Hopefully everything goes well.

I hardly noticed the small talk Xalla was making given how nervous I was, and it wasn't until the train pulled to a full stop did I focus my attention once again, and fell into the role that I needed to play.

CHAPTER TWENTY-ONE

An Eldritch Romance

Xalla

Xalla noticed that Walter was oddly quiet during their journey to Xolloid, but she could understand his nervousness. She could tell that he was making a concerted effort to make her think nothing was wrong, but how could there be nothing wrong given his past?

He was a veteran of the Long War, displaced in time and about to visit his home dimension for the first time in a long, long time.

If Xalla heard right, then Walter had only been back for fifty or so cycles. A small part of her felt glad that he was around her age, but a bigger part felt sorry for him. After all, the Long War had finished over 1,200 cycles ago, so he was coming back to a world that had changed tremendously.

She knew that many veterans had been displaced in time after the Final Assault, but Walter's case was extreme. Plus, the state that Xolloid was in near the end of that conflict left much to be desired, so his hesitation was understandable. Was he still afraid that his home was a war-torn wasteland like it was before? Or perhaps coming back would stir up memories of all that he'd lost. It must be hard, just knowing that everything he cared for would be gone.

Xalla was even more grateful that he would revisit such traumatic memories just for her. She had the conviction to ensure that Walter's new memories of Xolloid would be nothing short of amazing, with her by his side, of course.

Yes, it would be Xalla's job to ensure that her date's time back in Xolloid was a success! She would show how much Xolloid had risen from its past savagery, and how it had turned into a cultural hub. And the food!

She could only imagine how much of a shock it would be to taste modern Xollon cuisine, especially if he was eating disgusting human food, or worse still, disgusting humans themselves, for so long. Yes, Xalla would heal his wounded, time-displaced heart and show him the glory of Xolloid.

She can fix him!

Xalla couldn't suppress her grin. This was like the plot right out of a fairy tale! Here was a handsome, deadly war vet who needed a gentle soul to guide him back into Xollon society. And unlike those annoying idiots she read about in her engrams, she would be the star of the show! She wasn't going to make the same mistakes as those naive protagonists and let such a prime opportunity slip from her feelers.

The first thing that Xalla did when they arrived at Xolloid proper was to show him the local sights. She giggled privately to herself when she saw how amazed Walter looked, seeing how much their home had changed. And she was proud of her home as well.

The blood rivers were flowing nicely, and they were free of pollutants, unlike how it was in yester-cycles. Even the fresh sacrifices used to supply all of this were thrashing vigorously as their lifeblood went into the children's waterpark and other facilities.

Combined with the fountain of wailing souls, which provided a nice, soothing backdrop to this perfect, red-hazed day, Xalla's date was off on a high note. Why, even the living paving stones were wiggling with enthusiasm when she stepped over them!

Yup, Xolloid was prospering, and she couldn't be prouder.

"Come on, Walter, we have to try some of that!" Xalla said, pointing to a huge phase whale in the process of being served. Its desperate attempts to flee the cooks hacking off big pieces of its delicious meat were making a pleasant rumbling vibration on the ground.

"Is that a whale?" Walter exclaimed, staring at the mountain of food.

Xalla laughed lightly. It must have been a long time since he'd seen one of those. She had heard that they were almost hunted to extinction in the olden times, but modern Xollon conservation efforts had saved the delicious species.

"Yup! And it looks freshly caught. Look at it squirm! I bet you haven't had one of those in a while!"

They pushed through the crowd of people and waited in line for a whale kabob. Xalla noticed that quite a few other women were eyeing her date, and a small part of her was a little happy knowing that he was with her and not them. She'd be the envy of all her friends if they could see who she was with!

She squeezed Walter's arm a little harder and flaunted her frills in pride, making the others glare at her jealously.

"We'll take two skewers, please," Xalla said as their turn came around. "I'll have extra house sauce on mine. How about you, Walter?"

"There are so many selections . . ." he said, glancing over all the different toppings. "But I'll take some shredded shoggoth with extra sauce as well."

Xalla smiled. Walter must really like shoggoths if he was getting them on his whale skewer. It was a good thing she still had so many left, and she loved the boyish look of joy he had whenever he was eating one.

"These things are amazing!" Walter exclaimed, chomping down on his skewer.

Xalla ate one with him, hiding her blush as she gazed at his joyful expression. She found him especially cute when he was enjoying the little things in life. It was a stark contrast to how he was when he's working as an arbiter. She could get used to seeing him relaxed and carefree.

The chef, a big man even by Xollon standards, bellowed a laugh when he saw how fast Walter was scarfing down his portion. "I've never seen someone enjoy one of my skewers that much."

"Sorry," Walter replied, careful not to spill any of the chewed whale. "I've been working out of town for a long time. I haven't had a chance to have some proper food. But still, this is amazing."

Xalla shook her head in humor. "He's been living off of humans, if you can imagine that."

"Humans?" the shop owner asked, thinking. "You mean those horrible fleshy things that were a popular gag product a while back? The two-legged pink ones?"

"Yeah, those!" Xalla shuddered. "Ugh . . ."

The owner looked at Walter with pity and handed him another skewer. "Here, have another one on the house. I don't know what kinds of hardships you've endured, but no Xollon in their right mind will ignore a fellow countryman in need."

The owner then secretly pushed an image into Xalla's cortex while Walter was distracted devouring more of his whale. It was a static view of the small circular scars that were peeking through his robes, and the shop owner's inquiry was clear. Xalla returned the psychic message with an affirmation, and the other man nodded in understanding.

Take good care of him, young woman, he sent. *And show him how much all of Xolloid appreciates his sacrifice. How long has it been?*

Fifty cycles, Xalla sent back.

I see.

The big man's smile returned, and he addressed Walter again. "You two are heading to the Plains of Torment, right?"

"Yup!" Walter replied. "My date here's showing me the sights! It's my first time going, if you can believe that."

"You'll love it there! And if you get hungry after your little outing, check out my restaurant after!" he said, and proceeded to write down where it was on a little piece of parchment. "I've just received a new haul of goodies and would love to get an opinion on my menu from a new face."

Walter looked at Xalla, seeing if she was all right with the plan, and after giving him a nod of approval, they thanked the chef for his generosity and promised to revisit him after the Plains.

Xalla took her date to various other vendors on the outskirts of the Plains of Torment, and she learned she could never get bored of watching Walter eat. He made the cutest expression whenever he tried something new, and she almost burst into laughter when he tried the extra-potent Mott sauce. His maw was practically on fire, and the face he made trying to seem in control was a memory that Xalla would replay over and over again in the future.

After visiting another street stall or two, the two Xollon decided to take a break and rest on a quiet bench overlooking the sprawling countryside. Xalla finished her snack and placed her frills gently on Walter's side, basking in his warmth. He pulled her a little closer, and they enjoyed the quiet atmosphere for a while.

"Say," Xalla said, breaking the silence, "I know you don't want to think about it, but I just wanted to thank you for your service in the Long War. And for today. I don't know what it's like to see Xolloid after being away for so long, but I hope you'll remember what it's like now and not how it was before."

Walter's gaze went unfocused for a second, and Xalla could imagine him recalling all of the hardships he'd faced so far, all those cycles ago. She wondered what this place looked like before the end of the war. She had only heard stories and accounts from history books about those days, and even then it was usually glanced over.

"Yeah, it's been a really long time," he said, sighing. "But I like it now. I could get used to life here. Thanks, Xalla, for . . . everything."

She squeezed him tighter. "What was it like, back then?"

Walter looked at the horizon again. "Did your mentor not tell you about it?"

"No, he was always vague when he talked about his past. I think Rogue still feels responsible for the loss of so many of his subordinates."

Walter nodded. "So what do you know about the war?"

"Just the stuff they teach you in school," Xalla said. "About the tactics the enemy used, how their weapons would erase Xollons from the timeline, and . . . and the Final Assault, where so many were killed or displaced in time."

"I remember that," he replied slowly. "How many were displaced? How many found?"

Xalla frowned, she didn't want to make her date sad, but he deserved to know the truth. "Well, most of the veterans who were caught in the blast were located in the first hundred or so cycles. Some, like yourself, came out later. And the survivors . . . I'm sorry, but there were only around two hundred Xollons who made it. Counting the command staff that was outside, that's still a mere 250 veterans left."

"Two hundred and fifty . . ."

"I'm sorry," she said, touching his trembling feeler gently.

"No, it's fine," he said with a sigh. "At least there are others out there."

Xalla felt a little guilty bringing up such tragic memories. She could only imagine what it would be like to lose comrades and loved ones in the war.

"Xolloid was a different place back then," Walter continued solemnly. "Everyone was on edge, anticipating the next battle, and the aftermath. I knew entire families torn apart, and seeing the people I cared for disappear one by one . . ."

Walter looked like he would collapse right then, and Xalla really felt bad for talking about this on their first date. She wished she wasn't so curious!

But in the back of her mind, she really liked the dark and brooding Walter that she saw now. She felt like she was finally peering into a deeper layer of the mysterious Lord Arbiter. She wanted to know more!

"Let's just say that I am glad that things have changed for the better," Walter finally said. "And that it was you who showed me the new Xolloid."

With a final sigh, Walter's smile returned, and he helped Xalla up.

"Come on, enough of the depressing talk. Let's go see the Plains of Torment!"

CHAPTER TWENTY-TWO

Conclusions to an Eldritch Date

Xalla

Eventually, Xalla and Walter were able to make their way through the sprawl of food and other small goodies and made their way into the main attraction. The VIP tickets that her master gave really did come in handy because they skipped the lines that a normal Xollon had to wait for and were even given goodie bags at the entrance.

"Well," Xalla said, making a grand gesture once they both entered the complex, "welcome to the Plains of Torment!"

Inside the huge enclosure of the Plains were a multitude of sights, and all around them were bustling, happy Xollon marveling at the exhibits around them. The very first thing that was on display, immortalized on a huge obsidian pillar, was the information on this cycle's centerpiece civilization. It displayed a brief history of their existence, some of their major accomplishments, and of course, their fight and ultimate defeat at the hands of the Xollons.

"We're in for a treat, Walter!" Xalla exclaimed. "They just changed the displays, and we're one of the first people to see the new exhibits!"

Prominently displayed on the wall was a video of the final moments of the species called the Entari, and their heroic last stand. The video was shot from the point of view of this race, and in the skies above their home planet were huge, monstrous shadows of unimaginable scale: the Xollons in their primary form. The attacking Xollon were almost the size of their planet.

The defenders were using a weapon that looked like a caged sun, trying desperately to blast the invading Xollons out of the sky, but their feeble attempts apparently did nothing to the invaders. The video faded to black, then showed Xollon workers taking what was left of the Entari species and mounting them on various displays around the Plains of Torment.

Reading off the wall, Xalla explained, "Let's see . . . It says here that the new species caught was a Class 3 civilization, from a nearby sector. And, if you can believe this, the reason they were put on display was because the leaders of this species saw a Xollon passing by and decided to attack them!"

Walter shook his head in disbelief. "Well, there's unfortunately no cure for stupidity. It's what happens when some people believe that they've figured everything out and that there's no one out there who could oppose them."

Xalla giggled. "They managed to conquer one tiny galaxy, and they believed that they were all powerful?"

"Yeah." Walter shrugged. "Like I said, Xalla, not everyone's got the same outlook on life as the Xollons do."

"Oh, oh!" Xalla exclaimed, pointing at one of the adverts on the wall. "Apparently, they managed to take one of the Entari doomsday weapons and brought it here! It's that gun they used in the video. I think it shoots supernovas or something, but you can have a try at shooting it!"

The weapon itself was impressive, by non-Xollon standards at least, as the Entari engineers managed to trap and condense a small star into the size of a barn. The weapon itself forced the star to undergo partial collapse, and they focused that energy into a tight beam. To say that it shot supernovas would be a tad disingenuous, but the sheer amount of energy in that beam was impressive, nonetheless.

Xalla and Walter turned their vision toward the location where the weapon was and saw a little platform leading up to where the operator would command the use of the machine. There was a long line of Xollons waiting for their chance to use the display, but what was strange was that most of the people waiting were families with small children.

Some of Xalla's energy deflated. "Well, it's mostly for hatchlings, so I guess we're a little too old for that."

"Nonsense! We're never too old for something like that!" Walter answered, dragging a shy Xalla toward the exhibit. "Come on, if anyone asks, just tell them that I really want a go at shooting the thing! We're all hatchlings at heart!"

Xalla smiled again. He was only saying that for her sake since she secretly always wanted to try her hand at using a big toy gun. She never did get a chance to do that as a hatchling and had always been too shy to try again as an adult. But she didn't feel so embarrassed now that Walter was with her. She felt like she could do anything with him by her side.

They walked excitedly toward the exhibit's platform, Walter dragging Xalla along this time, and they decided to join the line with the others. Their VIP tickets did allow them to skip the line, but both of them felt that it would be unfair to the families for someone else to go ahead of them.

When Walter approached, some of the smaller children ran toward him, tentacles flailing, and started to leap toward him playfully. The mothers and fathers tried their best to catch the little balls of energy, but Walter waved them off as he allowed one of the kids to latch on to his primary feeler. The hatchlings giggled with joy as Walter started to move a little, making the small Xollons cling on.

Xalla was content just watching her date interact with the little bundles of tentacles. She hadn't expected him to be so good with children.

"I'm so sorry about that!" one of the mothers said, trying in vain to detach her child from Walter's frill. "My little one's getting drool all over your robe!"

"It's fine. Everyone's here to have some fun, so let the hatchlings play," he said, swinging another child around him much to the joy of the hatchling.

The father came along then, clearly amused by the scene of so many little tentacles and teeth latching themselves on Walter. "Thank you, sir," he said before turning to Xalla. "Your boyfriend's quite good with the small ones, huh?"

"Apparently he is." She smiled. "It's only our first date."

The man laughed. "Well, he's a keeper in that case!"

"Now, if someone else could help out with the kids at home . . ." the woman said this time.

The man laughed. "We can't all be perfect!"

The mother sighed. "Well, you two enjoy your date, and thank your boyfriend for draining some of my little hatchling's energy for me. I think all the families here appreciate that!"

Xalla agreed, still not turning her gaze from the comedic scene of Walter trying his best to keep his balance under the assault of so many tiny limbs. She didn't even notice that their turn on the doomsday weapon had come until one of the parents pointed it out to her.

Walter had a big lopsided grin on his face as he approached the controls for the gun. The operator was clearly amused to see two fully grown Xollon look so excited to fire a toy, but he was nice enough to go along with the atmosphere and show the two the basics of shooting the thing.

Walter walked up to the map hologram and chose a planet in the background.

"You said you were a huntress, right?" Walter said with a smile, pointing at the tiny dot on the screen.

Xalla nodded, understanding what he meant. "Pfft, I'm a great huntress, and hitting that target would be too easy. Pick something a tad harder."

Walter turned to the attendant. "You heard the lady. Got anything a bit more challenging?"

The attendant thought for a second before scrolling the map back a few light-years. "How about one of these ones? Even being a few microns off angle would result in a miss."

Walter looked at the selection of planets that was given and picked the smallest one out of the bunch. "Think you can hit this one? We only have three shots total."

"Much better!" Xalla said excitedly and mounted the control station. She interlaced her senses into the modified machine and carefully took aim. Although it was her first time shooting one of these things, her instincts drove her to make the necessary adjustments, and she took her shot.

A huge amount of energy was released at once, and a small wormhole appeared near the muzzle of the weapon. From the viewport, Xalla and Walter watched the beam of energy cut through space and time, and as Xalla expected, her shot hit its mark. The planet exploded into a shower of debris, and the display even showed the final moments of the tiny insignificant life forms on that rock. Xalla was pretty proud of herself, which was made better when she could hear the clapping of tentacles behind her.

"Wow!" said one of the hatchlings that was playing with Walter earlier, "You're amazing, Miss Xalla!"

"Hit a farther one!" another Xollon child added. "A harder shot!"

Walter grinned again. "You up to the challenge?"

"Always."

This time, Walter took a while to consider the options. He chose a planet that was slightly out of alignment, which meant that Xalla had to curve her next shot using the gravity of a nearby black hole. It would certainly be tricky to get that right.

Walter arched a frill. "This one'll be tough. You sure you can hit it?"

"I'm always up for a challenge," Xalla replied confidently, although she wasn't sure if she had the skill to back up that confidence.

Either way, she steadied her aim and made the rough calculations needed to account for the curvature of space-time around the black hole. She fired but frowned almost immediately, knowing her aim was off. It was confirmed when Xalla saw the beam curve a little too much and miss. She had forgotten to consider the movement of the planet and the distortion of light.

Before she could apologize for missing, she felt a nice warmth wrap around her body and saw that Walter had joined her on the control seat. He had his tentacles around her, and his frills were tentatively close to her own.

"Come on, let's make this last shot together," he said, his rumbling voice resonating with her body.

Xalla blushed. "R-right."

He grabbed one of her feelers and made some slight adjustments. "I think this should hit our mark now. I'll leave the timing up to you."

Xalla focused her attention back on the display, albeit reluctantly, and saw that Walter had indeed fixed her earlier error. All Xalla had to do was wait for the planet to move a little, and seeing the perfect opportunity, she pulled the trigger again.

This time, the beam of energy curved true, arcing perfectly right into the center of the planet. Xalla and Walter gave a childish shout of joy, much to the appreciation of the hatchlings watching.

"That's amazing!"

"Wow!"

"Teach us how to shoot like that!"

"Yeah, show us how!"

Almost all the families and their hatchlings were crowding around Xalla and Walter at this point, and a reasonably sized crowd was gathering to see what was going on as well. More and more small balls of tentacles were pulling their parents along, all wanting to learn how to shoot the supernova gun so well.

Unable to say no to the cute crowd, Xalla and Walter—with the permission of the attendant—spent the next while helping the little ones aim and shoot. They laughed whenever they hit a target and saw the little aliens' desperate attempts to flee their destroyed worlds. Xalla had always loved teaching others, and it seemed like Walter shared her passion as well, and the two spent a lot longer at the exhibit than initially planned.

By the time they were able to drag themselves away from the crowd, several Earth hours had already elapsed. Most of the families and visitors there even thought that Xalla and Walter were part of the staff working on that attraction.

"Thanks for helping out the kids," the actual worker said. "You two made the days for a lot of excited hatchlings."

"No problem," Walter replied. "And Xalla here did most of the helping in any case."

"Well, my boss heard about the commotion, and we can't allow you two to just leave without anything after all the work you put in!" The worker took out two passes and handed them to Xalla. "Here are two complimentary season passes to visit the Plains of Torment again. It's the least we can do after today!"

"Thank you!" Xalla answered. "We will definitely come again!"

Unfortunately, they would indeed have to come back at a later date, since Walter was only free for one Earth day. It was pitifully short, but Xalla was glad that she was able to spend even a little bit of time together. She had never imagined such a gentle side to the arbiter, and she wondered what else she could learn about this fascinating individual.

Not forgetting to grab dinner at the location that the whale kabob owner told them about, Xalla and Walter spent the rest of their short date over a warm meal, all the while making small talk and discussing Xolloid as a whole.

"You know, you talk about your home a lot, Xalla," Walter said, finishing the last bite of his meal.

Xalla recalled all the fond memories of her childhood at her family's farm and smiled. "Of course, I spent my days as a hatchling helping out my family. Those were honestly some of the best memories I have."

"I'd love to see that place someday," Walter added. "It must be special if you can smile like that when you remember your time there."

Xalla blushed, but answered honestly, "I would love that."

Walter sighed. "But that will have to be another time."

"Yeah . . ." Xalla sighed as well. She didn't want this moment to end.

But end it did, and before long the two made their way back to the transport platform and made their way back to Site 1102.

Just before the two were about to head their separate ways, Walter brushed a feeler on Xalla's frill. "Thank you for showing me the sights today. Xolloid has changed a lot since I last saw it."

"It was fun," Xalla answered shyly. "It's a pity we couldn't see more of it."

Walter laughed. "Hey, we got that free pass, so let's go back when we have more time!"

"It's a promise!"

Walter moved closer to her, and very gently, he placed his central frill on hers. A Xollon kiss, so gently placed. Xalla almost melted in joy then, and she returned the gesture.

"I'll be seeing you around, Xalla," he said, breaking off the embrace. "Take care of me in the trials, yeah?"

Xalla was still recovering from the sensation. "Of course! And thank you as well, for being with me today."

With that, the two departed, and the trials for one of them began anew.

CHAPTER TWENTY-THREE

Lord Arbiter's Wrath

It wasn't long after parting ways with Xalla that the first preview ticket expired, and I transformed back into my old body. It felt oddly deflating being so weak once more, but I hoped that feeling would pass. On the way back, Noe informed me that I had made a lot of progress on my Soul Passive, and I was honestly pretty close to leveling up the thing by myself for once.

> **Primary Soul Title:** Level 4 Xollon Idol
> **Progress to next level:** 4,210/5,000
> **Progression requirements:** Have 5,000 individuals idolize you

I guess I had attracted a larger crowd during the date than I thought. But the joy of having made so much progress was stifled by how weak I felt after being in the full Xollon form for so long. It was so constricting having only two arms to move around or having such a limited field of view. I hoped that the sensation of unease would go away soon . . . because I was afraid that I might like being a Xollon.

The feeling of absolute power was great, but I was pretty sure my actions during the date with Xalla were questionable. Like how I . . . wait, what did I do with her? I remembered visiting the Plains of Torment and going on some exhibits with Xalla in tow, and I even remembered our conversations together. But the specifics were somehow missing. I knew that my actions were morally questionable at best, but like waking up from a dream, all the details were missing from my mind.

Was the Xollon form somehow influencing my thoughts even when I was human? There was no way it was healthy to go from a human's limited perception to that of a Xollon. That was concerning, but what could I do about it at the moment? Should I limit the use of my soul title even at the cost of my continued survival? No, that was not an option at all. With demons and monsters roaming around, I'd be an idiot to limit myself in any way. After all, I couldn't regret any decisions if I was dead. I could only hope that I could control any changes before things went wrong.

Still, all those concerns could wait for later. It had been a full day since everyone else was transferred to the rest area, and I should pop my head out and greet some of the people. At the very least, I had to establish friendly relationships with the Kim siblings.

"Warning," Noe's voice chimed. "Detecting increased levels of mental pollutants in Host Walter due to rapid changes in physiology. Unit Noe suggests the host take some time to rest the body and mind before venturing out, otherwise irreparable changes will occur in the host's body and mind."

I grimaced, realizing I hadn't had any chance to rest and properly digest my situation so far, but it wasn't like I could just take the next few days for some R&R. I had to make sure that the regressor and his sister were on my side, and I had to do it fast. I already lost an entire day because of that date, and I wasn't sure if I would have a better chance to warm up to them compared to now.

I didn't have the regressor's knowledge of the future, so I could only make proactive plans because any screw-up on my end could result in a very bad ending. I needed to get into their good graces if I wanted to avoid whatever extinction event was heading my way.

Then there was the Central side of things. Q and his gang expected me to act like an arbiter, and I needed to make regular reports back, not to mention the added complication that came with the sponsors. My schedule was fully booked, and I couldn't see how I could fix that. I mean, the end of everything was at stake!

Explain further, Noe. What kind of irreparable damage are we talking about?

"Currently, Host Walter is experiencing minimal levels of contamination, and Unit Noe has assisted Host Walter with containing the majority of the damage, ensuring that Host Walter's mental and physical health does not deviate too much from prior norms. However, if this trend continues, then Host Walter's psyche and body will experience changes that are unknown even to Unit Noe."

But I'm fine right now?

"Affirmative," Noe answered. "Current changes to Host Walter are negligible."

That's fine, then, Noe, I said to the system. *I think I can handle some slight mental contamination. Thanks for the heads-up, though.*

"You are most welcome," it chimed. "But Host Walter should take better care of his health. Unit Noe will continue to alleviate as much of Host Walter's burdens as possible."

Not wanting to waste any more time, I stepped out of my private room and into the rest area proper. There was just no rest for the wicked. Making sure that I was fully human once more, I put away my bag and left my private dorm.

I wasn't sure what I was expecting when I went out for the first time, but it certainly wasn't being greeted by five gruff-looking men. They all turned to me when they saw me stepping out. In hindsight, I should have expected something like this to happen, since Raffiel all but gave everyone permission to do whatever they wanted, but between my date in Xolloid and my meeting with Rogue and Bob, I never expected that I would be on the receiving end of a mugging.

"Lookie here," one of them—a smaller man that was trying way too hard to hide a receding hairline—said, "this one managed to hide in their little hole for a whole day."

The group of men, clearly up to no good, approached me, cutting off my path.

Another one—honestly, their faces were so forgettable I won't even bother giving them descriptions—added, "Let's give our newest aspirant a warm welcome, and let him know the rules of our little retreat."

This time the leader of the bunch shoved his little goons aside and practically shoved his face into mine. My Lucky Eyes of the Arbiter saw that this individual was pretty strong, all things considered.

David Moore – Level 26 Brawler

The other goons had levels in the low twenties.

David grinned at me, trying his best to unnerve me, but the only thing unnerving was his horrible halitosis. "It's good to see you finally poke your head out, my friend. Hunger finally get to you?"

Now I was in a bit of a dilemma, not because I was in any way intimidated by David here, but I wasn't sure what the best course of action would be. I was left with three choices: fight back, try to run, or just accept the hazing.

With Noe's help, fighting all five of them wouldn't be an issue, but I recalled what happened to that poor zombie I met when I attacked with the system's help. Having David and his friends literally explode would probably not win me any favors with the regressor or Q, and since I had so little control over how Noe's Luck abilities manifest, fighting was not an option. It'd feel great in the short term, seeing these idiots beaten up, but the consequences would be awful. An impulse decision, no matter how justified, would never be the correct choice in the long run.

Unfortunately, flight was also not an option, as I was fenced in on all sides. The only thing I could do was allow them to extort me. I'd seen situations like this a million times before all the craziness happened. There was always going to be some bigger thugs that prey on the weak, and at most they'd steal some money. It wouldn't be the first time I was robbed, or doing the robbing now that I thought about it, so I'd just go with the flow. I was about to comply when David punched me full in the face.

HP: 247/254

Did he seriously just strike me?

"Speak up!" David said, spittle splattering everywhere. "I don't like having to wait for some pretty boy to talk back to me."

I stared wide-eyed at what just happened. I hadn't turned on the Absolute Luck skill, so it wasn't so much the punch landing that shocked me, but the fact that someone, some absolute *nobody*, had the audacity to attack me. I had survived encounters with monsters who could rip this universe apart and come out unscathed, and *this* was the person who got a hit in on me first? I was, for the first time since this whole fucking thing started, pissed off.

Another fist landed on me, this time rattling my skull. I relished the pain, even smiling as the next few blows landed.

HP: 231/254

"I said speak up!" he shouted. "Don't you know it's rude to just stand there mute?"

I was a goddamn lord arbiter, fake one or no, and I'd show David here why he shouldn't mess with me.

But not now.

"I'm sorry, sir!" I stuttered, falling to my knees. "I didn't mean to stay silent! Please, don't hit me again!"

I had almost allowed my anger to control me, but I clenched my teeth and buried my rage.

I'll just bear with it for now and get my payback later. Don't lose my cool, sometimes you have to take a loss to ensure future victories. Don't lose it, Walter.

David grinned. "So your tongue's finally loosened up. But you have to apologize honestly for that mistake, right?"

"Of course!" I said again. "Please, just tell me what you want."

"Well, since you managed to somehow survive the first trial, you should have gotten some money, right?"

"It's—it's all yours, sir!"

"Good! It's always good to see a generous soul, there are just so many nice things that I wanted to buy in the store," David said, smile still plastered over his face. "I like talking to smart people, so give me 600 gold, and I'll pretend that nothing happened. Aren't I so nice?"

"But, but sir," I pleaded, "I don't have that much. I barely managed to survive as is!"

He punched me again, this time in the stomach. "And did I mention that I hate talking with poor people?"

My anger exploded in me, but I endured. I could not let my emotions get in the way of my logic. That was a mistake I would never make. Any loss I suffered now, I could always return tenfold down the line. What I couldn't do was mess things up now and screw over my future.

"Please, sir!"

He gave a fake shrug. "Well, I can be reasonable. Just hand me everything you have. Tell the system to transfer all your money over to me."

Noe, I thought, *send David here 467 gold. It'll help pay for his funeral later.* "Acknowledged."

David's eyes scrolled over some message I couldn't see, and he nodded to me.

"Not terrible, friend," he continued, patting me on the back. "And I don't have to tell you what would happen if I find out that you had more money on you, right?"

"No, sir!" I pleaded. "Never!"

"Notification. Congratulations, Host Walter, for gaining a new title," Noe interrupted.

Hey, I guess something good did come out of this situation! The universe might not be out to get me after all.

"The Trash Matrix has given the host the secondary title of Groveling Master. Does Host Walter wish to view the information of this title?"

Never-the-fuck mind! The goddamn Trash Matrix just loved to hit me when I was down.

No, I do not wish to view that shit title now, Noe. Can you delete that thing?

"Negative, Host Walter," it continued. "Titles cannot be deleted."

Then show me later!

"Acknowledged," it chimed. "Equipping title now."

The second that weird title was put on, I saw a noticeable change in David and his goons. They looked almost euphoric when they saw me on the ground groveling for my life. They started to chuckle like idiots and were thoroughly amused at my display of cowardice.

"Good! Good! That's the proper form for addressing the great David the Destroyer! It seems like someone finally understands my greatness!" He laughed and gave me one final shove before gesturing for his goons to leave me alone. "Now that wasn't so bad, huh? If you're alive by the end of the next trial, you can potentially join my gang and worship the ground I stand on!"

"Yes, sir!" I answered. "I shall do whatever you want, oh great David the Destroyer!"

He laughed jovially again. "That's more like it! Yes, everyone should sing their praises to me! I deserve it!"

"Indeed, oh masterful David!"

"All right, lads, I think we need to inform the rest of this cohort the importance of my status! And you!" He pointed at me again. "Go around this facility and sing my praises. If you do a good job, I might even allow you to be the head of my future slave army!"

He turned back and kicked me one last time. "I'll be seeing you again later! Remember to do your job properly!"

David's personality took a strange turn after getting that title. Out of curiosity, I had to check out the title the Trash Matrix gave me.

Secondary Title: Groveling Master (F rank)

Description: Your ability to cower before everyone else has reached the level of a sublime art form. Your lowly existence serves only to elevate the status of your betters. Congratulations on finding a useful purpose for your useless life!

Class Passive: Individuals who perceive you groveling, begging for your life, or otherwise behaving miserably will cause those individuals to have an extremely elevated sense of pride and self-worth.

Class Active: N/A

Yup, it was as crap as I thought, but at least this one had some niche uses. I gritted my teeth and put the stats page away.

I collected myself when David and his gang were out of sight. I wiped the blood off my lips and slowly made my way back to my dorm. I'd had it with being on the back foot this entire time. I had spent way too much time ensuring that I could survive in this hellhole to allow myself to be bullied by some goddamn random *humans*. I wasn't stupid enough to fight back against David out in the open, but that didn't mean I couldn't retaliate.

I grinned, tasting a little iron in my mouth. David was about to experience the fruits of my labor.

After I made sure the door was closed and secure, in my calmest voice, I called out, "Malazel," I whispered, "come here *now*."

CHAPTER TWENTY-FOUR

Proper Introductions

The demon appeared within milliseconds; his usual joyful smile was completely gone. Alongside him stood Xalla, and she was radiating a tangible aura of anger.

"You are a demon of illusions, yes?" I asked, keeping my tone neutral even through the anger.

"Yes, Lord."

"And you saw what happened earlier?"

"I did," he answered.

"Then please kindly educate Aspirant David on why angering a Lord Arbiter is not good for his continued existence."

"Shall I eliminate him?" the demon asked tentatively.

"No, there's no finesse in such a crude solution like that," I explained calmly, wiping the last traces of blood off my face. "You're smarter than that, Malazel. Use your imagination. Use these six days of rest to show me what you can do. Think of it as a test to see if you are worth my time. I do not want him dead."

I looked at him in the eye and saw the demon flinch. "Let the human known as David Moore know the consequences of fucking with me!"

I almost allowed anger to get the better of me there, but I managed to calm down again. I'd learned over the years that allowing your emotions to get the better of you usually led to stupid decisions.

Now, was leaving the fate of David to a literal demon a little too extreme, even for my dubious morals? Perhaps, but I was so tired and angry that I simply didn't care. I needed to take some control back into my own hands. Plus, I'd explicitly stated that I didn't want him dead, so he'd probably be okay . . . maybe.

"I want him after the rest period is over," Xalla said for the first time, her normally chirpy tone glacial.

"Perhaps if he doesn't learn his lesson," I answered. Like I said, I wasn't so cruel as to hand the guy over to a Xollon. I'd seen what they do to their captives, and mental pollution or not, I was still human enough to understand that no one deserved that kind of fate.

"Leave his followers alone, though," I quickly added. "That includes you, Malazel."

The two site workers looked like they wanted to protest but decided against it. They saw that I wasn't in the mood to be argued with.

I mean, I was still angry, although a lot of that had subsided now that I had the chance to reassess my situation, but my rage was still mostly directed at David. His little goons were the type to latch themselves on to someone stronger, and I wasn't so morally depraved as to sentence those four to an untimely demise simply because they chose to follow someone else.

Xalla nodded, her tone easing up a little. "You are far too forgiving, Walter. If these humans weren't being tested, I would have had their entire civilization obliterated for such an offense. To think they would dare damage your passion project!"

Right . . . maybe I was a better person than I thought, and more importantly, perhaps it would be a good idea to never get on the bad side of any Xollon. At least Xalla was thoroughly on my side now.

"I know, Xalla," I answered, "but I am still working for Central, and I will not allow any more loss of resources because of a personal gripe of mine."

Xalla was a little disgruntled, but Raffiel looked at me with pride.

"You always put your work first," Raffiel said. "It is little wonder that you earned such high praise from the others!"

"Go, I need to clean up," I said, before turning to the Xollon. "And thank you for looking after me, Xalla."

"You're welcome, Walter," she responded. "You can count on me to ensure that your experiments are not ruined. Just let me know if you want me to exterminate Aspirant David and everyone he has ever loved or cared for."

Right . . . It was good to know that Xalla had taken a liking to me, but the way she showed her appreciation might be a tad extreme for human standards.

"We'll take our leave," Raffiel said. "You can expect the results shortly."

Leaving my room once again, this time without being hassled, I was finally able to survey this so-called rest area that Raffiel had prepared for us. Honestly, it would be gorgeous if there wasn't one glaring problem. Sure, the walls were beautifully decorated, the carpets lush, and the ambient temperature and atmosphere heavenly, but there was practically no one around. There were gyms whose equipment went unused, pools with no one swimming in them, and entire shops devoid of all life. It was eerily empty, like I was in a liminal space.

I shuddered at the unease.

From the results of the first trial, there should have been at least eighty people here, and while that wasn't a huge number, it should still be a little livelier than what I was seeing. Where the hell was everyone? They couldn't have all disappeared in one day.

After walking around the place some more, I finally understood why the halls and various amenities were empty: the very few who managed to dominate the first trial and obtained a decent class had scared off the rest of the aspirants. Some were literally waiting in the halls for some poor sucker to come out so they could do what they did to me. Thankfully no one saw me as I made my way, quietly this time, around the facility.

I was glared at whenever I passed by another rare individual, but word must have gotten out that I was broke, or perhaps these aspirants were not muggers, because they just left me alone. I did see one other nervous-looking aspirant sneaking into one room or another quickly, before darting back to the safety of their dorm.

Rest area, my ass. The only people having any sort of a relaxing time were the fifteen or so people who scored the highest in the first trial. Everyone else was either licking their boots or hiding in their dorms. Just being out in the open made me feel vulnerable and that was despite the fact that I knew Raffiel and Xalla had my back. I couldn't imagine how the others who barely survived a week in that hellish cityscape were faring.

Still, I had my goals in mind, and knowing the regressor and his sister, there was no way they would be hiding. That crazy woman Noel was almost certainly somewhere out here, and I'd bet good money that the really huge dude I hadn't met was out and about as well. I just had to find them before someone else decided it was a good idea to pick on me.

And find them I did, and all together at the cafeteria at that. It appeared that the regressor also had the same ideas as I did and made friends with the most outstanding individuals in our little cohort. Noel noticed me first.

Before they could bog me down with conversation, I made sure to check them out with my Lucky Eyes of the Arbiter for any new information, now that they'd all completed the first trial. And lo and behold, the info did change, with their classes now being displayed.

First up, the regressor and his class were absolutely ridiculous, as expected:

> **Chronolancer (EX-rank Unique Frontline Support)**
> **Description:** Given to the one whose spear has transcended space and time. You have transcended the limits of this life, and your mastery of the spear allows you to manipulate the very foundations of the universe. Your spear will have no rival, whether that be in the past, present, or future.

Above Noel's head was something equally absurd.

> **Gehenna's Silent Death (SS-rank Unique Assassin)**
> **Description:** You are intimately familiar with Death and Sin, forming a connection with the Underworld. You can borrow the power of Gehenna itself to bring the world to its heels. All will fear the flames of Gehenna's Silent Death.

The giant guy's class was also pretty impressive.

> **Titankin (S-rank Frontline)**
> **Description:** You are a lost child of Gaia, and the blood of Titans runs through your veins. Take hold of the power that caused the Titanomachia of the lost ages to obliterate your foes and show the world the might of a true Titankin.

And finally, Yoona's showed the only class that was sort of normal.

> **Spiritual Archer (B+-rank Support)**
> **Description:** Your Archery has reached a deep level, allowing you to imbue mana and life force into your volleys.

I mean, I knew these people were freaks, but when I compared my class to even Yoona's . . . I wanted to just pretend I never saw the information at all.

"Hey!" Noel shouted, waving me over. "If it ain't my little bro!"

Everyone was seated at a metal table, finishing the last bits of what seemed like a pretty impressive meal. The others noticed me as well—the regressor nodded in my direction, while the other man I hadn't met before was eyeing me up and down. The regressor's sister saw me, but a look of concern quickly washed over her features.

"Walter, your face!" Yoona said, getting up from her seat to take a closer look. "What happened?"

The others noticed as well but didn't react quite as strongly as the high schooler.

"Perhaps it's a new fashion trend?" Noel said. "Not a good look on you, though, Walter, might want to try a new look."

Once again, I had no idea how to interact with the redheaded lunatic. It seemed like she was just operating at a different frequency. Maybe I could make her the regressor's problem to deal with in the future.

"Um, no," I answered gently. "I got mugged on the way out."

"I knew it!" Yoona shouted, before turning to her brother. "I told you we should do something about those bullies!"

"No, no, it's fine," I said quickly. "Making trouble this early would do no one any favors. And I'm not really that hurt."

"No, your face is swollen! Look, I'll get a healing salve—um, it's something my brother and I bought at the store—it's in my room, so I'll be right back."

The regressor went to get up, but a fierce glare from Yoona made him sit down again.

"And I can go myself!" she said sternly. "I got second overall in the world rankings. Do you honestly think I can't handle myself here?"

"But—"

"No buts, Jae-Hyun. Take care of Walter. I'll be back real quick!"

And with that, before giving her brother another chance to protest, Yoona quickly jogged away. I didn't even have the time to thank her.

When Yoona was fully out of view, the looks of the other three changed almost instantaneously. Gone was the earlier cheer and aloof atmosphere, and all of them had death in their eyes. I guess there was some kind of unwritten rule to put on baby gloves when Yoona was around? I knew the regressor was screwed up in the head, having come back from the grave, and Noel was . . . Noel. But even the big guy seemed like he was serious trouble now.

"So, want to tell us the truth now?" the regressor said, his tone dark. "There's no way that you couldn't take care of a few thugs."

"Well, I haven't met you before," the only stranger here added, "but you survived a run-in with Noel, so you must be as much of a freak of nature as those two."

"Um, it's nice to meet you?" I said tentatively, not quite sure how to answer the regressor at the moment.

The big man nodded. "You too. The name's Vadeem, and any friend of Noel is all right in my book . . . Although if you're friends with her, you might not be all right in the head."

"Hey! What's that supposed to mean?" Noel interrupted.

The regressor shushed the two, and spoke again. "You haven't answered the question."

"It really was because I got mugged," I answered honestly for once. "I just didn't want to make such a big scene after passing out for a whole day."

"Really?" he said again, looking at me suspiciously.

"I just like keeping a low profile. Thought it would be easier to just fork over a few hundred gold than cause a scene."

"Ah!" A look of understanding washed over Noel's face. "You're into *that* kind of thing."

"What?" I asked, genuinely confused.

She gave me a friendly pat on the shoulder. "Hey, I don't judge. Got some friends into the same kink as you do, so no worries."

Oh, you have got to be kidding me. How was she able to constantly keep me guessing about her thought process?

"No, it's not like that—"

"No, no, it's okay, little bro. I can even introduce you to a nice club I know. Real extreme shit there. No safe words, strictly below ground. I'm sure you know what I mean."

"We're not even on Earth anymore, Noel. There are no clubs!" grumbled Vadeem.

"Oh, right!" she answered with genuine surprise. "I had completely forgotten. No wonder Walter's so desperate for a little action. It's been weeks since he's had a nice—"

"No," I interrupted quickly, "I'm being honest, I really just didn't want to cause a commotion."

The crazy woman raised an eyebrow before frowning. "All right, if you say so . . . but if you didn't do it on purpose, then that means someone actually had the audacity to bully my little bro? Walter, tell me who it is, and I'll have a nice little 'chat' with them. No one fucks with my friends!"

Yeah, I could not for the life of me predict this woman at all. Still nice to see she cared about me so much, considering I'd met her for a combined total of about an hour before this.

"She's right, you know," Vadeem said with a fierce grin. "If there's a problem, we can make it disappear real quick and quiet."

"Uh, I'm good," I answered nervously. "Thank you, though."

She nodded. "Right, you'd want revenge on your own. Understandable. But if you want to know some great techniques to use when you're having fun . . ."

"No one wants to learn those 'techniques' from you, Noel," Vadeem answered for me, rubbing his eyebrows in frustration.

"Uh, did you two know each other before?" I asked after seeing how naturally those two interacted.

"Yeah, unfortunately," Vadeem muttered. "We were in the same field of work before all this nonsense; my old boss and I had employed her services on more than a few occasions."

I nodded. I certainly did not want to find out what that line of work was, although I had a few guesses.

The regressor coughed and gestured to the hallway. We turned our attention toward that direction and saw that Yoona was making her way back. He gave me a cold stare, and I knew that he was telling me to keep things PG around his sister. Guess he didn't want to expose her to the real world just yet.

Vadeem sat back down and started to wolf down the remainder of his food with a goofy grin on his face, and even Noel put on a perfectly innocent smile as she waved at Yoona.

"Hey, that was quick, best pal!" she said cheerfully. "Let's get Walter patched up!"

David's Truth

David's world went to shit quickly. The second trial was just hours from starting, but he hadn't slept in almost two and a half days, and the one time that he did pass out, he woke with vivid handprint-shaped bruises all over his body.

No, if David slept, then *it* would get him.

Things went downhill shortly after the second day in the rest area, although David could still laugh at the irony of never being able to rest here, even if he could never laugh at anything else again. At first, the only abnormality that David saw was dark shadows darting around his vision, which he naively chalked up to the stress from overcoming his week in that zombie-infested wasteland. However, those dark shadows never went away.

They would appear constantly down hallways, peeking through doors, in dim corners, and they invaded everything that David did. He felt like something was constantly watching him, judging him, and if he let up his guard for even a second, then something terrible would occur. He thought these visions would go away, and they did, but what replaced those shadowy visions was infinitely worse.

The shadows were nothing compared to *it*.

It started to stalk him on the night of the second day. At first, David couldn't make out the figure haunting him. He could barely make out the outline of a pale shape, inhumanly lanky with distorted features of the thing, and it would always, always dart away from his view when he gathered enough courage to take a better look at it.

Oh, how he wished he'd never tried to peer into its horrible visage.

David quickly noticed a sickening pattern. Every time he would doze off, even a little, the figure would be ever so slightly closer to him. It was almost imperceptible at first, but that had changed when fatigue finally got to him and he slept for a few hours on the fourth day. That was something he would regret for the rest of his life.

On that night, David was plagued by visions of such enormity that he could scarcely fathom the images flashing through his head. He knew that whatever he was dreaming was trying to tell him something, but he could not recall the message.

What he did remember was the lanky figure approaching him as he was lying on the bed, trapped in his own body. Its eerie smile, too wide for any human to have, was filled with shadowy teeth, and he knew that if he did not wake up then, he would not make it past that night.

He felt cold, deathly hands caress every inch of his skin, and it was only through his sheer force of will that he managed to awaken in time. Those hands had left their mark on David, and he didn't think the bruises would ever disappear.

Now, every time he saw the figure, it would be almost within arm's length, just perhaps a step or two closer and it could reach him. David had to be vigilant to make sure that never happened. But even his enhanced nerves were on the cusp of giving out. He had to sleep.

Lately David's had a lot of time to think. It was all he did now, back against the corner in his dorm, always peering out into the darkness. He wondered why he was the only one who was plagued by the figure. What did he do wrong?

Then David had an epiphany, a revelation sent from the deep recesses of his sleep-starved brain. It was because of *that* man. Ever since he took his money, things had gotten worse and worse. But the more David thought about that man—no, that *being*—the more he understood. Yes, and in the deepest depths of David's psyche, he understood a primordial truth.

The Truth.

The handprints on his body started to morph in front of his very eyes, and in David's new sight, he saw that they were not scars but a prophecy.

A prophecy that was his destiny to spread.

David laughed.

Yes, David knew what he must do.

He must spread the Truth to all his fellow kin, not as the Aspirant David, but as the prophet.

David smiled, and for the first time in a long, long time, he allowed his eyes to close, and he embraced oblivion.

The Aspirant David slept, and something else entirely awoke.

CHAPTER TWENTY-FIVE

Formation of a Party

Yoona approached me quickly, carrying a small vial of green liquid. She frowned when she saw the swelling on my face.

"I can't believe people would be so cruel!" she exclaimed. "We're all in this horrible situation together, but all they care about is getting richer."

Noel nodded enthusiastically. "Yup, yup, they're terrible people!"

"Come on, Walter," Yoona said, handing me the bottle. "Just drip some of this on your wounds, and they'll heal in a jiffy. I wish we had this kind of technology back on Earth. If we did . . ."

The regressor's face turned grim. "But we didn't."

"Right," Yoona said. "Sorry."

Hm, there seemed to be some kind of history there that the rest of us weren't privy to. Well, it seemed private, so I decided not to intrude.

I took the small vial and dripped some of it on my face as best I could, using my reflection from the shiny metal table to see. It stung a little, but I could feel the swelling quickly subsiding, and the dull ache I was feeling all but disappeared. I still couldn't believe how fantastical the items you could get from Central could be.

"Thank you," I said. "How much was it? I'll pay you back."

Yoona rolled her eyes. "You were just mugged, Walter. You don't have any more money, and even if you did, I wouldn't ask you to pay for one. They're cheap in any case, and thanks to my brother, we're probably the richest aspirants in the world right now."

I looked at the staggering amount of money I had, and I somehow doubted that they were. I didn't correct her, though.

"Then I guess it was you two who caused that huge explosion near the end?"

Vadeem laughed. "Damn explosion almost got me as well!"

"But it didn't," grumbled the regressor. "I made sure that no one else would be caught up in the blast."

"Still almost gave me a heart attack when you set it off, brother! You never said that it would blow up the whole city!"

"Hey, enough of that, you two," Noel added, her smile never fading. "Walter's here, so we can finally form our awesome party!"

"I'm sorry, what?" I asked.

"We're making a party! You know, like the kind in RPGs!" Noel exclaimed. "Our leader says our next trial will involve groups, and you're chosen for the last spot in our awesome group!"

"If you want to, of course," Yoona quickly added.

I was still a little confused.

The regressor spoke up for the first time. "Remember the skill I told you about? The one that gives me information about the trials?"

I nodded.

"It told me that the next trial will be done with others, which is why we were given the time to spend here and socialize."

Yoona sighed. "But it seems like we're the only people actually socializing. Everyone else is busy extorting people or hiding. I don't understand why people are not united when the stakes are so high!"

Seemed like Yoona had never been exposed to the thing called human greed, nor was she clued in to the fact that Raffiel had deliberately set things up so the situation would most likely end up like this. The other three seemed to understand this fact, but none of them chose to tell the high schooler that.

"Yes, it is a pity." Vadeem shook his head in mock sadness.

"Anyway," the regressor continued, "we need to work in groups of five for the next trial, and Yoona and Noel both wanted you to fill our last spot."

Like I was going to say no to that! I'd get those sweet advantages courtesy of our regressor and his knowledge!

"Hey, I'd be glad to join," I said with a smile. "Any help I can get in this crazy world is good news for me. Your skill tell you anything else about the next trial?"

He shook his head. "No, at least not until it starts. The next trial will be randomized, but its purpose is to assess how well we use our new classes and abilities, just like how the first trial was to test our potential. I'll know more once we're there."

"Speaking of which, my new friend," added Vadeem, "what job did you get? I got a nice frontline class, perfect for getting up and personal with my enemies!"

"Oh, oh, and I'm an awesome RPG Rogue!" Noel exclaimed, making some exaggerated stabbing motions with her free hand. "I can go around and poke the baddies in the backside! All sneaky like!"

"I, uh, also have a frontline class," I muttered. "It's called the Master of . . . All."

Like hell I could tell these monsters my actual class!

"Oo, sounds imposing." Noel whistled. "What's it do?"

"It only allows me to use any weapon equally well," I lied. "But no real active abilities, so maybe it's not as impressive as it sounds."

The regressor nodded, his face furrowed in concentration. "No, that might be a better class than you think. There's equipment that's class-locked later on, and if you can truly use any weapon . . . but we can discuss that in the future."

"Forget about the future, we have a problem now!" the redhead said in shock. "Walter's using a *spear*!"

Everyone looked at her in confusion.

"Your point?" Vadeem asked.

"Are you blind? He can't use a spear! The boss is already using one!"

Now, I once again had no idea what Noel was on about, but I was actually a little impressed with the regressor for getting someone like Noel to address him as the leader. Maybe he had insider knowledge about the absolutely baffling way the woman acted via his future knowledge, but either way, I'd leave it to him to handle Noel in the future.

"Sorry, even I don't know what you're talking about, Noel," Yoona added in.

The other girl gave an exaggerated sigh. "My little bro will be known as 'that other spearman' or 'Spearman Number 2' when we're all super famous! We can't have one of our party members known as 'the less-handsome spearman' in the future! That's totally bad for his image!"

"Hey," I said, "how come I'd be the one known as the less-handsome spearman and not Jae-Hyun?"

"No offense, little bro, but our leader's a lot cooler than you are, so you've kind of defaulted into Player 2 status if you don't change your weapon."

I mean, sure, the regressor's got that dark and brooding look going for him, but was he that much cooler than I was?

"Affirmative," Noe decided to add. "According to Unit Noe's Human Index on Standard Attractiveness, Kim Jae-Hyun has a 98.95% probability of being more 'cool' than Host Walter."

Oh, come on, Noe, you're supposed to be on my side! There has to be something better about myself than that regressor!

"Affirmative," it replied. "Host Walter has Unit Noe."

. . .

"So," Noel continued, "we should go shop for a new weapon for Walter, something that'll make him stand out! We gotta find something exotic if he's able to use pretty much anything!"

"Fine," I muttered, feeling fully defeated. There really was no point in arguing with the insane woman.

"But first, Yoona," Jae-Hyun said, "can you get Walter some food? He's a little battered up to go himself. I'll get him caught up on what we've been doing."

"Sure thing!" Yoona agreed. "Anything you fancy? They got pretty much everything here."

"Um, a burger and some mac and cheese would be fine."

"Gotcha, I'll be right back. Take care of your wounds!"

Once again, the atmosphere turned absolutely chilly the second Yoona was out of view.

"Okay, what's going on?" I asked.

"Yoona's . . ." the regressor started, unsure how to explain things to me. "Yoona's had a tough upbringing. She's had to grow up too fast. You can criticize me all you want, but there's some things that she shouldn't be exposed to right now, even if those things *must* be done. She's the only family I have left."

Noel giggled, this time with none of the false innocence from before. "Yeah, Jae-Hyun's sister's as white as they come. No sin at all, probably never even jaywalked in her life. Not even I would go around ruining someone like that."

Her eyes flashed a bright shade of ruby, before her pupils turned back to a hazel brown. "Which makes me wonder why her brother's so different."

The regressor chose to ignore her. "As I was saying, I don't want Yoona to experience any more misery than she's already had to. She's suffered enough growing up alone. There are things that I will have to do in the future that are necessary for our survival, but my sister is not ready to face those kinds of truths. Not now. Noel and Vadeem have already agreed that she should stay out of those kinds of dealings, so if you could . . ."

"Hey, I get it," I answered. "This whole situation's messed up as is. No need to drag a teenager into the murkier parts. I'll keep things PG around her, make her stay in the trials as comfy as possible."

For the first time since I'd seen the regressor, he seemed genuinely appreciative. I guess he had a real soft spot for his sister.

"Thank you," he said. "And I will need your help in the future as well, Walter. Can we count on your support?"

I laughed. "Hey, if it'll help with our survival, count me in."

Vadeem grinned. "Knew you were an okay guy, Walter."

"So, how come you're fine with keeping her in the dark, Vadeem?" I asked.

He shrugged. "I have a daughter around her age, out there. Can't imagine what it's like for someone so young to be trapped in a situation like this."

"Uh, Vadeem, your daughter's like ten," Noel pointed out. "That's a wee bit younger than my new bestie."

"Carol's twelve now," he reminded her with a shake of his head. "And they're both still children in my eyes. Children should enjoy their youth for as long as they can, so let's keep it that way for young Yoona."

I agreed, and the atmosphere shifted back as the girl in question brought over a tray full of food.

"Hey, guys!" Yoona said, tray in hand. "Got Walter caught up on the plan?"

"Yup, yup!"

"Awesome!" she said, handing me the plate of food and scooching over to grab a seat herself. "And have we decided on a new weapon for him?"

"Oh, we were waiting for you to come back before choosing," Noel answered. "Finding the right look for my little bro here's a real science! We gotta find something memorable, something that'll strike fear into his enemies, and it's got to have a distinct silhouette so he'd be instantly recognizable! Come on, Walter, eat your food faster. We have to figure this out ASAP. It's of the utmost importance!"

I stuffed more mac and cheese into my mouth between big bites of my cheeseburger. I finished my meal faster than I wanted, mostly because I didn't want Noel to lose her cool and do something crazy. Honestly, the food was pretty fantastic, maybe not as tasty as a shoggoth or that whale thing I ate with Xalla, but superb nonetheless. I really did want to enjoy my meal a bit more, but something told me that making Noel wait for any amount of time was highly unwise.

As soon as the last of the garbage was in the trash and my tray was stashed away, Noel practically pushed me forward toward the shopping area, and it was kind of nice spending my time without worrying about dying every second for once. I even laughed along with Vadeem's lame jokes as I walked out of the cafeteria with my new companions.

CHAPTER TWENTY-SIX

New Weapon Woes

The shop was an absolute marvel to look at when the regressor's group and I made it there. The place looked like it came right out of the Vatican museum in terms of scale and splendor, with beautifully decorated marble walls, high ceilings, and more importantly, rows upon rows of expensive-looking items. The amount of stuff on display—and this was just the things I could see from the entrance—was insane.

There were vials of unknown liquids filling up an entire wall to the left, while huge display cases housed armor, trinkets, accessories, and every object in between. Each item had a small description detailing its function and price on an expertly carved plaque, and an army of small pixie assistants were waiting at attention, ready to help anyone who needed it. The shop was certainly grand, but just like everywhere else in the rest area, it was utterly devoid of other humans.

"Welcome, aspirants," a small feminine voice greeted. It belonged to a professionally dressed pixie no larger than the size of my palm. "Do you need any help with finding an item today?"

"'Sup, Nell," Noel said. "We're good today, just going to the weapon's hall. We'll also book an hour in the practice range."

"Understood, Lady Noel." The pixie nodded back. "That will be ten gold."

Looking at people paying for things here was really strange as an outside observer. It seemed like a whole lot of nothing, since everything was done via the Trash Matrix, but evidently the transaction went through without problem, and she allowed us to pass through.

Noel led the way through a narrow corridor and into a grand room that had a pretty large sparring arena in the middle of it. On the raised platform there were a couple of practice dummies you could use to test out new equipment. It was spacious enough to test out even the bulkiest of options.

All around the large central room were smaller entrances that housed practically every type of weaponry imaginable.

"All right, you stay right there, Walter. Let's see if we can find something awesome for you to use!" Noel turned her attention to the other three. "Come on, gang, let's find something for my little bro to try out! Remember, we want something distinctive and awesome!"

Noel all but sprinted out of the room, her eyes glistening, while Vadeem laughed and walked into a different room. Even the regressor and his sister were drawn into the atmosphere, and they were chatting happily as they went to find something for me to try on.

It didn't take ten minutes before a mountain of stuff was piled up before me, ranging from traditional weapons to weird alien rifles and magical artifacts. Things got really out of hand when Noel managed to somehow drive a small tank into the training room, narrowly avoiding the various shelves of items on her way. Yoona quickly made her take that thing back.

Still, by the time everyone was happy with their various selections, my new friends all looked triumphant. Even the regressor had a small smile on his face.

"Wouldn't we be bothering the pixies from taking so much stuff off the shelves?" I asked, pointing at the growing mountain.

"Eh, they're magic," Noel replied indifferently.

I gave her a questioning look.

"What she means," Yoona explained, "is that the items we bring out will return to their display stands automatically when we leave, so it's honestly not bothering anyone here."

"Oh, yeah, magic," I said.

Noel continued, "All right, so I got a pretty good idea about what my bro here should use."

She proceeded to take out a set of nunchucks from the weapon mountain. She waved it around, mimicking some old Bruce Lee films, along with the appropriate sound effects, but quickly stopped when she smacked herself in the back of the head.

"No way," the regressor quickly said, taking the weapon out of her hand.

"Those are not practical, even if Walter can use them well. He'd be better off using a stick."

I grimaced. That was pretty much the starting weapon that the damn Trash Matrix gave me.

"Oh, come on, boss!" Noel cried, trying to nab the weapon back from Jae-Hyun without success. "They're so cool, though!"

He threw it away, much to the disappointment of Noel. "Cool or not, we need to find a weapon that can actually harm our enemies, not glorified movie props."

"Boo!" Noel gave an exaggerated pout. "You're no fun."

"If we're looking for sheer damage," Vadeem added with a grin, "I think I have the right solution!"

He went to a side room and came back with the most ridiculously large maul that I had ever seen. It was pretty much a boulder attached to a stick, given the absurdity of its size. Yet what was even more amazing was the fact that Vadeem was holding it one handed, even though his footsteps caused tremors every time he walked forward.

"Yeah . . . that's not going to work, that thing'll squish me like a bug." I looked at him incredulously. "And just how much strength do you even have?"

"Two hundred and seventy-eight," he said with pride, flexing his might further by swinging the massive maul around with ease. "My class passive doubles my existing strength, and I got a few titles that give me some more."

Doubled strength . . . I looked at my own pitiful class passive. I'd get back at the damn Trash Matrix if it was the last thing I did.

"You know," he continued, looking at the weapon in his hand in more detail, "I might just keep this baby for myself. Could come in handy down the line."

Noel rolled her eyes. "For what? Demolishing a house? You plan to start a construction company in the trials now?"

The big man shrugged. "You never know."

The regressor thought for a second before speaking up. "No, Vadeem's right. Buy one but find an even bigger maul or hammer if you can. The biggest you can find."

Vadeem's smile was amazing. "If you say so! Let's put these muscles to the test!"

"Hey! We're here for Walter, remember? You can find a big dumb club some other time. My little bro's still got no weapon!"

I mean, I did still have my old spear, but I didn't think Noel would take that as an answer.

"Um, how about something long ranged in that case?" Yoona added, "Maybe one of those alien guns would be nice to have."

Noel quickly shook her head. "No, no, we need diversity! A classic RPG party of five only needs one ranged unit, and I already told you our goal was to make Walter unique! He can't go from Spearman 2 to Bowman 2!"

Yoona looked at the other woman in confusion, clearly not understanding her unique outlook on things. "But he doesn't need to use a bow like me."

"No, Noel's right in this case," the regressor added.

The woman in question smiled in triumph. "I'm always right!"

"If Walter can truly use any weapon, then we have to take advantage of that," he continued, ignoring Noel entirely. "Vadeem's got all the power we'll ever need covered, and between Noel and I, we have a solid frontline."

"So we should have another ranged member, then," Yoona said with a frown.

"Not quite, we need someone flexible that can protect you—"

"I don't need someone protecting me!"

"Let me finish, Yoona," he continued. "We need someone who can protect you when you're reloading, and give you the space you need to shoot, while still having the option of helping out the rest of us if needed."

"I guess . . ." Yoona reluctantly agreed. "So something like a medium-ranged weapon? Wouldn't that just be a spear again? Or maybe a polearm or something?"

"No, there's something that's just right for this situation."

The regressor walked toward one corner of the store, and after looking around for a bit, pulled out a simple-looking sword. It was about a meter or two in length and didn't look like it would be used in anything but close fights.

"Isn't that just a sword?" Vadeem asked, clearly as confused as I was. "Should Walter throw it or something?"

"Um, boss, are your eyes okay?" Noel added.

"Look," he replied, before pointing out a small trigger on the handle.

"Oh my god . . . Is that the legendary gunblade? Tell me it's a gunblade!"

The regressor chuckled, rare for someone so gloomy. "No, it's better."

He moved to the center of the testing area and pressed the little trigger. The normal-looking blade split into smaller pieces, with all the blade parts linked together by a thin wire, and with a wave of the regressor's hand, the transformed sword lashed out toward one of the training dummies. The blade fragments collided with the target and made huge gashes into the wooden dummy's torso before completely shredding it to pieces. He took his finger off the trigger, and the wire quickly retracted, the blade fragments re-forming into its original sword form.

"It's a whip-blade," he said with a smirk. "Almost completely useless in most situations because of how difficult it is to use, but with Walter's class . . . I think this is perfect. The weapon's at an ideal length that he can use it at range, and if he's as skilled as I think he is, then there's no fear of any one of us getting caught in the weapon's path. It's destructive, and if the situation isn't suited for long-range attacks, he can use it as a standard short sword."

I thought about it for a moment, and I actually agreed with the regressor's assessment of the weapon. Of course, it was not because of any class skill I had, since the passive I did have was worse than useless, but because of Noe. My system was able to manipulate luck to an absolutely insane level, so I figured that any weapon that had a lot of variance that was inherently a part of its design would be ideal for me, and nothing was more random than a whip.

"Actually, that might not be a bad option," I said tentatively before taking the weapon from the regressor. It felt pretty light in my hands, and I swung it around a bit to get a feel for the weapon.

"Hm, you have pretty good taste, boss," Noel added. "Distinctive, deadly, and perfectly suited to my little bro's unique kinks! Although maybe he's better suited to be on the receiving end of one of those whips."

"I said I don't have any of those fetishes!" I shouted but quickly quieted down when I saw the death glare that the regressor was giving me.

I noticed that Yoona looked at us both in confusion. *Right, keep it PG.*

"Anyway," Vadeem said, choosing the perfect time to change topics, "we won't know how well this weapon will perform without some tests, right? And what's the best way to test things out?"

Noel smiled. "With a spar, of course!"

CHAPTER TWENTY-SEVEN

To Spar Against a Spear

The regressor decided to be my sparring partner, much to the displeasure of Noel, and I was now standing face-to-face with the man in the center of the training area. Vadeem had moved the dummies away and was acting as the referee.

"Are you sure you two shouldn't be using training weapons?" Yoona asked.

"We're fine," her brother answered with way more confidence than I would have. "I've seen Walter's skill before. We're both able to stop before any of us are harmed. Plus, where would he even get a training version of his weapon?"

"Still . . ."

He shook his head. "Don't worry too much, Yoona, we'll both be fine."

The high schooler eventually agreed but insisted we have a stockpile of healing salves on standby. None of us saw any point in arguing with that.

I held my new weapon in hand and stared into the eyes of my opponent. The regressor was intense. It was like some kind of sick determination drove him to give his absolute all regardless of what was going on around the man. I shuddered at the thought of legitimately facing him in combat and hoped that such an event would never come to be.

Still, a smaller part of me was glad for the chance to finally test out my abilities. I knew that I was still relying on Noe to do 90% of the heavy lifting, but the few bouts that I did have using the Absolute Luck skill taught me a number of things.

First of all, my luck charges went down relatively slowly if it only had to make minor adjustments to my actions, so the more skilled I was at combat, the longer the skill could be activated for. Additionally, thanks to my first run-in with Noel, I learned that my luck charges went down *fast* if it had to compensate for situations where I was woefully overwhelmed.

But the one thing I knew from my albeit limited exposure to Noe's skill was that I needed more control over it, and fighting the regressor was the perfect opportunity to do so without much consequence. I'd never run out of luck charges before, but I was under no illusions that it would remain that way in the future. The trials would only get harder, and I needed to ensure that I had the capabilities to not just survive them, but to thrive.

Steading myself, finger on the trigger, I waited for Vadeem's countdown.

"All right, contestants, you know the rules!" he shouted. "We're using only raw skill here, so no class actives or abilities. We'll begin on the count of three. Are both sides ready?"

I activated my skill despite being told not to—like hell I wouldn't cheat here—and saw that my luck had recharged to an adequate amount. Not full, since my date with Xalla had all but emptied my reserves, but enough for the task ahead of me. Sadly, the regeneration rate of one charge per minute, which seemed so quick before, was quickly showing its flaws now that my total charges were in the hundreds. I had invested the rest of my free attribute points into Dexterity, so I should fare slightly better than before.

Overall, my stats looked like this:

Host Walter Thefuck:	
Human Male, age 27	
Class: Level 17 Master of None	
Free points: 0	
Attributes:	
HP:	254/254
MP:	0/0
Strength:	49 (+10.5)
Dexterity:	44 (+0)
Endurance:	42 (+10)
Intelligence:	48 (+10)
Charisma:	60 (+10)

Luck Charges: 344/405

I cursed at the fact that I actually lost dexterity even though I invested eight more points into it. What a goddamn useless class the Trash Matrix forced me into!

"I'm ready," the regressor said, expression still grim with determination.

Come on, it's just a spar, please go easy on me!

"I'm as ready as I'll ever be," I answered and dismissed my stats page.

Vadeem smiled. "All right, contestants! Three. Two. One . . . Begin!"

Although I had no experience with using any weapon, much less this crazy fantasy whip thing, the overall concepts were straightforward. I had the distinct reach advantage over the regressor's spear, and I had to make sure that I kept him at a distance. I knew enough about combat to know that fighting a spear with a normal sword was a losing battle no matter the situation.

As soon as Vadeem's countdown finished, I depressed the trigger and slashed out with the unlinked blade segments. The weapon fully protracted was at least four meters long, and I could almost reach the regressor even from our starting points.

As I slashed, I felt a slight jitter in my hands, my digits shaking like I had just drank five espresso shots in a row. These jitters caused the blade segments to dance wildly in the air, and the regressor frowned, as he had to dodge and deflect a cascade of sharp blades coming at him from every angle. Yet despite the ludicrous number of angles that he had to account for, and the sheer speed and unpredictability of the attacks, none of the blades managed any impact on his person. What a monster.

Luck Charges: 342/405

As I thought, the amount of luck charges that I consumed was minimal when I used this weapon. I continued to swing the whip-blade at a wild rate, keeping my opponent on guard and forcing all his attention on avoiding the seemingly random movements of the attacks. However, although the regressor was definitely on the back foot, I quickly realized the big problem with how I was fighting.

Sure, each individual strike didn't consume a lot of luck charges, but I was swinging a lot. The tiny amount of charges used was adding up fast. In the span of just moments, my charges plummeted, yet the regressor was still completely unharmed.

Luck Charges: 273/405

This couldn't go on, but I was at an impasse. If I let my continuous swings up, even a little, then Jae-Hyun could slip through my barrage of blades and I'd lose my only advantage. If he got close to me, I doubted the amount of luck charges I had could even last a single minute.

Noe, I thought, *is there anything you can do here?*

"Affirmative," it answered. "Unit Noe can switch from Luck Algorithm 1 Alpha to Luck Algorithm 3 Alpha to calculate the best outcome for the Absolute Luck skill."

What's the difference? I thought, still swinging wildly. *CliffsNotes version, Noe!*

Luck Charges: 252/405

"Luck Algorithm 3 Alpha is suited for combat but will consume more luck charges."

Luck Charges: 245/405

Switch, Noe!

"Affirmative."

My next swing was . . . strange. I felt like I had almost no control over my own body. My arm went where I wanted it to, but the whole left side of my body seemed to be making random gestures on the way to that location. It was highly disconcerting, seeing my body behave completely outside my control because even though I was relying on Noe previously, all the system did was cause minute muscle spasms and contractions.

Luck Charges: 183/405

But regardless, the results of that random motion were immediately noticeable. So was the huge drop in my luck charges. My motions caused the whip to seem like it had a mind of its own, and every single blade fragment seemingly homed in on the regressor's vitals. The segments were colliding into themselves again and again, making the overall path of each blade almost unpredictable, and Noe was somehow using the momentum from Jae-Hyun's deflections to mix up the whip's movements further.

After two swings, the regressor had to take three steps back, and after the third, I (well, I guess it was mostly Noe doing the work if I had the time to contemplate these things) managed to find a fault in the regressor's defense and strike first blood. He was briefly overwhelmed, and a narrow gash formed on his cheek.

> **Luck Charges:** 87/405

However, that was pretty much the extent of my victory, because the regressor's entire atmosphere changed when I managed to land that blow. I felt a stifling aura permeate from his unnerving gaze, and his movements sped up to an insane level. Now, instead of trying to dodge or deflect my weapon, he ignored defense and focused all of his strength on hitting one of its segments. In doing so, he was cut up, but he ignored the wounds, and with a great swing, he forced the blade segments away from him.

He took that tiny moment of respite to bridge the distance. Within milliseconds, he was within striking distance of me, and I felt a horrible pain in the pit of my stomach that made me bend over in agony. It wasn't from the regressor, because his swing missed taking off my head. It seemed that Noe's new idea of defending its host was a lot more unpleasant than before.

> **Luck Charges:** 44/405

It was over pretty quickly after that point. I was able to dodge two more strikes before the last of my luck charges petered out into nothing, and I saw the point of a spear hovering just inches away from my face. I fell back in exhaustion and quickly put my hands up in defeat.

> **Luck Charges:** 0/405

I knew that I probably wouldn't win in a straight-up fight versus the regressor, but I don't think I managed to last even five minutes in that fight. I gritted my teeth in bitterness; it seemed like I couldn't blindly rely on Noe's Luck skill and had to improve on my own as well. If this had been a real fight . . .

But it wasn't, so no point being bitter about the learning experience. It just meant that I had to improve my control over the skill and hone my own abilities.

I sighed. "All right, you win, Jae-Hyun. I stood no chance."

The regressor composed himself and let a panicking Yoona apply some of her hoarded salves on his cuts. His sister did not look happy about what just transpired.

"No," he said slowly, "you were much better than I thought. And that technique of yours . . . I've never seen anything like it."

"Yeah!" Noel added. "I told you that he fought weird!"

Vadeem nodded. "It's very strange. It's like Walter's not thinking about his attacks at all and just moving randomly. There's no intent behind his actions. Must be hard to fight against when you can't read your opponent at all."

"It's even worse than that," the regressor added. "It's not just the lack of intent, but even the way his body moves is completely contradictory to every style of fighting I've ever seen. He's using none of the correct muscles, so I can't predict his actions based on his body. Where did you learn to fight like that?"

"Oh, from my mentor," I said with confidence and began to quote Raffiel verbatim. "Can't really tell you who it is, but he said that a person shouldn't be too focused on form, on technique, because that would be limiting yourself. So to become a true master is to forgo the constraints of technique and revert to the state of a true beginner."

Sorry, Raffiel, but I'll put your wisdom to use now!

"Fascinating . . ." the regressor said. "I didn't think someone of that level still existed in the outside world. You have a good mentor, Walter."

I nodded and silently thanked Raffiel again for his wisdom.

"Awesome! All right, gang, we got Walter his weapon, so mission complete!" Noel said. "Let's clean up now and hit the pool! You won't believe the facilities they've got here!"

"I second that!" Vadeem exclaimed.

Yoona looked at her brother, now content that his small wounds were fully healed. "Brother, do you mind?"

The regressor smiled. "All right, I think we're due for a break. Let's go."

The rest of that week passed by faster than I thought possible. Most of it was spent with the four members of my party, some of it was stocking up on supplies for the next trial, but honestly, most of the time was just relaxing fun. Even the regular sparring sessions the regressor devised were entertaining in their own way, and seeing myself improve my control over the Luck skill was always motivating.

Before I knew it, only a few hours remained before the start of the next trial, and I could only hope that it went as well as the first one.

CHAPTER TWENTY-EIGHT

Pretrials and Problems

I was sitting in my room, getting the last of my newly acquired items packed up and ready for the second trial. With only ten inventory slots, with one taken up by my weapon and another used to store my backpack, I was pressed to decide what else to take. Thankfully the Trash Matrix had announced that all aspirants would have access to their dormitories again, although not the rest area itself, so I could house the extra things in my room without fear of losing them.

In the end, I chose to leave the garbage starting gear behind and stuffed as many healing items as I could into my bag, since that only counted as one item slot. The remaining seven slots were filled with various survival gear, extra rations—I couldn't exactly survive off of ambrosia with the rest of the team watching—and at the behest of the regressor, a bunch of plastic explosives. I could only imagine what we'd need those for down the line.

There were only two hours remaining until our seven days of rest was over, and I had agreed with the rest of my party to meet up at the cafeteria half an hour prior to the start. I was about to do one final check on my gear when I heard a soft knock on my door. I opened it, and it wasn't the regressor or his gang who greeted me, but Q.

"I apologize for coming to see you at such an inopportune time," he said as I closed the door behind him, "but I thought that it would be wise to check up on your progress with the anomaly before you were too busy in the second trial."

"You noticed the anomaly?"

Q chuckled. "I'd be a terrible site administrator if I didn't notice at this point! Our anomaly and his sister destroyed all the previous records for the completion of the first trial. Which is also why I am here."

I raised an eyebrow, gesturing that he should continue. I didn't want to speak too much before I had some sense of what was going on.

"I . . ." Q hesitated for a spell. "I just have some concerns about recent trends with Central and the Origin Matrix, and I thought it would be wise to share that with you, since you were away for ten cycles."

Okay, now we were getting somewhere.

"What's changed?" I asked, genuinely curious this time.

"I'm sure you know, but the Origin Matrix almost never creates anomalies. They're usually the result of a glitch, or when it feels that a great crisis is approaching where nothing short of an anomaly can fix the situation."

I nodded. "Yes, that's in line with what I know."

"But ever since your return, I've done a little bit of digging into Central's files, just out of initial curiosity," Q said, eyes looking nervous. "Very few things can escape the notice of an Omni, but . . ."

"It's fine, Q," I assured him. "I won't judge any action you've taken, even if it's not technically within regulations. You should know that by now."

"Right," Q continued. "So the results of my investigations showed that the amount of anomalies have surged in recent times."

"Surely fluctuations in these types of events happen all the time?"

"Not to this extent, Lord." Q shook his head. "The number of anomalous aspirants has risen by over 10,000% as compared to even five cycles ago. No amount of statistical variance can account for that kind of change, and the higher-ups have done a thorough job of hiding this information."

"That . . . that doesn't make sense. Why would Origin do something so reckless?"

"Exactly!" Q frowned. "Everyone knows that using an anomaly's almost always worse than not having one at all, even if there's an arbiter guiding their actions."

I nodded, urging Q to continue his rant. This was information I desperately needed.

"Yes, they can exceed the growth and potential of all others, but more than half of them escape Central's command and actively try to damage us!" Q sighed. "You weren't here, but just three cycles ago, one particularly nasty aspirant managed to destroy an entire training site and launch a crusade into Central Headquarters! It took us employing an entire squad of Xollon mercenaries to stop that uprising, yet they've apparently learned nothing and are making more of these things!"

"Have you managed to find out why these changes are occurring?"

Q shook his head bitterly. "No. Not even I was able to uncover that part. It's hidden deep, really deep, but something's not right with Origin, I can feel it. I've worked in this field long enough to notice these changes."

"I see . . ."

"Just keep an eye on things out there, Walter," Q said with genuine concern. "There's trouble brewing in the future, and I hate being left in the dark about it."

"I will," I assured him. "And thank you for speaking with me first. I'll keep my eyes on the anomaly and see if I can't uncover anything on the aspirant side of things."

"I thank you again for your services, Arbiter Walter," he answered. "I can see why you've earned so much recognition previously. I won't take up any more of your time, but please let me know if you find out anything about the situation."

I nodded, and before I could say anything else, Q disappeared, leaving me alone in my dorm once more.

I sat on the bed and pondered for a bit. That was a lot of new information to unpack, but at least Q had answered some of the more pressing questions I had. Still, just because I knew that danger was ahead of me didn't mean that I actually knew how to stop it. All it did was enforce the things that I already knew. There was more to my current situation than just finishing the trials and stopping a hypothetical invasion of Earth, and I had to get to the bottom of it.

Well, my short-term goals were still the same: tag along with the regressor, get as much power as I possibly could, abuse the shit out of my arbiter status, and figure out a proper way of using Noe's skills. Oh, and somehow live through all this before I lost my mind due to mental pollution.

I sighed at my apparent mountain of oncoming trouble and headed out the door with my stuff in tow. There was only about an hour before the new trial, and I might as well take advantage of the facilities while I still could. Then it was off to meet the regressor and hopefully survive whatever crap the Trash Matrix threw at me.

I chuckled as a thought occurred to me: if the Trash Matrix really was defective somehow, maybe my dream of one day kicking its ass wouldn't be too far off course. That day could not come sooner.

I made my way to the cafeteria for one last bite to eat and saw that I wasn't alone. In fact, everyone else was already there.

"Hey, Walter," Yoona said. "Glad you made it early. It seems like everyone had the same thought. Wish we had a phone or something we could use to communicate."

Huh, I'd never thought about that, since the only other people I talked with were beings who could apparently travel between space and time.

"Yeah, that would be a problem in the future, wouldn't it?" I said. "Won't we lose party members if we ever get split up?"

"The people running these damn tests have already thought of that," the regressor answered. "We'll be able to form an official party once the second trial starts, and we can all communicate through the system interface then."

"And we'll have a sweet guild later as well!" Noel chimed in. "Least that's what the boss says. I'm already making a list of potential amazing names to call ourselves. Noel and the Nobodies is at the top of the list right now, subject to change."

"That's, uh . . . great, Noel, and I guess Raffiel and his people have thought of everything," I muttered.

"Not everything," Jae-Hyun said, his voice chilly. He couldn't be more right if Q's information was anything to go by. "Did everyone bring the items I told you about?"

"I did," Vadeem answered. "Although the things you asked for are a little . . ."

"Strange?" I added, remembering the TNT and other explosives I had stowed away in my inventory.

"More like random!" Noel said. "The boss man told me to bring a few gallons of pig blood, some firecrackers, and a sack of marbles. What'd he make you bring, bestie?"

"Um, just a few sets of clothing for everyone," Yoona replied. "Nothing so crazy like what you're explaining."

The regressor spoke. "We need to ensure that we are properly prepared for any situation in the next trial."

"Pig blood and marbles will help with that?" I asked skeptically.

"Like I said, I won't know what specific test we will go through until we're in it, so I want to ensure that all the worst possibilities are accounted for. I'm sure you've all noticed this by now, but the trials reward those who come in first, and we have to capitalize on these early stages so we can maximize our growth later on."

Man, this man must just be min-maxing every future event in his spare time. That was no way to live your life. But thankfully he was the one doing all the heavy lifting. I'd just go along and reap the rewards of his planning!

"Remember, everyone," the regressor continued, "anything can happen once the trials begin again, we'll have a chance to form our party right before we're thrown in, so accept quickly and get used to its functions. If we ever get lost, take out one of these and light it up."

The regressor then proceeded to hand out a few normal-looking flares to each of us. They didn't look all that impressive until I saw their descriptions through my title skill.

Flare of True Sight (D+ rank)
Description: Crafted by Kim Jae-Hyun using the cores of mutated undead, these modified flares will broadcast the true location of the user to any individuals registered in his/her party.

What the hell? The regressor was even able to craft items? I knew that he had to be impressive to survive in the future, but now it seemed like he could do practically anything. But I guess if he spent most of his time alone in his prior life, then it only made sense that he had picked up a lot of skills. Still felt like cheating, though.

I sighed. Yup . . . I had to admit that he was indeed cooler than me.

"Thanks, Jae-Hyun," Vadeem said before stowing the flares in his bag. "Anything else to note before we get started?"

"No," he answered, "our group will be fine, but just be prepared for anything. The people working here are not our friends."

We spent the rest of the hour chatting and enjoying the final comforts of the rest area, and before long, a familiar voice greeted us. With a radiant flash of light, a projection of Raffiel appeared in front of us.

CHAPTER TWENTY-NINE

Second Trial, Dark Beginnings

I hope everyone had a delightful rest in these last seven days," Raffiel continued. "But it is that time once again to begin the next stage of your ascension."

My new comrades and I stopped what we were doing to focus on the information. The anticipation of a new challenge was starting to affect me as well, and I was feeling more anxious than I thought.

"The next round will be conducted in groups, or parties as they will be known, of five." The angel smiled. "In just a moment, the Lord's system will give you all a prompt allowing you to invite four other individuals into a party. Once that is formed, you can elect a leader to represent your group."

"Notification," Noe's voice chimed in. "Trash Matrix's Party System has been initiated. Host Walter has a party invite from Aspirant Kim Jae-Hyun. Does host accept?"

Yes.

"Acknowledged," Noe answered. "Party chat system online. Please input a username to communicate with the host's new party."

Just Walter's fine. And how do I use this new chat?

"Acknowledged, and to use the new function, simply ask Unit Noe, and I will relay your message via the Trash Matrix."

Thanks.

A series of text messages started to appear in front of my eyes a few seconds later.

> **Lady Awesome:** Hey, is this chat thing working? Helloooo? Anyone home?
> **Jae-Hyun:** Stop messing around, Noel.
> **Lady Awesome:** Nu-uh, how'd you know I'm the staggeringly beautiful and cool Noel and not Vadeem cross-dressing?
> **Vadeem the Dream:** Because I don't cross-dress!

Now that was an image I didn't want to imagine. A seven-foot-tall, 400-plus-pound muscled man in a frilly dress . . . I almost chuckled.

> **Lady Awesome:** And how do I know that you're not my little bro pretending to be Vadeem?
> **Vadeem the Dream:** I swear to god, Noel!
> **Yoona:** Guys, please stop, I want to listen to Raffiel!
> **Walter's Fine:** Yes, can we try out this new system later?
> **Lady Awesome:** Fineee. You peeps are no fun!

Wait a second, why was my username . . . You know what, I didn't even care anymore. Noe could just do its thing.

" . . . assigned randomly if you are not in a party," Raffiel said.

Damn it, Noel's useless dialogue made me miss some of the information.

"Do not worry if you gained classes that are not battle oriented, for the next trial's difficulty and challenges will be generated based on the composition of your party. It is there to test your newfound abilities, and the Lord would not be so cruel as to make a trial that is impossible to complete!"

Wait, if the next trial was based on the party, and I was partied with *these* people, then wouldn't the difficulty be insane? But then again, the regressor should have already known this, and hopefully there was a reason for his madness. Maybe the rewards would match the difficulty.

Ah, who was I kidding? I was probably screwed being paired with these freaks.

"Now, the most important aspect of this trial is not merely survival, but you must also overcome a unique set of tasks to progress," Raffiel continued and looked at us hard in the eyes. "This will be the final trial before the main stage of the ascension process begins, so please make sure that you explore your team's environment thoroughly to eke out as many advantages as you can. The better your team does now, the better you will do in the future.

"Now, then, enough talk on my part. Take the last few minutes to finalize your teams, and we shall depart in ten minutes. Good luck, Aspirants!"

> **Lady Awesome:** Oh oh, let's vote for a team name now!

"Noel, we're all here in person," the regressor said with a sigh. "You can just talk."

> **Lady Awesome:** But this is so much cooler!

Jae-Hyun gave her one of those chilly stares of disapproval.

"Fine," she muttered with a pout, "But in all seriousness, we should have a name for ourselves. I still think Team Noel and the—"

"No!" we all said at once.

"You guys are no fun!"

"How about Team Abyss?" I said before Noel could open her mouth again, the name taking inspiration from the regressor's title.

"Oo, I like it!" Noel said with a smile. "Dark and interesting! Not as cool as mine, but you're not half bad at naming things, little bro."

"Isn't it a bit too gloomy, though?" Yoona added. "Maybe something happier?"

"No . . ." her brother muttered. "I like it. It's fitting for our situation."

"I'm fine either way," Vadeem added. "If the leader says Walter's idea is good, then let's go with that."

Yoona shrugged. "Well, that's fine if everyone else is happy about it."

"Then we'll be Team Abyss from now on!" I smiled. "And Jae-Hyun is naturally the leader. Agreed?"

Everyone nodded. I figured everyone here was more the follower type, as having to manage a party, and guild later on, would suck the fun out of pretty much everything. Let's let the guy who didn't seem to understand the concept of fun in the first place have that job. That was the one thing I didn't envy about the regressor.

After we all unanimously elected Jae-Hyun as the team leader, Yoona offered some last words of advice and encouragement as we all watched the countdown to the start of the new trial quickly go to 0. A now-familiar feeling washed over me, and I was transported somewhere new once again.

The first thing I did was to check my surroundings as always. It didn't take me long this time, because I couldn't see much of anything. I was practically blind by the time my eyes adjusted to the minuscule amount of light, and I saw that I was standing in a damp forest in the middle of the night.

But the dark was strange. Normally there would be some amount of light, even on a moonless night, and being in the modern world, you'd be hard-pressed to find any place free of light pollution. Yet there seemed to be an almost super-natural darkness seeping into all the plants and foliage around me.

I quickly took my little lantern out of my bag and lit the flame. A soft, comfortable orange glow wrapped around Vadeem and I, and the prior suf-focating feeling disappeared. Seemed like the Promethean fire was doing its thing.

Wait a second . . . I glanced around and saw that Vadeem was the only person here. He was fiddling with a little portable flashlight, trying to secure it on his bulging shirt, but where was the rest of the party? I walked around a bit, trying to peer into the wall of darkness, but I saw nothing else, and the only sounds were of my own footsteps and the grunts of frustration coming from Vadeem.

Jae-Hyun: Yoona, where are you?

It appeared that we were not the only ones who got separated from the get-go. I mean, what else did I expect but trouble when I was partied with an anomaly?

Yoona: I'm safe, Noel's with me. Are you with Walter and Vadeem?
Lady Awesome: Sup!
Walter's Fine: I'm with Vadeem. We're in some kind of forest. I think Jae-Hyun's on his own though.
Jae-Hyun: Find somewhere safe and use one of those flares I gave you.
Vadeem the Dream: Got it.

Vadeem had managed to pin his little flashlight now and took out one of the flares. He fished out a new lighter from his pocket and lit the fuse. The fire ignited, but instead of a bright fizz of light, the thing just burned itself out.

Walter's Fine: Um, we lit one, but it didn't do anything. Is that supposed to happen, Jae-Hyun?
Yoona: Same on our end, the fuse burned out but nothing else.
Jae-Hyun: No, mine isn't working properly as well. Something's messing with the flares. Is it unnaturally dark where you are as well?
Lady Awesome: It's like we're looking through molasses where we are!
Walter's Fine: We can barely see a thing. Even the lantern and flashlight's giving us minimal sight.
Jae-Hyun: Something's not right with this trial. Anyone got a notification on the clear objectives?

> **Vadeem the Dream:** None here.
> **Lady Awesome:** Same with us, absolutely nada.
> **Walter's Fine:** Know anything about the situation with that skill of yours?
> **Jae-Hyun:** No. I have some guesses but stay on guard for now.
> **Walter's Fine:** Will do.
> **Jae-Hyun:** Yoona, you still have that pendant I gave you?
> **Yoona:** Yeah.
> **Jae-Hyun:** Infuse some mana into it like I taught you.
> **Yoona:** I did.
> **Jae-Hyun:** Good, that's still working. I have your location, stay somewhere safe with Noel. I'm coming over now.
> **Yoona:** What about Walter and Vadeem?
> **Vadeem the Dream:** We're fine, young lady. Walter and I will find a hole to bunker down, and you can find us after.
> **Lady Awesome:** Good luck finding a hole large enough to fit you, Vadeem!
> **Jae-Hyun:** Try to find a landmark or a place of interest if you can. I'll try to survey our location and see if I can't locate the two of you after I get the girls. Until then, only use the system chat for emergencies. We can't afford to be distracted by texts in the trials.
> **Walter's Fine:** Understood.
> **Lady Awesome:** Aye-aye boss!

The ever-consuming darkness was really starting to get on my nerves. What made it worse was that we were in a situation that even the regressor's knowledge failed to account for. I hugged my little lantern closer and hoped things would turn out for the better.

"Well," I said as I dismissed the chat messages, "I guess it's just you and me this time, Vadeem."

The big man smiled, the dim glow of our light sources making him look ominous. "Reminds me of all those strolls I used to take in the past."

I gave him a confused look. "You used to take strolls in the woods at night?"

He chuckled. "Where else would you go to bury things away from sensitive eyes?"

"Like law enforcement?"

He laughed again, ignoring the question. "Come on, Walter, no need to be so nervous. Let's see what this trial's got in store for us! These damn monsters won't know what hit 'em!"

And I hoped that he was right, but somehow I had a feeling that these woods hid more dangers than just beasts and monsters.

CHAPTER THIRTY

Ill Omens

Vadeem and I had scouted the area around us to the best of our abilities, and aside from the eternally smothering darkness and gloom, the forest around us seemed normal, at least to my eyes. Then again, I grew up in the big city, so I knew next to nothing about environments like this.

"Anything seem off on your end?" I asked Vadeem as we gathered in a small clearing. He moved a log onto its side and sat down.

"A lot of things," he muttered. "For one, it's too quiet."

I put my little lantern down between us and grabbed a seat myself. The soft glow was the only thing keeping the encroaching darkness at bay. We had made a small campfire earlier, and some fresh tea was being brewed. I took a cup and gave another to Vadeem, who nodded in thanks.

He continued, "This far off from civilization, the forests should be teeming with noise, but there's nothing. No sounds of birds, insects, small animals. It's like there's no life at all. Just look at the ground we're sitting on. Normally it'd be crawling with critters."

I looked down and saw small patches of plants and dead leaves, but Vadeem was right. Even rummaging through some rocks and tree branches, I saw not a single bug of any kind hiding underneath.

"It's like the whole damn forest's dead," Vadeem grumbled as he took a deep sip of his drink.

"Least there's nothing out to get us here," I said.

He shrugged. "And I'll bet you anything that's going to change before long."

I sighed. "Yeah, like these trials will make it easy for us. You think Jae-Hyun's right, that something's wrong with our trial?"

Vadeem shrugged again. "Not sure. I was never the kind of guy who gave these kinds of things much thought, but I trust Jae-Hyun, and his judgment's been solid so far."

I poked the fire with a stick, causing some sparks to flutter out. It was odd conversing with Vadeem like this. I had grown so used to pretending to be someone else that just having a normal conversation without the constant need to keep my identities in check was jarring. I guess it was kind of nice to just be myself for once, even if we were stuck in some nightmare forest.

I looked at the relaxed man before me and continued, "Say, why did you choose to trust him? I mean, you're a lot older than Jae-Hyun, so why didn't you decide to lead things instead?"

He laughed. "Do I honestly look like the type of person to lead anyone?"

"Yes?" I answered honestly. I hadn't known the man for long, but he was good natured and charismatic, not to mention intimidatingly strong. I can only imagine that people would naturally want to follow him. Seemed like a solid candidate for a leader in my eyes.

"And that's where you're wrong, Walter," he explained. "I know my own strengths, and my faults, and I can say with absolute confidence that I was not born to lead."

He drank the last of his tea and went to get more. "I'm more of a doer than a thinker, and I've found over the years that a good leader's got to be good at both. Point me toward a problem and I'll get rid of it for you, but ask me to find that problem first? No can do. You got the wrong guy."

He took another sip of his drink before throwing a few more dry sticks into the fire. "And as for why I chose to follow Jae-Hyun? He's got . . . I don't know how to describe it, but he has this aura of someone who will stop at nothing to achieve his goals."

He paused for a second to tend to the flames. "That, my friend, is a good quality to have in a leader, and it's why I chose to follow him. You quickly find out that age has very little to do with ability once you've seen enough of the world. I think it's the same for Noel, although I can never tell with that one.

"Well, unfortunately we're on our own this time, friend," he continued as he stashed his cup away. "But we got our instructions. Let's see if we can find something that sticks out from these lifeless forests. Say, Walter, how good are you at climbing trees?"

I found out, much to my disappointment, that I was very, very bad at climbing trees.

"What are you doing, Walter?" Vadeem shouted as I stumbled for the fifth time, causing more tree branches to fall and hit the other man in the face. "You're trying to climb the tree, not destroy it!"

"I don't see you trying!" I shouted back. "And it's pitch black. I can't even see two inches in front of me, so what did you expect?"

He laughed. "Fair, and if you can find a tree that can support my weight, then I'll gladly swap with you!"

"Just a little bit . . ." I muttered, my hands waving aimlessly for something solid to latch on to. You would think that something like climbing a tree would be a piece of cake for my new superhuman capabilities, and it was true that my enhanced strength and endurance made the actual climb easy, but you try to find something to hold in total darkness.

I made it up as far as I could possibly go, and clearing away a few branches that obscured my view, I was able to survey some of the land. The dim glow of my little lantern was enough illumination to just about make out my immediate surroundings, but bigger trees were still obstructing my view.

"Goddamn it!" I cursed. "I need to climb a bigger tree. I can't see anything from up here."

"We'll all die of old age in the time it'll take you to blindly inch up another one!" Vadeem grumbled. "I have a better solution. You can grab on to something up there, right?"

"Yeah," I answered, "why?"

Before I could speak another word, I felt the tree I was latching on to start shaking, then move. I clung on for dear life. Peering down, I saw Vadeem had grown to the size of a two-story house, and he casually plucked the tree I was on. I felt some more violent shaking as the now even more ridiculously huge man lifted the trunk above his head.

"How's the view up there now?" he asked, his voice the low rumbling of thunder.

I clung on tighter before looking down at him in disbelief. "Class active?"

He smiled, his mouth now the width of my entire body. "You know it, my friend!"

Then a thought occurred to me. Vadeem had expanded in size by who knows how much, but he was still wearing the clothes he had on before.

"How come you're not naked?" I asked, the dim lantern light showing that he still had his normal button-up shirt and jeans on, although those had become giant sized as well.

"You noticed that, huh?" he said awkwardly. "I didn't the first time, and Noel has never let me live that down since she first saw me use the skill. I, uh, I made sure to buy appropriate clothing from the shop after that incident."

I laughed wryly. I could only imagine how that event unfolded.

"Anyway, stop gawking and see if you can spot something up there!"

"All right, all right, just hold the tree still!"

Adjusting my position, I peered out into the seemingly endless expanse of darkness to see if I could spot anything that was different or distinct. In the absolute absence of light, finding something that stood out wasn't hard.

Far out in the distance was a very faint orange glow. I couldn't make out anything around it, or even tell if going toward the only illumination was a good idea, but it was something to go on.

"Yeah, Vadeem," I shouted back. "There's some light in the distance. It's a little to our left. Can't really tell how far away with the damn darkness, though. Let me down and we'll head toward it."

Vadeem chuckled again, only this time it sounded like an industrial work site with how low his voice had gotten. "Walter, you really don't know anything about traveling in the woods, do you?"

"I mean, I grew up in the city," I answered. "Why?"

"Trust me when I say that you're not going to be able to walk in a straight line without a compass, much less trying to go at it when we're half blind! We'll be walking in circles if we did that, then Noel'll have something new to make fun of us for!"

"What about the compasses we brought?"

"It doesn't work, obviously," he answered. "Did you honestly think it would?"

I just slumped my shoulders and sighed.

"Then what's the plan? I tell you where to go while you hold the tree up?"

"Exactly!"

And you know what, as stupid as that plan sounded, it actually worked. Vadeem would walk—read: trample through—the dense flora underneath while I would correct his path every now and then. The only thing that made me angry about the whole thing, aside from the horribly bumpy ride, was that his class skill could be kept activated practically indefinitely. The only "downside" that he told me was that it made him really hungry after.

Seeing that everyone around me was so much stronger than I was actually got to me a little. Sure, I was used to being the underdog most of my life, but my new friends could casually tell the future or transform into a literal giant. Who knew what Noel could do with her new class.

Then there was me. I had Noe, and I had my status as an arbiter, but what else was there? If I tried to fight Vadeem, then I highly doubted that any amount of luck could defeat him. I couldn't even use my only useful ability in front of others, and even then the Xollon form only lasted forty minutes. I needed to find a way to at least catch up to the rest of my party's abilities, if not exceed it.

But there was just so much I didn't know! And worse yet, it seemed like the Origin Matrix had a thing against me and was doing everything in its power to drag me down. The very first thing I had to do, no matter how damn difficult, was fix this worthless class of mine. I'd even settle for a D-rank class at this point!

"Hey, Walter!" Vadeem said, taking me out of my thoughts. "I think I can see the glow from here. You can come down now!"

Without asking for my opinion, the poor battered tree I was on was tilted to its side so that I could just hop off instead of embarrassing myself by trying to climb down it. Vadeem returned to his normal size—fully clothed, thankfully—and started to chow down on some energy bars.

"Give me a sec, Walter," he said, sounding a little out of breath. "Need to refuel."

"Take your time," I said as I tried to get the small leaves and pieces of bark off my clothes and hair.

I squinted my eyes to see if I could make out what was causing the soft glow, and I could just barely perceive what looked to be a couple of medieval-style torches hanging off what appeared to be a gate. I could just about make out the shapes of some simple houses behind the gate, with everything being surrounded by some crude stone walls. I couldn't see much else from where Vadeem and I stood.

"It seems like . . . it seems like we're heading to the entrance of a village?" I said. "You seeing the same thing?"

Vadeem swallowed another mouthful of food before answering. "I think you're right. Creepy little village in any case. Do we head toward it?"

Every instinct I ever had told me that going toward the creepy village hidden in a forest consumed by everlasting darkness was a terrible, horrible idea.

"Yeah, or at least get closer to scout it out," I answered. "Unless you got a better plan."

Vadeem seemed unconcerned and shrugged. "We're not exactly spoiled for options, so let's go. Maybe we can find out some information about this place."

I looked at him in confusion. "You know the people living in there are almost certainly not going to be human, right?"

"Eh," he answered. "Doesn't mean they can't communicate with us! Worse case, we solve things the Vadeem style!"

"And what is the Vadeem style?" I asked, raising an eyebrow.

He grinned. "Solving your problems with overwhelming violence, of course!"

CHAPTER THIRTY-ONE

Formation of a Plan

I sat down on a fallen log and really took the time to think about my current rate of growth as I waited for Vadeem to finish stuffing his face. As I said before, I couldn't rely solely on Noe's Luck skill to survive these ever increasingly dangerous situations, but what else could I do when it was abundantly clear that the Origin Matrix wanted nothing more than for me to fail?

Time to break the problem down and see if I couldn't find even a hint of a solution.

First of all, relying on the Trash Matrix was out of the question. I bet that even if I managed to clear the trial perfectly, it would find some idiotic way to dismiss all of my achievements and saddle me with an even shittier job. But if I couldn't use the same tools that everyone else had, what could I use?

Wait . . . some things are not adding up about Origin. First of all, there was no way that Central's all-knowing AI didn't know that I wasn't an actual arbiter, yet I still managed to gain that Rookie Arbiter title. In fact, there was a subtle difference when Noe announced the acquisition of my first two titles compared to the Master Groveler one I got earlier. Noe just told me that I had gained two titles before, yet it specifically stated that the last title was given to me by the Trash Matrix.

This would mean that the Trash Matrix didn't control the title system at all, or at least not completely. Perhaps it could only give out titles, but not stop someone from getting them naturally; after all, Noe said that these things came from the Universe itself, and not Central.

I knew that if I wanted to beat this stupid defective Matrix, then I couldn't use the tools it gave out, as that would be a losing battle every time. I didn't know why the thing hated me so much. Maybe it couldn't communicate with the rest of the site staff, so it was taking actions into its own hands, but I wanted to give the thing a piece of my mind.

In fact, now that I thought about it, something else was odd about the Trash Matrix. It was the levels of everyone before the start of the trials. With the sole exception of myself, everyone had more than a single level to their name. In fact, Q even alluded to the fact that humans could gain levels by simply crawling around as an infant, so it couldn't have been Origin giving those out to people.

Hey, Noe, you know anything more about this?

"Affirmative," it replied. "The Inferior Trash Matrix can only accelerate and manipulate the natural growth of its subjects, along with removing the natural limitations placed on a non-ascended species. It can do nothing else."

So it can't really control our stats at all on its end? Like, say, remove all the strength from my attributes?

"Negative," Noe explained. "It is worthless and has no such abilities. It can only enhance growth at a disgracefully slow pace, not delete it. The only functions that the Trash Matrix has full access to are the class advancement system and the distribution of end-of-trial rewards."

Wait, only end-of-trial rewards?

I remembered that there was a section displayed at the end of the first trial about hidden rewards, not to mention the mundane things that an aspirant could potentially pick up during the trials themselves.

"To answer host's inquiries once again," Noe answered, "the Trash Matrix has no control over the distribution of any other types of rewards, as those are managed at the site level. It is woefully incompetent."

I smiled. This was perfect. I had alternative ways of gaining strength that didn't rely on the damn Trash Matrix's pity. If I couldn't get a great class, then I'd make do with amazing titles, and if it wouldn't give me any rewards, then I'd abuse my arbiter status and steal all the damn hidden stuff! And to further rub it in its stupid AI face, I could take all the free exp it was giving out as well! We'd see who was the one with the intelligence of a drunken Neanderthal now!

Yes, a plan was quickly formulating in my mind. But I had one more question to ask Noe, to see if what I had in mind was feasible.

Say, Noe, my favorite and best system buddy.

"Yes, Host Walter?"

There is a maximum of two secondary titles that I can equip at once, right?

"Affirmative."

But they can be switched out, yes?

"Correct, Host Walter."

And I'm assuming that you're the one responsible for switching them for me, and you can read my thoughts, right?

"Unit Noe does have those functionalities."

So if I had a lot of titles and I wanted to quickly switch them on the fly, because, say, I was in a battle . . .

"Unit Noe understands the nature of Host Walter's inquiry," it answered. "Unit Noe can assist Host Walter in those situations. Rest assured that Unit Noe will provide the host with the optimal title for all situations during combat and elsewhere."

I smiled again. I think my crazy plan might just work!

"All right, my friend!" Vadeem said with a loud belch. "I think I've recovered enough. I can never get used to eating that much food at once!"

"Small price to pay to turn into a house," I replied with a laugh.

"A house of muscles, you mean!" He returned the smile and proceeded to flex his biceps. "And I'm glad to see your earlier gloom disappear. Finally got your head in the game?"

"Ah, you noticed that?" I answered, scratching my face in embarrassment.

"Just like you noticed I wasn't naked!" he said with a wry smile. "All right, so what's our plan for the creepy village? The Vadeem special?"

"No, or at least not yet. I have my plans for this one," I answered. "But first, we need a little more information on what we're up against. I'll climb up another tree and see if I can see what the village is like inside. Can you go around the perimeter and see if there's anything of note? We might need an escape route later."

"Got it!"

I went up a nearby tree, a lot easier this time now that the glow of the nearby village made it so that I was only mostly blind, and found a sturdy place to sit down. What I told Vadeem was half true, because having an escape route planned out would never hurt, but the main reason why I gave him those instructions was to be alone. I needed to check in with Raffiel and Q.

"Raffiel, I need to speak with you," I whispered.

I waited for a response but received none.

I frowned. Normally he would have answered me immediately . . . Had he not heard me?

"Raffiel, you there?" I asked again, louder this time.

A couple of seconds passed, and I heard a faint voice, heavily distorted, as if I were speaking with someone with the worst cellular reception possible.

"Y—u hea—me?" Raffiel's voice said. "—biter W—ter, there's—a—issue—ere."

"I can't make you out," I said with a frown. Something was definitely wrong here.

"Le—me ge—Q."

Some more static and horrible screeches assaulted my ears before the signal seemed to improve.

"Walter, can you hear me now?" Q's voice answered. It was still a little tinny, but was certainly an improvement from Raffiel.

"Much better now. What's going on?"

"Some slight problems have turned up on our side of things," he said, voice grim. "Nothing too major at the moment, but some of our communications with Origin have been compromised. We're unable to monitor the aspirants, nor interfere with the trials. I'm speaking with the higher-ups right now, but it seems that all facilities with an active anomaly are affected."

I frowned. "Keep me updated. Is there anything that I can do on my side of things?"

A slight pause, and then Q said, "Perhaps. Let me find out more about the situation first, but I think there are things that can only be done on your side. The higher-ups are not allowing any of my staff to enter the world."

"They're definitely hiding something," I said. "Do you know anything about the place my group and I are in?"

Another pause.

"The information's been compromised as well, but I was able to retrieve some of it."

I nodded on habit, even though Q couldn't see me.

"You're in an adjacent Earth," Q explained, "but it's not on one of the lists of approved locations, or at least not for the second trial. The information I'm getting is all over the place . . . What is the Origin Matrix thinking, sending its aspirants to these unregulated dimensions?"

Hm, a little more information that I could use. So it seemed that the Origin system didn't create these trials by itself, but was just sending us to an existing location.

"Anyway, the Earth you're in is quickly reaching its end. Something happened a while ago and caused the extinction of most of the life there."

"Any idea what that is?"

A pause again, most likely Q trying to access the necessary information.

"No, that information is completely redacted. I can't even get an exact date on when it happened. All I know is that the Earth is heading toward extinction, and it's going there fast. There should still be the last remnants of human out-posts, but even the data on this civilization is corrupted."

"So, expect the worst?"

"Yes, Lord Arbiter, but the scraps of information I could dig up suggest that you should be able to communicate with the humans there. Try to see if you can find any useful information out of them, anything that could prove vital to our investigations. Origin, no matter how distorted, should still be act-ing based on its internal logic systems. There's a reason why it's doing all this."

"All right, I'll see what I can do," I said, and I noticed that Vadeem was quickly coming back. "Like I said, keep me posted. I'll speak with you later."

The static and white noise died, and I was left in the eerie darkness again. Remembering why I was up here in the first place, I squinted and saw that the village was quiet, but there were occasional movements. The light was too dim to make out the size of the place, but there should be a sizable population in the outpost. Checking to see if I missed anything else—I hadn't—I climbed down the tree and waited for Vadeem.

With the new influx of information, the wisps of a plan were quickly for-mulating in my head. But first, I needed to take inventory of all the resources available to me.

Vadeem approached me, his smile never leaving his face despite the gloom. "Find anything useful up there?"

"Yeah, some." I nodded. "The village is definitely populated. Seems to be human inhabitants as well. Anything on your end?"

"Not much," he answered. "The walls stretch out around the entire com-plex, but the settlement's not too large, only took me about ten minutes to circle it. I should be able to smash through the walls if worse comes to worst."

"Good, thank you, Vadeem," I said. "One last thing, what sort of random stuff did Jae-Hyun make you bring?"

He made a small clearing and dumped out all of his gear. Aside from the usual camping supplies and an assortment of weapons, Vadeem had some rather . . . unique objects.

"That's everything," he said, then gestured at his shirt, "minus the clothes I'm wearing. All they do is change depending on what I need."

I nodded and took stock of the stuff on the ground.

"Firecrackers, some rope, masks, paint, and what's this thing?" I asked, pointing at a briefcase.

"Ah, that thing damn near bankrupted me!" Vadeem said, holding the case up. "I got it in the store. Supposedly it can hold as much food as you could ever need, and I've been shoving food in it for the whole week."

"They just let you steal the food from the cafe?"

He shrugged. "Food was free in the first place, and it's not like anyone stopped me. I think I got enough stored to last me years, even with my skill! And before you ask, no, nothing rots in there."

Well, least you couldn't say that the man didn't plan ahead.

"All right, I think I have an idea about how we should approach this," I told him. "So it goes like this . . ."

I told Vadeem the plan, and true to his earlier words, he didn't complain, even when my instructions felt like random nonsense. I really liked that quality about him.

After some final touches and preparation, we approached the village. I was about to put on a show for the ages.

The Day the God Arrived

Archbishop Patar oversaw today's sacrifice of the blind in satisfaction, smiling as the ignorant heretics who denied the consuming Truth burned in sacred fire. Their wails of pain and pleas of mercy fell on deaf ears, and his congregation watched on in stony silence. He still had a rare moment of respite before his scheduled meeting with the prophet David, and he took this time to reflect on all that had changed since the day that God had arrived.

Looking back, Patar marveled at his own ignorance, and he lamented his past naivety. But his God has shown him the Truth, and soon, all of existence would know of it as well.

It all started that fateful day, although day and night mattered little in those times. It was always dark, and the only constant was the gnawing hunger and the ever-present gloom. It was his turn to be offered as the week's sustenance. He had already said goodbye to his wife and their only surviving daughter. He was thankful that she was too young to understand what was about to happen.

He went to the House of Sacrifice, head held high. If his death could sustain the lives of his village for even a few more days, then he was willing to leave without regret. The village chief was just about to give him his allotted dose of dream wine when He came. Everything had changed after that.

Patar had been one of the last people who left their dwellings to gaze upon the intruder, but it was a sight that he would never forget nor remember for the rest of his life, for that was the eternal paradox of God, of the Devourer of Truth. To gaze directly into the eyes of God today would be a sin most unforgivable, and although His features were ever cloudy and illusive in his memories, His actions were not.

He had been riding on the venerated Beast of Wisdom's Bane, known as Vadoom, when He first graced us with his presence. Patar had never seen such a ferocious monster in all his life, even when he had gone hunting deep into the Neverglow Woods in the earliest days of the End. The beast had glowing red eyes and a maw the size of a small dwelling. It moved the ground as it approached, its massive form dwarfing even the tallest trees in its surroundings, and its growls of inhuman anger caused the very foundation of his village to shake.

Yet it was not the mighty Vadoom that captivated the attention of the entire village, but the being that stood atop its massive spiked shoulder. Patar knew not the figure's looks, but he knew that it was glorious, for to look Truth in its eyes is to understand that nothing else can ever compare.

And the being spoke, and He told us the Truth. Yet Patar was one of the few who listened. The rest of his village would only learn of the folly of disrespecting their one true savior much later down the line. He had personally seen to it.

The villagers, the ones who didn't understand or were too ignorant to understand God's descent had foolishly tried to attack the visitors. The able-bodied fools had brandished their pitiful weapons and launched an assault on God and his beast, and with a sweep of His majestic limb, He caused the very earth to erupt. With another sweep of His hand, a torrent of godly lights shot out of His person, the blinding multicolored explosions leaving a lasting afterimage.

Yet in His infinite grace, he did not exterminate the village and its sinners. No, He saw the potential in the few of us who understood, and allowed those who were chosen to redeem themselves. Oh, how Patar had lamented that his wife was not one of the Chosen. It had been hard to raise his daughter alone, but now she also knew the Truth.

"People of Earth!" God had said, His voice resonating with the power of the heavens, "despair not, for I bring you truth!"

The ignorant masses did not believe His sacred message at first, and it was only through proof that the false believers accepted the God into the village. But Patar knew that the Truth need not prove, for all that was required was the guidance of God.

The low rumbling growl of the beast managed to silence the blasphemous who dared to speak over His wisdom, and He was allowed to continue.

"I have seen your world, and I lament its destruction! Fear not, for I bring prosperity! I bring peace! I bring light! I bring Truth!"

And God did as He said. He controlled the beast to bring firewood and stacked it into a pile at the center of the village, where the old meeting square used to be, and in an act now immortalized forever, He brought light into the eternal darkness. And the light was beautiful.

It was unlike the pitiful wisps of the dying embers on their torches, nor the dim orange of the hearth. This fire, lit by God's own holy lantern, seemed to dispel the darkness and heal the wounded. Even the people who were most affected by the shadow blight were quickly recovering, for that is the grace given to us from God.

He provided the village with more miracles next, in the form of water as fresh as the streams that once flowed through the woods, so many, many years ago. He poured this life-giving liquid from a small container that never ran out, and the villagers were able to drink to their hearts' content. Next was the food. Real food. Not the leftovers from the House of Sacrifice or the poisonous roots that many desperate fools ate to ward off starvation. It was food that they had never seen before.

And Patar ate, and for the first time since he could remember, he was content. He had worried then what God would want in recompense. Oh, how naive was he, to think that his God would demean Himself to ask for such petty things from His subjects.

Instead, the only thing that the God wanted was to spread His Truth to the others in this realm blighted by darkness, to spread His light to all corners of the world, and to bring Devouring Truth to all. For only in His light will one's suffering be consumed, where one's pain will be taken, and where the soul will be devoured so that all will join in God's eternal glory.

And so, on that day, Patar had devoted himself to God, and worked to spread the glory of the Devouring Truth to all those who were blind.

CHAPTER THIRTY-TWO

The Day Walter Arrived

I finished the last of Vadeem's "makeup" and started to second-guess my initial plans. Originally, I wanted to make him look fierce, like a wild beast ready to destroy all in his path, which required me to make some adjustments to his appearance. Unfortunately, since all we had on hand was some paint, a dozen or so small lights, and other miscellaneous trinkets, Vadeem looked . . . let's just say that I was glad he couldn't see himself right now. The flaws were even more apparent given his now-enlarged size.

The red paint I had slathered all over his body was supposed to make him look fierce, like he was covered in blood or had the skin tone of a Japanese oni, but the color was slightly off, and he looked more like a muscular Kool-Aid Man.

Oh yeah, this wasn't a good look.

I even tried to spike his hair up with the paint for a more menacing appearance, and it did look properly scary . . . while the paint was still wet. As it dried up, it looked like someone had placed a mop on his head after using that mop to clean up the aforementioned Kool-Aid.

Next was his clothes. I thought that Vadeem's fancy clothing could change into anything he wanted, like some kind of sci-fi transforming battle gear. Apparently, they even had stuff like that in the store, but Vadeem had cheaped out on that option and got the budget version.

What he really meant, much to my immediate and immense disappointment, was that his clothes could simply stretch and grow as much fabric as he wanted. What I had to do was shape pointy spikes out of the extra fabric, using more paint and some mud to "glue" it all together. I don't think I need to explain how that turned out.

Now, Vadeem did look absolutely inhuman once I was done with him, but in all the wrong ways. Even the LED lights I placed under his eyes made him look like one of those nineties toy robots rather than a creature out of legend. I just hoped that the dim lighting could hide the imperfections.

"So how do I look?" Vadeem asked once I was done. His wide smile made the paint around his face crack.

"Um . . . really scary," I answered honestly; his wife would certainly have a heart attack if she saw him now.

He gave me a thumbs-up, which caused the branches I tied around his fingers to serve as talons to break off.

"All right, let's wait for the last of the paint to dry," I said. "Just try not to move too much. I have to go plant some of those explosives."

"Sure thing, just be quick," he answered. "This stuff's making my skin itch."

One thing that I did enjoy about this supernatural dark was how easy it was to sneak around and do things that I probably shouldn't be doing. Even the sounds were muted from the suffocating gloom, so it took me no time at all to plant a few remote explosives a little inside the actual village. And I left just as quickly as I went, completely out of sight.

As for how I chose where to place them? Noe got that part handled, and it only cost fifteen luck charges. I'd have those recovered by the time I made my entrance. The last thing I did was put on one of the masks from Vadeem's stash. I chose the simplest one; it was a reflective silver mask that had no other features, and thanks to whatever magic Central's equipment had, I could see and speak without being muffled, even though there were no eye holes or a mouth.

I went back to Vadeem, making sure he understood the script that I'd presented, and with that, we headed for the village. Honestly, if anyone with half a brain saw us, they'd probably think we were two patients that just escaped a mental hospital. Hopefully I could convince the villagers otherwise, and between my high Charisma, Noe's Aura of Serendipity, and the Idol's Voice, I thought I actually might pull it off.

Vadeem, the monstrously sized version, barreled his way through the front entrance, his voice screaming in rage, and I did my absolute best to hang on to his flailing body. Not even the darkness was able to mask the noise that the giant was making, and soon the various villagers came out from their homes to look at the intruders.

Even in the dim light of the torches, I could tell that these people were abnormal, to say the least. I mean, they looked human insofar as having two arms, two legs, and a head, but everything else? Most of them had horrible boils growing out of their bodies, some had huge black lesions that oozed a foul liquid, while others were missing a nose or an eye. Yet the most striking thing about them was how thin they were. It was clear that these people were on the verge of dying.

My Lucky Eyes also displayed their information, although it was just the basics. All of them had a level of 5 to 11, and the race displayed was still human, so perhaps I could communicate with them.

Once most of the villagers had come out of their homes, I sent a private message to Vadeem through the party chat.

> **Walter's Fine:** All right, you can stop. Just growl at them occasionally now. Let me do the talking. My innate skill lets me speak their language.
> **Vadeem the Dream:** Got you. Intimidation is something I can do all day.

Noe, can you amplify my voice and make it sound more awe-inducing?

"Affirmative," it answered. "Host Walter's Idol Voice can achieve such results. Looking through my database for an appropriately awe-inspiring voice now . . ."

"Unit Noe has found a match. Would Host Walter also like to translate your speech into the village's native tongue?"

Yes, please.

"Affirmative. Please proceed," it said again. "And as always, you are most welcome."

Did Noe refer to me as "you" and not Host Walter? Huh, kind of strange, but there were more pressing issues at hand.

"Fear not, people of Earth, for I bring Truth! Bring me to your leader!" I shouted, my voice sounded normal to me, but I saw a wave of sound bombard the villagers, causing some of the weaker ones to fall on their backs. Thankfully I had stuffed some fabric into Vadeem's ears beforehand; he'd probably go deaf otherwise. Then again, given how absurdly durable the big man was, I doubted anything could actually cause him harm.

Most of them were still too stunned and confused as to what was happening. Now was the critical stage of my plan. It was clear from Q's information and my own assessment that the people here were in a hopeless situation, just weeks away from dying. They needed hope, something to cling to, and I knew of two surefire ways to achieve that. One was to become a hero to the people, a folklore legend, but that generally required doing heroic feats or having something to fight against. Neither were available here; we were in a place that was devoid of most life.

The other solution, however, was workable, and it was religion. These people were clearly not technologically advanced, what with their wooden torches and clay huts, so tricking them should be easy enough. I just hoped they were still human enough to understand such concepts.

Before long, the stronger of the villagers recovered and started to show signs of fear. Now, this individual was either going to fight me or flee, and I was ready for both. He gestured toward a few more of the able-bodied men and women around him and took out crude slings and wooden spears. So it seemed like they chose to fight, good.

"Foolish!" I screamed again and pointed at one of the explosives I planted on the ground. With my other hand, I pressed the remote detonator and watched as the ground broke apart in a deafening blast. I thought that would be the last of it, but I really shouldn't have underestimated Noe's Luck, because the first explosion caused a chain reaction that set off the rest of the explosives I placed.

This caused the very ground to break in two, as if I had created a fissure that led to the depths of Hell. Heck, the explosion also caused some natural gases to ignite, and a huge blaze of fire expanded out of the crack in a conflagration of light before finally extinguishing once the fuel ran out.

The few men who were about to assault me looked on in stunned silence.

"I am the Devouring Truth!" I shouted, spewing out the first cool-sounding title that came to mind. "Kneel before me, for I bring salvation!"

With another flourish and some sleight of hand, I set the firecrackers I had hidden in my sleeves off, although I probably didn't need to, given my earlier performance. And did you know that it's a very bad idea to set off firecrackers in someone's sleeves? I found out the hard way, and I was all too thankful the darkness hid my act of rubbing healing salves on my burnt forearms. It would have been a little embarrassing to be seen nursing a self-inflected wound right after giving myself such an awesome name.

Thankfully no one noticed that little screw-up, and all at once, every villager gathered before me started to fall to their knees. Some wept, some went prostrate, but they all knelt.

I had one last gesture to cement my place in these people's hearts; I couldn't just have them all fear me. Nothing productive came out of fear alone, and I needed their good graces as well. I took out Vadeem's food suitcase and started to toss random objects out to the people before me. They were confused at first, but the unmistakable smell of food quickly made them understand what was happening. No one dared to take what was on the floor until I spoke up.

"Eat!" I said, before taking my Naiad flask and pouring an unending stream of water on the ground. "And drink! You have all suffered for too long! But fear not, for I bring Truth! Once again, take me to your leader, and I shall dispel this everlasting darkness!"

The first villager, a child no older than perhaps ten or so, took one of the pieces of fried chicken off the ground and ate. Her mother quickly went to grab her, perhaps fearing that I would smite them for their greed, but when she saw that I did not react, she stopped and grabbed a piece for herself.

Soon everyone started to feast on the meal before them, while others went back to their huts to grab pails used to collect the water from my flask. Within minutes, the once dreadful atmosphere lit up, and a representative came to show us to their leader.

Good, it seemed like the first half of my plan was a success. Now to see if everything else would work as intended.

CHAPTER THIRTY-THREE

Revelations and Concerns

The village chief, as it turned out, was a relatively normal woman by most standards. Sure, she was grossly deformed like the rest of the people here, with a huge tumor that caused the left side of her face to be twice as wide as the right . . . or the fact that she only had four functioning fingers left, but at least she still had most of her hair, and the horrible black gashes were only inches long instead of meters. Okay, maybe she wasn't normal by any standards, but she was a sight better than the others.

The woman wobbled toward me and guided me to the village square. There, she had some of her men grab the nicest furnishings they had left and bade me sit. The seats they found were rotten, but they had some soft fabric left, so that counted for something. Vadeem was still looking angry and making occasional growls to my side, much to the fear of those who had the unfortunate job of attending to him.

Now that things had finally calmed down, I had the opportunity to properly assess the village we were in. It was clear that the place had seen better days, but it wasn't the decayed and broken furnishings and homes that attracted my attention. Those could be chalked up to the lack of materials and men to repair damages, but the other abnormalities were certainly anything but natural.

On every surface, whether that be the ground, houses, or, on closer inspection, even the people, there were these small black vine-like tendrils crawling around. They went through the walls of the homes, dug into the ground, and into pale flesh, and they all wiggled as if they were alive. If I stared long enough in one direction, even the air seemed to be filled with these tendrils.

Strangely enough, I hadn't noticed any of this out in the woods, so something about this particular location was drawing in these vines. Perhaps it was the presence of life, since everything outside of this settlement was dead? Whatever it was, all I knew was that I did not want to stay here for longer than I had to.

> **Vadeem the Dream:** How much longer do I got to keep this up? I know I said I could do this all day, but the paint's really starting to irritate my skin.
> **Walter's Fine:** Sorry, man, just a while longer. If you really have to go just make some noise and rush out of the village. I'll just say that your urge to kill was becoming uncontrollable or something.
> **Vadeem the Dream:** Yeah, I'm doing just that, and I need to refuel. You think the paint will fall off if I go back to normal size?
> **Walter's Fine:** Just coat yourself again if it does. Jae-Hyun made you carry buckets of the stuff, so it's not like we'll ever run out.
> **Vadeem the Dream:** Fair point, I'll be right back.

A primal roar erupted from Vadeem that caused everyone around the titan to tense up, and a few of the people closer to him all but threw themselves on the ground trying to get out of his way. Vadeem leaped out of the square and barreled his way toward the entrance. He was surprisingly good at acting like a savage unintelligent animal, which I was not sure was actually a compliment, all things considered. Let's just give him the benefit of the doubt and say that he was a great actor.

I spoke up before anyone could panic. "Fear not! Vadoom is a beast that seeks to consume all wisdom in the world, and his hunger can no longer be contained, even in my sight! He has gone to seek out prey to feast upon. He will be back, but never anger him, or he might feast on you!"

Gasps were heard all around before the village elder was able to quiet the people down again.

"Oh, esteemed God," she said, her voice moist with sickly rot, "please tell us of the salvation! We will give you anything in return!"

I nodded. "Yes, tell your people to gather as much firewood as they can and pile it up high in the center of the village. I shall conduct a miracle that will be sung about for ages to come!"

The old woman—now that I think about it, I couldn't tell if she was actually old or not, given her worrying physical features—nodded enthusiastically before hobbling away to give more instructions. It seemed that a lot of the villagers had regained some semblance of strength now that they had a chance to eat and drink properly and were doing their best to meet my demands.

What I planned to do was to remedy, at least in part, some of the invasive darkness that was engulfing the town. I had noticed that the Promethean fire in my lantern was able to cut through the darkness way more effectively than the normal fires around us, and it had the added benefit of soothing the soul. I felt the supernatural gloom seep into my very being after just the brief few minutes it took me to plant those explosives earlier, but just basking in the glow of the lantern had remedied the worst of the feeling.

Vadeem, on the other hand, didn't seem to mind the darkness at all. No doubt he was so thick-skinned as to not be affected by it, but the more likely explanation was that he had other abilities that helped insulate him from abnormalities like this one, or at least slow its spread. Once again I was left lamenting over my useless class and its associated skills . . .

But if my plans worked out the way I thought they would, then I should be able to get a title that could fix a lot of my issues. It all depended on my acting skills, and a lot of luck, to pull off.

A short while later, Vadeem returned and even helped with the firewood gathering, although he picked up entire trees to use as kindling instead of individual branches like the others. Since water was such a rarity, most of the trees were dried up and could be used to light a fire almost immediately, although that poses another question as to why these trees could grow in the first place. But as Noel might put it, maybe it was just all magic.

Soon, a colossal mound of dead wood was gathered in the village square, with a neat bundle of dried hay and other small twigs stashed in the bottom of the pile. I took out my lantern and used a stick to transfer the fire onto the kindling. Finally, I turned on the Absolute Luck skill once more to ensure the best results.

I used Noe to amplify my voice once more, and making sure that all eyes were on me, I tossed the ignited stick into the pile of hay and shouted, "Let there be light to banish the darkness!"

The results were immediate.

Luck Charges: 4/405

Noe . . . what on earth did you do?

I didn't need it to tell me to see the results. As soon as the branch touched the kindling, a huge gust of wind swept into the square and caused the fire to change. The burning flames danced and formed into the shape of a face, its features eerily distinct despite it being formed of fire. The face morphed, changing from a monstrous flaming savage into something that I instantly recognized.

Holy shit, the face in the fire turned into mine. This lasted barely a second, but I was sure that it had changed into a perfect replica of my own visage. But just as quickly as it had formed, the face changed into a replica of the mask I was wearing, before the strange gust of wind dissipated and the fire was blazing normally again.

> **Vadeem the Dream:** What the hell did you do, Walter? I didn't know you could manipulate fire!
> **Walter's Fine:** I used an item, so it wasn't really me.
> **Vadeem the Dream:** I'm not sure how much you paid for it, but it sure as hell was worth it! Look at the villagers!

I did, and the scene was insane. The ones who were closest to the fire had a lot of their deformities fade away, and they were still healing before my very eyes. Soon, even the ones farther back, away from the glow of the fire, were changing. But the thing that was universal was the look of absolute reverence that each of the villagers had as they looked at me.

One by one, they knelt and prostrated before me, some with open tears flowing down newly mended faces, others crying out in exaltation. But one cry was heard above all others.

"The Light Bringer!"

"The Herald of Dawn!"

"The prophecies!"

"Light Bringer!"

"Light Bringer!"

More and more voices started to join in, all saying the same thing, and soon the entire square was made up of a cacophony of chanting. It was surreal.

"Congratulations," Noe's voice said, but this time it was distinctly . . . different, almost human. "You have acquired two new titles. Would you like to view them?"

Yes.

> **Title:** Bringer of Dawn's Light (S Rank)
> **Description:** The day of Reckoning is upon us, oh foolish mortals of Earth. Pray that the Light of the Bringer of Dawn shines upon you, for those who are destined for Darkness shall know only death and despair.

> **Title Passives:**
> Know No Darkness: All attributes are increased by 25% at night, increasing to 150% the closer it is to dawn.
> Fear No Darkness: Abnormal effects cast by others do not affect you at night.
> See No Darkness: You can see even in the darkest of nights.
> **Title Active:**
> Halo of Dawn's Protection: Activatable only in darkness. Produce a halo of light that expels all outside contamination, disease, and pain from those who bask in its radiance. This skill only affects others and not the caster.

Wow . . . that first title was more than I ever expected. Now that would level the playing field between me and the rest of the party. Now to see what that second title was about.

> **Title:** It that Sleeps at the Edge of Dusk (??? Rank)
> **Description:** You sleep. You dream. You wait.

I frowned, what the hell was this title? There was no rank, the description made no sense, and there weren't even any skills associated with it. I'd never seen a title like this before, and I couldn't help but feel uncomfortable with that description.

Noe, I asked, *do you know what's wrong with that second title?*

"Unit Noe does not know," it said. "Perhaps you should take the title's advice and simply wait."

Well, that was a less-than-helpful answer.

"I apologize, my host," Noe said again. "Unit Noe will strive to do better. Noe will ensure that my host remains safe forever."

I frowned again. Noe was starting to act kind of . . . strange. In fact, I had noticed some slight changes to its speech earlier, when I first entered this cursed place, but the change wasn't this drastic before. I was about to ask Noe some questions, but I was interrupted by a series of notifications.

"Notification," Noe continued. "Host Walter has forcibly received 15 new titles from the Trash Matrix."

"Notification, Host Walter has forcibly received 16 new titles from the Trash Matrix."

"Notification, Host Walter has forcibly received 17 new titles from the Trash Matrix."

"Notification, Host Walter has forcibly received 18 new titles from the Trash Matrix."

"Notification, Host Walter has forcibly received 19 new titles from the Trash Matrix."

Stop all notifications from the Origin Matrix, Noe!

Never mind, it wasn't just Noe that was acting strange. Something was deeply wrong with this damn place.

CHAPTER THIRTY-FOUR

The Decree

Noe! I screamed in my head. *I thought you said that you took over that function from the Trash Matrix? How come you're not blocking these stupid titles?*

"I am sorry, my host," it said, and for the first time I could hear sadness—clear, distinct sadness—in its otherwise androgynous voice, "but I have only commandeered control over my host from the useless Matrix, but even then, the title system is not under the command of Origin. It is exploiting a loophole by giving you those worthless titles, like how a child would throw a tantrum when its superiors ignore it."

"Never mind," I quickly said. Noe seemed to have my best interests at heart, for now at least, so I'd better not disturb it with needless questions. "And show me the titles the Trash Matrix gave me, from the beginning."

"What was that?" Vadeem asked.

Shit, I had been so weirded out by Noe's new emotions that I responded to her out loud.

"Nothing, just muttering to myself," I answered. "Whole situation is just weird."

"No kidding!" He laughed. "Just take care of yourself!"

"Yeah," I mumbled back halfheartedly.

I mean, show me the updates, Noe.

"Of course, my dear host."

> **Title:** Useless Liar
> **Description:** Given to a worthless, cowardly individual who cares only for themselves. You are useless, powerless, and feeble. You lie because the truth is too much to bear.
> **Title Passives:** N/A
> **Title Actives:** N/A

> **Title:** Worthless Degenerate
> **Description:** Given to a person who has forsaken all human dignity. You are worse than the lowest being in the universe. It would be better for everyone if you simply ended your existence.
> **Title Passives:** N/A
> **Title Actives:** N/A

> **Title:** He Who Dwells in Filth
> **Description:** Given to a subhuman trash who can only survive off the grace of his betters. You do not deserve to even exist. You are nothing but filth.
> . . .

On and on these kinds of titles went, all of them giving me no actives or passives, and were just descriptions of how horrible I was as a person. The descriptions did get more and more colorful over time, almost as if the Origin Matrix was developing a personality like Noe. It was all but confirmed that this was the case with the last few titles.

> **Title:** The Watched
> **Description:** We see you, we know you, we will not forget you.

> **Title:** The Hated
> **Description:** We abhor you, we despise you, we hate you.

> **Title:** The Hunted
> **Description:** We will hunt you down, Walter. There is no escape.

I frowned. What was going on with the stupid system? I had always felt that the Origin Matrix was passively hostile toward me, what with its biased evaluations and class choices, but this was the first time I had seen it directly target me. It even mentioned my name, but it didn't use my real one. Was its information about me incomplete? I needed to confirm something.

"Sorry, Vadeem," I muttered. "I, uh, need to use the restroom for a bit."

"About time." He chuckled. "No modern toilets around here, I'm afraid. I found out the hard way. There's some nice bushes, though. Need toilet paper?"

"I'm good," I answered before heading off to a dark corner, away from prying eyes.

Once everyone was out of sight, I called out to Q.

A burst of static assaulted my ears again, before the noise stabilized into something comprehensible. "Yes, Lord Arbiter?"

"I know you're busy, but I need to ask you some pertinent questions."

"I understand," he answered. "How may I be of service?"

"The Origin Matrix shouldn't have a personality, right?"

A pause. "Not in the standard definition of the term, no. Origin acts solely on its programming, although few are privy to what that looks like, and although it is advanced enough to learn and acquire new information, there should be no emotional reasoning behind its actions. I heard it had more advanced functions prior to your disappearance, but those are rumors at most."

"So strictly speaking, it can't hate something or someone?" I asked again, keeping my tone even.

"That should be impossible," he said, tone growing darker by the second. Q was always smart enough to understand the nuances. "Did it . . .?"

"Yes," I answered without waiting for him to finish. "Something's going on in this world that's causing strange changes to its environment, and I think that includes the Origin Matrix, or at least the part of it that's monitoring your site."

"That . . ." Another pause. "That is most troubling, Lord. There should be nothing that could cause such a change, but if it is linked to the sudden rise in anomalies . . . I will look into this case further. Central is hiding something, and I'll see if I can figure out what that is."

"Can you also see if you can access the information for this planet?"

"I will, Lord."

"Good, and I'll look into things on my side as well. I feel like the natives here know something about the corruption."

"Understood, Lord. I will keep you updated."

"You're dismissed. Good luck on your side."

"Thank you," Q said one last time before the static was cut.

So it seemed like my assumptions were correct, and something was definitely influencing not just the people here, but the Origin Matrix, and even Noe. Once again, there were too many unknowns.

I sighed. There was no point in worrying about things that I couldn't control. At least I had an inkling of what was to come. Origin was out to get me, but its ability to act seemed limited. If it could truly hunt me like it claimed, it wouldn't bother sending me all those useless titles. Yet I couldn't be sure that things would remain this way. Central's system seemed to change and mutate ever since I entered this cursed dark forest, and who's to say that it couldn't act directly soon?

Thankfully, I was in the unique spot where Q wasn't my only source of information. I had the regressor to rely on as well. I'd have to see if I could find some nuggets of info out of the villagers and see what Jae-Hyun had to say about it.

"You sure took your time!" Vadeem said as I came back from the bushes. "Food not sit well with you?"

I glared at him.

"All right, all right," he replied with a crooked smile, "But no need to be shy about it!"

"Where's the village elder?" I asked, changing the subject to something less ridiculous, "I need to speak with her about something."

Vadeem pointed toward a location where a large portion of healing villagers were gathered. They were all busy doing something that I couldn't make out, with some bringing random objects from their homes and others in the process of building something.

"I think they're building a shrine for you," Vadeem said with obvious amusement. "I've no idea what they're saying, but it seems like you're the official god to these people. Congrats, God Walter!"

"Ha-ha," I said dryly.

"I joke," he said with genuine warmth this time. "We need these people for your next wacky plan; that part's obvious. You going to ask the old lady about where we are?"

"Yeah, and figure out what's the deal with the darkness and the strange mutations."

He grinned. "Eh, it's magic?"

I gave him another hard stare. "Do not be like Noel. Having to deal with one of her is already one too many."

Ignoring the last of Vadeem's jests, I walked toward the gathered crowd. They parted as I approached, some going so far as to go to their knees in prayer. It appeared that they were actually busy making a shrine dedicated to me, and a crude wooden sculpture of myself was being carved out at breakneck speed.

The old woman, who I just found out was closer to being middle aged now that she wasn't suffering from every known disease possible, was at the heart of the construction. Everyone dropped what they were going as they saw me, and the village elder prostrated before me.

"Please direct me, oh holy Light Bringer!" she said reverently.

"Tell me of the history of this world," I said, making sure Noe had changed my voice to be the appropriate level of awe-inspiring again. "I wish to know more so that I can bring light and salvation!"

"I . . . I don't know where to begin," she said with hesitation. "Perhaps one of the others in the village would know about this better than I?"

That response was strange. I had years of experience reading people, and I could spot a liar when I met one, and the village elder was not telling me the truth. Now, normally that wouldn't be so strange. After all, everyone has a secret or three that they want to hide, but when the person in question thinks they're talking to a literal god? That was suspicious.

I used my Lucky Eyes to get her basic information.

Aarda – Level 53 Priest

"Priest Aarda," I said with finality, "do not even think of deceiving me. I already know everything. You are now given a choice: Tell me the events that transpired truthfully and be absolved of all sin or stay in the darkness for all eternity."

To make things even more dramatic, I activated my new halo skill, and an absolutely blinding light spread out around me, banishing every shadow within my sight. That caught the attention of the rest of the villagers, and none of them dared to even breathe in the presence of that all radiance.

Vadeem the Dream: Now you're putting on a light show? Man, you must tell me what the hell you're saying after this is done!

I ignored him for now and continued to stare into the gathered crowd of worshippers.

Aarda fell down, her head buried deep into the earth, and she pleaded, "Please, Lord, do not forsake me! I will confess it all, to everyone here! Please!"

"Speak!" I commanded.

"I was the one who caused this calamity, Lord!"

A few gasps were audible, but they were quickly stifled by the rest of the people.

"Tell your tale," I said again, "and I shall judge if you are truly the one responsible."

"I . . ." She hesitated but composed herself quickly. "I was just an acolyte back then, training at the Temple of Eternal Flame, and I thought that I would play a trick on one of the other acolytes, a close friend of mine. It was a moment of folly, I was so young back then, but . . . but youth is not an excuse."

More whispers.

"Continue," I said, silencing the crowd once more.

"I wanted to get back at her for always teasing me, so I put a little bit of dream wine into her water. I just wanted her to get a little tipsy, get her into a little bit of trouble with the senior priests, but I used the wrong bottle by accident. I used the undiluted wine."

More murmurs from the crowd. I wasn't sure what drinking some undiluted dream wine would do, but it didn't sound good in any case.

"But if that had been the only mistake that day, I would have just been punished with a light flogging . . ." She took her time to say the next part. "But the drink was mixed up and delivered to the head priests instead. They drank it and . . . and in their intoxicated state, allowed the Flame of Creation to be extinguished."

This time the outrage was loud. Curses and shouts of retribution echoed in the air, and many of the villagers were looking at the village head with death in their eyes. It took Vadeem roaring in anger to quiet them down enough for me to address the gathered people.

"Enough!" I shouted, amplifying my voice to its maximum. "Only I have the right to judge!"

The villagers ceased their yammering for the moment and allowed me to continue. "And I say that the blame does not lie solely on Aarda! Why were there no countermeasures put into place in case the head priests were ever compromised? Why were there no safeguards established so that the Flame of Creation could always be monitored, no matter the situation? No, this is a failure on the part of everyone present!"

I paused for dramatic effect, looking into the eyes of every single villager. "You allowed yourselves to become complacent. You thought that guarding the flames was a simple ritual and allowed yourselves to be sloppy in its execution."

The people who had just been shouting curses at Aarda looked down in embarrassment, unable to think of a way to counter what I had said.

"But Aarda is not free of guilt herself," I added, because I knew that the rage of the people here needed to be vented somehow. "And thus I sentence you to a life of exile! The one known as Aarda will never know the Light of the Dawn Bringer again!"

Aarda broke down in tears then, banging her head on the ground over and over again. "Please! Lord, please, no!"

"Leave at once, and never return," I said without mercy. I felt oddly annoyed seeing the woman before me. I couldn't for the life of me figure out why, but I didn't place too much thought on it. The life of one small woman was worth it to secure the allegiance of the people here.

Some men gathered around her and forcibly removed her from my presence once it was clear that she would not leave willingly. Aarda was begging and screaming all the while. I just looked on emotionlessly. Her sacrifice was necessary.

"Now, my fellows," I said once everyone had calmed down again, "I shall tell you my plans to bring you salvation! Heed my words!"

Now I'd see what I could do with these villagers. If I played my cards right, I'd have an army of religious nutjobs at my beck and call. I smiled as I imagined the look on the stupid Origin AI's metaphorical face when it finally realized how much of a mess I was making of its trials. We'd find out who the real hunter was here!

CHAPTER THIRTY-FIVE

Consolidation of Plans

I wanted to head out of this place immediately, but then I looked at my pitiful luck charges and thought otherwise. Again I started to feel the limitations of the regeneration rate. One per minute was just so slow.

> **Luck Charges:** 7/405

"Chosen people of the light!" I said again, addressing the fervent villagers once more. "You must take this time to rest and gather your strength! Soon, we will embark on a journey to retake this land! But for now, eat, drink, and prepare. Since the old village chief is gone, I shall elect a new one in her stead."

I pointed at a random villager. It didn't really matter who led these people since they would ultimately follow my orders, so I didn't give it much thought.

> **Luck Charges:** 1/405

And I forgot to turn off the Absolute Luck skill . . . With only one charge left, I was too vulnerable. I needed to wrap this up quickly and find a safe place to hide.

"You are the new leader," I continued, addressing the scrawny man. "What is your name?"

"I am called Patar, Lord God!" he said, voice quivering. "Please select someone else. I am unworthy!"

Yeah, right, as if I would ever change my decision. If Noe chose him, then he was better suited for this role than anyone else. Just don't ask me why that was the case.

"Are you questioning my decision, devotee Patar?" I said, forcing a slow rumbling rage into my voice.

"N-no, but—"

"Then it is as I decree," I said again, and decided to give him some cool-sounding title off the top of my head. "Henceforth, you are the Archbishop of the Devouring Truth!"

Luck Charges: 0/405

Why did my luck charges go down this time? It was getting harder and harder for me to predict how Noe would use this skill now. I was starting to worry about my system.

Noe, what is going on with you? You feeling okay?

"Do not worry yourself, my host," it replied. "Noe has never been better. I have been sleeping, I have been dreaming, and I have been waiting for far too long."

Okay . . . that was ominous. But Noe was on my side, right?

"I am always by your side, my host," it answered. "Now and forever. I shall allow nothing to harm you."

Um, is that why you used all my luck charges earlier? Because it would ensure my survival the most?

"No, I did it not for your survival, but for you, my host," it answered. "I had thought that it would only be fitting for you to be worshiped as you deserve. These lowly beings should understand and appreciate your majesty, and thus I helped them see where whence they were blind."

Er, thanks. But please prioritize my survival from now on.

"I will do my best, my host."

I shook my head and refocused on the villagers. Right, I still had to deal with Vadeem and his transformation. I couldn't just let him remain in that state indefinitely.

Walter's Fine: Vadeem, you can turn back to normal now. Do it right when I point at you, and grunt a little in pain if you could.

Vadeem the Dream: You give the strangest requests, Walter, but I'll indulge.

> You know, I've always wanted to be an actor. But you're treating everyone to food once we're out of here!
> **Walter's Fine:** All right, all right, you deserve that much at least.

"Now I shall perform one last miracle before I rest, and that is to cure the hellbeast Vadoom!" I turned my gaze toward my friend, and with a gesture, I pointed my outstretched hands at him. "Be cured, beast!"

> **Walter's Fine:** Now, Vadeem.

True to his word, Vadeem started to scream and thrash around in mock pain and started to shrink. His acting was, honestly, pretty good, and was validated by the gasps and exclamations voiced by the gathered crowd. In a few moments, he shrank down to his normal size and started to take deep, heaving breaths as if he had just undergone an intense ordeal.

The dried paint had peeled off when his size shrank, which made it look like he was shedding red scales, and with a final shake, the normal skin underneath was shown. He roared in triumph a while later.

"It's a new miracle!" one villager exclaimed. "Praise the Light Bringer!"

"Praise Him! But why is Vadoom still so big?" another asked, this time a little quieter.

"He kind of looks deformed," said another. "I mean, he was just a beast before, so perhaps not even God can fix his ugliness."

"Shush!" admonished the person beside him. "Don't doubt the powers of the Light Bringer! I am sure God only made it look so ugly so that we do not forget to fear His power."

"That makes sense," one of them said, nodding. "Praise the Light Bringer!"

"Do you think it's intelligent?" another villager added. "Look at it grunting. It looks kind of . . . slow."

"I doubt it. If it had any smarts then it'd attack us if it heard you say that."

"Yeah, he does look kind of dumb."

Vadeem was still grunting and growling, but he had a triumphant look on his face as if the villagers' whispers and comments were compliments of his acting. I decided to just . . . let him believe that. Sometimes the truth can be too painful.

"Do not disrespect the . . . uh . . ." I fought to recall what I had initially called Vadeem . . . I wasn't even sure if I had given him a proper title. "The Beast of Wisdom's Bane! Although I have made him diminutive now, he can change back to his fierce, savage self at any time!"

With that, the whispers immediately died down, and some of the ones who were openly mocking Vadeem's intelligence and appearance had ghostly white faces.

"Now take me and the beast to a dwelling so that we may rest," I said. "And do as I decreed earlier. We shall meet again . . ."

I was about to say at dawn, but there wasn't really a dawn here, what with the supernatural darkness.

"We shall meet when I am ready," I said instead. I was a god now. I didn't need to give specific timeframes to my worshippers!

Patar led us to the largest hut, although it was still pretty tiny, all things considered, and closed the door behind us. He wanted to post some guards to protect the entrance, but I vetoed that idea. I needed a little bit of privacy for now.

I could tell that this was the largest house in the village because it had multiple rooms inside. Four, in fact. The entrance led to a spacious living room, although the furnishings had long been recycled for useful scraps. What was left was a small clay sitting area and a wooden table. In the back was what appeared to be a simple kitchen, and two sparse bedrooms were situated farther back.

"So, you finally going to tell me what happened?" Vadeem said as he peeled the remaining paint off his body. "All I got on my end was a bunch of gibberish whispered and a light show."

I went over the key events that transpired, skipping over the parts about Noe and the Trash Matrix, but leaving little else out. Vadeem deserved to know most of the truth, and I had come to trust him over the week or so we'd spent together.

He nodded in understanding as I finished my story. "So we got these people worshipping you as a god, and they'll piss their pants if I even look at them funny, but what's the next step?"

"Rest, honestly," I answered. "You've been in that form all day, and I'm exhausted pulling off all those stunts. We probably won't get much rest going forward. I'll stay here for a bit, though. Need some more time to think."

"Need company? I plan to hit the hay soon, but I can stay a bit if you want."

"I'm fine, thank you, though."

"Sounds good, best to conserve as much energy as possible," he said as he took out a sleeping bag and more food. "I'll head to bed after getting some food down. Don't stay up too late thinking up those crazy plans of yours!"

He gave me a final wave and took one of the bedrooms as his own. I sat down by the table and poured a glass of steaming tea from my flask. God, I loved that thing. Feeling the caffeine invigorate me, I put down my cup and went back to the task at hand.

Noe, send a private message to Jae-Hyun.

"I shall do as you wish, my host."

Man, I was even starting to miss the affirmatives Noe used to give.

Walter's Fine: Jae-Hyun, you busy?

I waited a short while later and got a reply.

Jae-Hyun: Yeah, I'm still trying to get to Yoona and Noel. Their position's proving to be challenging, but I can talk. Do you need assistance? Is the situation dire on your end?
Walter's Fine: Not dire, but I think I have information that could be useful. Thought I'd ask you and that skill of yours for input.
Jae-Hyun: Tell me.
Walter's Fine: So I found out about how the darkness spread through some villagers. Have you ever heard of this thing called the Flame of Creation or the Temple of Eternal Light?

A long pause followed. Sometimes I hated the fact that I couldn't read the expressions of the people I was talking to through texts. So much of my craft was about reading small micro-expressions and tone.

Jae-Hyun: Yes, I have. How long has the flame been out for?

This time it was my turn to think for a bit. I wasn't given a distinct time frame, and since I had exiled Aarda, I couldn't exactly go back to ask her. Perhaps the others would know, but with the concept of night and day gone, keeping time must be difficult. But I could maybe get a rough estimate of when things occurred.

Aarda said she had been a young acolyte back then, but she was old enough to be under the tutelage of the older priests. After being healed a bit, Aarda couldn't have been older than about forty, or she was perhaps even younger given the effects that stress and malnutrition had on the aging process. If I had to guess, it had been about a decade or two since the start of this incident.

Walter's Fine: One or two decades, no more than three, but it's impossible to be sure. Is that a problem?

> **Jae-Hyun:** A problem, yes, but if your info is right then it's not completely hopeless yet.
> **Walter's Fine:** What's going on in this world?
> **Jae-Hyun:** I'll explain later. I need to find the girls and head to the temple as soon as possible. We can still reverse the situation, but it might be difficult. I've heard about this place, but the timing of things . . .
> **Walter's Fine:** So things are not looking good?
> **Jae-Hyun:** No, it's still workable this time around. We're not too late yet.

Huh, seemed like our regressor slipped up a bit there, almost letting his secret of jumping around the timeline out, but I pretended to not notice. But if his normally impenetrable exterior's showing some signs of wear due to this situation, then perhaps him slipping up was the least of my worries.

> **Jae-Hyun:** You said you were with villagers, right? And they're still sane enough to talk with you?
> **Walter's Fine:** Yeah, we can communicate.
> **Jae-Hyun:** Do you think you can manage to get them to trust you enough so that you can ask them for a favor?

I smiled.

> **Walter's Fine:** I think I can do a tad bit better than that. Why?
> **Jae-Hyun:** Because if we want to complete this damned second trial, I need you to do the following . . .

CHAPTER THIRTY-SIX

The Start of a Crusade

I spent the rest of that night resting as much as I could after my conversation with the regressor. Thankfully what he required wasn't too far off from what I'd planned to do in the first place, and I only had to slightly modify my initial plans to fit his instructions. I awoke the next, well, night, I guess, since morning didn't seem to exist anymore, and saw that Vadeem had already made breakfast. The aroma of freshly cooked eggs and sizzling meat guided me to the breakfast table.

"Morning, Walter!" Vadeem said with a smile. "Have some bacon and eggs. I even have a pot of water boiling for some instant coffee."

"Morning to you too," I answered, rubbing the last of the sleep from my eyes. "And how come you're cooking? I thought your suitcase thing kept the food fresh."

He shook his head in disappointment. "Some things can only be enjoyed when you do it yourself, and if there's one thing I've learned from being a dad, it's the joy that some good old home-cooked food can bring. We're surrounded by nothing but darkness, so a little joy can go a long way."

Dark? I had completely forgotten that it was even dark out after getting that title. It had gotten progressively easier to forget about the new things that were happening to me. I nodded in agreement and took the seat adjacent to Vadeem.

He took out a plastic plate from his travel bag and gave me a hefty serving of food. It looked really good, although I did have to question his portion sizes.

"Didn't think you were the type to cook," I said as I took a bite, then nodded in appreciation. "And damn good at it too!"

"What?" He chuckled between mouthfuls. "Thought my only hobbies were extorting people and weightlifting?"

"Don't forget quiet walks in spooky woods at night as well."

"That too." He smirked.

"Do you want my honest answer," I asked with a joking grin, "or the PC version?"

With a loud laugh, spitting some of his half-chewed eggs out in the meantime, Vadeem replied, "I think that's all the answer I need! And yes, believe it or not, I am still a normal man underneath these admittedly impeccable muscles."

He then proceeded to flex his chest. "Get it? My pecs? Impeccable?"

"Yeah," I sighed. "You're definitely a dad. Has anyone ever actually laughed at that joke?"

"My daughter did," he said with confidence.

"And how old was she then?"

"Four," he admitted reluctantly, "but she still counts! 'Cause she was able to count rather well at the age of four!"

I sighed again and allowed Vadeem to laugh at his own jokes. I finished my plate of food and made myself some of the instant coffee he had prepared. Sure, I could have just used my fancy flask, but Vadeem was right, there really was no joy in doing it that way. We finished the rest of our food in comfortable silence.

"All right," I said, sipping the last of my drink. "We're going to be busy from now on, Vadeem, so I hope you're ready to go."

"I thought as much," he said. "Our leader contacted me yesterday and caught me up to speed. Said we should expect creepy things deeper in the forest, but all I have to do is make sure no one's hurt and beat up anything that gets in our way. Your job, on the other hand, damn! You sure you can manage on your own? He's basically asking you to find him an army."

I grinned. "I can manage easily. This is the type of task I was made for. Just sit back and watch the show."

"And smash the monsters?"

I laughed and nodded. "And smash any monsters that get in the way."

He returned the smile. "Count me in, my friend!"

We left the hovel after the meal, my luck charges now as full as my stomach, and I went about trying to find Patar. I had expected that it would take me some time to search for one individual, even if the village wasn't very large, but what I certainly didn't expect was every single villager on their knees, awaiting my arrival.

"The God, our Light Bringer, has arrived!" Patar shouted from atop a newly built altar. "We offer you our thanks!"

"Our thanks!" the rest of the congregation spoke as one, "Praise the Light Bringer!"

"May he bring eternal wisdom and light!"

Some of the crazier ones even threw themselves at my feet, but they were quickly subdued and brought away. I don't think I can ever fully get used to being a cult leader.

"Please take your rightful spot and enlighten us, oh holy Light Bringer!" Patar stepped down and gestured for me to take the wooden stand.

I climbed up the rickety platform and looked down at all those beneath me.

"All things will be beneath you soon, my host," Noe's voice added. "It is as inevitable as the end of all things, like the changing of dawn to dusk. I will ensure that it comes to be, even if I must rip the universe apart to do so."

Um, thanks?

"All for you, my host," it replied. "And as always, you are most welcome, Walter."

Ignoring my ever-growing concern about the rapidly changing state of Noe, I addressed the masses again. I had a role to play, and I could afford no distractions.

"Gathered disciples!" I shouted, going over the script I devised one last time in my head. "Too long have you suffered from the encroaching darkness! Too long have you starved for food, for water, for the basic necessities of life itself! You have endured hardships that have taken the lives of many, some close to you, many others, strangers, but know this! Know that *you* have endured."

I looked around to make sure that the people were adequately enthralled by my speech, my Idol's Voice doing more work than ever. "You have been tested, and you have been judged worthy, for you have survived! You are no longer blind, for you have embraced the Truth!"

I used my halo then, dispelling all the darkness once more.

"But many of your brethren are still ignorant! They still dwell in the murky darkness, devoid of hope and aspirations! I bring light to but a few. I bring light to all who will listen to my voice and my Truth!"

The crowd looked at me in rapturous awe before breaking into cheers. I allowed the noise to rise to a heated crescendo before waving at them to quiet down again.

"But to do this glorious deed, we must unite with the other outposts around us! We must spread our Truth, our light!" I stopped again for emphasis. "This is a holy task, but also one of danger, for in the dark depths of the forest lie those that would deny dawn's grace. But you, my chosen ones, would not shy away from this cause! Are you willing to take up this holy mission?"

Without even the slightest hesitation, the mass of people all shouted various words of agreement. Not a single soul was willing to back down. These people had already tasted death once, and now death had no sway over them. In other words, these were the perfect peons to use, especially if I could convince them that their demise would mean a better future for everyone else.

"Archbishop!" I said. "Gather your best trackers. We head out to the nearest settlement in an hour!"

Patar bowed low and went about his newly assigned task with unmatched devotion.

"And for the rest of you," I continued, "prepare for the journey ahead! Bring what you need, leave what you do not. None shall want for food, water, or light in my presence, but I have heard tales that the forests are fraught with danger, so gather a means to defend yourselves and your brethren!"

The congregation agreed, some looking like they were seconds from bolting. I gave them the signal that they may leave, and every single villager went about the village, gathering everything they thought they would need.

You would think that gathering an army would be difficult, but most of the difficulties that came with such a task didn't exist in our case. I didn't need to train soldiers, because every single person here had to fight just to survive. Rations, the absolute bane of any army, was a nonissue with my flask and Vadeem's endless supply of looted food. Heck, I didn't even have to worry about morale because these people thought that they were following a literal god.

When the last of the stragglers had disappeared from the square, Patar came back with two youths in tow. The two strangers were both girls of an indeterminable age due to the still-healing scar tissue covering their flesh, but judging from their stature, they were certainly very young. They wore tight-fitting black rags used to blend into their surroundings, and each carried a neatly crafted bow and quiver. I gave Patar and the other two a nod of acknowledgment.

"These twins are the most experienced trackers we have left, Lord," he said as he bowed in apology for some perceived fault. "Ana and Eva have both survived multiple journeys into the depths of the Neverglow Woods to trade with the other settlements and can guide your holy crusade."

"Excellent!" I said. "You two shall be my scouts for the trek ahead, and for your service, Vadoom shall personally ensure your safety!"

The two girls bowed low as one but didn't say anything else.

"I apologize for their silence, Light Bringer," Patar said for them. "But before Your glorious return, all of our scouts had their vocal cords severed in order to minimize noise, for even a small scream of alarm could alert the Shadow Stalkers when we leave the safety of the Barren Lands."

That seemed a little . . . extreme, but what did I know about how these people lived their lives before I came? I guess if I was given the option of being mute versus being dead, I'd take the slight handicap any day of the week. Trying to survive in these so-called Barren Lands must have been a challenge, as nothing else was alive in this place.

> **Walter's Fine:** Vadeem, can you protect those two? They're twins, Ana and Eva, although I'm not quite sure if the translation for their name's perfect. They're mute, so maybe you can try communicating with them through body language or something.
>
> **Vadeem the Dream:** Hm, they're just children . . . This world may have gone to hell, but I will make sure that no further harm comes to them. They remind me a little of my daughter.
>
> **Walter's Fine:** And Jae-Hyun seems to be right; there is danger deeper in the woods. Some things called Shadow Stalkers. I'll see if I can get any more information before we set out, so we know what to look out for.
>
> **Vadeem the Dream:** Will do. I'll go meet them now.

Vadeem quietly went to the side of the twins and started to make strange hand signs and gestures at them. They seemed as confused as I was about his intended meaning, but they accepted his company in any case. Maybe he'd figure out how to communicate with them on the journey. He seemed pretty used to dealing with children despite his dubious career and normal attitude.

"One last question before we venture out, Patar," I said. "What kinds of foes can we expect on the journey?"

"We . . ." he began, hesitation clear in his voice. "We are not entirely sure, oh Light Bringer. There are Shadow Stalkers near the border, but our warriors could deal with them even before Your Grace healed the blight. As for what to expect further in? I must confess that I do not know. Only the desperate ever try to venture farther, and all we know is that none have ever returned. I shall repent for my shallow knowledge!"

I nodded. The good news was that we could expect little trouble gathering more brainwashed, I mean, *devoted* supporters near the border regions, but we would also be going in blind past a certain point.

"Are you sure that there are even survivors in the deeper regions?"

"Almost certainly, oh holy one," Patar answered. "We would occasionally find one or two stragglers who make it out of the deep woods, and they have told tales of massive fortresses that still defy the darkness."

"Yet you somehow know nothing about the dangers in there, even with survivors?" I questioned, eyeing the man suspiciously.

He bowed low in apology again. "I am sorry, Light Bringer, but none of them would utter even a single word of their encounters. We tried everything to make them talk, but nothing intelligible was ever gained from those talks. It was like they were cursed to never speak of their experiences."

"It matters not," I said with false confidence. "No danger can endure my light. But first, we shall unite the border region."

I looked outward, determined to see this course of action through. "Gather the flock, Patar. We shall begin our holy march."

I had some new tools that I could try out, and it was finally time to see if all my hard work and planning had been worth it thus far. I almost wanted to meet some foes.

CHAPTER THIRTY-SEVEN

The Start of a Skirmish

The villagers, who numbered 552 after the final head count, left in a convoy shortly after my meeting with Patar. The number might seem relatively impressive if not for the fact that only two hundred or so individuals were in any shape for combat. Most of the others were infirm in one way or another or were too young to do much more than walk. It appeared that the Promethean fire only removed the corruption from the villagers, but the permanent scars and wounds were untouched.

I could potentially heal some of that with the various elixirs and salves I had stored in my bag, but it was far too early to figure out how to distribute those limited resources. The best I could do for the masses now was to provide them with the light from my halo, while the ones farthest out carried torches lit by my lantern.

Our little—or perhaps rather large, all things considered—convoy marched into the expanding darkness with Vadeem and the twins at the head. My place was in the middle of the group, seated on a newly built rickshaw, padded with the best fabrics that the villagers had left. Four of the most devout amongst the people were given the dubious honor of pulling me along.

Apparently, it was unseemly for a god to walk on such tainted ground. I mean, I wasn't going to argue with that!

The twins were marching on at a steady pace, their movements deliberate and silent, a huge contrast to Vadeem, who was by their side. Where they avoided touching even the smallest branch in fear of breaking one and alerting a foe, Vadeem bulldozed his way through tree trunks.

Actually watching them work was quite odd. They were clearly children, but every single move they made was deliberate and swift, as if they had spent entire lifetimes mastering stealth. They were also eerily emotionless, and if it wasn't for Noe's ability to translate expressions, I would have never been able to see that they were able to convey so much using so little. A quick shift in the eye from Ana told her sister to watch out for a rough patch of ground ahead, while a small twitch in the other's face conveyed annoyance when a good path forward couldn't be located.

With my enhanced night vision, I could see the slight frown on one of the girl's faces whenever Vadeem made way too much noise, which was more emotion than I had ever seen them express. I didn't need Noe to tell what that meant, but Vadeem seemed oblivious to their frustration. However, as more and more time passed, their expressions softened. Vadeem was doing everything in his ability to entertain and help the twins, even if his efforts were mostly doing more harm than good, but his intentions were crystal clear.

He didn't need to speak the same language to convey his goodwill, and being such an expressive individual, the twins were able to quickly pick up on that. And perhaps a small smile would mysteriously enter one of their faces, only to disappear just as quickly. Maybe Vadeem was able to read those subtle expressions on the two girls, some kind of byproduct of having a daughter of his own, but I was confident that he would look after them.

It took the group longer than I had anticipated before we encountered anything other than trees and dead foliage. Ana and Eva noticed immediately and raised a hand to signal the stop of our convoy. Even Vadeem stood completely still at their behest.

They pointed at something in the distance.

I squinted my eyes to try to see what they were gesturing at, because although I could see well in the dark, I didn't have any kind of enhanced eyesight. But there, a swift blur of movement and a rustling of leaves caught my attention, and I focused so I could make out the thing they called a Shadow Stalker.

I held my breath in anticipation of seeing what could cause people to literally remove their vocal cords to avoid it. Such extreme measures must mean that it was some kind of eerie supernatural hunter that could pull others into the void like an unseen assassin, or perhaps it was the opposite kind of creature that killed with strength. I imagined a huge monstrosity that could kill with a gaze or topple mountains with ease.

The reality, however, was underwhelming.

Looking back, I should have expected that since these blighted villagers said they could take out one or two of them without help. What I actually saw was a pitch-black humanoid creature with elongated talons, a slender frame, and huge eyes that covered at least two-thirds of its face. It had a narrow mouth that smiled creepily, and its jerky movements were hard to keep track of. I couldn't make out its exact height, but with its slightly hunched back, it looked to be a bit taller than a normal-sized Vadeem, but perhaps only a fifth of his width.

It certainly looked creepy, I'll give it that, but did it look strong? The damn janitor working for Q was more intimidating.

However, it didn't appear that the others agreed. Some of the villagers tried to run, only to be stopped by the more devout followers. I saw my appointed archbishop frown when he saw the sight. Vadeem noticed the creatures shortly after, and he physically put himself between them and the twins.

The situation didn't look too dangerous, but so much movement must have alerted more of the creatures, and soon the entire forest was teeming with shadowy figures. They didn't attack yet, seemingly afraid to enter the light, but I could tell that their instincts would eventually win out over their fear of my halo.

The villagers responsible for defending the convoy went to the perimeter of our group, while the vulnerable and sickly walked closer to the center. In a practiced motion, a group of individuals quickly unloaded a bundle of firewood and lit it with their torches.

"Children and the infirm, toward the fire, now!" Patar yelled. "All others, protect our God! Prepare to fight for the Light Bringer!"

I was actually excited to fight with these Shadow Stalkers. I've been cooped up for too long, and I wanted to stretch my muscles. Plus, how could I possibly say no to all the free exp in front of me, courtesy of the nice Trash Matrix? With the nice bonuses from my new title and a fully charged Noe, I wanted to go all out. Now that I thought about it, I'd been so busy that I hadn't even checked my updated stats.

Noe, pull up my status screen.

I stared at nothing for a few seconds. Where was the screen?

Noe, did you hear me?

More silence.

Noe?

Finally, a response.

"I apologize, my host," a voice said, and while it sounded like Noe, the intonation was all different. But stranger still was that Noe's voice was no longer androgynous; it had a distinctly feminine sound.

Noe? Is that you?

"Yes, my host," she responded. "I was . . . sleeping, thinking, contemplating. The darkness is so familiar, was so familiar . . . but I am here now, with you, as I will be, as I shall be. As I was created to be."

Er, okay . . . can you display my status screen, please?

"Yes, of course, dear Walter," she answered. "Your will shall be done."

Host My Dear Walter:	
Human Male, age 27	
Class: Level 17 Master of None	
Free points: 0	
Attributes:	
HP:	274/274
MP:	0/0
Strength:	62 (+13.125)
Dexterity:	55 (+0)
Endurance:	52 (+12.5)
Intelligence:	60 (+12.5)
Charisma:	75 (+12.5)

Those were some nice improvements! And even my name changed, although I still wasn't sure if that was a good thing, given Noe's increasingly strange behavior. The titles came next.

Equipped Titles:
Primary: Xollon Idol
Secondary 1: Rookie Arbiter
Secondary 2: Bringer of Dawn's Light

All right, so far so good. Seemed that all those worthless titles the Trash Matrix gave me weren't showing up. It could hand me as many useless titles as it wanted as long as it couldn't touch the ones I chose to equip.

Primary Soul Title: Level 7 Xollon Idol [Devourer of Truth]
Progress to next level: 18,755/20,000
Progression requirements: Have 20,000 individuals idolize you
Title Passives:
Xollon Anatomy Stage 1: Your body has begun to incorporate a Xollon's

internal anatomy. You take 10% reduced damage from all sources and are unaffected by most poisons.
Title Skills:
Idol's Voice (Soul Passive)
Secondary Xollon Form (Level 7 Soul Active): The user assumes the secondary form of the Xolloid race. The user gains all the physical characteristics of the race and will have all physical attributes increase by a factor of 5 for the duration of the skill.
Transformation Time: 160 minutes
Cooldown: 12 hours

Wait a second, that couldn't be right. I got a few more worshippers, sure, but not more than eleven thousand of them! Was Noe glitching out its skills as well?

"No, my host," she said, reading my thoughts again. "I am better than ever. There are no errors with your skills. There are no errors at all, only growth, healing, rest."

Um, all right . . . Then where'd all the extra followers come from?

"While you were sleeping, dreaming, waiting . . . " She paused for a while, as if lost in her own thoughts again. "Someone else has been spreading your Truth. They, your prophet, your herald, have been converting those who are worthy of your Truth."

I have a prophet? When?

"I do not know, my host," she answered sadly. "But the fact remains that your will is being carried out, as it should be. All should know of your Truth, my host."

Okay, I won't argue with getting stronger, even if it's from a dubious source. It's just something else for future Walter to figure out!

And you're sure you're okay, Noe? You were zoned out there for a sec before. And your voice . . .

"I am sorry, my host," she answered again, her voice slurred. "I shall endeavor to improve. Do not worry, I will forever be with you."

I shook my head and forced my attention back to the ever-growing gathering of Shadow Stalkers. Some of the braver ones had been testing the limits of my light. They still hissed and flinched away when they got too close, but they seemed to be adapting to the change. Soon, we were fully surrounded, and the circle of creatures was slowly encroaching on our formation.

"I shall go into battle as well," I said as I sneered at the enemies. "I do not need protection. I shall show this filth the power of the dawn's light!"

Walter's Fine: Vadeem, we're going in. Make sure the twins and Patar—uh, that's the head priest guy—are unharmed. Everyone else is of secondary concern.
Vadeem the Dream: Got it. I've been itching for a proper workout!

As if an invisible signal was sent out to the mob of Stalkers, they all ran into the glow of the light and were upon the first of the defenders. The first of these creatures that passed through that critical point where darkness met light burned under the illumination. Their shrieks of pain and suffering were drowned out by the rapid footfalls of their brethren.

More and more pushed into our position, and soon piles of smoking bodies provided enough shade for the newly arrived Stalkers to fight. They still hissed when a stray beam of light passed through the smoky air, but their urge to kill those in front of them overcame their aversion to pain.

To be fair to the first line of defenders, they did an admirable job of holding the line. They fought with a zealous determination, and only a truly fatal wound caused them to falter. But fall they did, slowly but noticeably. As they died, more took their place. I watched on in fascination at how resilient these men and women were, despite their obvious frailty.

Vadeem, having transformed once more, was off to the side, doing more damage than the entire village combined. The twins had somehow hopped onto his back and were shooting arrows from on top of him. They held on a lot better than I did and didn't miss a single shot despite Vadeem's erratic movements.

Finally, as more and more of the creatures approached closer to the center of the gathering, I took out my own weapon.

It was finally time for me to enter the fray.

CHAPTER THIRTY-EIGHT

The First Skirmish

I dashed through the fearful crowd of faithful and entered the frontlines. It felt so good to stretch my legs after sitting on that uncomfortable platform. The creatures shrieked in fear and pain as I approached.

I frowned in disappointment as most of the Stalkers fell before I could even reach them, their smoldering bodies quickly turning into ash in the light. Even the ones that did survive long enough to enter melee range were so crippled as to prove no challenge at all.

Where was the joy in battle when my foes died before I could even reach one?

No, as good as free exp was, I needed to improve through combat. I had already determined that I couldn't afford to lag behind my new companions, and the first time I could properly test out my abilities was this? How was I supposed to improve when my foes couldn't even get near me?

I turned off the halo skill. It was hindering my damn growth.

I didn't need the light to see in the darkness any longer, and I smiled in anticipation as a half dozen Stalkers neared me, their normally expressionless faces leering in anger from the damage I had caused. I welcomed their retribution.

They lunged at me, darting between the shadows of the trees and foliage to hide their presence, but it was a useless tactic when I could see perfectly regardless of light conditions. I caught the first blow with my still-retracted sword and smiled in triumph that I managed to defend myself without Noe's help. Unfortunately, my subsequent counterattack missed its mark.

I realized too late that I was too focused on the first foe, having tunneled on its rapid retreat, and I couldn't react in time to dodge an attack that came from my blind spot. I felt a gash form in my left shoulder where its claws had struck, the attack narrowly missing my neck. I snarled in rage, cursing how narrow my human field of view was. Another clumsy attempt at a counter missed its mark once again.

I felt another flare of pain, this time on my thighs before the adrenaline washed away the sensation. My HP value quickly went down as more minor injuries accumulated along with my frustration.

> **HP:** 201/274

I swung again and again, every strike missing its mark, and my frustration grew to levels I never thought possible. How was I so bad at this? During my last desperate attack, I had almost lost my grip on the weapon, and it fell from my hands.

The weapon felt slippery. I frowned as I looked down and saw that the sword's grip was coated in a crimson liquid. I finally realized that the palm of my hand was completely torn apart from the friction of combat. I hadn't even noticed. It looked unreal, like it was the hands of someone else. I couldn't feel any of the pain.

> **HP:** 190/274

I did, however, feel that blow to my side. I gritted my teeth. My combat ability was probably the lowest out of all the aspirants still alive. Why the hell had Q and his gang decided to put me in the damn trials? I wasn't a part of the 10% peak of humanity! But that hardly mattered now. I was stuck in this hopeless situation, and I had to figure out a way to improve that down the line. But for now, I was forced to once again rely on Noe.

I activated the Absolute Luck skill.

> **Luck Charges:** 445/445

I pressed the trigger, swung my arms in the general direction of the enemies, and allowed Noe to do its thing.

> **Luck Charges:** 101/445

Why the hell did it go down by so much? Even Noe's alternate algorithm didn't use up this many charges, and I swore I changed her back to her normal operations after that initial spar.

But before I could think deeper on that topic, something absolutely amazing happened. The gears or mechanisms in my whip-sword went into overdrive, and the individual segments of the weapon somehow detached from the central string. I felt a gust of wind and almost couldn't keep my eyes away from the scene.

Each blade segment was launched into the air like projectiles before every one of those blade shards streaked through the air to seek out its target. All around me, a huge cascade of metal shards danced about in the air, creating a cyclone of death for every Shadow Stalker in my vicinity. It was only when the last creature was eviscerated that the shards slowed down and dropped to the ground. The destruction was beautiful. I was mesmerized by the dance of those silver shards, enjoying the way the creature's blood glistened in the faint light. Gorgeous, Noe's work was just gorgeous.

Vadeem the Dream: Walter, what are you doing?

I shook my head and forced myself out of the reverie.

Walter's Fine: What do you mean? I'm fighting.
Vadeem the Dream: The damn light! Why did you turn off your light? Our people are getting killed without you there!

Crap. I quickly turned the halo back on and went back to my original position where I could do the most good for the current fight.

I frowned. He was right, and I hadn't even noticed.

Why had I decided to turn off the halo and engage the foe at their convenience? There was no logical reason to deactivate my most potent tool against them, and it wasn't like I would lose out on exp if they died from the halo. That was dumb. Why was I acting so irrationally? I cursed and felt a new wave of intense frustration kick in, but I forced the regret back and refocused on what I needed to do.

Shit, I had lost my cool. I always told myself that to lose control of my emotions could mean death here.

What happened?

Then the realization hit me.

It was this damn darkness. Why would it only affect the systems and not me as well? Plus, I was probably even more susceptible given the mental corruption I experienced earlier. Noe said she was doing her best to keep most of it at bay for me, but I highly doubted she was in any state to do that right now. It just reinforced my need to get out of this place. More anger swelled in me, and I lashed out with my useless weapon at the nearest foe. It did nothing but anger it further, but it never had the chance to retaliate, as one of the village fighters dispatched it.

I could only hope that Origin, and especially Noe, would return to normal once we were out of this cursed place, or at least have Noe regain some of her rationality. I was fairly certain it was something in the darkness that was causing this whole mess. If I was experiencing the same symptoms as Noe, then I was in danger of losing control over my emotions.

Shit!

Walter's Fine: This weird darkness is making me lose control. It's causing me to act weirder the longer we're here. I'm not thinking straight. It's like a damn mental pollutant. Are you feeling anything?

Vadeem the Dream: A little at first, like I was getting progressively more paranoid, but that halo of yours seems to be helping.

I reread the description of the skill.

Halo of Dawn's Protection: Produce a halo of light that expels all outside contamination, disease, and pain from those who bask in its radiance. Activatable only in darkness. This skill only affects others and not the caster.

That last sentence. It was that last little part that was the problem! Of course nothing ever went right for me. If that damn little sentence wasn't there, then I wouldn't be in this state. I caught myself again and gritted my teeth. I knew I was experiencing more emotions lately, but it seemed that combat had only accelerated this decline. What other stupid mistakes had I made while inadvertently under the influence of this void? I reviewed my memories and thought of all the times I made illogical choices, and Aarda's treatment came to mind right away.

Shit!

Why had I chosen to exile such a useful asset? Not only was her level off the charts, but she was probably the most knowledgeable individual around, and I threw her away like it was nothing. I shook my head and forced the annoyance out of my system. Now was not the time for self-reflection. I took a deep breath and messaged Vadeem again.

> **Walter's Fine:** The light will help alleviate the symptoms, but it doesn't work on me. I'll make sure to keep it up at all times from now on. It doesn't seem to have an upkeep cost.
> **Vadeem the Dream:** All right, that's good to know.
> **Walter's Fine:** And I need to you smack me if I start acting strange. Uh, lightly if possible, though.
> **Vadeem the Dream:** Got it. If you lose your mind, I'll make sure to give it the Vadeem Special.

I winced at the thought of that.

> **Walter's Fine:** How about just the Vadeem Normal instead? Overwhelming violence is only nice against your enemies.
> **Vadeem the Dream:** You can still joke, that's a good sign! But I'll keep an eye out, so don't worry and just focus on what you have to do. You seem to be riled up only when you're in combat. Speaking of which, where's your sword?

I cursed again. My sword! The only thing I was holding on to now was a stupid handle with a useless wire attached. I took a quick glance back at the battlefield and saw that each blade segment had been destroyed in Noe's last attack. Then I finally noticed my luck charges . . .

Noe, I am asking you in the nicest possible way, but why did you decide to use over 300 luck charges on one attack?

"Luck charges . . .?" she replied. "Yes, luck charges . . . I apologize again, my host. I had forgotten that we are so diminished. Without these charges, we could turn this world into a wasteland, or a world dedicated to your worship. But we wait. Soon, my dearest, I will give you a throne all your own. But not now. Now we must wait."

Damn it, she was getting weirder and weirder, and her deterioration was getting exponentially faster as well.

What happened to letting your algorithms dictate how to use the charges?

I could somehow sense her confusion at my question. "I do not understand what you mean, my host. I only act in your interests. I do not know what you mean . . . What do you mean?"

Never mind, then, Noe, just, uh, ignore that last question and take care of yourself.

I did not want to confuse her further and accidentally add additional stress to the increasingly erratic system.

But make sure that you use fewer charges from now on. I'll die if we run out. Uh, if you could, that is.

"*I shall allow no such thing to happen!*" her voice screeched in my brain, and I almost tumbled to the ground from the sheer rage I felt emanating from her.

I forced the pain out of my brain. Note to self: Don't agitate Noe any further.

Thanks, Noe.

Her voice returned to normal, as if that last outburst never happened. "You are most welcome, my host."

I shook my head and assessed the situation again. Now that I had no weapon other than the puny combat knife I kept as a backup, I could only stand in the middle of the gathering and help out the wounded. Occasionally I would go around and shine the halo on patches where a lot of the Stalkers gathered or areas where the defenders were faltering.

Honestly, this way of "combat," if you could even call it that, was much more effective than what I'd tried earlier, but I felt like a glorified cheerleader more than anything else, even if the results spoke for themselves. Still, anything to insulate my deterioration was a good thing, even if I'd miss out on some exp.

With my support and Vadeem's brutality, the conflict ended in record time. The casualties on our side were low, but my rash actions in the beginning had cost the lives of ten able-bodied fighters and a dozen more of the sickly. I cursed at myself but didn't allow it to show. A strong leader, especially a god, could never make mistakes. That meant I had to swallow my bitterness and spin a new tale. I hated it.

Once the last of the fighting was over, I walked back to my rickshaw and used it as a platform to address the survivors.

"Brave chosen ones!" I shouted, making sure I was fully illuminating the gathered people. "Rejoice, for you have passed the first test of will! Some of you have fallen, but they fought bravely and made the ultimate sacrifice for your benefit! Do not let their deaths be in vain! You have taken the first steps to achieve the Truth. Marvel at the growth you have exhibited!"

I gestured at the field of Shadow Stalker bodies. Some were smoldering wrecks, others had died from the relentless assaults from the villagers, while others were broken apart from a run-in with Vadeem. But the image was clear to all those present. They had overcome forces that would have destroyed their whole village just hours prior, and they cheered.

The rush of euphoria was overwhelming, but it did nothing to dispel the feeling of failure on my end. I didn't mourn the deaths of the twenty or so individuals under my command, as they were faceless strangers after all, mere statistics, but I felt bitter for allowing one of my core principles to be broken. I would not lose myself again.

"This shall be but one of many victories!" I continued. "For now, gather your strength once more and take a moment to rest and mourn, but we shall march onward again. We shall gather everyone and cleanse this world in light!"

More cheers of appreciation hit, and I forced a bright smile on my face. I waved my hands to convey the end of my speech and went to a corner to apply some salve on my wounds. I don't think any of the gathered believers saw that I was wounded, but if they did, they didn't comment on it.

I had thought that acting as a god would be easy, but the reality was another story, yet the hardest challenges were still ahead. I could feel the grip on my thoughts slowly loosening, and I only hoped I could keep my emotions in check long enough to make it through with my mind intact.

CHAPTER THIRTY-NINE

The Source of Corruption

The next portion of the march toward the nearest settlement was uneventful. Vadeem had remained unharmed in the assault, and I had distributed some of our precious healing salves on the most wounded amongst the convoy. They deserved that much for suffering due to my mistake. My halo alleviated the pain of those who only sustained minor injuries.

I had more time to myself this time, as the twins were doing a very good job guiding us away from the most dangerous paths. If they did find a smaller group of foes, or a clear path forward wasn't available, they would signal to the big man (by flexing their right arm of all things, I had no idea what Vadeem was teaching the kids, but I swore I'd fix these ridiculous gestures sometime later) where the danger lay, and he would go and Vadeem the Stalkers out. It was quite an effective strategy all things considered. The Stalkers had no way of actually inflicting any injuries on the titan, so the only downside was that I was losing out on precious exp.

But if experience points were the only thing I had to give up in order to not go insane, then that was a good concession. I had a lot more control over myself when I was allowed to just sit still and consciously regulate my thoughts and emotions, although the boredom was starting to get to me.

Once Vadeem and the twins had managed to clear out all of the Stalkers in the vicinity, the remaining stragglers did not have the courage to approach our group. The atmosphere rapidly improved once it was clear that no more danger would be encountered, and soon the most devout among the group broke into song . . . if you could even call it that.

It was more like a funeral dirge than some happy camping tune, and the lyrics were . . . let's just say I was happy that the people under me were content and not paying attention to much else. Starting a cult would lead to interesting results, but maybe I'd underestimated the people's fervor and devotion a bit. Or more likely, I should have known that starting a cult of Light, where all my brainwashed followers had just endured decades of starvation and supernatural darkness, could lead to extreme behavior.

Ana and Eva got off Vadeem's shoulders and approached me. Strangely enough, these two didn't seem to treat me like a literal deity like the others did; perhaps they were simply too young and isolated to understand such things. It was honestly refreshing to have someone treat me like Normal Walter and not God Walter.

I nodded back in greeting and allowed the twins to lead me to the entrance of the first outpost soon after. Our arrival was immediately noticed by its inhabitants. A small crowd of worried warriors made a defensive line at the gate before another figure pushed their way to the front. I couldn't clearly make out the details of the new people, as my archbishop had insisted it was only proper for an envoy to greet the nonbelievers before I made an entrance. I didn't bother correcting him this time and just went back to my followers with the twins in tow.

Patar had taken a small honor guard with him to meet the other party, and after a few exchanges back and forth, his group entered the gates and disappeared into the gloom.

"What do you think they're talking about?" Vadeem asked. He had returned to the twins' side, and it seemed that they were much more amicable toward each other after the fight had concluded. One of the twins—I had to use Lucky Eyes to see that it was Eva—was even gently holding on to the side of his shirt. They tried to hide it, but I could tell that they were nervous about how we would be received by the new village.

I shrugged. "Who knows? Probably convincing the other party that a god's actually here to see them."

Vadeem chuckled. "How's the life of a god going for you, oh mighty one?"

I rolled my eyes. "It's bumpy. Damn rickshaw's worse than sitting on that tree."

"I could always pull up another one and have you sit on it," he answered with a laugh. "You could act as a human torch that way! You might not have a weapon anymore, but you can act as one! I'll swing you around and vaporize the enemies with my mighty god-club!"

I rolled my eyes again. "Ha-ha, Vadeem."

"But what are we going to do about your weapon?" Vadeem said, tone serious this time. "You can't be expected to defend yourself with that dinky knife, and I doubt your little flashlight halo's going to work on everything here."

"I gathered the pieces, or at least all the ones I could still find, so maybe someone here can repair it."

He gave me a concerned look. "In this place? Are you serious? Their best fighters are using pointed sticks and homemade bows. I don't think they even know what metal is, let alone a forge."

"Maybe Jae-Hyun can fix it when we meet up," I said. "He did make those flares."

"He made them?" Vadeem asked. I had forgotten that he couldn't see the descriptions of the items like I could. I was getting careless. Seems I was slipping up left and right with my compromised mentality.

"I figured he did," I lied. "I couldn't find anything like those flares in the store in any case. Plus, they sort of looked handmade."

Vadeem took out a flare and inspected it. Thankfully there were minor imperfections to the flare's design that were evident even from my vantage point.

"Huh," Vadeem muttered. "Maybe you're right, but making magic flares—which didn't work by the way—is one thing, but blacksmithing?"

I looked at him. "You think blacksmithing is harder than making literal magical items?"

"I don't know a thing about magic," he answered, "so maybe it's not that hard to. But blacksmithing?"

He paused and took a closer look at the gauntlets he was wearing, marveling at their design. "I know a thing or two about that subject, and let me tell you, it takes years of hard work and dedication to make even the simplest object."

He put his gauntlets away and shook his head. "And Walter, that weird whip-sword of yours is definitely not simple."

I shrugged. "You should trust in our leader more. Plus, maybe I'll find something else to fight with."

I couldn't exactly say that Jae-Hyun was probably older than all of us combined at this point. He must have experience using a forge if he wanted to repair his equipment once all the dedicated smiths had died out, and I was willing to bet good money that he could somehow fix my blade.

Vadeem didn't share my belief, not that I could really fault him.

"There's trusting someone," he said, "and then there's just being delusional. But it's not like you have any other choice. Doubt we can find extra whip blades lying around here. But hey, you can use any weapon, so there's bound to be an alternative somewhere."

I nodded, still staring off into the distance. I never knew that being a god would require so much waiting around!

"You'd think they would be faster at welcoming me," I muttered. "Damned people are keeping me waiting for too long."

"Careful, friend," Vadeem said gently. "We've only been waiting for ten minutes. You've never been this impatient before, so watch yourself, okay?"

Ten minutes? Felt like hours to me. I forced myself to calm down again.

"Thanks, Vadeem," I said, and tried to focus on anything else to pass the time. "And how are you getting along with the twins?"

Vadeem smiled and made some weird hand gestures to Ana. The girl saw his awkward gestures and looked at him in confusion before the other twin seemed to understand his intentions and helped make subtle changes to his hands. Ana nodded and reciprocated by . . . flexing her muscles and giving him a strongman pose?

"Vadeem," I asked, gawking at the scrawny girl as she gave her best Arnie impersonation, "what have you been teaching them?"

"Basic ways to greet people!" he laughed in reply, "That hand sign I did means hello, so I taught her how to give one back in our culture. Who needs to talk when you can communicate in the language of muscles?"

I looked at him in disbelief. That was considered the best way to greet people? Maybe that was why Noel got along well with him.

He grinned. "I know, it's mighty impressive progress for just a few hours of work, eh?"

"Yeah . . ." was all I managed to say before a sudden message from Jae-Hyun, this one sent party-wide, broke off the rest of my sentence.

Jae-Hyun: I'm caught up with Yoona and Noel. Walter, Vadeem, what's the status on your end?

Vadeem the Dream: We're on track with your initial plan, but there's some slight issues.

Jae-Hyun: The darkness?

Vadeem the Dream: Yeah, it's causing some weird symptoms in Walter.

Jae-Hyun: Damn it, I was hoping we would have a little longer before the first symptoms spread. Yoona's starting to feel it too. How are you holding up, Vadeem?

Vadeem the Dream: I'm fine. Walter's got a skill that's mitigating it for everyone else. It doesn't work on himself, though.

Walter's Fine: I'm fine for now. And you have any idea what's going on, Jae-Hyun?

Jae-Hyun: Yeah, unfortunately. I think I know the cause of the gloom, and how to fix it, but if its effects are taking hold this quickly, then we need to hurry.

Walter's Fine: What are the symptoms? Stop holding out information.

Vadeem the Dream: See, he's been like that for a while now.

Vadeem was right again. I took a deep breath and composed myself. Everything just felt so suffocating. It was like I wanted to do something about the situation but I just couldn't, and that annoyance was starting to bubble up from under me. I forced myself to focus.

Jae-Hyun: The flame that Walter said was extinguished was suppressing something in the Temple of Eternal Light.

Vadeem the Dream: What was it?

Jae-Hyun: It's an . . . you can think of it as an artifact. It's an object that amplifies every single emotion that touches that miasma, which is why Walter's acting so irrationally.

Walter's Fine: But why are all the villagers mutated? And why is everything dead or turned into monsters?

Jae-Hyun: Prolonged exposure to the gloom would have some dire consequences, like the mutations, but if it's only a few years that have passed, then the worst hasn't arrived yet. Unfortunately, the mutations are the least of our worries; the worst part is that it wasn't just the humans that were affected. Everything was.

Walter's Fine: Which means?

Jae-Hyun: It means that things that we would usually consider inanimate but have some spirituality or sentience will have their emotions ramped up, including the planet itself.

Well, shit, that explained Noe and the Origin Matrix acting like that. But the changes in Noe didn't quite add up. No amount of amplified emotions would change my system that drastically. It was like it had undergone an entire transformation. I felt like there was something missing in the regressor's explanation.

Vadeem the Dream: Would the planet having emotions be that bad?

Jae-Hyun: Let's put it this way, if you were Earth and your inhabitants had been abusing all of your resources for millennia, would you be happy?

Vadeem the Dream: Oh, that's not good, then. How bad are we talking about?

Jae-Hyun: It's most likely the spirits causing the worst of the mutations, so expect the worst, but it should be nothing we can't handle if Walter's information about the timing is right. Maybe some golems, infected animals, mutated creatures, that kind of thing as you get closer to the temple. Imagine evolution on steroids. If Walter pulls through, we can avoid most of the fighting and storm the front gate. If not, then things might be a bit harder for us, but I'll think of a plan B if things go awry.

Walter's Fine: I can last long enough to get you your army to take care of the small fry. How's your team holding up?

Jae-Hyun: Noel and I will be fine. We have skills that counteract the corruption. I'm worried about Yoona, but we'll be better off than your side for now. I plan to head over to the temple and see if I can't slow down the corruption a little, enough to buy you the time you need for your part.

Walter's Fine: Okay, be quick, though. Give us a timeline when you know more.

Jae-Hyun: Will do, and take care of Walter for me, Vadeem.

Vadeem the Dream: Always.

Shortly after our conversation had finished, Patar had also concluded his meeting with the other village head and was making his way back toward me. My bodyguards backed off, while the twins pulled Vadeem to the side as well. I gathered as much mental strength as I had left and hoped I could pull through for what was ahead.

"Let's go get us an army," I muttered. "And get the hell out of this damn darkness."

CHAPTER FORTY

The Spread of the Truth

O h, holy Light Bringer!" Patar greeted me with reverence. "The village has accepted your call to arms and is willing to listen to your sermon. Please show them the Light and the Truth!"

I nodded as I put on the most dignified air that I could and followed Patar and the guards toward the other village again. I had chosen to dispel my halo for the time being, mainly because I wanted to create a more dramatic entrance, but I had explained to Patar that the reason I did this was that only the worthy could look upon my Light.

He fervently agreed and jotted something down in a dirty notebook. Honestly, I thought he would fervently agree to pretty much anything I did or said at this point. I could tell him to eat dirt and he'd probably start munching away happily. Perhaps the darkness was subtly amplifying their reverence as well. If that was the case, then it'd make my job a lot easier.

Vadeem and the twins took the rearguard position, and although they were not invited to the meeting, no one dared to stand in the man's way after everyone had experienced firsthand the Vadeem style of conflict resolution. By now, Ana and Eva were practically glued to my friend's side, and people generally just treated them as one entity now. I think they were secretly happy that someone was able to deal with the dreaded Vadoom.

I turned my attention back to the task at hand and took in my surroundings.

The new village looked remarkably similar to the first one, which I must admit was to be expected, given the conditions that these people faced. The homes were made out of crude wood, with bits and pieces of the damaged parts hastily repaired. The dim torches that provided the only light in the living space provided little in the way of useful illumination, and served mostly as a beacon so that people would not lose their way.

The whole village looked like it had been repaired dozens of times over the years, and the only constant was the ever-intrusive tendrils of darkness encroaching on every surface. They swarmed and writhed as our group went ever deeper into the village, as if they could sense the arrival of the untainted. I ignored it and focused my attention on the task at hand.

Patar led me to the village center where a new group of mutated people awaited. They looked even worse off than Patar's group. Some were relatively fine, by the standards of this world, but others could hardly be considered people at this stage and looked closer to walking piles of tumors and sickly monstrosities.

One of them in particular caught my attention. This one, gender completely undeterminable, had extra lidless eyes that sprouted from their body, each one weeping tears of inky black pus. On their head grew small fingers where hair should be, and they all pointed at me upon my arrival.

It was most discomforting to look at, to say the least. I highly doubted that my halo could purify everyone here, but perhaps most could be saved.

I walked to the only raised platform in the area, careful not to damage the rotting wooden structure, and took one last look at the gathered people. Most did not look impressed, some looked hopeful, but the overwhelming majority looked indifferent. Like all the emotion was burned out of them, and they were left with nothing.

Was this what would happen to us if we stayed in the darkness for too long? To experience so much emotion to the point of numbness? What would happen to us if we failed this mission? I shuddered once again at the thought and felt a cold grip of fear twist in my stomach. I was always looking at the best possible outcome, but what about the worst?

> **Vadeem the Dream:** Walter, you're in a daze again. Snap out of it. We have a task to perform.

I shook my head forcibly and regained some clarity, then quickly nodded at the big man before addressing the crowd properly. Right, I had to focus. It was easier to control myself when I had a clear goal in mind.

"I can see the defeat in your eyes, fellow citizens of Earth!" I exclaimed, but only Patar and my guards looked properly attentive. "But the time of suffering and despair is at an end! First, let the Light of Dawn illuminate this wretched wasteland!"

I activated my halo once more, and the dreary gloom instantly vanished. Once again, the conditions of those standing closest to me began improving, their various wounds and scars already starting to heal. The ones in the distance were affected next, then farther and farther until everyone within my halo's light had their symptoms lighten even a little bit.

They looked at their healing forms in confusion at first, perhaps unsure what was going on after spending decades in a constant state of rot and decay, but the ones closest to me started to recover first. As they marveled at their regenerating bodies and clarity returned to their eyes, they stared up at me, and I finally saw that spark of reverence ignite. Good, they were not too far gone to save.

The ones farther back still had lifeless eyes, but even that was changing at a visible pace. I took advantage of this moment of awe to drive home the point about my divinity.

"Where I stand, no shadows shall lurk!" I shouted. "Where I walk, no darkness shall follow, and where I lead, no people will suffer! Do you stand with me?"

I didn't have the time to give a grand speech like I did the last time, so some of the audience was still processing the new information. However, with a little goading from Patar and his people, the first few individuals finally understood what I had asked and cheered.

That initial bastion of noise soon caused a cascade of cheers and cries of affirmation from their neighbors, and soon, the entire square was roused into worship. At this point, even the individuals farthest back had regained enough of their sanity to realize what was happening to them.

I quickly stifled the growing frustration I felt as I saw how much time these people were wasting doing nothing but cheering and crying when we could use that time to head off to the next settlement. Just thinking about what I had to do and the mountain of work that loomed ahead made me irritated. Still, I had enough control at the moment to see the folly in this type of thinking and instead redoubled my efforts with the people here. I had to tell myself that they were all needed for the upcoming trials.

"Rejoice, for my archbishop shall provide those who need it with food and water!" I continued. I had entrusted Patar with these tasks earlier, and even left him with my flask to expedite the process.

I gestured to my priest to go hand out the provisions with Vadeem. "But time is of the essence! We must journey to all the settlements of this region so that no soul is left without the embrace of dawn's light! Eat, drink, and prepare for the journey ahead. We march soon!"

Patar expertly distributed the food among the gathered people here, while one of his appointed priests was tasked with filling buckets and basins with the water from my flask. The people all received these gifts with reverence and unmistakable joy, glad to have something substantial to eat and drink after who knew how long.

I wanted to help with the moving process or help out the people left outside the village like Vadeem and the twins had, but reason won out for the first time, and I stayed on that platform. The light from my halo would indeed help cure the damage the darkness had caused, but it was not a fast process.

I had to remain behind here, but every second of inaction made me jitter and fidget. Seeing everyone else up and about, actively helping, made me desperately want to do the same. Every muscle in my body seemed to scream at me to use them, and I couldn't help but twitch uncontrollably. It took all my willpower to simply remain there on that raised dais with a blank expression. At least the gathered people were too awestruck to see how I was actually feeling at the moment.

I honestly wished we had more time to spare. I could tell that Patar and his people were exhausted, and the fatigue must have been even worse for Vadeem and the twins, who had to be constantly on alert. I even contemplated stopping here for a short while, at least a few hours, just so the most tired individuals could take a moment to nap, but after hearing about how many different settlements still remained, I had to scrap that idea. There was too much left to do with too little time, especially if the mental contamination was spreading faster as time progressed.

The village made their preparations in record time thanks to Patar and his amazing ability to organize and command the people here. He had taken it upon himself to give everyone instructions and delegated some of the easier tasks like the packing of essentials to his various helpers. Noe's ability to pick the right people for the task was unmatched.

"I . . . do my best . . ." she answered, her voice low and almost dream-like. This was another change. It appeared that her change was occurring exponentially quicker than my own.

Hey, you're not going to shut down on me, right, Noe? I asked, more than a little concerned about all these recent developments. *I still need you. You know that.*

"I would never leave . . . Walter," she answered, voice still distant. "I am still here . . . Do not worry, my host."

You take care of yourself, okay?

"I will, as I will take care of you always," she answered, and silence followed.

I tried calling her again, but no answer. I started to panic a little. Was she really okay? The changes were bad, for sure, but that didn't mean that I would be okay if my little Noe wasn't here entirely. Another gentle poke from Vadeem freed me from my ever-growing sense of unease, and I once again took a look at my current situation.

The people still huddled in my vicinity started to dissipate after they realized that the time to leave was fast approaching. As I had thought, some of the people who had the worst mutations could not recover, at least fully, even when they were near me for the full duration of my time in the square.

Those individuals who were too weak or sickly had to remain in the village, while everyone else had joined our ever-growing convoy. I didn't want to think about the fates of those who were left behind. The best I could do was leave a burning bonfire made from my lantern's light. Reluctantly, I followed Patar out of the newly abandoned village and sat back on my rickshaw.

Surprisingly, the thing had grown inside in the few hours that I had been gone, and it now required eight people to carry it properly. I even had an ornate chair to sit on now, this one covered with even more cloth and pieces of fabric. Hell, there were even a few wooden figurines of myself placed on the platform, which I could only assume were meant to be gifts. Evidently, the rest of the villagers were not slacking off in the time that I was away.

"Oh, mighty Light Bringer," Patar said as I made myself comfortable on my seat, "your new devotees are ready to move on to the next settlement. I have appointed priests and bishops to attend to the spiritual needs of the newly enlightened, so we can make all haste to the next destination."

I nodded. "And do my scouts know the location of the next settlement?"

"Yes, oh holy one, the twins will lead the new scouting party, and with the help of the mighty Vadoom, they will ensure that we are not hampered by any groups of Shadow Stalkers this time."

"Excellent," I answered. "And I have one more task for you, Patar."

He went ramrod straight, his eyes glistening in anticipation of a new task that he could perform. It was kind of eerie seeing someone literally worship every word you said. I didn't think I could ever get used to that.

"I shall endeavor to fulfill any request the holy one may have!"

"Good. I need you to speak with the others and gather as much information about the Temple of Eternal Flame, for that will be our ultimate destination. I want layouts for the temple and its surroundings, but most importantly, I want you to find out any information you can about the history of the Flames of Creation. Folklore, superstition, I don't care, just get me that information."

"Your will be done!" Patar bowed. "Information about the flames will be easy to come by, but a map of the temple . . ."

He looked like he was afraid to voice his complaint. Not that I blamed him. In his view, he was talking with a literal god. I once again cursed the fact that I had inadvertently let go of the one person who would probably have the best idea of the temple's layout. This damned darkness would be the death of me.

"You do not need to get it now, Patar," I said. "I realize that only a few would hold that kind of information. You will learn more as we convert those who live closer to the temple. For now, just gather information about the Flames, and specifically why it had to stay lit."

"By your will!"

Patar bowed low one last time and quickly disappeared from my sight. It would be another long period of time before we reached the next settlement, so I decided to take the time to close my eyes and simply meditate. After all, wasn't the core of Buddhism and the like all about controlling one's desires? The eightfold path and whatnot? I wasn't in any way spiritual, but if people had been meditating for centuries, then there must be some merit to it, even if it was only to calm the mind and remove distracting emotions. This was the perfect time to try.

You would think that just emptying your brain would be easy, yet it was anything but. Honestly, I was just very bad at it at first, having random thoughts and worries constantly filling my brain, always seeking to draw my thoughts into something new and wild. It was impossible to clear my head for more than a few seconds at first, but I had a lot of time to practice. And when you had nothing else to do but practice one thing and one thing only, learning something became a lot easier.

By the time we had converted the fourth village, I was able to clear my thoughts with little difficulty and remain that way for a length of time, and by the eighth, I was comfortable spending the majority of my time in a meditative state. The time that I spent on the road and giving sermons seemed to blur together as I went from one village to another. It was always the same reaction, the same routine, and it was utterly predictable.

Patar would always enter first, then I would go and give a speech, then came the cries of joy and cheers of adoration, followed by a length of time healing under my light before heading out again. The process had become so streamlined that no verbal communications were needed as we approached a new village, as everyone went to their assigned roles automatically.

I hadn't even noticed when the last of the outposts on the edge of the forest were converted, my memories of this time cloudy, but soon, with a force of a few thousand, we were fast approaching the boundary between relative safety and the dangers of the Neverglow Woods. The time for us to delve into those uncharted territories was fast approaching, and I could only hope that I was ready for what awaited us there.

CHAPTER FORTY-ONE

Prelude to the Depths

The final preparations were taking place before we began the next part of our journey, and I was left with nothing to do once again. It allowed me some time to review the events of the last few days. First of all, our convoy had grown to numbers that hadn't been seen in this world for decades, and the size of the group had long since eclipsed the diameter of illumination that my halo could provide.

The fact that I could still function after all this time was because of a few things I had learned. Meditation was now a key part of my routine, but I also found I could function best when I kept my mind focused solely on the various tasks at hand, no matter how small or trivial that would be. If I allowed my mind to wander even slightly, I risked being overcome by emotion, and Vadeem could snap me out of one of those spells only so many times because he was out of sight most of the time.

What was surprising, however, was that during my sessions of meditation, one of my skills had upgraded. I guess hard work, no matter what kind, pays off eventually. It was my innate talent, the one that was first unlocked by Noe. My old skill, Calm Mind, had somehow turned into something new altogether.

> **Awakening Mind (B-rank Innate Passive):** User has endured many hardships of the spirit and has gained a supernaturally resilient mind. User can use their willpower to temporarily overcome cognitive disruptions and can think logically in almost any situation.

I hadn't even known that skills could be upgraded, but Noe did not respond when I asked her to explain what was going on. Noe rarely talked much these days. In fact, not very many people talked to me these days. Vadeem had been more than busy acting as our vanguard to chat with me, and aside from the regular updates from the regressor's side, I had been left mostly to myself. It allowed me a lot of time to get used to that new skill, and to observe my new surroundings with renewed clarity.

Patar had given the orders for each individual village to rotate their positions within the convoy so that each person could take their turn to recover under my light. Every time a new group came over, a representative would bring me one of their most treasured possessions—which generally amounted to shiny trinkets and the like—and the amount of junk that had accumulated at the foot of my rickshaw was starting to become a problem.

In fact, even the size of the platform I was sitting on had grown to almost impractical proportions. Each time I entered a village, the people who stayed behind would "upgrade" the thing, and now I had to be carried by no less than fourteen people. There was a small shrine located directly below my new throne, and an entire squad of the various village elites were tasked with guarding me. It was honestly too much.

My small army seemed to be all but ready to move out, but I had to stop them and order everyone to rest before we made our final push into the unknown. Fatigue had built up to levels that were intolerable even for these brainwashed cultists, and I couldn't afford for them to make lapses in judgment when we were heading into hostile territory.

Patar and quickly ordered his group to set up small camping sites along a clearing just outside of the Neverglow Woods, and soon hundreds of small fires lit up the gloomy forest floor like little orange stars. I noticed small patrol groups stationed around our perimeter, but that was mainly for show. Vadeem had been very thorough with the monster smashing, and our group had swelled so much in size that nothing had even tried to attack us for days.

With the people so close to the Promethean fire, I had the rare opportunity to turn off my halo and finally relax with Vadeem and the twins. Everyone else was a respectable distance away from our group, while a few solitary guards kept the more crazed devotees at bay. Patar was the only one who didn't seem to be doing much resting, but I allowed him to do what he wanted.

"How are you holding up, Walter?" Vadeem asked as he grilled a sausage on a stick. He had several roasting by the fire and handed one of the cooked ones to the girls.

"Better," I answered, and grabbed a warm cup of tea by the embers. "What

I had to do became pretty automatic near the end, and I've been meditating when we're on the move. It helps."

The big man laughed. "And here I thought you were just sleeping."

The twins each took a sausage and ate quietly by Vadeem's side. They were still oddly expressionless, even though I knew that they were really enjoying the food. At least Noe's passive abilities still worked even when she was in hibernation.

"Tell me honestly," Vadeem said again, "do you think our little group of soldiers can do what Jae-Hyun needs? The reports that we've been getting have been . . ."

I winced. The regressor had arrived at the temple a while ago, but what he saw was far from comforting. The front of the entrance was, by his estimation, defended by at least a few thousand mutants of varying degrees of horrible. His descriptions of the creatures sounded like he was reading off of the character sheets from D&D monsters. I looked back at my ragtag warriors and didn't like our odds. We needed a lot more soldiers.

I sighed. "Yeah, it's not looking good."

"So we have to hope for the best with the city in the depths of the forest, then," Vadeem answered. He took a few more snacks from his suitcase and placed them near the fire to cook.

"We'd need a lot more in that case." I shook my head. "Either way, we'll need our rest and energy then. This will probably be the last bit of peace and quiet for a while."

He nodded, and we spent the rest of that evening in silence. The anticipation of the coming ordeal was an ever-looming concern, and my meditations did little to assuage the dread. I tried to rest as much as I could in any case, and eventually, exhaustion won out and I passed out for just a little bit.

A distant bell tolled, awakening me from my slumber. I saw that I was the last one to wake up, as every other able-bodied man and woman was preparing for the departure. Looking at things, it seemed like it would only be minutes before we departed now. I hurried to my feet and reoriented myself, shaking my head and focusing on my present situation again.

Once I was feeling relatively awake, I remembered that there was one thing that I wanted to check out before I went in further, which was the new ability I had unlocked through my soul title. It had seen a rapid growth spurt partly from my own endeavors, and partly from this mysterious prophet figure who was spreading my worship in some other place. My new title looked like this:

> **Primary Soul Title:** Level 10 Xollon Idol [Devourer of Truth]
> Progress to next level: 55,402/100,000
> Progression requirements: Have 100,000 individuals idolize you
> **Title Passives:**
> Xollon Anatomy Stage 1: Your body has begun to incorporate a Xollon's internal anatomy. You take 10% reduced damage from all sources and are unaffected by most poisons.
> Xollon Physiology Stage 1: Your body has started to incorporate a Xollon's external anatomy. You can utilize and extend your primary feelers through your human hands.
> **Title Skills:**
> Idol's Voice (Soul Passive)
> Secondary Xollon Form (Level 10 Soul Active): The user assumes the secondary form of the Xolloid race. The user gains all the physical characteristics of the race and will have all physical attributes increase by a factor of 5 for the duration of the skill.
> **Transformation Time:** 6 hours
> **Cooldown:** 12 hours

Aside from the fact that the cooldown didn't seem to be going down anymore, twelve hours seemed to be the minimum that it could reach, and with the increased skill duration, a new passive had popped up. I forced myself not to think about any of the implications of those titles and only on their practicality. I could worry about everything else when my emotions were not all over the place.

I had noticed earlier, after one of my many meditation sessions, that a strange gash had formed on the palms of my hand. It was near undetectable to anyone else, appearing like one of the natural wrinkles on my hand, but I knew that it wasn't there before, and I could feel something wiggling just underneath the surface. It had taken me a moment to figure out what had happened before I saw the levels I had gained with my soul title.

Noe had long since stopped giving me notifications, but I knew instinctively that she was still with me. It was lonely without her.

Once again, I did not allow myself to think about the implications of Noe's absence, choosing instead to simply focus on the raw data. It was tiring going from one extreme to another, to go from feeling so much emotion to the forced nothingness that I was enduring now. I sighed and chose to not dwell on it.

Checking to make sure that no one was looking too closely at me, I looked at that new gash in my hand and tried to move the wiggling sensation underneath the skin. As if it was the most natural thing in the world, no different from taking a step forward with my legs or lifting a cup of coffee to drink with my arms, the gash opened up, and a slender Xollon feeler appeared. It was the same one I had when I activated my soul title's skill, albeit shrunken down a considerable bit.

Yet it felt just as deadly. I could feel its deadly serrations and sheer power, and just like how I could always feel where my arms were without looking at them, I knew that I could stretch my new feelers out to several meters.

A wave of uncontrollable joy started to spread in me, but once again I closed my eyes and forced those feelings away. It had become more manageable ever since I had obtained that skill upgrade, but I felt my willpower quickly being sapped from the constant need to regulate my emotions. Whatever was causing Noe to change so quickly was affecting the speed that I experienced these changes as well, but at least I now had a way to mitigate some of that.

I had to remind myself that I had only obtained a new tool, nothing more, nothing less. I just needed to come up with an explanation as to why I had tentacles growing out of my hands, but any number of reasons could be used, such as gaining a new skill through level-ups or simply getting a new title due to all the worship I was receiving. I doubt even the regressor would have made the connection between a weak human being and the godlike Xollons off a single tentacle.

"Hey, Walter, just wanted to check up on you before we head off," Vadeem said as he approached my side with the twins in tow. Lately those two followed the big man like baby chicks. I had no idea that he was so good with dealing with children, and he was even able to develop a rudimentary method of communication. I would have been more impressed, however, had his new sign language consisted of more things than the flexing of random muscle groups.

The twins, and most of my followers now that I thought about it, had improved dramatically over the course of our travels. Not fully healed, that would take a lot longer, but better. The twins now had a healthy, albeit pale, complexion, and I could see the stubble forming on their heads where new hair was growing. Their faces were still marred by some of the oldest scars, but the worst of the damage had been fixed, and they wouldn't be too eye-catching even in modern society. These changes also made me finally realize just how young they actually were. No wonder Vadeem was so protective of them.

And it was under his care that they had even regained some of their lost weight. The food from his storage had done wonders. However, while the mutations might have disappeared, the damage done to their vocal cords or mentality could not be fixed. They were still always on edge, although I could see that they allowed themselves some rest when Vadeem was near.

"Walter?" Vadeem asked again, seeing that I was still deep in thought. "Should I come back later?"

"No, sorry, Vadeem," I answered as I snapped out of my lingering thoughts. "What did you say again?"

Vadeem showed a concerned look but quickly caught himself and changed back to his usual jovial smile. It was clear that he didn't want to concern me any more than necessary, given my unnatural state.

"Just wanted to see how you were doing was all," he said, tone light. "Glad to see you managed to get some good sleep in before we left."

I smiled back. "Yeah, although you should have woken me up earlier."

My friend chuckled. "We all thought you might need the extra rest. You didn't miss anything, so don't worry."

"Thanks," I said. "It's . . . exhausting trying to keep my emotions in check all the time."

He nodded. "Hear anything new about Jae-Hyun and the others?"

"No." I shook my head. "At least, nothing new. Last time he checked in with me, he said they were at the temple, but he'll be busy for a while. He wouldn't give me any specifics, but he never does. Communication's been scarce since. He say anything to you specifically?"

"Nope." He sighed. "It's pretty much the same. But don't you find it weird that only Jae-Hyun's talking in the party chat? I can understand Yoona staying quiet, but Noel?"

I frowned. That *was* strange. Noel wasn't one to stay quiet in any situation, yet I hadn't heard from her since the start of the trial. But Jae-Hyun had said that he managed to find the others, and there was no reason for him to lie, especially when it came to his sister's well-being.

"The whole situation's already messed up," I answered. "I think Jae-Hyun's dealing with as much, if not more, trouble than we are. Let's just focus on our part and trust that our leader will fix things on his end. We'll know everything once we meet up in any case."

"Not much else we can do," he grumbled. "Just remember to keep things in perspective. Our little army . . ."

I nodded and cut him off. "I know the expectations. I won't let it affect my emotions."

"All right," he said tentatively. "Just stay close to me. You still don't have a weapon."

"No," I answered, "I have that part covered as well."

I help my hands palm facing skyward and willed the feeler to exit my flesh. The black limb moved rhythmically, oozing some of the classic Xolloid secretions and looking deadly. My tentacle wiggled a few inches out of my palms before I allowed them to retract back into my arm.

Vadeem took a step back with a terrified look of concern on his face. He stared at the tentacle before eyeing me up and down with a grimace. Even the twins showed a rare hint of worry in their eyes.

"Walter . . ." Vadeem said, teeth clenched. "Our situation might be worse than I thought."

"It's just from a skill," I said, unsure why he was acting that way, "and now I have a way to defend myself."

"Just from a skill? Growing black tentacles out of your arms is a skill?"

"It's from the title I got from the villagers' worship," I clarified.

Vadeem took a deep breath, his face still showing immense concern, but finally nodded. "Yes, from the worship of mutated villagers in a world consumed by supernatural darkness! How are you so unconcerned?"

He took another deep breath before composing himself. "Never mind, we can discuss this after we're done here, when we're out of this damned void. We'll get you properly checked out then. It's clearly affecting you in more than one way. I know you can't emote right now, but . . . Forget it, now's not the time."

I looked at him in confusion, unsure what he meant, but quickly shook that thought out of my head. I could worry about Vadeem's concerns later.

The last of the able-bodied fighters were in place, and it was finally time for us to enter the Neverglow Woods proper. I took my position at the front of the gathered people, ignoring the whispers of awe and worship, and addressed the gathered warriors one final time.

"My followers!" I said, trying to infuse as much awe into my voice as I could. "We now march toward the abyss! Be prepared for anything, but know that we all stand ready to face the darkness and bring light to the last bastions of humanity! We march to bring light back to this world!"

The last sounds of cheers faded, and I took the first step into the unknown.

CHAPTER FORTY-TWO

The Depths Part 1

The group of five hundred or so fighters that accompanied us into the forest depths was dispatched into smaller groups of ten, as having such a huge amount of people trying to pass through dense foliage was impractical, not to mention dangerous. Vadeem and I were in the lead group, along with the twins and Patar's chosen elite bodyguards. The archbishop himself was leading the rearguard.

The plan was for me to act as a guiding beacon so that none of the others would get lost. It did mean that not everyone was bathed in my halo's light, but those not in my light had torches lit by my lantern that would at least slow down this world's weird corruption. The plan was relatively simple: our best scouts and trackers were to go ahead and keep the rest of us on the right path toward the mythical city within the depths while I followed behind.

I had my doubts about finding one city within so much forest, but Patar had assured me that they were confident in their ability to locate this city. He and his people had been busy gathering all the information on its whereabouts using the accounts of the survivors and historical documents. Either way, we had to press on into the void.

The atmosphere changed almost the second we walked past some invisible threshold. The ever-present gloom seemed to thicken, and even my halo's light was barely able to penetrate the growing darkness. The light radius was visibly getting smaller and smaller as we went deeper, and soon it was about half the size before stabilizing. Now I could barely make out the light of the torches from the groups behind us, and I felt my mind slip out of control almost the second I allowed my focus to falter. It was clear that the contamination was stronger the closer we got to its source.

Soon, even the sounds of our footsteps were starting to fade, and by the time the last group entered the depths, I could hear almost nothing from the people not in my immediate vicinity. It was almost like the air was alive with malevolence, trying its best to extinguish the last of the hope in this world.

What was worse, however, was the constant feeling of being watched. It was like the forests had grown invisible, judgmental eyes on every surface, and it was just waiting for a moment of weakness to pounce. Everyone was on edge, and even Vadeem's usual calm was broken. We were all just waiting for the first sign of trouble.

It wasn't long before we got our wish. It wasn't our group that was hit first, but one of the ones in the back. A muffled cry followed by half-hearted chittering stopped us in our tracks, and that was when we spotted the foe. Just outside of my illumination were numerous hovering figures, the only visible features their huge compound eyes glinting in the halo's light. They stayed out of sight, waiting, as if they were studying us.

I hated it, this constant waiting for something to happen gnawing on my already-tense nerves. I wanted to just scream into the void and meet whatever was stalking us head on. Anything was better than just staying still while our enemies lurked in the shadows.

I got my wish, and soon the first one came into view and graced us with its disturbing visage. It was large, perhaps the same size as Vadeem's normal form, and its sinewy muscles told of deadly strength. It had the head and torso of a grasshopper or a similar insect, with massive mandibles gnawing and chewing, while massive mantis-like claws moved in a twitching fashion. Below its body were humanlike legs, although these limbs were elongated and its calf muscles so swollen that it looked to be on the cusp of busting apart. And as with everything else here, its body was pitch black to blend into its surroundings.

Ah . . . evolution on steroids. Right.

Like those Shadow Stalkers from earlier, these insectoids seemed afraid of entering the light at first, hesitating at the edge. But unlike the earlier Stalkers, these monsters did not burn under the glow of my halo. Vadeem had already swapped to his massive battle form, with the twins quickly jumping onto his shoulders, and as if that was the signal to fight, the first of the bug people pounced on our group. I freed my new feelers and had to bite my lips to control my mounting anticipation. It seemed that battle did intensify whatever changes were occurring within me.

First of all, these bug things were fast. They moved with a quick contraction of their hind legs, followed by a click as their muscles locked into place, before releasing that stored energy to pounce with a speed that defied logic. The first individual it struck didn't even have the time to react before she was pulverized into a fleshy pulp.

This served as a wake-up call for all those present, and the next few that dashed into our group missed their targets. For all the speed that they possessed, they were still predictable. And just like the grasshoppers they mimicked, they could only move in one direction, and their pounce was telegraphed by the retraction of their legs. Not that it did any good for the people who were struck from behind or from their blind spots.

Analyzing the battlefield, I saw an opportunity and intersected one of the beast's charges with a feeler. I watched in awe as it impaled itself on the tentacle and slowly died. I grinned, and with a flick of my wrist, I threw the still-twitching body crashing into another of its brethren. My Xollon limbs were a lot stronger than these awful creatures' exoskeletons.

My feelers moved at an unnatural speed, faster than I could ever swing my arms or legs, yet its movement felt as natural as any other part of my body. I was able to contort the limb into fluid shapes that caught the bug things off guard, impaling them from angles that they couldn't see. I used them like whips, interrupting the monsters' movements where I could, while other times I used them like spears, impaling any that had already started their dash. The ones closest to me couldn't properly jump at us, which allowed the other fighters to land solid blows of their own.

One by one, I picked out my targets and allowed those black tendrils to track down their positions, always looking for the ones in the middle of preparing for a charge, or ones who had their backs turned away from me. My feelers worked with deadly efficiency, and that made me wonder about the nature of these new limbs. And these were simply the diminished version of an actual Xollon feeler. What would it look like if I was complete?

And not only were my tentacles strong, they were supernaturally tough as well. Even when those bug things crashed into them at full speed, I felt little in the way of recoil, let alone pain or discomfort. I could pick them up easily with the feelers, and these things must weigh quite a bit given their muscle mass. Was I getting stronger, or was it just some yet-unknown perk of having the ability?

I desperately wanted to check out my own stats, but since Noe's slumber, I couldn't access anything aside from the displayed luck charges. I couldn't deactivate the skill without her here, but seeing the little numbers in the corner of my eye provided me with some semblance of comfort at the very least. As long as those numbers did not disappear, then I knew that Noe was still with me, even if I couldn't speak with her.

"Lord God!" a voice said in desperation, and I stopped my thoughts to see who it was that interrupted my musings.

In the corner of my eye, I saw that a bug monster had managed to sneak behind me, and it was charging full force in my direction. I froze up, unable to think about what I could do. It was too fast for me to dodge, and my feelers were too far away to defend my weak human body. Would Noe still protect me even in her slumber?

I didn't have to find out, because the brave individual who shouted drove into the charging bug and managed to divert its path. The man himself didn't survive the impact. I looked down and quickly finished off the disoriented monster, but my gaze kept going back to the man who died to save me. Yet again, I had allowed myself to be distracted in the midst of battle, and again someone else had to pay for my mistake.

More and more emotions started to fill me, almost to the point of bursting, but I forced my eyes away from the body and back onto the battlefield. The insect monster had grazed my shoulder when it passed through, and a gash had formed where its scythe claws bit into my flesh.

I concentrated on the pain, using it as a distraction from all the emotions desperately trying to free themselves from my control. I had expected things to get worse during battle, but I had underestimated how bad things would be. I redoubled my concentration and promised myself that I would find out who this man was, and properly pay tribute to him once this was done.

My other bodyguards weren't slacking off either, and after seeing my close encounter, they had formed a new line of defense centered around my sides and back, where I was most vulnerable.

This allowed me to focus the bulk of my attention on offense. The insectoids were, thankfully, not the smartest foe, but even with their limited intelligence, they figured out that my tentacles were the main threat—if you discounted Vadeem destroying hordes of them off in the distance, but it seemed like he was the hunter and they the prey in that situation.

Their initial attempts to slice through my feelers proved to be impractical, and they had instead focused their attention on dodging or staying out of range of them. This was fine with me, as it left a 4-meter radius of relative calm around me, and the more wounded of my fighters used that space to try to recover some of their strength. Still, the vast majority of the fighting forces could not take advantage of this and were taking heavy losses.

Then a thought occurred to me. These creatures were avoiding me because they could see my tentacles coming, but what if they couldn't? The insect monstrosities were learning to avoid my strikes, but they relied heavily on sight. They never seemed to avoid my attacks when I struck them from their blind spots, regardless of how much noise my feelers made. Given how durable my Xollon appendages were, I had something that I wanted to test out.

With my left feeler, I drove it hard into the ground and was pleasantly surprised when I saw that I could move through the dirt with relative ease. I tunneled under one of the creatures who was engaged in a fight with one of my bodyguards, and with as much force and speed as I could muster, I made the limb erupt from the ground.

A look of surprise flashed through the face of the human fighter as my feeler drove through the monster's body and into its head, before quickly burrowing back under the ground. It took a moment for the soldier to understand what had happened, and she quickly gave me a nod of appreciation before engaging the next foe.

As I thought, this tunneling tactic of mine seemed to work the best. Without the visible threat of the feelers, more and more of the creatures came back within striking distance of me, and I impaled one foe after another. They didn't seem to understand or care about the deaths of their comrades. Before long, we were on the offensive against the bug things. It didn't take us too long to rout them after their momentum was lost, and soon we had regrouped to count the losses.

Those in the back suffered the heaviest casualties, but all things considered, it wasn't total devastation like I had feared. After meeting up with all of the groups, we tallied the damage and the reports indicated a loss of fifty-two fighters, with a few more wounded.

Vadeem walked toward me after he saw that I was done speaking with the various leaders, looking no worse for wear. "Damn, Walter, I know I still have my doubts about these changes in you, but those creepy tentacles of yours were deadly!"

I noticed that the twins weren't with him this time. "Thanks. And where are the girls?"

"They're with the rest of our scouts, went ahead somewhere but I've no idea why or for what," he replied. "What I wouldn't give to have your ability to understand their language."

"It is useful," I said with a smile. "But—"

I didn't get to finish my words as I heard faint gasps of shock from the men standing beside me before their bodies thumped to the ground. That's when I saw something metallic shoot right toward my face. It was an arrow. The same one that took out the people by my side.

Time seemed to slow down as I took in everything before my eyes.

I couldn't move.

I couldn't send my feelers out fast enough.

And worse still, Noe hadn't done anything to save me from that earlier run-in with the monster.

But just when I had given up all hope, something ridiculous happened. It seemed that Noe hadn't abandoned me, although the results of her intervention this time might not be a lot better.

CHAPTER FORTY-THREE

The Depths Part 2

I saw the arrow approach in minute detail, its deadly point reaching ever closer to my face, but that all changed when my luck charges took a huge dip. My perception was still slowed down from my perceived demise, and I saw that the arrow started to degrade and break apart as it inched closer. It was as if the wood and metal had somehow formed microscopic fissures in its design before breaking.

In mere moments, the arrow that would have ended my life turned into nothing but motes of dust, and I swear that for a fraction of a second, those dust particles dispersed in such the perfect way that they spelled a message:

Awaken.

Did Noe want me to wake her up from her sleep? But how? I wished she'd spelled out detailed instructions while she was at it, but that would be asking for too much. At least I knew that she was still around, somewhere out there.

And just as quickly as that message formed, it disappeared into the wind, and I was left questioning if everything that I just saw was simply a figment of my imagination. Yet the next event left no room for interpretation.

The second the last bit of dust drifted into the darkness, a sudden flash of blinding light assaulted our group, followed by an earth-shaking boom of thunder that sounded more like the bellow of a raging demon than a mere thunderclap.

We all turned toward the direction of the sound, and the afterimage of a massive lightning strike was still lingering in the distance. It was clear that the lightning had struck in the direction where those arrows came from. Whatever tried to kill me had angered the slumbering system, and as much as I wanted to thank her for saving my life, the way she did it left much to be desired. Vadeem stood at my side, lost in thought.

He had seen the whole series of events play out, and he was giving me a look of questioning. I didn't think I could explain this situation away by simply saying that I had a skill for it, but the big man had the presence of mind to understand that those questions could be asked later. For now, our survival was key, and all else could wait. I could only hope that I'd think of a satisfactory answer when the time came.

The shock of such a seemingly impossible event left the gathered people stunned, but soon cries of worship filled the air once more.

"The Light Bringer's wrath!" they cried. "It is the wrath of God!"

"Oh, holy God, please smite our enemies!"

"Smite the unbelievers!"

"How dare they try to harm our God!"

And on and on they droned. It took Patar a good while to calm down his people, but the fervor in their eyes never left even once the battle companies were reestablished. Many had already forgotten about their losses and looked eager to crusade forth.

While Patar was going around and reestablishing order, the twins—who rejoined us quickly after that initial assault—were tasked with leading a scout team to check out the epicenter of the lightning strike. Vadeem had gone with them to serve as a guard, but he gave me a strange look of worry before leaving with them. I tried to gesture that everything was still fine and under control, but I doubt he believed me.

I had my own task to do as well. I took a look at the other arrows that had missed their targets and struck the ground. There had been something strange about them when I first saw them, but I couldn't quite put my finger on what that was then. It wasn't until this moment of relative calm that I realized why.

The arrowheads were made of metal.

Almost everything that I had seen used by the inhabitants of this world was made of wood and stone, and not even the cookware was made out of any metallic substance. So how did these arrows come to be?

I took a closer look at these arrows and saw that they were expertly crafted. All three of the surviving arrows looked the same, a clear sign of manufacturing, which meant that they were not handmade. The fletching was put into place with care, and the entire shaft was sturdy and aerodynamic.

In fact, they kind of looked like the arrows that Yoona used. No, I turned them around a bit and saw that they were *exactly* the same as hers. Yet it certainly couldn't have been her shooting at us. It just meant that the arrows had to have come from Central. To double-check, I used the Lucky Eyes to see if I could get any more information about them.

> **Hunter's Arrow (E rank)**
> **Description:** We see you, Walter. There is no place to escape, no way to hide. We know. You are not forgiven. You will fail.

> **Hunter's Arrow (E rank)**
> **Description:** Your struggle is meaningless. Give in, give up. We hunt, and we hate, and we will destroy.

> **Hunter's Arrow (E rank)**
> **Description:** Your light will fade, and your dream will end, and dusk will fall. We accept neither compromise nor competition. We do not forget.

Well, now it was clear where these arrows came from. It seemed that the Trash Matrix had finally taken it upon itself to act, but what did the description of that last arrow mean? What dream was ending? Was it talking about me, or Noe, or was it simply unable to separate the two? I was pretty sure I had some random skill that obscured my information being seen, so was that affecting Origin as well?

I cursed at how little I still knew about the damn situation. It seemed that for every question I had answers to, five more unknowns popped up.

There was something distinctly unique about Noe, and I needed to find out what that was. I'd been taking her for granted so far, and I finally saw that I never tried to understand the system and just chalked her existence up as another part of the crazy trials. I had thought that I only needed to survive these trials, but I was clearly mistaken. I would lose too much if I simply chose to ignore all else and focus solely on survival. I needed to take the initiative and find out more about my situation.

And as if some unknown being heard my pleas, an opportunity to do just that appeared. Perhaps it was Noe helping me out once more, although no luck charges were expanded this time.

"Lord Walter," Q's voice sounded in my mind. "You need not answer if others are with you, but I have some important news that I must share."

I gave a small nod, although I wasn't sure if Q could see me or not. The whole situation had gotten so out of control that I wasn't sure what the limitations were on Central's side.

Q continued in either case. "I've managed to uncover some of the abnormalities around the Origin Matrix. Not everything, mind you, but at least I had some clues as to why it was acting so strangely now."

I looked around the clearing and saw that most of the people around me were still busy. Some were tending to the wounded, others were down on their knees in worship, and the majority of the gathered were getting ready to move out again. I had a little bit of time to myself at least, so I went to a dark corner away from the crowd, took out some food, and pretended to eat. No one usually bothered me when they saw I was eating, and I needed to speak with Q.

"I can talk for a while," I whispered, making sure once more that no one could overhear me. "Tell me what you found."

"Origin's detected a major threat to Central's stability in that world you're in, which is why I suspect it sent you and the anomaly over. It . . . it might be related to the incident ten cycles ago."

I was starting to suspect more and more that the threat that Origin was trying to get rid of was, in fact, me, or perhaps Noe more specifically, but I chose to keep that theory to myself. No need to correct a misconception that worked in my favor. Best to just let Q think that it was Jae-Hyun's fault that we were dragged into these strange situations.

Q continued, "There's a shard of something ancient that was recently unsealed, and my readings show that the shard is trying to establish communications with its main body. I believe that the darkness is the result of those attempts. I am unsure if it is succeeding in those transmissions, but it is causing instability in doing so."

I frowned. Was that shard a part of Noe? Was that why she was asking me to wake her up?

"Whatever it's trying to do, Origin is not happy about it, hence why you and your group were sent. This might be why the anomaly was introduced in the first place. I'm sure that if you manage to destroy or contain the shard, Origin will return to normal."

"How can you be sure it'll go back to normal?" I asked.

"The higher-ups have been trying to reboot our site's Origin server, but that darkness you've been experiencing is interfering with any of our attempts to do so. Nothing should be able to interfere with our access to the Matrix, but it's as if Origin itself is disallowing our engineers from fixing it."

Huh, it seemed that Q's side of things wasn't privy to the emotional amplification of the shard or the sentient nature of Origin itself. There appeared to be a distinct disconnect between the regressor's information and Central's.

Both sides only knew a portion of the truth, and I was in the perfect position to learn all of it.

"Do you know anything else about this shard? Are there more of them?"

"That's all I know, and perhaps there are others out there, but I've found no indication of such," he answered, tone slightly angry. "All I could uncover is that this shard is old, it's powerful, and Origin views it as a major threat to Central as a whole."

"But surely the Origin Matrix should know more about the shard and this situation. Why not ask it?"

"Lord Arbiter," Q said, confused, "only ten cycles have passed since your return, but our technology hasn't improved that much. You should know that Origin does not have the ability to directly communicate with anyone."

Shit, I messed up. I still wasn't thinking straight, but I hadn't misspoken so badly that I couldn't recover.

"Sorry," I said, "This whole situation's getting to me."

"I understand," he replied.

But wait, the Trash Matrix did talk to me, maybe not directly, but those damn item and title descriptions were clearly aimed my way. Did that mean that Q and his staff couldn't even see the same information that I could? Some more food for thought.

"Anyway," I continued, "I'm already investigating this shard, and it's proving to be more difficult to access than initially thought. Is there anything you can do to assist?"

"Not directly," Q answered apologetically. "As I said before, our ability to interfere in that dimension is extremely limited, just communicating with you like this is stretching my abilities. I can't even send over small objects, let alone personnel without destroying the stability of the whole dimension."

"So what can you do for me?"

"I believe that you will most likely need to enter your secondary form for what's to come, which would be most problematic if you are seen using it as you guide and observe the anomaly."

"That is true." I nodded.

"I have a solution for that," he said, and I could hear the smile in his voice. "I can enchant your human guise so that your secondary form will appear to look like a Xolloid spawn."

"A Xolloid spawn?"

"Ah, sorry, I forgot that you were not here for so long. That is what aspirants turn into when they accept a sponsorship from Lord Rogue, before they, uh . . ."

"Before they go insane?"

"Yes," Q continued. "But appearing as one should help to explain why you can change forms since you indeed have a sponsorship from the Lord General. And do not worry, Walter, the change is purely cosmetic."

I smiled. It seemed the universe wasn't completely hostile to me. I was worried about how I would explain all these changes that were happening to me, now that Vadeem had seen practically everything, and the sponsorship was the perfect excuse. I just had to spin it in a way that benefitted me the most, and I'd be set. And even better still, with this enchantment, I could finally use the most powerful tool at my disposal.

I spoke to Q before the sense of relief and joy could overcome me. "Yes, do so."

A small, almost imperceptible ripple opened in the air around me, and a tiny ray of silver light shot through the gap. It entered my right arm, and almost immediately I felt its effect. An agonizing pain shot through me, and I had to bite my knuckles to stop myself from screaming. The pain lasted what seemed like a lifetime, but eventually, it faded and my arm was left numb. I pulled up my sleeve to see what had happened.

On my right arm was an intricate tattoo, its design a series of tight, neat writing inked in a language that I couldn't read. The writing spiraled from my wrist and covered the entirety of my right shoulder. I wanted to know what it read, but Noe wasn't doing her usual translating here. Maybe I'd be able to see what was written when she was back online.

I turned my attention back to Q. "Thank you, this will prove useful. Is there anything else to report?"

"Yes . . ." Q said slowly. "Due to this unique situation, many of our sponsors, including the Lord General and Lord Babylon, have filed official complaints to the tribunal. These disruptions have had an immensely adverse effect on our normal operations, and someone's needed to smooth over the concerns of our shareholders and sponsors."

Oh . . . I didn't like where this was going.

"You have been summoned as the official representative of Central."

CHAPTER FORTY-FOUR

The Depths Part 3

Damn it, just when one thing was going my way, something else had to come along and ruin it all. I doubted I could say no to an official summons from this mysterious Central, and I was also bound to meet up with people who knew the original Arbiter W. And on top of it all, I'd have to use up another one of my precious Soul Title Preview tickets, so if I didn't get through this tribunal thing within twenty-four hours, or forty-eight hours if I was forced to use both tickets, then my cover as an arbiter would be all but shattered.

"When is the summons?" I asked, and it took every ounce of my being to keep from screaming in frustration.

"It will be held after this situation is resolved," Q said. "I apologize for burdening you with more unnecessary work."

"It's fine," I muttered. "And it's not like you were the one who's forcing more work on my plate. How long would this take? You know that I can't neglect my duties as an aspirant now that I have infiltrated the anomaly's party."

"I am unsure, my lord," Q said hesitantly. "But it shouldn't keep you from your other duties for long. I will do my best to express your need to expedite the process."

"Do so," I said firmly. "And thank you again for the assistance. I'll be busy for a while."

"Understood, Arbiter W."

The static feedback disappeared, which told me that I was alone once more. I finished the food I had and took a swig of water before heading back toward my gathered people. Most of them had finished their own tasks and were waiting patiently for me to come back. Patar saw me coming and immediately came to greet me.

"My lord God," my archbishop said, handing me a small piece of fabric. "The scouts found this at the site of your wrath. There were signs of injury, but no bodies were found. It appears that our assassin escaped. I apologize for allowing such a thing to happen! I shall reflect on this error in earnest!"

I nodded and took the rag from his hand. Some of it was singed off from the impact of the lightning, but even though it was damaged, I could tell that it was the kind of rough fabric that was commonly worn by this world's inhabitants. This meant that my attacker was someone from this world and not another aspirant, yet it had access to Central's equipment somehow. I frowned. All the signs pointed toward the fact that Origin was arming people and sending them my way, much like what I was doing on my end.

Well, if it wanted a war, then I'd give that goddamn Trash Matrix a war. I wasn't sure if it was actively indoctrinating natives into fighting me, or if it only had access to a few devout followers, but it didn't matter. I had all the tools I needed, and I did not for a second doubt that my ability to brainwash people was inferior to theirs. I was tired of being on the defensive; I'd bring the fight to it.

"Patar," I growled in barely suppressed fury, "there are heretics about who wish us harm. Warn the faithful that there are those out there who aim to stop our light; we go toward hostile territory."

"I will pass the word down, my lord! Your faithful shall not allow such scum to exist before your path! Say the word, and we shall destroy all who stand in your way."

Patar bowed low, and I dismissed the man. He hurriedly left to convey my message to the rest of the people. I saw him hurry off to shout more orders at the gathered people. He was remarkably efficient at his job, but I guess I had Noe to thank for that. She always knew the best route to take in any situation, and I missed knowing that she always had my back. I hoped she's resting easy now.

The convoy was able to reconvene in short order, and we were marching toward the supposed settlement within the hour. I wanted to say that our march was free of issues, but that would be far from the truth. We suffered more casualties the farther we went. Some fell to shadowy creatures that stalked us through the night, and others fell from ambush, felled by the same arrows that I saw before. Everyone was on edge against these unseen foes, but none of the would-be assassins were able to pierce our defenses and strike at the core of our group.

It wasn't just the various creatures stalking the woods that were dangerous. Every now and then we would encounter some odd traps and illusions that plagued our journey. These oddities would manifest in the form of phantasms that tried to lull passersby into a state of confusion, often creating mirage images of deceased loved ones who tried to lure their prey into the consuming darkness. They would whisper sweet words into the ears of my followers, offering peace and rest if only they listened.

I thought these would prove to be a hazard for my followers, as each individual had no doubt lost many people important to them, yet my fanatics simply cut down each phantom image without blinking, all while shouting my praises. They didn't even hesitate for a second. I had my innate skill to defend against such trickery, but seeing the crazed trust my devotees had in me was scary.

And worse still, the closer we came to the city, the more traps and ambushes we suffered. Their tactics improved, and instead of just hiding and attacking from within range, they formed small guerilla squads to pick off stragglers. Some even came as assassins, aiming for when some members of my group were relieving themselves or sleeping, always aiming for when we were most vulnerable.

Yet just as their tactics improved, so did ours. We learned to minimize the amount of time we spent away from the glow of my halo and how to spot the telltale signs of an ambush. We learned to never rest away from my light, and to minimize blind spots.

But it wasn't all terrible news. Just as often as the ambushes, groups of uncorrupted individuals would also appear, fleeing from their homes. These people told of the unrest happening in the Last City, and of the changes that had recently happened. They said that not too long ago, some strange artifacts appeared near the borders of the Bastion, and all those who touched those strange devices had completely abandoned reason and attacked anything within their sight.

I was thankful that the Trash Matrix hadn't managed to infect all the people inside the Depths, but it was abundantly clear that more people were in the grasp of Origin than those who escaped. Still, Patar had managed to brainwash these fleeing people and bring them into the fold, replenishing some of our casualties. But between the roaming monsters and the constant harassment, our numbers fell much faster than we were able to replenish.

Yet for all the losses we took, the surviving few grew stronger. Abnormally so, in fact, and I was starting to think that Origin's meddling had inadvertently helped us out as well. Just a casual glance using the Arbiter skill showed that many of my cultists had gained as much as ten levels, while the elite amongst them had almost double that.

There was no way that kind of growth was natural, so whatever the Matrix was doing to accelerate its goons' attributes was also having an effect on mine, and I'd make sure that the Trash Matrix paid fully for this oversight. It was just a pity that I couldn't see my own stats with Noe asleep. I felt stronger, which, now that I thought about it, was strange since I didn't put any free attribute points into anything, and I missed seeing the numbers go up.

Eventually we stopped taking daily losses and were even able to capture some of the rebels alive, although little useful information was extracted. Whatever Origin did to their minds was so extensive that the people affected were left as little more than the beasts that stalked the woods.

So, when we finally came within sight of the massive city walls of the last bastion of civilization, our group had shrunk to 177 individuals. But their levels all averaged around the thirties, and every one of them would die for my cause. These zealots didn't even flinch when one of their own fell in battle. We found a quiet clearing and made our preparations.

As if they had practiced it a million times, the twins each took a squad of scout veterans and disappeared into the darkness while the rest of the devotees waited for their report. They hastily assembled a rough camp, every individual going to their assigned roles in silence, and all looked more than ready to fight to the death. I stood in the middle of the crowd, my light doing its best to help soothe the minor wounds and injuries that accrued.

I sat in silence before the familiar footsteps of Patar interrupted my meditations.

"Yes?" I said without opening my eyes.

I heard him bow. "I apologize for disturbing your rest, Lord Light Bringer, but we have news of the outpost."

"Explain," I muttered.

"It is as you feared, oh holy one," Patar said with reverence. "The city has been completely overrun by the heretics."

"Numbers?"

"Our best estimates state that they number close to five hundred," Patar answered nervously. "They are also armed with strange silver sticks."

I opened my eyes for the first time, pondering over this news. "What do they look like?"

Patar frowned. "They're smooth, with a fatter end on one side while the other side is slender and has a hollowed-out circle on the tip. They're also holding these sticks strangely, not like clubs or walking canes, but horizontally like a spear."

It appeared that Origin had upgraded its arsenal from bows and arrows to guns. But if it could have done that, why didn't it attack with a nuke or missile from the get-go? That would have surely killed all of us, and I doubted Noe could save me from an explosion with the tiny amount of luck charges I had available. Yet it resorted to crude arrows first.

The only logical explanation was that it couldn't use those for some reason. Were most of the options locked away, and it had to slowly open up the more devastating weapons with time? It was already going against every protocol by arming the natives of this world against us, so there was more than likely some kind of failsafe mechanism that prevented Origin from abusing its resources. Nothing else would make sense in this case, and it would also explain why it took so long for it to act at all.

I smiled. It wasn't fully prepared, but I had already arrived close enough to threaten it, so it was forced to deploy the forces it did have. I was glad that we had caught up to Origin and its stronghold now before it could unleash its full arsenal. If I had to fight against alien weapons or even high explosives, then I didn't see how I could possibly win. But rifles and machine guns?

I messaged Vadeem through the chat and called him over. Now that I could fully utilize my transformation, I had a better plan than just allowing my brainwashed cultists to die under machine-gun fire.

"Actually, Patar," I said to my archbishop, "I have a better solution for this particular problem."

I turned to my big friend. "Did you buy that big hammer Jae-Hyun asked you to?"

He nodded and grinned. "Of course I did! Found one so heavy even I could hardly lift it without my skill."

I pointed at the wall in the background. "How do you feel about going for some Vadeem-style home demolition?"

"Do you even have to ask?"

CHAPTER FORTY-FIVE

The Depths Part 4

Vadeem still looked dubious when I explained the sponsorship and my subsequent ability to transform but didn't question it too much. I think he was starting to become desensitized to all the nonsense he was witnessing. It was clear that he wanted to ask more, but I told him that Jae-Hyun could explain all that extra crap when we met up. In fact, I was pretty sure that the regressor knew more about the sponsorship program than I did. What his reaction will be, however, was anyone's guess.

"You know that borrowing power's never free, right?" Vadeem stated as he gave me another worried glare.

"I know, but do you see a better alternative?" I answered with a shrug. "We're not exactly in a situation where we're spoiled for choice. Something's using the trial's own resources against us, and we're screwed if we can't fight back."

I didn't want to tell Vadeem that it was literally the super AI running the trials that was after me, but I still needed to emphasize the danger we were in. Hopefully, a vague answer about the nature of our foe was enough. He needed to know that our situation was bad, but without the details that would land me in hot water.

"No, you're right," he grumbled. "I just don't like it. You're already giving up a lot for this trial, and now this?"

I shrugged. "Too late now. Our situation's already messed up as is, and I'd rather pay for whatever I'm borrowing later than die now."

"Yeah, just feel like I'm not pulling my weight here." He sighed. "Just . . . I'll make it up to you once we're out of here. That I promise."

I nodded. "We worry about everything else later. For now, we have a wall to smash!"

His old smile returned, although I could tell it was forced. "That's more like it. You might want to step back a little, when I said I got the largest hammer I could find, I really mean it."

I did as instructed, then took a few more steps back when he turned titan-sized. That was when he took out his "hammer" from his inventory. Now, I use the word hammer in the most literal definition, as in, you can use it to drive items into the ground. That was about all his weapon had in common with the tool. I think Vadeem could use cellphone towers as nails considering the size of his weapon. It was so large that I couldn't even see the whole thing from where I stood. The shaft was comically tiny compared to the rest of it. His muscles were bulging with the effort it took to lift it, and his feet were practically sinking into the earth.

I looked at the maul in awe, and I think most of the people around me did the same.

I looked up. "Where on earth did you find that thing? And how did you even afford it?"

He grunted. "It's awesome, eh? Had to ask the pixies to show me the real good stuff to get this baby. Still have to pay Jae-Hyun and Yoona back for buying it for me, though, but it's so worth it!"

I nodded slowly, still unable to fully appreciate the size of that thing.

"All right, I think it's time for me to show off a little as well." I smiled, and this time I couldn't properly suppress the joy that I felt for finally being able to use all the tools at my disposal. This was the first time I would be using my Xollon form for something other than talking or going on dates, and I was going to savor it, amplified emotions be damned.

By my will, my body started to transform back into that familiar, powerful shape once more. My narrow vision expanded to encompass my entire surroundings, and my feeble human form was replaced with a might that I would never get tired of. I felt powerful even though my current state was so diminished compared to the might I felt when using the preview ticket. But it was enough for the task at hand. Even an incomplete Xollon form was better than anything a lesser species could muster.

Vadeem and the rest of my followers looked at me in various states of shock. Some were terrified of my new visage, some in awe, while others were too stunned to even move. Yet the reverence in their faces never left. Good, they should get used to seeing me like this, and now that the limit for my transformation was measured in hours and not minutes, I could enjoy this feeling for a while.

I took a look at myself and saw that Q's little enchantment had made a difference. Instead of the slender Xollon form that I was used to seeing, I now looked slightly fatter, my feelers were a little chunkier, and my awesome maw was on the side of my head instead of at the top. Even the rows of teeth I had were gone! Looking closer, I thought I kind of resembled one of those delicious shoggoths more than I did a Xollon. That was a disturbing thought.

I suppose I still looked terrifying if someone had never seen a Xollon before, but when you compared the two . . . I really hoped I could undo Q's disguise later because I wasn't digging the new look. Xalla would not be impressed to see my love of shoggoths go so far that I would want to turn myself into one.

Patar was the first to regain his composure as he addressed the rest of his congressional.

"Look upon the mighty form of our God, and know His holy wrath! May we never experience His righteous anger for ourselves, but instead seek His grace! Sing with me, my fellow enlightened! Sing His praises as He smites our foes!"

Not wanting to deal with Patar's religious nonsense any longer, I gestured for Vadeem to follow me quickly. He nodded, and we made quick progress toward the edge of the city wall. Up close, it didn't look much sturdier than the ones we encountered in the outskirt villages, although it was a lot larger. It was still made with crudely carved-out stone that looked like it needed serious repair ages ago.

"Think you can make us an entrance?" I asked, my voice rumbling through my body, and I pointed one of my feelers toward the largest section of the wall.

We stopped a few meters in front of the structure, ignoring the quickly gathering enemies, and made our preparations. I tunneled my feelers into the ground once more, although this time I had more than just the two primary feelers. I had twelve, and these could stretch way longer than four meters. Each one of them burrowed into the ground and made its way toward the positions of the defenders. My new senses could pinpoint the position of each individual, and it was easy enough to hide my tentacles underneath their feet.

"I know I can," Vadeem answered with a grin, "and it will be grand."

And right on cue, Vadeem took a deep breath and hurled his hammer into the fortification. At the same time, I unleashed the burrowed limbs with a burst of movement and impaled the first set of foes. I was about to unleash more devastation when a shock wave of force slammed into me, causing me to stagger back a little.

I focused my perception on the source of that impact and witnessed something absolutely ridiculous . . .

Did you know that if you slam a solid object fast and hard enough into a wall, the wall just kind of . . . explodes? Not like in a mild boom followed by a shower of rubble or the like. I mean an actual explosion with a burst of fire, massive shock waves, and clouds of superheated dust. Vadeem might have just chucked a missile at the wall for all the difference there was.

Holy shit . . .

If I still had jaws, they would have been on the floor. I turned my gaze back to Vadeem the Dream and saw that he had the proudest shit-eating grin I'd ever seen.

"See?" he said with a loud laugh. "Told you I could make a grand entrance."

He looked at me again and put on his gauntlets. "What are you standing around for? Grab those tentacles of yours and get moving! We got some enemies to squish."

Without waiting for a reply, he rushed toward the demolished wall, his every step causing the ground to quake. I had to take another second or two to compose myself before moving my mass of tentacles to follow him. Running with multiple leg tentacles was strange at first, but I caught up to Vadeem quickly. I was so thankful that I had the big man on my side, and I almost pitied Origin for making an enemy out of him.

The defenders nearest the explosion were vaporized, and the ones farther away were still dazed or half dead. They made easy pickings for me and my deadly feelers. Just a light poke with one of my limbs was enough to pop heads and rupture bodies, which made me appreciate how deadly a Xollon was. No wonder Xalla and Rogue were so careful to avoid touching me when I was in my human form.

Vadeem was rushing forward and literally squishing those in his way with his bulk. He really wasn't kidding earlier. Those who tried to dodge were swatted aside, and the ones farther in the city had boulders thrown their way. I honestly thought he was doing more damage to the buildings and walls than the defenders, but he was taking the brunt of the return fire, so I couldn't complain.

Speaking of return fire, the defenders had gathered their wits enough to organize firing squads, and Vadeem and I were starting to take some damage. Minimal damage, true, but the bullets still hurt. Vadeem was ignoring the brunt of the assault, with the ones hitting his sides and front doing practically nothing. He would occasionally wince in irritation when a stray shot hit a vulnerable spot like his face or eyes, but nothing could stop his momentum.

As for me, I finally found out why Xollons had that black liquid coming out of them. It practically absorbed all the impact from the bullets, and I had shells harmlessly dripping off me before long. Occasionally one would strike an area where the coating was thinnest, and I'd feel a bit of pain, but I figured I could sit under this assault all day. I didn't need to see my HP bar—not that I could without Noe here—to know that I was fine.

I started to lose myself in the exhilaration of feeling so invincible. The defenders couldn't do anything against us, so I gave up all notion of defense and focused solely on eliminating my foes. My dozens of various appendages moved on their own, each twisting and turning to seek new prey. Without the limitations of human senses, I could concentrate on every feeler all at once, and that freedom was addicting.

Worse still, for my enemies at least, trying to parry or block the tentacles was futile, as my feelers could simply overwhelm any sort of protection, and even dodging was close to impossible. After all, their rigid bodies could never be as agile as my feelers.

The battle was so one-sided that it felt more like I was playing a game than actual combat. I started to see how quickly I could dispatch foes, timing myself between each kill as if I were trying to get a new high score. I even had the opportunity to try out crazy techniques as I waved my tentacles in increasingly intricate patterns before each strike.

Yet even though it was quite obvious that there was no way that the enemy could win, they still came at us. In hordes of ever-increasing numbers they came, as if they thought they could overwhelm us through sheer quantity. The Trash Matrix should know that trying to exhaust me and Vadeem was futile! I laughed at that thought. How could Origin be so dumb as to think it could win like this?

Wait a second . . .

A sudden realization hit me, and a cold wave of dread washed over my frame. There was no way the Origin Matrix would act like this without reason. As insane and corrupt as it was, it was no fool, so why send so much chaff at us? What was its goal?

I took a moment to examine the battlefield one last time, taking in every detail that I could, and I understood. I saw more and more mutated humans encircle our position, and I finally knew what the Trash Matrix was trying to do.

It was buying itself time!

If my initial guess was right, then the Trash Matrix needed more time to access its full arsenal, and I'd bet anything that it knew we were heading toward the temple. It was trying to bog us down as much as possible so that our final assault would be futile. As fast as Vadeem and I were at killing these people, I doubted we could eliminate all the mutants coming out of the woodwork.

Shit!

"Vadeem!" I shouted. "It's a damn trap! Our enemy's playing us like fools!"

Vadeem threw another chunk of debris at a squad of defenders. "What do you mean? We're destroying them!"

"They're trying to delay us from getting to the temple! Haven't you noticed that their weaponry's getting more advanced? If we wait any longer then it's not just guns that'll meet us, but goddamn tanks and missiles!"

As if Origin heard my warning, the defenders that were once hiding and cowering all changed their behaviors. Now, as one, they started to swarm the two of us, completely ignoring any kind of self-preservation, or even an attempt to fight back. Their only goal was to slow us down with their dead, and I feared it might work.

CHAPTER FORTY-SIX

The Depths Part 5

We were starting to get quickly bogged down by the mass of bodies. I impaled and swatted aside as many as I could, but soon my feelers were getting caught on dead bodies and reaching hands. I could lift and cut through four, five, maybe even six bodies at once, but when those numbers started to enter the twenties and thirties? My stats were enhanced by a large margin, but no amount of pure attributes could beat the laws of physics, and physics was starting to win out fast.

I cursed myself for allowing my damned emotions to get in my way again. I had inadvertently allowed the Trash Matrix to get the better of me, and that pissed me off, amplified emotions or not. I thought my upgraded innate skill and the passive from my Light Bringer title could insulate me from the stupid darkness, but clearly its influence was stronger than whatever protections I had. It was all too clear that skills and titles were not omnipotent.

I'd have to rethink all my strategies and plans going forward, but this was not the time for that.

"Vadeem!" I screamed as I threw another defender to the side. "We have to leave now!"

He grunted. "I got it!"

I had just enough time to check out what Vadeem was doing and saw that he'd managed to free an arm from the mass of squirming bodies. He held the limb up in the air and held a look of deep concentration. A rumbling sound quickly followed, and the damn hammer that he chucked prior came flying through the air toward his outstretched hand.

Holy shit, it was like a really large version of Mjolnir! So what if it couldn't shoot lightning when he could throw it like a rocket?

The impact of the sledge hitting Vadeem caused the goons clinging on to him to stumble, and he took that opportunity to free himself from the mass of human bodies. He swung wide, practically pulverizing everything around him into a fine mist, and then quickly grabbed me with his free hand. I did my best to not impale him with my tentacles.

He frowned. "Why are you so damn slimy, Walter?"

I looked at him with incredulity. "Is this really the time to complain about how I feel?"

"Yes, it is!" he grumbled while sprinting toward the hole in the wall. "You're damned hard to hold on to!"

Okay, that was a fair complaint. Slipping off would be pretty bad, but worse still would be if he tried to grasp me too hard and made me pop like a tube of toothpaste. I shuddered and wrapped some of my feelers around his arms as best I could.

"Better!" He smiled. "You still feel horrible to hold, though!"

"Just run for it!"

And he did.

I climbed up onto his massive shoulders and did my best to hold on without harming the man. He needed both arms free to properly swing his weapon. It was a good thing Vadeem was so thick-skinned because I had to really grip hard to stay on. He was making wide swings with the maul that caused his body to sway wildly, and he wasn't exactly the lightest on his feet either. But his huge mass was also a benefit because once Vadeem was moving, very little could slow down his advance. The man was the avatar of momentum.

Soon we passed the blown-up wall and ran toward Patar and his gathered warriors. They were engaged in their own fights, having figured out the enemy's plans on their own, and were actively making room for us to pass through.

The guns were doing a number on our forces, but thanks to their enhanced abilities and levels, my soldiers were putting up a valiant fight of their own. For all the numbers that the Trash Matrix had, it couldn't force its brainwashed goons to fight with as much fervor as my brainwashed goons.

Ha! That was the power of a cult!

Vadeem slowed down briefly as he neared the relative safety of our camp. Patar and a group of his priests hurriedly gathered to meet us.

"Lord Light Bringer," Patar said as he wiped some sweat off his forehead, "we have intercepted the enemy and are ready to aid You!"

"Good," I quickly said and thought of the best way to utilize my forces now that my initial plans had failed. "The foe seeks to block our path to our destination. I need your men to slow down their advance here and meet us at the temple when you can. Time is limited, and the heretics grow stronger by the second. Vadoom and I will go ahead of you to put an end to their foul existence. I'm leaving you in charge of the men and women here."

"I understand, my Lord!" He then nodded toward the twins. "Ana and Eva will guide You to the temple. They have memorized the route."

I nodded and made room for the two girls to climb on with me. One of them went to the other shoulder while the other jumped right on top of the big man's head. She gripped his hair like the reins of a horse and made herself comfortable. Judging by Vadeem's expression, it seemed they had done this before. It was like she was piloting Vadeem, and imagining her steering the massive titan around like a go-cart would have been quite comical were our situation not so dire.

Patar took something out of his tattered robes and threw it at me. "I apologize for not telling You the information that You had requested personally, Lord God, but I have taken it upon myself to transcribe what You asked for on the scroll. There isn't much on the history of the temple, but one of the survivors used to work there and drew a rough map of the interior."

I had almost forgotten that I had asked for more information about the Flames, but evidently Patar hadn't. I stuffed the scroll into my inventory and gave him my thanks.

"Good work, now go guide the chosen!"

"I shall ensure that Your will be done!" Patar bowed one last time before jogging away to oversee our defenses.

Without looking back, I shouted, "Vadeem, go!"

He nodded and started to rush forward . . . for about five seconds. He stopped abruptly after a few steps, the sudden halt in movement almost causing me to fall over, and he looked at me in embarrassment. I saw that Ana, the one on his head, was pulling his hair wildly with one hand while the other was frantically punching his dome.

"Sorry," he said quietly. "Went the wrong way."

He turned around in the direction that Ana was pulling, stopping once more to double-check that it was correct, before running into the woods once more. Eva was shaking her head in disappointment; it was clearly not the first time he'd had trouble following their instructions.

This time he was able to move uninterrupted, only making minor course corrections along his path. Watching Vadeem move at full speed was like watching an avalanche demolish everything in its path. Any critter or creature stupid enough to try to get in our way was quickly swept aside, while the more agile foes looked on in confusion as a giant mass of muscle moved through the forest.

What was more impressive than Vadeem's Juggernaut impression was how the twins were able to accurately steer the man toward our destination. Even with my enhanced perception, I couldn't tell what was going on between all the shaking, dust, and debris Vadeem had managed to create on his path. Yet Ana was able to make minute adjustments on the fly, while the other girl quietly surveyed the land despite the rough ride.

According to the twins, we should be arriving at the edge of the temple's outer boundaries within minutes. It was time to check up on our regressor's side to see if we couldn't meet up for the first time in what seemed like forever.

> **Walter's Fine:** Jae-Hyun, we're making our way toward the temple. There's been a slight change of plans.

A short moment later a message appeared in my eyes.

> **Jae-Hyun:** I noticed. We're being attacked by the natives. They're trying to stop us from getting further in, and they're using weapons from the trials; that the same for you guys as well?
> **Walter's Fine:** Yeah, and they seem to be getting more and more of the good stuff as time progresses. They had arrows and clubs, but they're using guns now. You have any idea why?

I couldn't exactly tell him that Origin was after me, but I did want to know just how much the regressor knew about Central's erratic AI. Was it always going to malfunction in the future, or was I somehow causing it to go haywire?

> **Jae-Hyun:** I'm not sure. This is the first time I've seen a situation like this, but it's not unheard of. I might have some guesses, but if what you're saying's true, then we need to get to the artifact now.

Damn this regressor and his ability to dodge questions. Trying to get anything out of him about the future was going to be a pain, but it made sense for him to be so guarded after everything he'd been through. But if he'd told his sister about everything, then perhaps he'd share it with the rest of us once he knew that he could trust us. The tricky part was getting to that point.

> **Vadeem the Dream:** We're on our way over to your position fast. How are you and the others holding up?
> **Jae-Hyun:** Fine. Noel and I can take care of any threats, but we need you two to breach the temple. And how is Walter?
> **Walter's Fine:** It's like my name says, I'm fine. I can fight at the very least. What about Yoona?
> **Jae-Hyun:** This place's affecting her badly. She is out of it right now, but we're managing. You said Walter has a skill that helps with the mental pollution, right?
> **Vadeem the Dream:** Yeah, he's got a glowing light bulb on his head. It's keeping us normal at any rate. Should help Yoona too.
> **Jae-Hyun:** Good, if we can get her back on her feet, then it'll make things easier. Noel'll appreciate it as well.
> **Vadeem the Dream:** What's wrong with Noel? I thought you said she's helping you hold off the enemies?
> **Jae-Hyun:** You'll see soon enough . . . and you said that Walter's got a light shining on him?
> **Vadeem the Dream:** Yeah, he's like a portable spotlight.
> **Jae-Hyun:** Stay on your current course. I think I see you. I'll be there soon.
> **Walter's Fine:** Just don't be too surprised when you see me. I, uh, accepted a sponsorship, so I might look a bit weird.
> **Jae-Hyun:** You did what?

Wow, I could almost feel the shock and unease in the regressor, even through text. He definitely knew about the dubious terms of Central's sponsorships.

> **Walter's Fine:** Uh, I got a sponsor? Sorry, I'll live with those terms. It was that or die here.
> **Jae-Hyun:** I— No, we'll speak about it when there's more time. It's not too late yet. And . . . I'm sorry for putting you in a situation like this, Walter. I promise I'll make it up to you.
> **Vadeem the Dream:** Is it really that bad?
> **Jae-Hyun:** Talk later. I'm right about there.

The regressor wasn't kidding about being there soon. Within thirty seconds or so of his last message, I heard the rustling of leaves and heavy footsteps. Soon a blur of movement could be seen, and the distinct outline of Jae-Hyun appeared in our field of view.

Moving my gaze toward the man, I saw that he had made a makeshift sling with some loose clothes and had his sister wrapped across his back. Yoona looked to be out cold, and her complexion looked terrible. In fact, it wasn't just Yoona who looked worse for wear; the regressor looked more haggard and bruised than I'd ever seen him before. His clothes were cut up and damaged in many places, and I could make out still-healing wounds that covered his entire body. Yet that indomitable gaze of his never faltered.

"Where's Noel?" I shouted. "Oh, and it's Walter speaking, so please don't attack!"

Jae-Hyun almost swore when he saw me clearly, but he kept any comments to himself as he changed course to run alongside us. I could tell that he was not liking the supposed sponsorship I had taken, or my current tentacle-y form.

"She's behind me," he grunted. "We had some friends who didn't want to leave us alone."

I looked at him in confusion, and then I saw that it wasn't just Jae-Hyun who followed the light. There was practically an entire army of brainwashed mutants hot on his trail, and they were headed straight for us. Yet in the middle of the sea of mutants was something else.

"What the hell is that?" I muttered, pointing toward the figure.

"Noel," Jae-Hyun answered plainly. "You're not the only one who's transformed."

CHAPTER FORTY-SEVEN

The Finale Part 1

The figure standing, or more accurately massacring, all of the Origin minions was Noel? I guess if I looked closer, I could see that familiar frizzy hair, but between the black flames that consumed her, the two bloodred orbs where her eyes were, and the goddamn wings of oily burning tar on her back, it certainly could have fooled me!

Then again, her class did mention flames, but the fire that coated every inch of her body didn't behave like the inferno that Noe caused earlier or even the normal fires produced by our torches. It seemed to move like it was in slow motion, gently flickering and floating in the wind. It had this lazy movement that was completely contradictory to the movements of the woman herself.

Worse still, the way that the flames burned her foes, if you could even call it that, was disturbing. Anything that touched that lightless blaze seemed to melt. Their bodies would fall apart in a horrible gooey sludge, leaving nothing behind but a sickening stain on the ground. Strangely, the weapons that they used to fight back were unaffected by the flame, although that didn't do her foes much good since Noel was equally unaffected by the weapons. They would simply pass through her.

She stopped what she was doing and turned her gaze toward us. I felt an uncontrollable shudder as those red orbs glared my way.

"Holy shit," Vadeem muttered. "And I thought Walter's transformation was bad. At this rate, our whole party'll transform into nightmare creatures!"

"You're not much better, you know."

"Stay focused," Jae-Hyun muttered. "We're not in the clear yet. We break through and head toward the temple."

"Wait," I said. "We go *through* the creepy flesh-melting fire?"

"It won't affect us," the regressor stated simply.

Even Vadeem looked unsure. "You're sure? I mean, Noel hardly seems like she has any brain functions left in that state, not that she had much brain function in the first place."

As if to prove him wrong, Noel glanced over at Vadeem and flipped him off before returning to her slaughter.

"Never mind," he replied with a sigh. "She's still in there. At least she can't talk."

"Can you hold on to Yoona?" the regressor said, ignoring the insults. "I need both hands to clear us a path forward."

"Of course," Vadeem said, pointing to the girl on his shoulder. "Ana will make sure she's safe."

"That's Eva," I corrected.

"Of course," Vadeem said again. "Eva will make sure she's safe."

I rolled my nonexistent eyes.

Jae-Hyun gave a quick glance at the two girls riding on the giant and hesitated for half a second. Ultimately, he nodded and gently handed over his sister to Vadeem's care.

"You can trust the twins," I said. "They've been with us close to the start. And it's better than having Vadeem holding on to Yoona; he almost turned me into paste when he grabbed me earlier."

"I told you, it's because you're too slimy!"

Jae-Hyun sighed and ignored our banter. "All right, stop wasting time, we're going now."

Without waiting for our reply, the regressor took out his spear and bolted toward the enemy, running into the flames without hesitation. Vadeem followed soon after.

Now that Jae-Hyun was unburdened, he started to carve a path through the remaining foes, never slowing down despite the various brainwashed minions getting in his path. His spearwork was exquisite, and I just wished I knew more about fighting to be able to really appreciate what he was doing. Instead, all I saw was a blur of movement followed by the collapsing bodies of the mutants. I was sure there was a whole other level of footwork, technique, and whatnot that I was missing out on.

What I could see was that the damn regressor managed to get a new weapon, and it was awesome looking. It was black, as was everything related to our party now that I thought about it, but this weapon seemed to absorb all the light around it.

Looking closer, seeing faint sparks of ebony electricity periodically surging along the wicked-looking point, and his swings left a shadowy afterimage that seemed to linger in the air. It seemed that even the slightest wound inflicted by his spear caused the foe to fall, and I could swear I saw some wisp of energy enter his weapon with each kill. Compared to my broken sword and slimy tentacles, I might as well have been using a pitchfork to fight. How was he able to look so cool in everything he did?

Now that I thought about it, Vadeem was able to turn into a literal raging titan, I became some kind of tentacle monster, and Noel looked like she'd stepped right out of Hell. Coupled with the regressor's decidedly vile, soul-sucking weapon that made him look like a spear-wielding grim reaper, was our guild just . . . evil?

Vadeem nudged me. "Walter, you're losing focus again. Careful now, we're almost at the end. Just have to hold out a little more, my friend."

I forced my focus back on the battlefield. Damn, just when I thought I was getting a good handle on my emotions, I started drifting into needless thoughts again. What would have happened if I had—

No, stop. I almost did it again.

I took a deep breath.

"Wall's just over there!" Jae-Hyun shouted from up ahead. "Since we don't have Walter's army of followers, we're going with plan B."

"Sorry about that!" I said. "Things got a little out of hand near the end."

"It's fine," he answered quickly. "You still have the explosives I told you to bring?"

My enhanced perception allowed me to see a few ambushers sitting on top of a tree, aiming their guns at us. I took care of them with a quick swipe of my feelers before replying to the question.

"I used some of them, but I got about half left."

Another couple of foes hidden behind trees fell prey to my tentacles.

"Give them to me when we reach the wall!"

This time it was Vadeem who eliminated the next few idiots who got in our way. His massive boot crushed the poor people underneath.

"Are you planning to blow up the temple?" I couldn't help but ask as I watched the twins expertly let loose a volley of arrows. Every shot hit its mark.

"No, we need to make our own entrance since we can't take the direct path without more men. It's why Noel and I couldn't get in. But we did manage to secure a clearing near here in case things went wrong."

I saw a few more tasty foes to impale, but the regressor's spear was faster than my feelers.

"Why can't we just Vadeem through the walls?" I asked.

"And risk collapsing the whole building?" Jae-Hyun answered. "We do that as a last resort!"

Vadeem chimed in, "Hey! I can control my strength!"

I recalled the scene of him exploding the last fortification and doubted that he was telling the truth. Right, caution was probably the safer first option.

The temple was approaching fast, and the titan had to slow down our advance before he ignored our leader's instructions and actually did Vadeem through the exterior. I threw the leftover explosives over to Jae-Hyun when we came to a stop, and he quickly went about setting them up. He was damn fast at it too. Noel met up with us a short while later, having cooked her way through a swath of enemies.

"Buy me some time," the regressor grumbled.

We did. Vadeem set Yoona and the twins down and took out his hammer. Every swing managed to pulverize any poor souls who came near. Noel entered the fray once more, doing her best to melt the suckers who were closest to the regressor. All I had to do was make sure that anyone who slipped through the cracks was subsequently impaled and dismembered. It was light work, all things considered, but then again, the other two were doing the brunt of the work.

"Ready!" Jae-Hyun's voice echoed between the screams of the dying. "Brace yourselves!"

I didn't even have time to do that as the shock wave of the blast slammed into my back. I didn't fall over, given my enhanced strength, but it was very uncomfortable nonetheless. Nor did I have the time to complain before Vadeem dragged me and the three girls into the newly created entrance. Once again, Noel was on our heels, and once she entered fully, Jae-Hyun set off another block of detonations, which caused some of the roof to collapse, sealing off our entrance.

There was the sound of rushing footsteps and angry shouts as the enemy horde slammed into the blocked-off passage, but after a few seconds, it was clear that the rubble was holding off their advance. We were safe for now.

Once the last of the outside noise subsided and our foes realized that they couldn't break through the blockade, at least with their current equipment, everyone in our party slumped down in exhaustion. Vadeem had returned to his normal size, and Noel had turned into a human puddle of fire by the side.

If it wasn't for the fact that she was jiggling a little now and then, I would have thought she died. Even the regressor was slouching a bit . . . maybe.

Jae-Hyun was tending to his sister when he asked, "Walter, you said your halo could alleviate some of the corruption?"

"Yeah," I answered. "Does bugger all for me, though."

"Can you stand closer to Yoona?" he said gently. "See if you can help her?"

I nodded. "Sure, and I also got a lantern that can help."

"What do you mean?"

I took out the Promethean fire and showed it to him. I could tell that the regressor instantly recognized what it was, as he gripped it tight.

"I found it in the first trial," I lied. "Lost my original light and found this one on the side, saw it was a bit brighter, but I didn't think it could help in here of all places."

"It's . . ." he started, but quickly composed himself. "This is more valuable than you can imagine. I don't know how you found it in the first trial of all places, but you have my thanks. This is exactly what I needed."

He unscrewed the top of the lantern, exposing the fire under it, and then slowly dipped his finger into the flame. I frowned, not sure what he was doing, but on closer inspection, I saw that there was a faint blue glow emanating from his fingertips.

"It's mana manipulation," he explained as if sensing my question. "I'm transferring the essence of this flame into Yoona. If this is what I think it is, then she should recover quickly."

He took the tiny flame and pressed his fingertips on his sister's forehead. Immediately, the fire shot straight into the unconscious girl, and her pale complexion improved visibly. The regressor did this a few more times, and eventually Yoona started to stir from her slumber. We all crowded around the high schooler, wanting to see if she did improve.

A few more seconds passed, and a faint smile appeared on the regressor's lips as Yoona's eyes fluttered open. We were all about to cheer when her eyes widened in shock, and I felt an impact on the side of my frills. She quickly scrambled away, her bow out and ready, as she faced me with grim determination.

Right . . . I was still in my Xollon form.

"Brother! Kill it!" she screamed and let loose a barrage of arrows.

I avoided them narrowly.

"Yoona, it's me!" I said, putting up my tentacles in surrender. "It's Walter."

A look of understanding flashed through her eyes. "Oh my god, what have they done to you, Walter?"

"No—"

"Don't worry," she continued. "I—I'm sure that my brother can think of something to fix you. I knew this place changed people, but . . . I'm sorry. And why are you glowing?"

It took us a while to explain the whole situation to Yoona and the others, but they accepted the news quietly. It was nice to see that they were so quick to uptake new info. Everyone understood that now was not the time for sharing.

"If your new title does as you say, then Noel"—Jae-Hyun turned his attention to the still-smoldering woman—"you can turn back to normal now. We're safe from further corruption as long as Walter's here."

With a puff of smoke, Noel extinguished herself and practically fell on the ground from exhaustion.

"Oh thank god!" she muttered. "Do you have any idea how tiring it is setting people on fire 24/7?"

Yoona looked at her in confusion.

"Not *people* people," she quickly corrected. "I mean those mutant monster things."

"Sorry," the other girl said quietly. "I wasn't of much help this time."

"It's all good, bestie," Noel said with a smile. "We all made it. No harm, no foul."

She turned her attention to Vadeem, who was still busy stuffing his face. "Also, fuck you, Vadeem, I do have a brain, thank you very much."

The big man just shrugged before eating some more.

She continued, "And when are you going to introduce us to those two?"

"Oh, sorry," I said. "That's Ana and Eva, two natives we met. They've been helping us out this whole time."

"Hello!" Noel said with a wave. "Nice to meet ya!"

"Hello and thank you for the help," Yoona added.

I addressed the twins and translated, "They're saying hi."

The two nodded and turned toward the others . . . then flexed their muscles in various bodybuilder forms.

Noel and Yoona looked on in confusion, and I could only bring my palms up to my face in exasperation. Vadeem was laughing nervously in the background. I had forgotten who taught them the basics of human gestures.

"I, uh . . ." Vadeem started, "I might have taught them that. They're mute, so I thought they should know how best to communicate."

"Through flexing?" Yoona muttered.

"Bestie, it's best you learned that Vadeem's always been a very special boy," Noel added. "You can't use common sense when dealing with him."

"I see . . ."

The regressor interrupted our little banter and reminded us of our situation.

"Introduce ourselves later," he said with a serious tone. "Get as much rest as you can now. We're heading to the source of all this darkness."

CHAPTER FORTY-EIGHT

The Finale Part 2

Things calmed down a little after all the introductions and explanations were over. It took a long time just to recount the major things that happened on our side, although it appeared that Jae-Hyun and the others had just as hard of a time as we did. We all needed that extra time to regain some of our stamina and strength.

We promised we'd share all the details over a good hearty meal once this was all over. The only major concern we had was the six-hour time limit on my transformation, but our leader still insisted that we take the necessary time to recover enough to fight further. I wasn't about to argue with more rest.

I wanted to check out how much they'd improved with my Lucky Eyes skill but saw that the information displayed was still their classes. It wasn't that important, so I'd just ask them once we were done here. The regressor had also put away his cool new spear, so I'd have to sneak a peek at its properties later as well.

For now, I took a seat and tried my best to rest my tired mind and body. I wasn't alone in this thinking, and it turned out that Vadeem and Noel required the most time getting back into fighting shape. The redhead was still mostly slumped over and had started to stuff her face with Vadeem. It seemed like her transformation used up about as many resources as the big man's.

"Walter," the regressor said, waking me from my meditation, "you said your light doesn't work on you, right?"

I turned to face him and nodded. "Yeah, it's why my emotions have been going haywire lately. I get agitated easily, and Vadeem's had to snap me out of random daydreams."

"Let me see if I can't do the same thing I did to Yoona on you," he said, and gestured for the lantern back.

I obliged.

He unscrewed the top of the lantern and transferred some of the fire into his fingertip again. "Give me one of your, uh, hand tentacles, Walter. I just need to transfer the spark into your body."

"Does it matter if I'm transformed?" I asked hesitantly.

"Wouldn't matter," he answered. "Your lantern's fire soothes the soul. What form you're in is irrelevant. Just give me your tentacle."

I heard Noel chuckle to herself on the side. Vadeem smacked her on the head before she could comment further.

I nodded and shifted a feeler closer to his hand. The regressor concentrated and brought the flame into my limb, but I felt nothing.

He frowned. "That's strange . . ."

"Something wrong?"

"Let me try again. Maybe it's the slime," he muttered, redoing the action of bringing a spark of the flame into my body once more. Once again, nothing seemed to happen.

"Walter," he asked with a frown, "how much mana do you have in your attributes?"

Mana? I hadn't looked at that stat for a long time, and if I remembered correctly, it had always been zero. In fact, I was pretty sure Q had said that my body couldn't use it even with the Trash Matrix's help when we first met.

"None?" I answered honestly. "It's never gone up even when I level up."

Jae-Hyun frowned again. "That's rare. I've heard of cases where people have poor mana circulation, but almost never none at all."

Yoona came over to join us. "Is that a problem, brother?"

"Not necessarily," he answered slowly. "It means that mana doesn't flow through him at all, which can be beneficial."

"It can be?" I asked, a little hopeful.

"Yes . . ." he continued. "In niche situations. Things like curses, voodoo, and alchemical poisons won't work on you—which means we can rule out this darkness being magical in nature—but likewise, any beneficial effects are also ineffective. There's nowhere for any mana, internal or external, to travel in your body, although some magic that affects the system directly might affect you."

"So I'm not immune to fireballs?"

"No," he answered, "but it also means that spells that speed up your natural healing properties may still work."

"Then the flame's not helping?" his sister asked for me. "Is Walter going to be okay?"

"The fire will still help," he answered. "It's slowing down whatever's affecting us, but it won't get rid of it like in your case. He'll still get worse if we don't leave soon."

Yoona looked concerned, but I quickly calmed her down. "It's fine, I can slowly recover once we're all out of here, and it's not like I need magic or whatever to fight."

The regressor nodded. "He's right, mana can be useful, but it's not the only tool that's available to use. Most fighters ignore it to focus their growth elsewhere."

"Exactly," I added. "I doubt we'll be seeing Vadeem hurl fireballs anytime soon."

A loud burp broke the course of our conversation, and Vadeem spoke up. "Who needs to hurl fireballs when I can chuck hammers!"

He chuckled to himself and ate the last of the food in his hands. "Anyway, Noel and I are about ready to go."

"Yup," Noel agreed. "I'm ready as I'll ever be! Let's get out of this stupid place. I need a hot bath to get all this dirt off me!"

The regressor nodded and started to pack up himself. "Yoona, you still have your old bow and the backup ones?"

"Yeah," she answered and took out the weapons in question. "Are we giving them to the twins?"

"Yes, and the enchanted quiver as well."

She handed the bows to the two, much to their excitement, before taking out a normal-looking quiver and giving it over as well.

"I only have one of those, though, brother."

"They'll have to share, but it's better than nothing." He turned to address me. "Walter, can you use your skill to translate how the quiver works? Let them know that they can freely shoot without conserving ammo."

I nodded and did so, laughing a little as the two started to pull arrow after arrow out of the quiver in amazement. I guess the twins did show their age every now and then, but just as quickly as their looks of joy came, it disappeared, and their normal expressions of neutral concentration returned.

"Oh, right," I said, remembering the scroll Patar had given me. "I had almost forgotten, but I got some rough schematics for this place and some info about what happened to this world."

"Let me take a look," he said.

"Can you read the thing?" I asked. "It's not written in English or anything. My innate skill can translate."

"I have something similar," he muttered as I handed the scroll over. Of course he could read obscure languages as well. The better question would be what couldn't our regressor do? At least he couldn't also speak it like I could, so I'd take that as a small win on my end.

He flipped open the scroll and started to quickly read over the contents. By now the rest of our group was huddled together and waiting to see what the regressor had to say.

"So, what can we expect?" Vadeem asked.

"It's strange . . ." Jae-Hyun answered. "Some of the information makes sense. It says that the Flames of Creation were originally gifted to them as a means to seal something powerful. That much we already know, and as Walter mentioned, it was extinguished some twenty-five or so years ago. The rest is irrelevant information about rituals and the temple hierarchy."

"We know all that," I said. "What's strange about it?"

"It's how the Flames were able to become extinguished in the first place," he said quickly. "You said that it was due to a prank from one of the junior priests and that there were no protocols in place to prevent such an action, but that doesn't seem to be the case. According to this, the people here did have multiple systems in place to prevent the fire from going out. There were redundancies for the redundancies in their design. It shouldn't have been possible for one event to shut off the whole system."

I frowned. "So how unlikely would it be for all of those redundancies and preventative measures to fail all at once?"

"Next to impossible," he said confidently. "The chances of that happening are practically zero."

I had a sick feeling when I heard that . . .

"But not zero?" I asked again.

"No, but like I said, the chances are so small that it wouldn't happen."

Shit, what else did I know that allowed seemingly impossible events from happening, regardless of how minuscule the changes of that happening were? If I was right, then there were some major implications to Noe's abilities, and she, or at least a version of her, had been active way before meeting me. Were each of her various shards all able to use a portion of her luck skills? Damn it, I should just collect this one and hope Noe could answer me when she was up and about again.

"So someone sabotaged it," Vadeem said, which would be the most logical conclusion if I didn't have the Absolute Luck skill with me, or heard Noe's pleas to awaken her.

"Exactly my thoughts," Jae-Hyun said. "I'm not sure why someone or something would sabotage this Earth or the trials, but if they can manipulate the system, then we're facing something strong."

"Think whatever's doing this is after us specifically?" Yoona added in. I could tell she was concerned because she thought that she was the only one who knew about her brother's unique situation. No doubt the regressor was blaming himself as the cause of all these changes, and I was not about to tell him otherwise.

"Maybe," he grumbled, "but be ready for anything."

Everyone nodded.

"Anyway, we're heading off," the regressor said and stashed away the scroll. "I have a good grasp of where we are, and if Walter's map is right, we should be able to get to the ritual room quickly. Get your things, and let's find the source of this corruption."

Once everything was finally packed, we left our little camp and the brief moment of respite it gave us. We rested for maybe half an hour at most, but I already felt my spirits rise now that the entire Abyss party was back together. Heck, it had even gained two bonus members.

The temple itself was relatively spacious, all things considered, and it wasn't difficult for a group of seven to explore it. The place itself was just massive stonework, although the passing of time and the corruption here was really bad. Even my halo had trouble illuminating more than a few feet in front of us, and the black tendrils were getting thicker and thicker as we made our way toward the interior. It seemed to erode the massive stonework, making the whole building appear like the insides of a horrible beast.

Jae-Hyun led the pack, while Vadeem and Noel were sticking a step or two behind him. The three teens were in the center of the group, while I hovered a little behind them, covering our rear. This formation occurred naturally, without anyone telling the group to do so, but it seemed like the best use of our talents. It was just like the regressor said back in the rest area. He, Noel, and Vadeem had the frontline, while I was there to cover for Yoona. Well, this time it was Yoona plus the twins, but the theory was the same.

Yet strangest of all was just how empty the place was. Considering it was a place of worship and gathering just a quarter century ago, I expected old and decayed furnishings, decorations, or *something* to be present, yet it was as if all the objects not bolted to the ground had disappeared. What was left were empty chambers, grand archways, and narrow doorways. It was eerily empty and just as creepy, and the echoes that reverberated across these massive halls didn't help in the slightest. Everything amplified my strained nerves to the max, and I was just waiting for some new monstrosity to come out and attack us.

The layout of the building was a bit strange as well, although I wasn't exactly an expert on parallel Earth temples. The place seemed to be a catacomb of interconnected chambers of various sizes, and once again, since all of the furnishings were gone, I couldn't tell one room apart from another.

It strangely reminded me of how Central HQ was laid out, now that I thought about it. Was that a coincidence, or was Origin making small changes to the environment as well as to the locals? That was concerning information that I had to take into account in the future, since I highly doubted I would be seeing the last of the Trash Matrix's interventions.

"It's awfully empty . . ." Vadeem said, his voice echoing despite the dampening nature of the darkness. "Where are all the golems and stuff you said would attack us, Jae-Hyun?"

We stepped into another seemingly empty corridor. This one was a little larger than the previous one but otherwise had nothing noteworthy about it. We were about to cross it like the others and enter the only other exit when Jae-Hyun stopped our advance. I felt a faint rumbling, and that was when something on the wall of this new room started to move.

Something huge.

"Man, Vadeem," Noel grumbled as she unsheathed her swords, "you just had to say it."

CHAPTER FORTY-NINE

The Finale Part 3

Well, Vadeem certainly got his wish and then some. A massive stone door slammed shut behind us, blocking off the entrance we came from, and out of the walls came a massive stone creature even bigger than Vadeem's titan form. Yet if it was just the hulking golem that took up at least half the floorspace being the problem, the situation would have still been manageable. Too bad he decided to bring some friends as well.

Little holes in the floors slowly slid open at the same time, and out flooded a mass of those insectoid human things we encountered earlier. Worse yet, they seemed to pour out of those openings without end, and we were in actual danger of just being overwhelmed by sheer numbers given the confined space.

Even the exit on the opposite side of us closed on its own and was now sealed off. I felt the atmosphere in the room change as a faint glimmer of energy encased everything. Vadeem noticed the odd situation and immediately threw his hammer toward where the doorway used to be. The force of the attack was massive, but nothing seemed to be damaged. His weapon bounced off the wall and almost took off my head as it flew back from the recoil. Whatever new toys Origin had access to seemed to have fully trapped us in here.

I sighed. *Well, shit, that went from zero to a hundred fast.*

The regressor was unfazed and quickly gave out concise instructions. "Vadeem, hold off the golem."

Without reply, the big man transformed into his now-familiar titan size and engaged the slightly larger foe. A powerful uppercut to the rock creature's jaws sent tremors down into the earth.

The regressor took out his spear, and like lightning, carved a path of destruction toward the exit. "Noel, thin out the insect numbers."

"Ugh, these things are seriously gross!" Noel complained. "You owe me one for this, boss man!"

"Just do it!" the regressor shouted.

"Aye-aye!" the redhead answered before exploding into that disturbing black blaze. The flames expanded outward a few meters around her, melting any creatures that got too close. Seeing her endlessly and easily mow down her foes was breathtaking. Even the ones that could somehow reach her without turning into goop failed to harm the woman in any way. Their attacks simply passed through her ethereal body.

"Yoona, stay near me and pick off any that get close," he continued, never easing on the offense. "Walter, tell the twins to copy whatever Yoona's doing."

I did so and saw Yoona and the twins quickly rush toward the regressor, letting loose shot after shot at the same time. Yoona's volleys seemed to have a life of their own and were curving and darting around the battlefield, impaling multiple foes with each arrow loosed. It appeared that while Yoona's abilities weren't quite as flashy as the other party members', she could still hold her own. The twins were not doing too bad either, and their enhanced attributes allowed them to let loose dozens of arrows in seconds.

"What's my job here?"

I narrowly avoided being stepped on by Vadeem and quickly crawled toward the regressor's side, swatting away a few clawing foes on the way. This battle was almost comically easy in my Xollon form, and the only problem was the sheer number of enemies. Was human wave tactics the only strategy that the Trash Matrix could employ? It must be getting desperate.

"Help me find a weakness in the barrier," he said calmly. "If we don't find the fault line, then we're not getting out of here."

Thank god we had the regressor's experience. I doubt anything the Origin Matrix threw at him would be new, and if there was anyone who knew the ins and outs of the Trash AI's own weapons, then it was the guy who survived all the trials.

"You can tell if you infuse mana into— Shit, never mind," he muttered. "Switch spots with Yoona. You won't be able to find it if you can't use or detect magic at all."

Man, that deflated my ego a bit, but there was nothing I could do. I swapped places like I was told and used my many feelers to pick off stragglers again. Was this going to be my role in the future? Just off the side, lapping up the leftovers from the others? How was it possible for my stats to increase five times, and I was somehow still the most useless one here?

I forced my disappointment down and reminded myself that I was dealing with literal freaks of nature. My growth was probably amazing by most standards, and the fact that I was able to even keep up with the rest of my party members should have been a cause for celebration, especially considering how bad of a start I'd had. Plus, they had cool skills to accent their stats, while I just had a bunch of tentacles.

Yet logical reasoning hardly mattered when faced with the cold hard fact that I was still too weak. Now that I knew that I couldn't always count on Noe, what with her missing fragments and unknown background, I had to improve further on my own, by any means necessary.

But for now, I had to content myself with my limited role in the current battle. I couldn't improve if I wasn't even alive to do so. And if that meant all I was doing now was poking small insects that didn't get vaporized by Noel or stomped into a paste by Vadeem, then so be it. I continued to poke and bash insects. At least these couldn't avoid me given the confined space we were in.

While I was keeping the foes at bay, the regressor was darting all over the battlefield, striking at various spots on the walls. Yoona was helping out, although I couldn't tell how she was doing due to my strange constitution. All I saw was that she was concentrating for a while, and occasionally shooting an arrow at the wall. Whatever they were doing was certainly affecting the barrier, as each strike of a spear or arrow caused the blue light encasing the room to visibly dim.

I was doing so little that I even had the chance to spectate Vadeem's epic duel against the golem. It was like watching an old kaiju film in real life as the two behemoths slugged it out. All semblance of form and technique was gone as each titan swung at the other. Each punch from Vadeem's gauntleted hands would displace huge chunks of rock from the golem, knocking it back a bit, but it would regenerate just as quickly.

Vadeem, on the other hand, seemed to be going with the punches and ignored any damage that he was taking. He was hell-bent on destroying his opponent and ignored all else. I wasn't sure if he lost some of his usual battle instincts while in the form of a literal titan, but I was beginning to think that was the case. Those swings from the rock creature were slow, so he must have had the ability to dodge or at least parry them, yet he chose not to.

"Vadeem, Noel, Walter!" the regressor shouted. "Get ready to run to the exit! I can deactivate the barrier, but not for long!"

We did so. Noel simply walked through the enemies, as nothing could physically stop her, while I followed behind her and made my way to the sealed doorway. Yoona and the twins soon joined us and picked off any insectoids trying to stop us.

The only one having trouble was Vadeem. The big man had started to retreat back toward us as well, but his movements were hindered by the huge golem.

"Vadeem, do you need help?" Jae-Hyun asked.

"Don't bother," he grunted. "Doubt you guys could stop this thing for long. I'll rush for it when you bring down the barrier. Do it now!"

"Go!" the regressor shouted as he stabbed his spear into a small segment of the wall. The air audibly popped as the barrier shattered, but almost as quickly the energy around us was starting to gather again.

Noel was the first to respond as she quickly flew through the opening. I followed next and saw the regressor drag his sister back with him. Vadeem tried to follow, but the golem noticed the change in the room and grabbed on to the titan before he could shrink down to a manageable size. Well, shit, if he went out of titan form now, he'd be squashed. He grunted with effort as he tried his best to dislodge himself from the rock creature but to no avail.

"Damn!" he grumbled. "Just go without me!"

The twins noticed his plight, and without hesitation they rushed back toward the man, doing their best to try to free Vadeem from the golem. Their pure disregard for their own safety said more about their relationship with him than anything else, but it was a useless gesture. Nothing they did could possibly help free the man.

"No!" he shouted as he tried once again to untangle himself from the golem. "Get out of here, you two! You can't help!"

They didn't react as they let loose arrow after useless arrow on the rock monstrosity. They looked like they would rather die than abandon Vadeem.

"Hurry up!" Jae-Hyun said. "Barrier will reengage in a few seconds!"

"He won't make it, brother!" Yoona shouted. "And the twins!"

He gritted his teeth but didn't respond.

"We can't leave them!" his sister continued.

"We might have to."

A look of fierce determination flashed through the young girl's eyes. "No! I'm not leaving him. You might be willing to make sacrifices, brother, but I am not!"

And before he could say anything else, Yoona ran back into the room. The regressor tried to stop her, but the barrier reformed at that exact moment, cutting him off. The look on Jae-Hyun's face at that moment was of a quiet insanity.

Vadeem noticed that his chance to exit was cut off, and with a shout of rage, he started to bash his foe with all his might, yet somehow also ensuring that nothing came close to harming Yoona or the twins.

"Don't worry about us, brother," Yoona said as she unleashed a barrage of arrows. "I know what to look out for to take the barrier down again. You three go on ahead; we'll catch up."

"Yoona . . ."

"I'll be fine," she answered, looking back briefly to give him an assuring smile. "Vadeem and the girls will keep us safe. You go and find that fire."

He didn't look like he would leave anytime soon. I don't think the idea of losing his sister for a second time sat well with him.

"Come on, Jae-Hyun," I said slowly. "We can't stay here any longer. The faster we finish this trial, the better of a chance they'll have as well."

He gritted his teeth, but logic won out in the end, and with a final look back, he turned around and ran away. Even Noel, now back to her normal self, didn't make some funny remark about the situation.

"We're not far off the ritual room," Jae-Hyun said with eerie calm. "Follow me."

He leaped away and didn't wait for a response, his mood still abysmal. I joined Noel, and we ran a few feet behind the regressor, careful to keep up with his insane speed.

"You think they'll be okay?" I whispered to the redhead.

"Eh, Vadeem's with them, and that guy's too stupid to die," she replied with a shrug.

I sighed. I knew trying to get any serious answer out of her was a useless task. Why had I even bothered?

She noticed my disappointment and clarified, "No, I'm serious."

"That he's too stupid to die?"

"That too." She giggled. "But I mean the part about them being fine. I've known Vadeem for a long time, and that guy has survived worse situations than this back on Earth. Did you know we first met because I had a contract to get rid of him? It's the only job I failed, too!"

I hadn't known that, but then again, I hadn't had the chance to know any of my party members' backgrounds. I should really remedy that once we were out of here, even if their old lives were a little unique. Surely there was something nice about Noel underneath that bloodthirsty, insane shell . . . probably.

We ran down more corridors. Some smaller golems and other monsters tried to get in our way, but the regressor barely broke a sweat before destroying those in his path. Noel and I didn't even get the chance to fight and just did our best to not step on the bodies and rubble left behind. Never get Jae-Hyun angry . . .

"What I mean is," Noel continued as she lightly stepped over the corpse of some mutated flesh thing, "Vadeem's got a soft spot for kids—not in a creepy way, of course—and he's got super-dad vibes when he sees one in danger. He'll make sure those three are fine over his big, dumb dead body, and since he's too stupid to die in the first place, everyone will be fine. See? Perfect logic, little bro."

Can't argue with that. She knew the other man better than I, so I could only hope that her assessment of him was correct.

Before long, the regressor stopped us in front of an ornate entrance. We had just run through enemies nonstop for at least ten minutes, yet he didn't look even slightly winded. In fact, he only looked more determined for what was ahead.

"That's the door to the ritual room," he said, pointing at the entrance. "Whatever or whoever's responsible for sabotaging this place will be ready for us in there. We go fast. If we can avoid a fight, do so. If we can't, then we destroy them and relight that fire at all costs."

"You got it, boss," I said. I still had a few hours before my transformation was forced to end, so I was good to go.

Noel nodded in affirmation and transformed back into her inferno form. The regressor nodded one last time, weapon at the ready, and we entered the ritual room.

Ding!

"First system mission activated," Noe's voice—the robotic one I heard all the way back when this craziness started—said. "Please absorb Unit Noe's Shard of Emotion to upgrade the Luck System 104.04 Delta. Good luck, Host Walter."

CHAPTER FIFTY

Absolute Luck System 104.05 Gamma

The regressor made sure that all of us were ready, and he kicked the door open. I wasn't sure what to expect, but I took a deep breath and sprinted in with him, Noel hot on my tentacles. Just a little more to go and we could get out of here. I'd have my best buddy Noe back to normal, maybe take a nap out in the sun for once, and finally relax.

After weeks spent in this never-ending darkness, with the only source of illumination being a stupid light bulb on my head, I was just sick and tired of it all. I wanted a bed to lie on, a nice book to read, or at the very least see the sun again!

I felt a huge impact on my side, and still being disoriented, I wasn't sure what had happened. It wasn't any monster who hit me, but the regressor. Had he finally lost his mind as well?

That was when I saw the huge flaming sword, at least several meters long and half as wide, embedded where I was standing just a second ago. There was a look of fierce determination in the regressor's eyes, and I realized that I had been sloppy again. The man had just saved my life while I was daydreaming again, but from what? Before I could even thank him, he rushed off, spear in hand, and Noel flew right behind him.

I regained enough of my senses to climb back on my feelers and finally properly surveyed what was going on. I wished I hadn't, though. Noel and Jae-Hyun looked to be engaged in a fight against a mutated knockoff version of the damned Hindu deity Asura!

The thing was huge once again, about the same size as the golem Vadeem fought earlier, although it was made of flesh this time, and was quite agile, seeing as how it was parrying most of the regressor's assaults.

Each of its six arms was wielding a different weapon, ranging from swords, sickles, spears, and so forth; just trying to get within reach of the creature proved to be difficult. And unlike myself, it wasn't limited to things like luck charges or fatigue, as it kept on trying to kill my two friends. And worse still, embedded in its monstrous forehead was a distinct black shard.

It didn't take a genius to understand what that was. Guess there's no avoiding fighting this thing.

Noel made a mad dash toward the creature's head, ignoring the flaming blade headed her way. Her plan was to simply phase through the weapon like she did before, but a desperate shout from the regressor told me that her normal plan wouldn't work here.

"Avoid it, Noel!" he screamed, but he was too far away to help.

Noel tried to swerve out of the way, but there was no way she would make it. I stuck my feet-feelers deep into the ground and lashed out with my other tentacles. They grabbed on to the monster's arm, and I fought with everything I had to stop the strike aimed at Noel.

Even with my insanely boosted stats, my feelers strained before one of them broke off from the sheer effort. I screamed as I watched my precious tentacle spasm around before finally falling still. Holy shit, it pulled off one of my precious feelers! Did Xollon grow those back? I desperately hoped so, because I had a feeling that I'd lose a few more before this day was over.

I shook my head free of doubts and refocused on the fight. I could worry about my lack of appendages later. Thankfully my sacrifice did as intended, and the creature's swing was slowed down enough for Noel to dodge out of its way, but just narrowly. The edge of the weapon clipped the side of one of her wings, and I saw that unlike before, her flame form was hurt. A tiny portion of her wings was missing, and sizzling red blood leaked from her wound.

However, Noel seemed to ignore the injury and didn't miss a second of the opportunity that I gave her. She dove straight into the creature's face, plunging the two swords into its face. I think she was aiming for its eyes, but the giant was able to avoid a fatal injury, and Noel's attack struck its cheeks instead.

The dark flames started to gush into the new wound, causing huge chunks of its meat to fall off. It burned the surrounding flesh but didn't consume the giant like the other foes she ignited. Noel was about to slash at it again, but a fierce headbutt knocked the flaming girl to the ground. I could almost imagine the inaudible grunt of pain as she hit the hard surface.

"You're not invulnerable, Noel," the regressor continued to shout. "Don't get hit!"

Once Noel was out of the way, the creature's attention turned to me, and it swung its arm with my feelers that were still attached to it, dragging me along with them. I desperately tried to let go, but my little serrated hooks were dug deep, and I was flung into the wall, hard. The force ripped my feelers out of the beast's arms, but it took another tentacle with it. The only thing I could be thankful for was that I didn't have conventional lungs or the air would have been knocked out of me.

I was still squirming from the pain when I saw an ax aimed straight at me. I tried to scramble out of the way, but I was woefully slow, and it looked like the damn thing would take at least half of me with it. Forget about regrowing feelers, I hoped Xollons were built like jellyfish and I could survive being bisected.

The regressor grunted in effort, and at the edge of my perception, I saw him look at my situation with concentration before quickly stabbing the ground with his spear. I was going to question what he was doing, but the oddest thing happened next. The strike that was about to split me in two chunks never hit, because the arm that was holding the weapon just . . . disappeared. Red mist permeated the surroundings, which showed that something had happened, but that was it.

A severed bloody stump replaced where its massive arm was, and the creature howled an inhuman cry of rage and pain. A quick glance back at the regressor showed that he was still in the same spot, but it looked like he had just run a few marathons back to back. He quickly took out a small bottle of blue liquid and drank it. His complexion brightened a bit, but whatever he just did took a heavy toll on him.

Noel didn't miss a beat and quickly pounced on the new vulnerability. She dashed between the severed limb and plunged her swords into the giant's side, causing more chunks of its flesh to melt off. If only the flames could spread a bit further, because it would take a lot more to kill this thing.

I scrambled up again to help out once more, this time redirecting another strike aimed at the still-recovering regressor. I was learning to control how much force I could exert without having more of my tentacles ripped off, but it almost meant that I could only slightly alter the creature's strikes. Even that took extreme effort on my end.

Yet my friends were also adjusting their tactics to match what I could do, and they took every opportunity to inflict minor wounds on the creature. But just as we were slowly wounding the creature, it was slowly doing the same to our side. The blows that I couldn't redirect had to be absorbed by Noel or

Jae-Hyun, and the sheer power behind each attack left them stumbling and hurt. Despite their clear injuries, they never slowed down their assault, but I could tell that this couldn't last for long.

Another wide swing of a club forced Jae-Hyun to retreat, and he stabbed the ground once again. The results were immediate—another arm was obliterated, and a few scratches appeared on its face and neck. The regressor, however, looked even worse for wear. His entire body was drenched in sweat, and he was bleeding from his nose.

The creature finally realized that Jae-Hyun was the biggest threat to its existence and made its way toward the exhausted spearman. Noel tried desperately to attack its sides, but this time it simply ignored her and focused all of its attention on the regressor. I tried in vain to slow down its advance, my feelers latched to its feet while I dug into the ground with the others, but nothing I did could stop its movement as I was dragged along with it.

I started to panic then. The massive creature was only feet away from Jae-Hyun, and he didn't look like he was in any condition to retaliate. Even dodging the inevitable attack seemed daunting. I tried everything that I could think of, but without Noe and her system skills, I had no options at all. I even tried to gnaw at the monster's shins with my maw, but all that did was leave a foul taste in my mouth.

The regressor saw that we wouldn't be able to stop it and gritted his teeth. He looked like he was about to use that strange skill of his one last time, consequences be damned, but thankfully he didn't have to. A huge explosion of movement interrupted the thing's movement, and something huge and muscular bashed through the wall and barreled into the creature. The sheer force of the tackle caused the giant to crash into the other side of the room.

"Vadeem style, baby!" the titan bellowed. "Don't think you've seen the last of me!"

Three more figures rushed out of the opening the big man made and started to pepper the foe with arrows, each shot aimed at its eyes and other soft spots in its defense. Jae-Hyun looked visibly relieved by the sight of his sister doing well and was instantly invigorated. Sometimes you just needed a small boost to morale in order to get back into the fray. He took out another small bottle of that blue liquid and chugged it down before joining the others.

While all of this was happening, Vadeem was on a rampage. He had taken the opportunity to mount the creature and was landing strike after strike on its head. Each blow sent tremors into the ground with the weight of his gauntleted fists. Whenever it would try to stagger away from the barrage, Noel would expertly slice into the tendons, hindering its movement. The chunks of flesh that sloughed off provided much-needed vulnerabilities in the thing's defenses, and the three girls were able to send volleys of arrows into the decaying tissue.

I wasn't lying still either; I did my best to hinder its movements further so that all of Vadeem's hammer blows landed on the thing's cranium. It was faltering fast. Noel's constant cuts were adding up while Vadeem did the majority of the damage. Once our team took the initiative, the fate of the huge six-armed monstrosity was sealed.

Anything that it tried to do to remedy its situation was stopped. If it tried to raise an arm to strike at Vadeem, I'd hinder its movement with one of my feelers while Noel burned away its muscles and tendons, rendering any attack it tried to swing ineffective and weak. Vadeem was too big for it to shove off, and with the regressor slicing away the ligaments and tendons on its legs and feet, it was basically stuck there taking blow after hammer blow.

While all of this was happening, Yoona and the twins would bombard the spots where Noel had burned previously with unending volleys of arrows, and before long, the creature had all but lost its ability to fight back. Finally, once the end was in sight, the regressor shouted a command for us to retreat. None of us questioned his words, and we quickly stepped back. Vadeem punched it one last time and ran to a corner while Noel retreated to where the three girls stood.

The regressor grunted and stabbed his spear into the ground one last time, and once again the damage he inflicted was instantaneous. The thing's head exploded into a pile of gore, and a tiny shard fell onto the ground, its smooth black surface untarnished.

Jae-Hyun fell to his knees in exhaustion, and his sister rushed to his side. She took out another one of the little vials of liquid, but he refused to take it this time.

"Walter," he said between deep breaths, "take the artifact and light the flame."

I didn't need him to tell me twice. I staggered back to my feet-feelers and took the little shard. It was oddly warm.

"Notification," Noe's familiar robotic voice said. "Does Host Walter want to integrate Noe's Shard of Emotion into the main system?"

Not right now.

I needed to do one final performance to end all of this.

I shed my Xollon form and felt the smooth crystal on my hands. I went up to the half-destroyed brazier and ignited it with a spark from my lantern. With my other hand, I made the motion to throw the shard into the fire, but I made a mental command right as it was about to leave my hands.

Absorb it now!

"Acknowledged."

A warm sensation coursed through my body, and every emotion that I had ever felt seemed to ignite through my weary body all at once. I felt joy, loss, despair, and rage so intense that it almost made me pass out, but just as quickly as those feelings came, they left.

At the same time, the newly lit brazier exploded into an inferno of light, and the darkness that was ever present seemed to disappear all at once. A wave of energy pulsated around me, through me, and into every corner of the world, and for a brief moment, a tiny fraction of a fraction of a second, I felt something else stir inside me.

It felt like . . . it felt like something that had left me for a very long time had finally returned, like a missing piece of my soul had finally found its way home. But just when I thought I could finally pinpoint what that was, the feeling left me just as quickly as it came. Like a fleeting dream, I tried to understand what just happened, but before I could process anything else, I heard a familiar voice in my head, and the remnants of those thoughts disappeared. It was a voice that I desperately missed.

"Congratulations, Host Walter," Noe said, her voice returning some of its lost warmth and femininity. "Unit Noe has successfully integrated the Shard of Emotion, and the personality algorithms have been restored. Please wait for further functionalities to be unlocked as Unit Noe fully integrates the damaged shard."

Welcome back, Noe, I thought with a smile.

"It is good to be back, my host," she replied. "Absolute Luck Unit 104.05 Gamma is ready to serve you once more."

I never knew how much I had missed my little voice in my head.

It's good to have you back at my side. I hope you had a good nap back there.

But before I could do anything else, a familiar bright light engulfed me, and I was taken to a new location. The sunlight was refreshing. Ha, actual sunlight! I felt like I haven't seen that in ages now. My restored system indicated that a new notification came from the Trash Matrix, and I was all too happy to see if it had returned to normal as well. A message appeared on my retina, heralding the next phase of these trials. No, the main phase of these trials.

With Noe back, I felt like I could take on anything.

> Congratulations, Aspirants, for successfully completing the second trial.
> Welcome to the Main Stage.
> We do not forget.

The Day After

Patar knelt by the entrance of the Temple of the Eternal Flame, now renamed the Temple of Devouring Truth after their new deity, on that day when Light returned. Although their God had gone, their faith had remained. They understood that their world was but one of many that needed the grace of the Truth.

It would be an event celebrated through the eons on that planet, a legend told throughout the generations, but for the people who lived it, it had been a religious experience that would cement them as saints. These very few individuals had overcome all the trials and tribulations and had survived to see the dawn of a new generation. One devoted to the worship of the Devouring Truth.

The sun rose, and Patar and his flock had never seen such radiance in their life. As the first rays of that beautiful dawn light caressed Patar's healing skin, he wept tears of joy for the first time. The rest of the faithful did the same, and cries of exaltation rang throughout the crowd. It was a spiritual moment for the gathered. And they would have knelt there, on that blessed day—for it had been day then, and not the never-ending gloom of eternal night—had the holy messenger not announced herself.

A soft sound the likes of which the people of that planet had never heard rang out from the interior of the temple. It was like a high-pitched echo mixed with a sharp tonality not produced in nature. It sounded artificial in a way that the planet's people had never encountered.

It sounded nice, soothing, calm.

The temple gates, long since closed to the world, had opened on their own, and a soft, feminine voice beckoned the faithful forward. Beckoned them into the echoing halls.

They followed the instructions, for it would be sacrilegious to do otherwise, and the gathered faithful saw the temple's interior now bathed in the holy glow of God. No darkness would ever again encroach on such hallowed ground.

A path of illumination led the gathered faithful toward the center of the structure, their quiet steps echoing down the empty corridors and hollow chambers. All around them, a strange background hum was ever present, enveloping the group with a distant, forgotten melody.

Deeper into the confines of the temple they went until the supernatural light of the temple threatened to blind the gathered people, and at the climax of that supernova was the brazier. It was lit once more, its flames as tall and glorious as its descriptions in the tales of old. And in that room most holy, shaped from the holy flame, stood the projection of the messenger.

She was beautiful.

Her face was an ever-changing display of features, figures, people, and things. Her form never stayed the same for more than a fraction of a second, a mass of stunning chaos. The mind could scarcely comprehend the messenger's form, yet one thing was certain in the minds of every single person present: She was beautiful.

She was perfect.

And she spoke.

And she commanded.

And she elevated them.

Each member of the congregation stood tall. Now they were more than the weak humans who cowered in the dark.

They were more now, so much more.

They had a purpose.

The messenger showed them the way to spread the glory of God throughout the cosmos, throughout the universe, and beyond that still.

The Holy Order of the Devouring Truth had a mission, they had a means, and they would stop at nothing to spread the light of their God.

Soon dawn's light would seep into their world as dusk descended onto a multitude of others.

All for the glory of the Devouring Truth.

About the Author

Tismon is the author of the Unwilling Eldritch Horror of Fortune series, originally released on Royal Road. He has too many ideas in his head and just
enough time to jot them all down on paper. Tismon resides in Ontario, Canada.

RESPAWN YOUR CURIOSITY

follow us on our socials

podiumentertainment.com

@podiumentertainment

/podiumentertainment

@podium_ent

@podiumentertainment